Nora Roberts is the *New York Tim*
more than one hundred and ninet_
storyteller, she creates a blend of warmth, humour and
poignancy that speaks directly to her readers and has
earned her almost every award for excellence in her field.
The youngest of five children, Nora Roberts lives in western
Maryland. She has two sons.

Visit her website at www.noraroberts.com

KEY TO PHOTOGRAPHS

Page vi top: Lily Dora Alexander, undated photograph, possibly on honeymoon in early 1914

Page vi bottom: Major Graham Chaplin washing in A Company trenches at Pont Ballot, outside Armentières, December 1914, taken by Captain Fred Davidson, RAMC

Page xviii: Graham Chaplin as 36-year-old captain, in Cameronians' rifle green doublet with shako, 1909

Page 18: Colonel Philip Robertson, standing centre, in discussion with Captain Ronald MacAllan, on horse, and others during the retreat from Mons, August 1914, taken by Lieutenant Robert Money

Page 38: Lieutenant Ernest Hobkirk and Major Graham Chaplin enjoying a cigarette in freezing conditions, Houplines trenches, November 1914, taken by Lieutenant Robert Money

Page 60: as page vi bottom

Page 79: Major Graham Chaplin, Captain Francis Hamilton, Major Richard Oakley, Captain John Stormonth-Darling and Lieutenant Ernest Hobkirk with local housekeeper outside billets in Bac St Maur, near Armentières, November 1914, taken by Lieutenant Fred Davidson, RAMC

Page 103: Major Graham Chaplin, far left, with Captain Thomas McLellan, far right, flanking unnamed soldier and Lieutenant Douglas Moncrieff Wright, in A Company trenches outside Armentières, taken by Lieutenant Robert Money

Copyright: the photographs on pages 18, 38, 103, 233, 273 and 378 are used by kind permission of South Lanarkshire Council, which oversees the Cameronians archive at Low Parks Museum, Hamilton.

Nora Roberts

The Magic of Christmas

MILLS & BOON

All rights reserved including the right of reproduction in whole or in part in any form. This edition is published by arrangement with Harlequin Books S.A.

This is a work of fiction. Names, characters, places, locations and incidents are purely fictional and bear no relationship to any real life individuals, living or dead, or to any actual places, business establishments, locations, events or incidents. Any resemblance is entirely coincidental.

This book is sold subject to the condition that it shall not, by way of trade or otherwise, be lent, resold, hired out or otherwise circulated without the prior consent of the publisher in any form of binding or cover other than that in which it is published and without a similar condition including this condition being imposed on the subsequent purchaser.

® and ™ are trademarks owned and used by the trademark owner and/or its licensee. Trademarks marked with ® are registered with the United Kingdom Patent Office and/or the Office for Harmonisation in the Internal Market and in other countries.

This edition published in Great Britain 2018
By Mills & Boon, an imprint of HarperCollins*Publishers*
1 London Bridge Street, London, SE1 9GF

THE MAGIC OF CHRISTMAS © 2018 Harlequin Books S.A.

The Playboy Prince © 1987 Nora Roberts
Charmed © 1992 Nora Roberts

ISBN: 978-0-263-26727-3

9-1117

MIX
Paper from
responsible sources
FSC™ C007454
www.fsc.org

This book is produced from independently certified FSC™ paper to ensure responsible forest management.

For more information visit: www.harpercollins.co.uk/green

Printed and bound
by CPI Group (UK) Ltd, Croydon, CR0 4YY.

3

The Playboy Prince

For Tara Bell, with hope that her wishes come true.

Chapter 1

The stallion plunged over the crest of the hill, digging hard into the earth and kicking up dust. At the peak, he reared, powerful forelegs pawing the air. For an instant, horse and rider were silhouetted against the bright afternoon sky. One looked as dangerous as the other.

Even as hooves touched earth, the rider's knees pressed to the stallion's side and sent them both recklessly racing down the sheer incline. The track there was smooth, but hardly gentle with a wall of rock on one side and a drop into space on the other. They took it at full speed and gloried in it.

Only a madman rode with such arrogant disregard for life and limb. Only a madman, or a dreamer.

"*Avant*, Dracula." The command was low and challenging as was the laughter that followed. The tone was one of a man who considered fear a banquet and speed the wine.

Birds, startled by the thunderous pounding of hooves on dirt, flew from the trees and bushes on the cliff above to wheel screaming into the sky. Their noise was soon lost in the distance. When the path veered to the left, the stallion took it without a pause. The edge of the road gave way to cliffs that spilled sharply for seventy feet to the white rocks and blue sea. Pebbles danced off the dirt to shower soundlessly into the empty spaces.

The rider glanced down but didn't slow. He never even considered it.

From that height, there was no scent of the sea. Even the sound of waves crashing was indistinct, like thunder far off and still harmless. But from that height, the sea held a danger and mystique all of its own. Every year she claimed her tribute in the lives of men. The rider understood this, accepted this, for so it had been since the beginning of time. So it would continue to be. At times like this he put himself in the hands of fate and backed his bet with his own skill.

The stallion needed no whip, no spur to drive him faster. As always, his master's excitement and confidence were enough. They tore down the twisting path until the sea roared in their ears and the cry of gulls could at last be heard.

To the onlooker, it might seem the horseman was fleeing from devils or racing to a lover. But anyone seeing his face would know it was neither.

If there was a gleam in the dark eyes, it wasn't one of fear or anticipation. It was challenge. For the moment, and the moment only. Speed whipped the man's dark hair as freely as the horse's dark mane.

The stallion was fifteen hands of coal-black energy, wide at the chest, powerful at the neck. The horse's hide glistened with sweat, but his breathing was strong and even. Astride him, the rider sat erect, his tanned, narrow face glowing. His mouth, full and sculpted, was curved in a smile that spoke of both recklessness and pleasure.

As the path leveled, the stallion's stride lengthened. Here, they passed whitewashed cottages where clothes flapped on lines in the sea breeze. Flowers crowded for space in tidy lawns and windows were opened and unscreened. The sun, still high in the sky after noon, flashed its brilliant light. Without slackening, without needing his master's light hands on the reins to guide him, the stallion sprinted for a hedge as high as a man's waist.

Together, they soared over it.

In the distance were the stables. As there were danger and deadly attraction in the cliffs behind, so were there peace and order to the scene ahead. Red and white, and tidy as the lawns surrounding them, the buildings added another touch of charm to a landscape of cliffs and greenery. Fences crisscrossed to form paddocks where horses were being exercised with far less drama than Dracula.

One of the grooms stopped circling a young mare on a lead when he heard the stallion's approach. Crazy as a loon, he thought—but not without grudging respect. This horse and this rider, merged together in a blare of speed, were a common sight. Even so, two grooms waited at attention for the stallion to slow to a halt.

"Your Highness."

His Highness, Prince Bennett of Cordina slid off Dracula's back with a laugh that echoed the recklessness. "I'll cool him down, Pipit."

The old groom with the slight limp stepped forward.

His weathered face was passive, but he passed his gaze over both prince and stallion, checking for any sign of harm. "Your pardon, sir, but a message came down from the palace while you were out. Prince Armand wishes to see you."

Not without regret, Bennett handed the reins to the waiting groom. Part of the pleasure of the ride was the hour he normally spent walking and brushing down the stallion. If his father had sent for him, he had no choice but to forgo pleasure for duty.

"Walk him thoroughly, Pipit. We've had a long run."

"Yes, sir," said the groom who'd spent three-quarters of his life with horses. Among his duties had been seating Bennett on his first pony. At sixty, with one leg game from a fall, Pipit remembered the energy of youth. And the passion. He patted Dracula's neck and found it damp. "I'll see to it myself, Your Highness."

"Do that, Pipit." But Bennett loitered long enough to loosen the cinches. "Thanks."

"No thanks necessary, sir." With a quiet grunt, Pipit hefted the saddle from the stallion's back. "Isn't another man here who has the nerve to deal with the devil." He murmured in French as the horse began to dance in place. In moments, Dracula settled again.

"And there isn't another man I'd trust with my best. An extra scoop of grain wouldn't hurt him this evening."

Pipit took the compliment as no less than his due. "As you say, sir."

Still restless, Bennett turned to walk from the stables. He could have used the extra hour to cool himself down as well. Riding fast, riding reckless, satisfied only part of his thirst. He needed the movement, the speed, but most of all, he needed the freedom.

For nearly three months he'd been tied firmly to the palace and protocol, the pomp and procedure. As second in line to Cordina's throne, his duties were sometimes less public than his brother Alexander's, but rarely less arduous. Duties, obligations, had been a part of his life since birth, and were normally taken as a matter of course. Bennett couldn't explain to himself, much less anyone else, why sometime during the past year he'd begun to fret and chafe against them.

Gabriella saw it. Bennett thought perhaps his sister even understood it. She, too, had always had a thirst for freedom and privacy. She'd gained a portion of that two years before when Alexander had married Eve, and the weight of responsibility had shifted.

Still she never shirked, Bennett thought as he passed through the palace's garden doors. If she was needed, she was there. She still gave six months of every year to the Aid for Handicapped Children while keeping her marriage vital and raising her children.

Bennett dug his hands into his pockets as he climbed the stairs that would take him to his father's office. What was wrong with him? What had happened in the past few months that made him want to slip quietly out of the palace some night and run? Anywhere.

He couldn't shake off the mood, but he managed to tame it as he knocked on his father's door.

"Entrez."

The prince wasn't behind his desk as Bennett had expected, but was seated beside a tea tray at the window.

Across from him was a woman who rose to her feet at Bennett's entrance.

As a man who appreciated women of any age, of any form, he took an easy survey before turning to his father. "I'm sorry to interrupt. I was told you wished to see me."

"Yes." Armand merely sipped his tea. "Some time ago. Prince Bennett, I would like to introduce Lady Hannah Rothchild."

"Your Highness." Her gaze swept down as she curtsied.

"A pleasure, Lady Hannah." Bennett took her hand, summing her up in seconds. Attractive in a quiet way. He preferred less subtlety in women. British from her accent. He had an affection for the French. Slim and neat. Invariably, the more voluptuous caught his eye. "Welcome to Cordina."

"Thank you, Your Highness." Her voice was indeed British, cultured and quiet. He met her gaze briefly so that he saw her eyes were a deep and glowing shade of green. "Yours is a beautiful country."

"Please, sit, my dear." Armand gestured her back to her chair before he lifted another cup to pour. "Bennett."

Hannah, with her hands folded in her lap, noticed Bennett's quick look of dislike at the teapot. But he sat and accepted the cup.

"Lady Hannah's mother was a distant cousin of yours," Armand began. "Eve became acquainted with her when she and your brother visited England recently. At Eve's invitation, Lady Hannah has agreed to stay with us as Eve's companion."

Bennett could only hope he wouldn't be expected to escort the lady. She was pretty enough, though she dressed like a nun in a gray, high-collared dress that came a discreet two inches below her knees. The color did nothing for her pale, British complexion. Her eyes saved her face from being plain, but with her dark blond hair pulled back so severely from her face, she put him in mind of the old Victorian companions or governesses. Dull. But he remembered his manners and treated her to an easy, companionable smile.

"I hope you enjoy your stay as much as we'll enjoy having you."

Hannah gave him a solemn look in return. She wondered if he was aware, and thought he was, of how dashing he looked in casual riding clothes. "I'm sure I'll enjoy it immensely, sir. I'm flattered the Princess Eve invited me to stay with her while she awaits the birth of her second child. I hope to give her the companionship and help she needs."

Though his mind was on other matters, Armand offered a plate of frosted cookies. "Lady Hannah has been very generous to give us her time. She's quite a scholar and is currently working on a series of essays."

Figures, Bennett thought, and sipped at the hated tea. "Fascinating."

The smallest of smiles touched Hannah's lips. "Do you read Yeats, sir?"

Bennett shifted in his chair and wished himself back to his stables. "Not extensively."

"My books should be here by the end of the week. Please feel free to borrow anything you like." She rose again, keeping her hands folded. "If you would excuse me, Your Highness, I'd like to see to the rest of my unpacking."

"Of course." Armand rose to lead her to the door. "We'll see you at dinner. Be sure to ring if you require anything."

"Thank you, sir." She curtsied, then turned to extend the courtesy to Bennett. "Good afternoon, Your Highness."

"*Bonjour*, Lady Hannah." Bennett waited for the door to close behind her before dropping onto the arm of his chair. "Well, she should bore Eve to tears within a week." Ignoring the tea, he took a handful of the small iced cookies. "What could Eve have been thinking of?"

"Eve became very fond of Hannah during her two weeks in England." Armand walked to a scrolled cabinet and, to Bennett's relief, took out a decanter. "Hannah is a well-bred young woman of excellent family. Her father is a highly respected member of the British Parliament." The brandy was deep and rich. Armand poured it sparingly.

"That's all well and good, but—" Bennett stopped abruptly as he reached for the snifter. "Oh good God, Father, you're not thinking of trying for a match here? She's hardly my type."

Armand's firm mouth softened with a smile. "I think I know that well enough. I can assure you Lady Hannah was not brought here to tempt you."

"She could hardly do that in any case." Bennett swirled the brandy, then sipped. "Yeats?"

"There are some who believe literature extends beyond equestrian handbooks." Armand drew out a cigarette. There was a knot of tension at the base of his neck. He forced it to concentrate there rather than allowing it to spread.

"I prefer the useful rather than poetry about unrequited love or the beauty of a raindrop." When that made him feel small and ungracious, Bennett relented. "But in any case, I'll do whatever I can to make Eve's new friend welcome."

"I never doubted it."

His conscience soothed, Bennett moved on to more important matters. "The Arabian mare should foal by Christmas. I'm betting it's a colt. Dracula will breed strong sons. I have three horses that should be ready to show in the spring, and another I think should be taken to the Olympic trials. I'd like to arrange that within the next few weeks so that the riders will have more time to work with the horse."

Armand gave an absent nod and continued to swirl his brandy. Bennett felt the familiar push of impatience rising and fought it down. He was well aware that the stables weren't high on his father's list of priorities. How could they be with internal affairs, foreign affairs, and the very tricky politics within the Council of the Crown?

Yet, didn't there have to be something more? The horses not only gave pleasure, but added a certain prestige when the Royal House of Cordina possessed one of the finest stables in Europe. For himself, it was what he considered his only true contribution to his family and country.

He'd worked for the stables as hard and as menially as any groom or stable boy. Over the years, he'd studied everything he could about breeding. To his delight, he'd found within himself a natural skill that had added spark to his education. Within a short time, Bennett had turned a good stable into one of the best. In another decade, he was confident it would have no equal.

There were times when Bennett needed to discuss his horses and his ambitions with someone other than a stable hand or another breeder. Still, he understood, and always had, that that person would rarely be his father.

"I take it this isn't the time to discuss it." Bennett took another small sip of brandy and waited for his father to reveal whatever weighed on his mind.

"I'm sorry, Bennett, I'm afraid it isn't." The father felt regret. The prince could not. "Your schedule this next week. Can you tell me about it?"

"Not really." The restlessness was back. Rising, Bennett began to pace from one window to another. How close the sea seemed and yet how far away. He wished for a moment that he was on a ship again, a hundred miles from any land, with a storm brewing on the horizon. "I know that I have to go into Le Havre at the end of the week. The *Indépendance* is coming in. There's a meeting with the Farmers' Cooperative and a couple of luncheons. Cassell fills me in each morning. If it's important I can have him type up the highlights for you. I'm sure I'm cutting at least one ribbon."

"Feeling closed in, Bennett?"

With a shrug, Bennett tossed off the last of his brandy. Then the easy smile returned. Life, after all, was too short to complain about. "It's the ribbons that do it. The rest, at least, seems worthwhile."

"Our people look to us for more than governing."

Bennett turned from the window. Behind him the sun was high and bright. Whatever he might sometimes wish in his secret heart, the royalty he'd been born with cloaked him. "I know, Papa. The problem is I don't have Alexander's patience, Brie's serenity or your control."

"You might need them all soon." Armand set his glass down and faced his son. "Deboque will be released from prison in two days."

Deboque. Even the name caused fury to churn in Bennett's stomach. François Deboque. The man by whose orders his sister had been kidnapped. The man who had planned assassination attempts on both his father and his brother.

Deboque.

Bennett pressed a finger to the scar just below his left shoulder. He'd taken a bullet there, and the trigger had been pulled by Deboque's lover. For Deboque. By Deboque.

The bomb planted just over two years before in the Paris Embassy had been meant for his father. Instead it had killed Seward, a loyal assistant, leaving a woman widowed and three children fatherless. That, too, had been Deboque's doing.

And in all the years, nearly ten now since Gabriella's kidnapping, no one had proved Deboque's involvement in the kidnapping, the conspiracies or the murders. The best investigators in Europe, including Bennett's brother-in-law, had been brought in, but none of them had proved that Deboque had pulled the strings.

Now, within days, he would be free.

There was no doubt in Bennett's mind that Deboque would continue to seek revenge. The Royal Family was his enemy if for no other reason than he'd been held in a Cordinian prison for over a decade. Neither was there any doubt that during that decade, he'd continued to deal in drugs, weapons and women.

No doubt, and no proof.

Guards would be added. Security would be tightened. Interpol would continue its work, as would the International Security System. But both Interpol and the ISS had been trying to nail Deboque with murder and conspiracy to murder for years. Until he was gotten under control and the strings to his organization severed, Cordina and the rest of Europe were vulnerable.

Hands in pockets, Bennett strode out to the garden. At least they'd dined *en famille* that evening. It had relieved some strain, even though little could be said in front of Eve's new friend. He doubted if anyone that quiet and prim would have picked up on any tension around the table. She had answered when spoken to and nursed one glass of wine throughout the meal.

He would have wished her back to England a dozen times if he hadn't seen how good she actually was for Eve. His sister-in-law was three months pregnant with her second child and didn't need the additional strain of talk of Deboque. Two years before she'd nearly been killed protecting Alexander. If Lady Hannah could keep Eve's mind off Deboque, even for a few hours a day, it would be worth the inconvenience of having her in the palace.

He needed to talk with Reeve. Bennett drove his balled

fists into his pockets. Reeve MacGee was more than his sister's husband. As head of security, he would have some answers. And Bennett certainly had the questions—dozens of them. More was being done than the placing of extra guards. Bennett refused to go through the next weeks blindly while others worked to protect him and his family.

Swearing softly, he looked up at the sky. The moon was cloudless and half full. Another time, with the scents of the garden wafting around him, he would have itched for a woman to watch the sky with. Now, filled with frustration, he preferred the solitude.

When he heard the dogs bark, his body stiffened. He'd thought himself alone; he'd even been sure of it. In any case, his aging hounds never barked at family or familiar servants. Half hoping for a confrontation, Bennett moved quietly toward the sound.

He heard her laugh and the sound surprised him. It wasn't quiet and prim, but rich and delighted. As he watched, Hannah leaned down to stroke the dogs, which pressed against her legs.

"There now, what a lovely pair you are." Smiling she bent farther still to nuzzle. The moonlight slanted over her face and throat.

Instantly, Bennett's eyes narrowed. She hardly looked plain and subdued at the moment. The moonlight accented the hollows and contours of her face, enriching the soft English skin and deepening the already deep green eyes. He would have sworn that he saw both strength and passion there. And he was a man who recognized both in a woman. Her laughter floated out again, as rich as sunlight, as sultry as fog.

"No, you mustn't jump," she cautioned the dogs as they circled her. "You'll have mud all over me and how would I explain that?"

"It's usually best not to explain at all."

She snapped her head up as Bennett spoke. He saw surprise, or thought he did, but it passed quickly. When she straightened, she was the calm, unremarkable Lady Hannah again. He chalked up the passion he'd thought he'd seen to a trick of the light.

"Good evening, Your Highness." Hannah took only a moment to curse herself for being caught unaware.

"I didn't know anyone else was in the garden."

"Nor did I." And she should have. "I beg your pardon."

"Don't." He smiled to put her at ease. "I've always felt the gardens aren't enjoyed nearly enough. Couldn't you sleep?"

"No, sir. I'm always restless when I travel." The dogs had deserted her for Bennett. She stood beside the flowering jasmine and watched him stroke them with strong, capable hands. She was well aware that numerous ladies had enjoyed the same easy touch. "I'd seen the gardens from my window and thought I might walk awhile." In truth, it had been their scent, exotic and alluring, that had urged her to loiter after she'd noted the layout of the space.

"I prefer them at night myself. Things often look different at night," he continued, studying her again. "Don't you think?"

"Naturally." She linked her hands together just below the waist. He was marvelous to look at, sun or moon.

When he'd strode into his father's office that afternoon she'd thought that riding clothes suited him best. The dogs came back to press their noses against her joined hands.

"They like you."

"I've always been fond of animals." She unlinked her hands to stroke. He noticed for the first time that her hands were delicate, long and slender like her body. "What are their names?"

"Boris and Natasha."

"Suitable names for Russian wolfhounds."

"They were given to me as puppies. I named them after characters in an American cartoon show. Spies."

Her hands hesitated only a heartbeat. "Spies, Your Highness?"

"Inept Russian spies who were forever after a moose and squirrel."

He thought he saw it again, the flash of humor that lent something special to her face. "I see. I've never been to America."

"No?" He moved closer, but saw nothing but a young woman with good bones and a quiet manner. "It's a fascinating country. Cordina's become closely linked with it since two members of the Royal Family have married Americans."

"A fact that disappointed a number of hopeful Europeans, I'm sure." Hannah relaxed enough for a cautious smile. "I met Princess Gabriella several years ago. She's a beautiful woman."

"Yes, she is. You know, I've been to England several times. It's strange we never met."

Hannah allowed the smile to linger. "But we did, Your Highness."

"Boris, sit," Bennett commanded as the dog lifted a paw toward Hannah's dress. "Are you sure?"

"Quite sure, sir. Then you'd hardly be expected to remember. It was several years ago at a charity ball hosted by the Prince of Wales. The Queen Mother introduced you to me and my cousin Lady Sara. I believe you and Sara became...friendly."

"Sara?" His mind backtracked and zeroed in. His memory, always good, was faultless when it came to women. "Yes, of course." Though he remembered Hannah only as a vague shadow beside her glamorous and bold cousin. "How is Sara?"

"Very well, sir." If there was sarcasm, it was well coated with manners. "Happily married for the second time. Shall I send her your regards?"

"If you like." He dipped his hands into his pockets again as he continued to study her. "You were wearing blue, a pale blue that was nearly white."

Hannah lifted her brow. She didn't have to be told that he'd barely noticed her. The fact that he hadn't, yet still remembered the color of her gown gave her a moment's pause. A memory like that could be useful—or dangerous.

"You flatter me, Your Highness."

"I make it a policy not to forget a woman."

"Yes, I can believe that."

"My reputation precedes me." The frown was there, then gone, to be replaced by a careless smile. "Does it concern you to be alone in the garden, in the moonlight with—"

"The Royal Rake?" Hannah finished.

"You do read," Bennett murmured.

"Incessantly. And no, Your Highness, I'm quite comfortable, thank you."

He opened his mouth, then laughed and shut it again. "Lady Hannah, I've rarely been put so neatly in my place."

So he was quick—another point she'd have to remember. "I beg your pardon, sir. That certainly wasn't my intention."

"The hell it wasn't, and well done." He took her hand and found it cool and steady. Perhaps she would prove to be a great deal less dull than he'd anticipated. "I should beg your pardon for baiting you, but I won't since you obviously hold your own so well. I'm beginning to see why Eve wanted you here."

Hannah had learned long ago to block off any form of guilt. She did so now. "I became very fond of her in a short time and was delighted with the opportunity to stay in Cordina for a few months. I confess, I've already fallen in love with little Princess Marissa."

"Barely a year old and she's already ruling the palace." Bennett's eyes softened as he thought of his brother's first child. "Maybe it's because she looks like Eve."

Hannah withdrew her hand from his. She'd heard the rumors that Bennett had been half in love, or possibly more than half in love, with his brother's wife. It didn't take even so talented an observer as she to hear the affection in his voice. She told herself to file it away. It may or may not have its uses later.

"If you'll excuse me, sir, I should go back to my room."

"It's still early." He found himself reluctant to let her go. It was unexpected that she would be easy to talk to, or that he would find himself needing to talk to her.

"I'm in the habit of retiring early."

"I'll walk you back."

"Please don't trouble. I know the way. Good night, Your Highness." She merged quickly with the shadows while the dogs whined a bit and thumped their tails against his legs.

What was there about her? Bennett wondered as he bent to soothe his pets. At first glance she seemed almost bland enough to fade into the wallpaper, and yet... He didn't know. But as he walked back toward the palace with the dogs at his heels, he resolved to find out. If nothing else, probing a bit beneath Lady Hannah's quiet breeding would keep his mind off Deboque.

Hannah didn't wait to see if he followed her, but walked quickly through the garden doors. She'd been born with the talent to move quietly, so unobtrusively she could easily be missed in a group of three people. It was a talent she'd honed to a skill and which served her well.

She moved up the stairs without a sound, never looking back. If you had to check whether you were being followed, you were already in trouble. Once inside her own room, she locked the door and slipped out of her practical pumps. Because the woman she professed to be would never leave her clothing scattered, Hannah picked them up, and with only a brief look of distaste, placed them neatly in her closet.

Checking only to see that her curtains were drawn, she peeled off the unflattering cocktail dress.

Although she thought it deserved its day in the garbage, she carefully hung it on a padded hanger.

She stood now, a slimly curved woman with milk-pale skin and long legs in a skimpy lace-edged teddy. Drawing the confining pins from her hair, she let it fall heavily to her waist with a sigh of pure pleasure.

Anyone who knew Lady Hannah Rothchild would have been stunned by the transformation, so complete, so ingrained was the role she'd played for nearly ten years.

Lady Hannah had a passion for silk and Breton lace, but confined it to nightwear and lingerie. Linens and tweeds were more fitting to the image she'd worked hard to create.

Lady Hannah enjoyed reading a pot-boiling thriller in a steamy bubble bath, but she kept a copy of Chaucer on her nightstand and if asked, could quote and discuss a handful of obscure passages.

It wasn't a matter of split personality, but necessity. If she'd given it any deep thought, Hannah would have been able to state that she was comfortable with both of her selves. In fact, more often than not she thoroughly liked the plain, polite and marginally pretty Hannah. Otherwise, she could never have tolerated the sensible shoes for extended periods.

But there was another part to Lady Hannah Rothchild, only daughter of Lord Rothchild, granddaughter of the Earl of Fenton. That part was not quiet and unassuming, but shrewd and sometimes reckless. More, that part had a taste for danger and a mind that absorbed and stored the most minor detail.

Combined, those parts of Lady Hannah Rothchild equaled an excellent and highly skilled agent.

Ignoring her robe, Hannah opened her top drawer and drew out a long, locked box. Inside was a strand of pearls handed down from her great-grandmother with matching earrings her father had had reset for her twenty-first birthday. In the drawers of the box were several other pieces of jewelry befitting a young woman of her class.

Hannah pulled a notebook out of the false bottom and taking it to the rosewood writing desk, began to write her daily report. She hadn't gone into the garden merely to smell the roses, though she had lingered too long because of them. Now she had the complete layout and no longer had to rely on the information fed her. She took the time to draw a sketch of the palace, including the doors and windows most easily accessible. By the following day, or the day after at most, she would have a schedule of the guards.

It had taken her little time to form a friendship with Eve. Securing an invitation to the palace in Cordina had been as easy as asking for one. Eve missed her sister and the familiarity of her own country. She'd needed a friend, one she could talk to, one who would share her delight in her daughter.

Hannah had obliged.

She felt the quick trickle of guilt again and ignored it. A job was a job, she reminded herself. She couldn't let the fondness she felt for Eve interfere with a goal she'd begun to work toward two years ago.

With a shake of her head, she made her first notes on Bennett. He wasn't completely what she'd expected, Hannah thought now. Oh, he was as charming and as attractive as his dossier had said, but he'd given the dull Lady Hannah his time and attention.

An egotistical womanizer, Hannah reminded herself. That had been her own conclusion after doing her research on him. Perhaps he was a bit bored and entertained thoughts of distracting himself with a vulnerable and accessible woman.

Narrowing her eyes, Hannah looked back on the way he had smiled at her. A man of his looks, position and experience knew how to use that smile or a soft word to enchant a woman of any age and any class. The fact that he'd done so, with astonishing regularity, was well documented. Perhaps he would try to add another jewel to his crown by seducing her.

She remembered the way he'd looked in the moonlight, the way his eyes had warmed when she'd bantered back with him. His hand had been firm and hard when it had taken hers—the hand of a man who did more than wave regally to his people.

With a shake of her head, she brought herself up short. It wouldn't do to consider a dalliance with Bennett for enjoyment, but for its usefulness. Thoughtfully, she tapped her pencil on the pad. No, a romance with Bennett would only lead to complications, no matter how advantageous it might be in the long run. She'd keep her eyes down and her hands folded.

Carefully, Hannah hid the notebook again and replaced

the false bottom. The box was locked, but left in full sight if anyone searched her dresser.

She was in, she told herself with a growing sense of anticipation as she looked around the room.

When Deboque walked out of prison in two days' time, he'd be very pleased.

Chapter 2

"Oh, Hannah, I'm so glad you agreed to visit awhile." With her arm hooked with her new friend's, Eve strolled behind the backdrop at the theater. Her body remained slender during the early months of her pregnancy, but her dress was cleverly cut to conceal even the slight weight gain. "Alex doesn't find it as necessary to pamper me to death now that you're here. He finds you so sensible."

"I am sensible."

Eve's low chuckle flowed into her easy Texas drawl. "I know, that's the beauty of it, but you're not always telling me to sit down and put my feet up."

"Men sometimes look at pregnancy and childbirth as a traumatic disease rather than a fact of life."

"That's it exactly." Delighted with Hannah's dry wit, Eve drew her into her office. With Gabriella so often in America and her own sister visiting only rarely, Eve had indeed yearned for another woman to relax with. "Alex keeps expecting me to faint or get overly emotional. I never felt better in my life, except perhaps when I was carrying Marissa."

Tossing back her fall of dark hair, Eve perched on the edge of her desk. Here, at least, she could still claim some measure of the privacy she'd given up when she'd married a prince. Though she never regretted the sacrifice, she always enjoyed stealing a bit of her own back.

"If you hadn't come, I'd have had to fight him tooth and nail to continue working. He only agreed because he felt you'd keep a close eye on me when he's busy."

"Then I won't disappoint him." Hannah took quick stock of the office. No window, no outside access. With a smile, she chose a chair. "You know, Eve, I really admire you. The Fine Arts Center always had a good reputation but since you took over here, this theater has become one of the most important in Europe."

"It's what I've always wanted." Eve looked down at the diamond-encrusted band on her finger. Even after two years it sometimes astonished her to find it there. "You know, Hannah, some mornings I'm almost afraid to wake up; I think that I'll find out it was all a dream. Then I look at Alex and Marissa and think, they're mine. Really mine." Her eyes clouded a moment with both fear and determination. "I won't let anything or anyone hurt them."

"No one will." Eve's thoughts were on Deboque, Hannah surmised. The princess was bound by duty to keep some fears to herself. "Now, not to pamper, but I think we could both use some tea, then you can show me what sort of job I can do around here."

Eve brought herself back with an effort. Nightmares of Deboque, a man she'd never seen, continued to plague her. "Tea's a wonderful idea, but I didn't bring you to the Center to work. I just thought you'd like to see it."

"Eve, you of all people should understand that I need something to do or I'll be bored to death."

"But I'd hoped this could be a vacation for you."

The guilt shimmered a bit. "Some people aren't meant for vacations."

"All right then. Why don't you watch rehearsals with me for an hour or two and give me an honest opinion?"

"I'd love to."

"Great. I'm worried about the opening. We only have a couple of weeks left and I've had nothing but trouble with this playwright."

"Oh, who is it?"

Eve rose and took a deep breath. "Me."

Hannah drank her tea and stayed in the background. It didn't take long for her to see that Eve was respected not only as the wife of the heir, but for her knowledge of theater. She noted too that guards, unobtrusive but in force, were always close at hand. When the princess was in the theater, every entrance was blocked, every interior door was double guarded. Hannah was also aware that a special unit of security checked the Center daily for explosives.

While seated mid-theater with Eve, Hannah watched the rehearsal. She'd always had an affection and respect for actors, as she understood the effort and skill that went into characterization. Now, while lines were cued and staging set, she matched the members of the troupe with the information she already had compiled on each of them.

They were certainly talented, Hannah thought as she found herself drawn into the rhythm and emotion of Eve's play. The sets were still incomplete, but the players needed no more than Eve's words and their own skill to make a statement. Each one of the actors had a reputation in theater and a complete security check.

But it had been an actor—Russ Talbot—who'd nearly carried out Deboque's revenge two years before. Hannah couldn't forget that it was a strong possibility that someone other than herself had been planted. Deboque was known for covering his bets.

"She's wonderful, isn't she?"

Drawn back, Hannah looked over at Eve. "I beg your pardon?"

"Chantel O'Hurley. She's exquisite." Shifting in her chair, Eve leaned on the seat back in front of her. "She rarely makes a stage performance, so we're lucky to have her. I'm sure you've seen her films in England."

"Yes." Hannah gave her full attention to the curvy blonde center stage.

Chantel O'Hurley. Hannah paused to recollect everything she'd read in the actress's file. Twenty-six. American film star. Residence, Beverly Hills. Daughter of Frances and Margaret O'Hurley, traveling entertainers. Sisters, Abigail and Madelaine. Brother, Trace.

Hannah frowned and continued to watch. She had full background information on the entire O'Hurley family, except the brother. There her sources had closed tight. In any case, Chantel O'Hurley was a talented actress with an impressive list of screen credits and no known affiliation with any political group. Nonetheless, Hannah would keep an eye on her.

"She's found the heart of it," Eve murmured. "I'd finished the play and was trying to work up the courage to produce it, when I saw her in her last film. I knew immediately she'd be the perfect Julia." On a long breath Eve leaned back again in an unprincesslike slouch. "I can't believe she's here, reciting my lines. There isn't an emotion that voice can't pull out."

"I'm sure she's honored to be performing in a play written and produced by Princess Eve of Cordina."

On a half laugh, Eve shook her head. "If the play had been lousy, I could have been Empress of Europe and Chantel wouldn't have accepted the part. That's what I'm hanging on to."

"A member of the Royal Family doesn't write lousy plays."

At the sound of the voice behind her, Eve was springing up and reaching out. "Alexander! What are you doing here?"

"I, too, have an interest in the Center." He kissed the hand he held before turning to Hannah. "Please, sit, I didn't mean to disturb you."

"No." Eve sighed and glanced back at the stage where rehearsals continued. "You meant to check up on me."

It was, of course, the truth, but Alexander only shrugged. In the dim light, Hannah saw his gaze sweep over his wife's head to the guards placed at several strategic points. "You forget, *mon amie*, that I am still president of the Center. In addition to that, my wife's play is in rehearsal. I have a small interest there as well."

"And you came to be certain I wasn't staying on my feet." Over the frustration came the tug of love. Eve rose to her toes to kiss him. "Thank you. Hannah, tell His Highness I've been taking care of myself in the four hours and forty minutes since he last saw me."

"Your Highness," Hannah began dutifully, "the princess has been taking excellent care of herself."

A smile softened his features, but he continued to stand protectively near his wife. "Thank you, Hannah. I'm sure the credit goes to you."

With a low laugh, Eve tucked her hand throughAlexander's arm. "Hannah, you can see that I wasn't joking when I said that Alex thinks I need a keeper. If you hadn't come I have no doubt he'd have hired a two-hundred-pound wrestler with tattoos."

"I'm glad I could save you from that." What was this? Hannah wondered. A tug of envy? Ridiculous as it seemed to her, she recognized the emotion as she studied Alexander and Eve. So much in love, she thought. The power of it all but cast an aura around them. Did they realize, could they realize, how rare a thing they'd found?

"Now that I've interrupted," Alexander was saying, "I was hoping to convince you to join me for my luncheon with the American senator."

"The Yankee from Maine."

With a smile, Alexander stroked her cheek. "My dear, it continues to fascinate me how your country divides itself into sections. But yes, the Yankee from Maine. We should be finished by three and be back at the palace when Marissa wakes from her nap."

"But you had a meeting this afternoon."

"I canceled it." He brought her hand to his lips. "I wanted to spend some time with my family."

The glow of pleasure all but lit up the theater. "Give me five minutes to get my things. Hannah, you'll join us?"

"If it wouldn't inconvenience you, I'd really like to stay and watch the rest of the rehearsal." Her mind was already shooting ahead. Alone, she could take a casual tour of the complex. If there were vulnerabilities, she'd find them.

"Of course, stay as long as you like." Eve bent down to kiss her cheek. "We'll have a car wait for you at the stage door. Five minutes," she repeated to Alexander before she dashed off.

"What do you think of the play?" Alexander asked Hannah as he took the seat beside her.

"I'm hardly an expert on the theater, Your Highness."

"In private, please call me Alexander."

"Thank you," she murmured, aware that this gave her an intimacy rewarded to few. "There's an intensity, an immediacy in the dialogue that makes one care deeply about the characters. I don't know the end, but I find myself hoping Julia wins even while I'm afraid she won't."

"Eve would like to hear that. The play—and other things—have her very tense right now."

"You're worried about her." In a gesture that was pure instinct, Hannah placed a hand on his. "She's very strong."

"I know that, better than most." But he'd never been able to block off the memory of how her body had stiffened, then gone limp in his arms when a bullet had struck her. "I haven't told you before how very grateful I am that you came to be with her. She needs friendship. I changed her life, selfishly perhaps because I couldn't live mine without her. Whatever can be done to give her a sense of normalcy, a sense of peace, I'll do. You understand the obligations of royalty. The limitations. Even the risks."

"Yes, I do." Hannah left her hand on his another moment before removing it. "And I understand a happy woman when I see one."

When he turned to her then, Hannah saw the strong resemblance to his father. The lean, almost scholarly face, the aristocratic lines, the mouth that was held firm. "Thank you, Hannah. I think perhaps you'll be good for all of us."

"I hope so." She looked back at the stage, at the players, at the roles. "I do hope so."

Alone, Hannah watched for another half hour. Yes, the play was good, she decided, even gripping, but she had other games to play.

The guards remained, but with no royalty present they were more for the purpose of keeping others out than monitoring those already in. Lady Hannah was already established as the princess's confidante and companion. Trusted by Prince Armand himself, she wasn't followed when she rose and slipped through a side door.

There was a miniature camera concealed in a lipstick case in her handbag, but she didn't use it now. Her training had taught her to rely on her powers of observation first, her equipment second.

A building the size of the sprawling Center wasn't easily secured. Hannah found herself giving Reeve MacGee a nod of respect as she walked through. Heat sensors as well as hidden cameras. But the sensors were activated only when the Center was closed.

Security passes were required at the door for members of the cast and crew. On the night of a performance, however, entrance could be gained for the price of a ticket. Deboque would step from behind bars in a day's time.

As she walked, leaving one corridor for the next, Hannah drew a blueprint in her mind. She'd studied the layout of the Center on paper before, but preferred to walk in it, to focus on it, to touch the walls and floor.

Too many blind corners, she thought. Too many small rooms used for storage. Too many places to hide. Even with Reeve's expertise, the building could be vulnerable with the right plan of attack. But then, Hannah believed any building could be.

She turned into Wardrobe, pretending a casual interest in the costumes. Did the guard at the door know everyone by sight? How easy would it be to replace one of the technicians? A photo was affixed to the pass, but makeup and hairpieces could take care of that. How often had she, or another like her, gained access to a place by faked credentials or a clever disguise?

Once inside, a man could disappear easily. If a man on the security panel could be bribed or replaced, so much the better.

Yes, she'd put that scenario in her report and let her superiors chew on it awhile. She'd add to that the fact that no one had checked her bag. A small plastic explosive could be easily carried and easily planted.

She walked from Wardrobe into a rehearsal hall walled with mirrors. With a little shock, she stared at her reflection on all sides. Then, as she had in the garden, she let out a low, easy laugh.

Oh, Hannah, she thought, how miserably dull you are. Turning to the side, she shook her head. No, maroon did nothing for her, and the high-necked jacket with its bulky belt only made her look unattractively thin. The skirt came well below the knee to hide her legs. She'd braided her hair today, tightly, then had circled the braid at the base of her neck.

Being a part of herself, it was the best cover she could have conceived. She'd been too skinny as a child, with unmanageable hair, and knees that were forever scraped. Her facial bones had been prominent even then, but in the young girl's face had seemed too sharp, too angular.

Then when the other girls had begun to bloom and curve, Hannah's body had remained stubbornly straight. She'd been bright and athletic and cheerful. Boys had patted her on the back and called her a good sport, but they hadn't been interested in taking her to any dances.

She'd learned to ride, swim, shoot skeet and to put an arrow in a bull's-eye from a hundred paces, but she hadn't dated.

She'd learned to speak Russian and French and enough Cantonese to surprise even her father, but she'd gone alone to her own graduation ball.

When she turned twenty, her body changed, but Hannah hid the late blossoming under dull clothes. She'd already chosen her path in life. Beauty turned heads and in her field it was always best to go unnoticed.

Now, she looked at the results in the wall of mirrors and was satisfied. No man would desire her. It was human nature to look at the physical shell and draw emotion from that long before you dipped beneath to the intellect or soul. No woman would envy her. Dull was safe, after all.

No one would suspect a plain, bookish woman of excellent breeding and quiet social manners of deception or violence. Only a select few were aware that the woman beneath was capable of both.

For a reason she couldn't name, that thought made her turn away from her reflection. Deception had been with her all of her adult life, and yet she couldn't quite dismiss the twinges of guilt she felt whenever Eve looked at her as a friend.

It was a job, Hannah reminded herself. No emotional attachments, no emotional involvements were permitted. That was the first and most important rule of the game. She couldn't afford to allow herself to like Eve, to even think of her as anything but a political symbol. If she did, everything she'd worked for could be lost.

The envy had to go as well, Hannah reminded herself. It was a dangerous lapse to let herself look at the love between the prince and Eve and wish something similar for herself. There was no room for love in her profession. There were only goals, commitments and risks.

There would be no prince for her, royal or otherwise.

But before she could prevent it, her thoughts turned to Bennett and the way he'd smiled at her in the moonlight.

Idiot, she told herself and began tightening a few loose pins. He was the last person she should think about in a personal way. If for no other reason, there was his dossier and the astonishing list of women who'd been part of his life already.

Use him, certainly, her mind went on. But don't think about him as anything but a means to an end. Romantic fantasies had ended for her at sixteen. Ten years later, in the middle of her most important job, was hardly the time to begin to weave them again. She would do well to remember that the stiff-lipped, proper Lady Hannah would never see His Royal Highness Prince Bennett de Cordina in a romantic light.

But the woman within dreamed and for a moment strained against the confines she'd built herself.

Hannah turned to look back at the mirrors when she heard the footsteps.

Immediately alert, she cast her eyes down and walked from the room.

"Ah, there you are."

At Bennett's voice, Hannah gave an inward curse, but curtsied. "Your Highness."

"Taking the grand tour?" He walked closer, wondering why she looked as plain as a maiden aunt and continued to intrigue him.

"Yes, sir. I hope it's all right."

"Of course." He took her hand, willing her to look directly at him. There was something about her eyes.... Or perhaps it was her voice, that cool, always composed British tone. "I had some business in town. Alexander suggested I swing by when I'd finished to see if you were ready to go back."

"That's very kind of you." And oh, how she would have preferred a silent, anonymous driver who'd have given her the opportunity to assimilate her report on the drive back.

"I was here." He felt the restlessness layer over him

as she drew her hand back to her side. "If you'd like to see more, I'd be happy to take you around the rest of the Center."

Hannah weighed the pros and cons in a matter of seconds. Another quick look might add something, but she'd already gone through the main theater twice, once with Eve and once alone. It might begin to look odd if she went through again with Bennett.

"No, thank you. It is a fascinating place. I've never seen a theater from this side."

"Eve's territory. I confess I prefer front row center myself." He took Hannah's arm and began to lead her down the hall. "If you hang around her for any length of time, she finds something for you to do. With me, it's usually moving boxes. Heavy boxes."

With a laugh, Hannah slanted him a look. "That's one of the best uses a woman can find for a man."

"I can see why Eve took to you." He'd come simply to do his sister-in-law a favor, but now found himself glad. Outward appearance aside, Lady Hannah was anything but dull. For perhaps the first time in his life, Bennett was beginning to look beneath the physical. "Have you seen much of Cordina yet, Hannah?"

She noticed he'd dropped her title, but decided to let it pass. "Only snatches so far, sir. Once I'm a bit more familiar with Eve's routine, I plan to explore a bit. I've heard your museum has some excellent exhibits. The building itself is reported to be a fine example of post-Renaissance architecture."

He wasn't interested in exhibits, but in her. "Do you like the water?"

"Of course. Sea air is very beneficial for the constitution."

With a half laugh, Bennett paused at the top of the
stairs. "But do you like it?"

He had a strange talent for looking at a woman as
though he were seeing her for the first time. And looking as though it mattered. Despite her training, Hannah
felt her pulse rate accelerate. "Yes. My grandmother has
a place near Cornwall. I spent several summers there as
a girl."

He wondered what she would look like with her hair
down and the sea wind teasing it. Would she laugh as
he had heard her laugh in the garden? Would he see that
light flash in her eyes again? Then he realized it didn't
matter how she looked. He went on impulse, knowing he
might regret it.

"I have to go into Le Havre in a couple of days. The
drive runs along the coast. Come with me."

If he'd asked her to step into the storage room and neck,
she would have been no less surprised. Surprise turned
quickly to caution and caution to calculation. But beneath
it all was the simple pleasure that he wanted her company.
It was the pleasure that worried her.

"It's kind of you to ask, Your Highness, but Eve may
have plans."

"Then we'll check with her first." He wanted her to go.
He found himself already looking forward to spending a
few hours with her away from the palace. Perhaps it was
for the challenge of it, the challenge of picking away at
that prim, proper exterior and finding what, if anything,

lay beneath. Whatever the reason was, Bennett didn't question it. "Would you like to go?"

"Yes, I would." Hannah told herself it was because it would give her the opportunity to study him more closely, for professional reasons. She told herself it would give her the chance to see how well security worked away from the palace and the capital. But the truth was as simple as her answer. She wanted to go.

"Fine, then we'll fix it, and you can stand through the long and wordy welcoming ceremony with me."

"Hate to be bored alone, do you?"

Laughing, Bennett took her hand again. "Yes, I can see exactly why Eve brought you to us." Her hand was an inch from his lips when the murmur of voices came from below. Glancing down, more than a little annoyed, Bennett spotted Chantel.

"The anger has to show," she was insisting, walking so quickly the director had to lengthen his stride to keep up. "Julia is not a passive woman. She doesn't hide what she feels no matter what the consequences. Dammit, Maurice, I'll make it subtle. I know my job."

"Of course you do, *chérie*, that I don't question. It is simply that—"

"Mademoiselle." From the top of the stairs, Bennett looked down. Hannah had a firsthand glimpse of how he smiled at a truly beautiful woman. Without thinking, she drew her hand from his and linked her fingers together.

Chantel, reaching one hand up to draw back her pale blond hair, tilted her head back. Even so dispassionate an observer such as Hannah had to concede that few women could claim such a combination of glamour, beauty and sexuality. Her lips curved. Her eyes, a deep, dreamy shade of blue, smiled with them.

"Your Highness," Chantel said in her rich, smoky voice as she dipped into a formal curtsy. She started up the stairs and Bennett started down. In the middle, they stopped, then Chantel reached up to touch his face before bringing him closer for a lengthy kiss. Above them, Hannah felt her teeth snap together. "It's been a long time."

"Too long." Bennett cupped her hand in both of his. "You're lovelier than ever. It's astonishing."

"It's genes," Chantel claimed, and grinned at him. "My God, Bennett, what a beautiful man you are. If I wasn't a cynic, I'd propose."

"If I wasn't terrified of you, I'd accept." They embraced again with the ease of old friends. "Chantel, it's good to see you again. Eve was turning handsprings when you agreed to take the part."

"It's a good play." Chantel gave a matter-of-fact shrug. "Even though I adore you, I wouldn't have come all this way to take a role in a bomb. Your sister-in-law's a talented woman." Chantel cast a look over her shoulder at the director waiting respectfully at the bottom of the stairs. "You might mention to her that I'm fighting to preserve the integrity of her Julia." As she turned back, she spotted Hannah standing on the landing. "Friend of yours?"

Glancing back, Bennett held out a hand. "Hannah, come meet the incomparable Chantel."

The stiffness in her movement only suited her character, Hannah told herself as she started down. All unremarkable women tensed up when slapped in the face with great beauty. She stopped on the step beside Bennett, but kept nearly a foot of space between them.

"Lady Hannah Rothchild, Chantel O'Hurley."

"How do you do?" Formal and proper, Hannah held out a hand. Chantel kept her face passive as she accepted it.

"I do fine, thank you." As a woman, as an actress who understood angles and role-playing, she wondered why someone with such good bone structure and a flawless complexion would deliberately make themselves appear plain.

"Lady Hannah is keeping Eve company for a few months."

"How nice. Cordina's a beautiful country. I'm sure you'll enjoy it."

"Yes, I already am. I also enjoyed watching you rehearse."

"Thanks, but we have a way to go." Chantel tapped a finger on the banister and wondered why she felt such instant distrust. Dismissing it as overwork, she turned back to Bennett. "I have to run. Try to make some time for me, darling."

"Of course. You're coming to dinner Saturday with the rest of the cast?"

"Wouldn't miss it. I'll see you there, Lady Hannah."

"Goodbye, Miss O'Hurley."

After giving Bennett a quick pat on the cheek, Chantel descended the stairs again and let the director trail behind her.

"She's quite a woman," Bennett murmured.

"Yes, she's very beautiful."

"There's that, too." Without looking at her, Bennett

took Hannah's arm again. "I suppose I've always admired her willpower and ambition. She's determined to be the best and isn't afraid to work for it. Every time I see her on the screen, it's breathtaking."

Hannah dug her fingers into her purse and reminded herself she was supposed to be unassuming. "You admire ambition, Your Highness?"

"Nothing's changed for better or worse without it."

"Some men still find ambition in a woman unflattering, or at least, uncomfortable."

"Some men are idiots."

"I couldn't agree more," Hannah said dryly, dryly enough that he lifted his brow as he gazed at her.

"Why am I never quite sure whether or not you're insulting me, Hannah?"

"I beg your pardon, sir, I was simply agreeing with you."

He stopped again. From the stage came the murmur of voices, but the hall was deserted. Bennett took her chin in his hand, ignoring her jolt of shock, and studied her face. "Hannah, why is it when I look at you I'm not convinced I'm seeing all there is?"

Alarm bells went off in her head. Her face paled a bit. She knew it, but thought, hoped, he would take that as natural. Not by another blink did she show concern. "I don't know what you mean."

"I wonder." He moved his thumb over her jawline, then just beneath where the skin was softer yet, and warm. "Yes, I wonder more than I should about you, Hannah. Do you have an answer for that?"

There were amber flecks in his eyes, turning what

might have been plain brown into something tawny and compelling. He had the mouth of a poet and the hands of a farmer. Hannah wondered how it was possible to combine the two as her heart, always so steady, began to drum against her ribs.

"Your Highness—" It was both the lady without and the lady within who fumbled.

"Do you, Hannah?"

He saw her lips part. Strange, he hadn't noticed how attractive her mouth was before—soft, just a bit wide and beautifully shaped without cosmetics. He wondered if it would taste as cool as her voice or as rich as her eyes.

She had to stop this, here and now. The yearning building inside her could only be destructive. Even as she longed to reach out, she cast her eyes down. "No, sir, except that many times men are intrigued with a woman simply because she's not what they're accustomed to."

"We'll see." He backed off, though the effort it cost him was a surprise. "I'll take you back now, Hannah, and we'll both give it some thought."

Chapter 3

Hannah was given free run of the palace and the grounds. She had only to ask and her bath would be drawn or her bed turned down. If she developed a craving for hot chocolate at three a.m., she could pick up the phone beside her bed and request it. As a guest of the Royal Family, she was afforded every amenity the palace could offer.

And as a guest of the Royal Family, she was afforded her own guards.

Hannah considered them only a slight nuisance. It was a simple enough matter for someone of her talents to make them think she was tucked safely away in her rooms while she was somewhere else entirely. However, the fact that she was being watched made it difficult to set up a meeting with her contact on the outside.

Using the palace phones was out of the question. Too many extensions made it a risk that even a casual, coded conversation could be overheard. She'd briefly considered smuggling in a transmitter, then had rejected the notion. Transmissions could be traced. She hadn't spent two years of her life to get to this point to see it all wiped away because of some electronic foul-up. In any case, she preferred meetings of such importance to be face-to-face.

Two days after she arrived in Cordina, she mailed a letter. It was addressed to an old family friend in Sussex who didn't exist. Its destination was one of Deboque's many branches throughout Europe. If for any reason the letter was intercepted and opened, the reader would find nothing more interesting than a chatty note describing Cordina and the weather.

Once the letter reached its destination and was decoded, it would read differently. Hannah had given her name, her rank in the organization and had requested a meeting, detailing the time, date and place. The information would be fed back to the Cordina contact. All she had to do was get there, alone.

One week, Hannah thought once the letter was on its way. In one week she would well and truly begin what had been started so long ago. She had plenty to do to keep her busy in the meantime.

Princess Gabriella and her family were visiting the palace that evening. The staff had been in an uproar for the better part of the day, more, Hannah guessed, because the children were descending than for any other reason. Hannah had heard that the priceless collection of Fabergé eggs was to be put out of reach.

She spent the day quietly enough, visiting Eve and Marissa in the nursery, lunching with several members of the Historical Society, and in the lull of late afternoon, exploring the cellars for vulnerabilities.

Now, she clipped on her pearls and prepared to join the family in the main drawing room. It would be interesting to see them all together, she thought. In that way she could judge the interactions as well as the individuals. Before too much time had passed, she had to know them all as well as she knew herself. One mistake, one bad judgment call, and all could be lost.

"Come back here, you little demon!"

Hannah heard a loud laugh, a thud, then rushing feet. Before she had a chance to open the door to see for herself, it burst open. Barreling through it was a small boy with a thatch of dark hair that may or may not have been combed in the past week. He gave her an amazing grin, showing more than one gap before he scooted under her bed.

"Cachez-moi, s'il vous plaît!" His voice was muffled by the skirt of the spread before he disappeared.

Hannah opened her mouth again only to see Bennett filling the doorway.

"Did you see a small, miserably mannered boy?"

"I, ah—no," she decided on the spot and folded her hands. "I did think I heard someone go running past. What are you—"

"Thanks. If you see him, lock him in a closet or something." He started off down the hall. "Dorian, you nasty little thief, you can't hide forever."

Hannah walked to the door and looked out to see Bennett turning the corner before she closed it. Moving back to the bed, she crouched down and lifted the skirt. "I think it's safe now," Hannah told him in French.

The dark hair poked out first, then a sturdy little body

dressed in short pants and a white linen shirt that were streaked with dirt. If Hannah hadn't already seen his picture, she would have taken him for one of the servants' offspring. But he was royal.

"You are English. I speak excellent English."

"So you do."

"Thank you for hiding me from my uncle." Young Prince Dorian bowed. Though he wasn't yet five, he executed it perfectly. "He was angry, but he doesn't stay that way long. I'm Prince Dorian."

"Your Highness." Hannah curtsied. "It's a pleasure to meet you. I'm Lady Hannah Rothchild." Then unable to resist, she bent down to his level. "What did you steal?"

Dorian glanced at the closed door, back at Hannah, then grinned. Digging into his back pocket he pulled out a yo-yo. It might once have been blue, but now it was the gray of old wood with a few chips of brighter paint still holding. Hannah studied it with appropriate respect.

"This is Bennett's—His Highness's?" Hannah corrected.

"*Merveilleux, n'est-ce pas?* He's had it since he was five." Dorian turned the toy over in his hand, marveling that it had once been new and shiny when his uncle had been just the age he was now. "He gets angry when I go into his room and play with it, but how else am I going to be able to make it work?"

"Good point." Hannah barely resisted the urge to ruffle the royal head of hair. "And one would doubt he plays with it himself very often."

"He keeps it on a shelf. It isn't that he really minds me looking at it," Dorian explained, loyal to the core. "It's just that when I try to make it work, the string gets all tangled and knotted up."

"It takes a little practice."

"I know." He grinned again. "And I can only practice if I steal it."

"Your logic is flawless, Your Highness. May I see?"

Dorian hesitated only a moment, then graciously handed it over. "Girls usually aren't interested in such things." He made a grimace of masculine disgust. "My sisters play with dolls."

"Everyone has different tastes, I suppose." Hannah slid her finger into the loop, wondering how long it had been since Bennett's had fit there. The string wasn't as old as the toy itself. By her guess, it would have been replaced more than a dozen times over the years. On impulse, she let the yo-yo slide down, dangle, then brought it neatly up.

"Oh, nicely done." Charmed, Dorian watched her with wide eyes.

"Thank you, sir. I used to have one of my own. It was red," she remembered with a half smile. "Until my dog chewed it up."

"Can you do any tricks? I tried Round the World once and broke a lamp. Uncle Bennett scolded me, but then he tossed out the pieces himself so no one would know."

Because she could picture it so well, Hannah smiled. A loud roar, but little bite, she decided and wished she didn't like him the better for it. "A trick?" As she considered she took the yo-yo up and down. Then, with a quick flick of her wrist took it Round the World. When it snapped back in her palm, Dorian laughed and climbed on her bed.

"Do another, please."

Calling on memory, Hannah Walked the Dog and had the young prince bouncing on the bed and calling out for more.

"Well done, Lady Hannah," Bennett said from the doorway. "Obviously you have hidden talents."

Hannah had to bite off an oath as she brought the yo-yo back. "Your Highness." Toy in hand, she curtsied. "I didn't hear you knock."

"I didn't." Bennett pushed away from the doorjamb he was leaning on to walk to the bed. Unrepentant, his nephew grinned up at him.

"Isn't she wonderful, Uncle Bennett?"

"We'll discuss the Lady Hannah's attributes later." He gave Dorian's ear a twist before turning around. "My property, if you will."

Fighting to keep a straight face, Hannah handed it to him.

"This might seem to be nothing more than a simple child's toy," Bennett began as he slipped it into his pocket. "But in fact, it's an heirloom."

"I see." She cleared her throat on the laugh, but it escaped anyway. Hoping she looked contrite, she stared at the floor. "I beg your pardon, sir."

"The hell you do. And he was in here all along wasn't he?" Bennett pushed his nephew flat on the bed and sent him into a fit of giggles. "You let me go running off all over the palace looking for this petty thief when all the time he was hiding behind your skirts."

"The bed skirts to be honest, sir." She had to clear her throat again, but managed to speak calmly. "When you rushed by with so vague a description, I had no idea you were looking for Prince Dorian."

"I admire a good liar," Bennett murmured as he moved closer. For the second time he caught her chin in his hand. But for the first time, she saw all of the arrogance he was capable of and felt all of its attraction. "And I grow only more intrigued."

"Lady Hannah can do a double Round the World."

"Fascinating." Bennett slid his hand away slowly as he turned back to his nephew. If he'd listened for it, he might have heard Hannah's slow sigh of relief. "I thought we had an agreement, Dorian."

Dorian's head drooped, but Hannah didn't notice that the light in his eyes dimmed in the least. "I only wanted to see it. I'm sorry, Uncle Bennett."

"Sure you are." Bennett hauled him up by the armpits, scowled, then kissed him soundly. "Your mother's downstairs. Don't slide in the halls on the way to the drawing room."

"All right." On his feet again, Dorian bowed to Hannah. "It was a pleasure meeting you, Lady Hannah."

"And you, sir."

He sent her a gap-toothed grin before he dashed off.

"Sweet talker," Bennett muttered. "Oh, you might think he's all charm, but he has a black heart."

"Strangely enough I was reminded of you."

With one brow lifted, Bennett rocked back on his heels. "Indeed, my lady, that is strange."

"He's a scoundrel, without question. And you love him."

"That's beside the point." Bennett stuck his hand in his pocket. "As to the matter of the yo-yo."

"Yes, sir?"

"Try to wait until I'm five feet away before you laugh in my face."

"As you wish, Your Highness."

"It was a gift from my mother when I was ill one summer. I've bought the little devil a dozen of them, but he keeps stealing mine. He knows if I don't get a son of my own by the time he's ten I'll make him a gift of it."

"I have a redheaded doll my mother gave me when I broke my wrist in a fall. I kept it when I outgrew all the others."

It wasn't until he'd taken her hand that she realized she'd told him something he didn't need to know, something she'd never told anyone else. Even as she warned herself such lapses were dangerous, his lips brushed her fingers.

"You, Lady Hannah, have a kind heart as well as a clever tongue. Come, walk downstairs with me and meet the rest of my family."

Reeve MacGee would be a formidable obstacle. Hannah had thought so before, but seeing him with his family, she was sure of it. She knew his background from the time he'd entered the police force as a rookie through his less publicized work for the United States government.

His involvement with Cordina and the Royal Family had the ring of romance, but Reeve was no poet. He'd come out of a self-imposed retirement at Prince Armand's request when Gabriella had been kidnapped. Though she'd escaped, her time in captivity had left its mark.

Amnesia had plagued her and Reeve had been enlisted to protect her, and to investigate.

There had been no doubt that Deboque had been pushing the buttons, but though his lover had been captured and imprisoned, she'd never implicated him. Like other powerful men, Deboque inspired loyalty. Or fear.

During the time that Gabriella was struggling to regain her memory, she and Reeve had fallen in love. Although Reeve had refused to accept a title when they married, he'd agreed to head security in Cordina. Even with Reeve's experience and skill, the palace had been infiltrated once again.

Two years ago, Alexander had nearly been assassinated. Since that time, Reeve had managed to block any and all attempts on members of the Royal Family. But Deboque was about to walk out of prison. With freedom would come more power.

Hannah watched Reeve now, seeing a quiet, introspective man who plainly adored his wife and children. He would use everything available to protect them from harm. So much the better.

With her hands folded and her skirts smoothed, Hannah sat and listened.

"We all know your play's going to be a wonderful success." Gabriella, with her hand caught loosely in Reeve's, smiled at Eve. Her rich red hair was styled with casual chic around a face that remained delicate and lovely. "That doesn't mean we don't understand you have to worry about it."

"I'm at the point now where I wish it was over." Eve drew Marissa into her lap.

"But you're feeling well?"

"I'm feeling fine." Eve let Marissa climb down again. "Between Alex's pampering and Hannah's eagle eye, I can hardly lift a finger without a doctor's certificate."

"It's so good of you to come." Gabriella smiled at Hannah before she sipped some sparkling water. "I know firsthand how comforting it is to have a friend nearby. Are we keeping you happy enough so that you're not homesick?"

"I'm very happy in Cordina." Hannah kept her back straight against the sofa.

"I hope you'll come out to the farm while you're here."

"I've heard a great deal about it." Gabriella had been kidnapped there while it had still been an overgrown plot of land. "I'd love to see it for myself."

"Then we'll arrange it." Reeve spoke quietly as he lit a cigarette. "You're enjoying your visit so far?"

"Yes, I am." Their eyes met and held. "Cordina is a fascinating country. It has a fairy-tale aura perhaps, but it's very real. I'm particularly interested in visiting the museum."

"I think you'll find we have some very unusual exhibits," Armand put in.

"Yes, sir. I did some research before leaving England. I have no doubt that my time in Cordina will be an education."

Marissa toddled over, still a bit unsteady on her year-old legs, and held her arms up. Hannah placed the child in her lap.

"Your father is well?" Reeve asked her through a haze of smoke.

Hannah jangled her pearls to entertain the baby. "Yes,

thank you. It often seems that the older I get, the younger he gets."

"Families, no matter how large or how small, are often the focus of our lives," Reeve said quietly.

"Yes, that's true," Hannah murmured as she played with the baby. "It's a pity that families, and life, aren't as simple as they seem when we're children."

Bennett sat relaxed in his chair and wondered why he thought if he could read between the lines, he'd discover a great deal more than small talk.

"I wasn't aware you knew Hannah's father, Reeve."

"Only casually." When he leaned back, his smile was easy. "I heard that Dorian stole your yo-yo again."

"I should have locked it in the safe when I heard he was coming." Bennett patted the slight bulge in his pocket. "I'd have given the little devil a run for his money, but he had an accomplice." He turned his head to look at Hannah.

"I'll have to apologize for my son—" Gabriella's lips curved as she lifted her glass again "—for drawing you into his crime, Lady Hannah."

"On the contrary, I enjoyed it. Prince Dorian is charming."

"We call him other things at home," Reeve murmured. The woman was a mystery, he thought. The harder he looked for chinks, the fewer flaws he saw. "With that in mind, I think I'll go out and look for the bunch of them. Adrienne's at the age where you can't be sure she'll mind them or urge them to wade in the fountain."

Bennett glanced toward the terrace doors. "God knows what havoc they might have wrought in the last twenty minutes."

"Wait until you have your own." Eve rose to take Marissa from Hannah. "You'll spoil them rotten. If you'll excuse me, I want to go up and feed Marissa."

"I'll go with you." Gabriella set her glass aside. "I thought we might talk over the plans for the Christmas Ball. You know I want to help as much as I can."

"Thank God I don't have to beg. No, Hannah, please, sit and relax," Eve continued as Hannah started to stand. "We won't be long."

"See that you're not." Bennett took out the yo-yo to pass it from hand to hand. "Dinner's in an hour."

"We all know your priorities, Ben." Eve bent to kiss his cheek before she left the room.

"I could use a walk myself." Rising, Alexander nodded to Reeve. "I'll help you round up the children." They were barely out the terrace doors when a servant appeared in the doorway.

"I beg your pardon, Your Highness. A call from Paris."

"Yes, I've been expecting it. I'll take it in my office, Louis. If you'll excuse me, Lady Hannah." Taking her hand, Armand bowed over it. "I'm sure Bennett can entertain you for a few moments. Bennett, perhaps Lady Hannah would enjoy seeing the library."

"If you like to look at walls of books," Bennett said when his father was gone, "you can't do much better."

"I'm very fond of books." Taking him at his word, Hannah rose.

"All right then." Though he could have thought of a dozen better ways to while away an hour, he took her arm and led her through the corridors.

"It's difficult to believe that the museum could have

finer paintings than you have here in the palace, Prince Bennett."

"Le Musée d'Art has a hundred and fifty-two examples of Impressionist and Postimpressionist paintings, including two Corots, three Monets and a particularly fine Renoir. We've recently acquired a Childe Hassam from the United States. In return my family has donated six Georges Complainiers, a Cordinian artist who painted on the island in the nineteenth century."

"I see."

Noting her expression, Bennett laughed. "As it happens, I'm on the board of the museum. I may prefer horses, Hannah, but that doesn't preclude an affection for art. What do you think of this?"

He paused in front of a small watercolor. The Royal Palace was beautifully, almost mystically painted. Its white, white walls and turrets rose behind a pink mist that enchanted rather than concealed the building itself. It must have been dawn, she thought. The sky was such a delicate blue in contrast to the deeper sea. She could see the antiquity, the fantasy and the reality. In the foreground were the high iron gates and sturdy stone walls that protected the palace grounds.

"It's beautiful. It shows love as well as a touch of wonder. Who was the artist?"

"My great-great-grandmother." Pleased with her reaction, Bennett drew her hand into the crook of his arm. "She'd done hundreds of watercolors and had tucked them away. In her day, women painted or drew as a hobby, not as a profession."

"Some things change," Hannah murmured, then looked back at the painting. "Some things don't."

"A few years ago I found her work in a trunk in one of the attics. So many of them had been damaged. It broke my heart. Then I found this." He touched the frame, reverently, Hannah thought. She looked from his hand to his face and found herself caught up in him. "It was like stepping back in time, generations, and discovering yourself. It could have been painted today, and it would look the same."

She could feel her heart moving toward him. What woman was immune to pride and sensitivity? In defense, she took a small step back. "In Europe, we understand that a few generations are only a blink in time. Our history stands before us, centuries of it. It becomes our responsibility to give that same gift to each new generation."

Bennett looked at her and found her eyes almost impossibly deep. "We do have that in common, don't we? In America, there's an urgency that can be exciting, even contagious, but here, we know how long it takes to build and secure. Politics change, governments shift, but history stands firm."

She had to turn away from him. It would only cloud the issue if she thought of him as a caring, sensitive man rather than an assignment. "Are there any others?" she said with a nod toward the painting.

"Only a handful, unfortunately. Most were beyond repair." For reasons he could only be half-sure of, he wanted to share with her things that mattered to him. "There's one in the music room. The rest are in the museum. Here, have a look." With his hand guiding her again, he took her down the hall into the next wing, their footsteps echoing off the mosaic tile.

Leading her through an open door, Bennett took her into a room that seemed to have been fashioned to accent the white grand piano in its center.

There was a harp in the corner that might have been played a hundred years before, or last week. In a glass case were antique wind instruments and a fragile lyre. The flowers were fresh here, as they were in every room in the palace. Trailing blossoms of jasmine spilled out of glossy, Chinese red urns. A small marble fireplace was swept and scrubbed clean with a pile of fresh kindling stacked as though inviting the match.

With Bennett, she walked across an Aubusson carpet to look back in time. This painting was of a ball, festive in bright colors and bold strokes. Women, gloriously feminine in mid-nineteenth-century gowns, were whirled around a gleaming floor by dashing men. There were mirrors that reflected the dancers and doubled them while a trio of chandeliers glistened overhead. As Hannah studied it, she could almost hear the waltz.

"How lovely. Is this room here, in the palace?"

"Yes. It has hardly changed. We'll have the Christmas Ball there next month."

Only a month, she thought. There was so much to be done. In a matter of hours Deboque would be out of prison, and she would soon learn if her groundwork had been clever enough.

"This is a beautiful room." Hannah turned. Keep your conversation light, she warned herself. Keep your mind light, for now. "In our country house there's a small music room. Nothing like this, of course, but I've always found it so relaxing." She wandered to the piano, not so much to examine it as to give herself distance. "Do you play, Your Highness?"

"Hannah, we're alone. It isn't necessary to be so formal."

"I've always considered the use of titles as proper rather than formal." She didn't want this, she thought quickly. She didn't want him to close that gap of rank between them.

"I've always considered it annoying between friends." He walked behind her to touch her lightly on the shoulder. "I thought we were."

She could feel his hand right through the neat linen of her dress, through the skinny silk strap beneath and onto her flesh. Fighting her own private war, she kept her back to him. "Were what, sir?"

He laughed, then both hands were on her shoulders, turning her to face him. "Friends, Hannah. I find you good company. That's one of the first requirements of friendship, isn't it?"

She was looking up at him, solemn-eyed, with the faintest blush of color along her cheekbones. Her shoulders seemed so strong under his hands, yet he remembered how soft, how delicate the skin along her jawline had seemed.

Her dress was brown and dull, her face unpainted and unframed. Not a hair was out of place and yet he got a flash of her laughing, her hair unbound and her shoulders bare. And the laughter would be for only him.

"What the devil is it about you?" Bennett muttered.

"I beg your pardon—"

"Wait." Impatient, as annoyed with himself as he was with her, Bennett stepped closer. As she stiffened, he held his hands up, palms out as if to reassure her he meant her no harm. "Just be still a moment, would you?" he asked as he lowered his head and touched his mouth to hers.

No response, show no response. Hannah repeated it over and over in her head like a litany. He didn't press, he didn't coax or demand. He simply tasted, more gently than she'd had known a man could be. And the flavor of him seeped into her until she was all but drunk with it.

His eyes remained open, watching hers. He was close, so close she could catch the scent of soap on his skin. Something that brought images of the sea. Hannah dug her fingers into her palms and fought to keep from showing him the turmoil within.

God, she wanted. How she wanted.

He didn't know what he'd expected. What he found was softness, comfort, sweetness without heat or passion. Yet he saw both in her eyes. He felt no driving need to touch her or to deepen the kiss. Not this first one. Perhaps he already knew there would be others. But this first one showed him an ease, a relaxation that he'd never looked for in a woman before.

He was man enough, experienced enough, to know there was a volcano inside of her. But strangely, he had no desire to push it to the eruption point, yet.

Bennett broke the kiss simply by stepping back. Hannah didn't move a muscle.

"I didn't do that to frighten you." He spoke quietly, for it was the truth. "It was just a test."

"You don't frighten me." He didn't frighten the woman he could see, but the one within was terrified.

It wasn't quite the answer he'd wanted. "Then what do I do to you?"

Slowly, carefully, she unballed her hands. "I'm afraid I don't understand what you mean, Your Highness."

He studied her another moment, then spun away. "Maybe not." He rubbed a hand along the back of his neck wondering why such an unassuming, placid woman should make him so tense. He understood desire. God knows he'd felt it before. But not like this. Never quite like this.

"Dammit, Hannah, isn't anything going on inside of you?"

"Of course, sir, a great number of things."

He had to laugh. He should have known she would put him in his place with logic. "Call me by my name, please."

"As you wish."

He turned back. She was standing in front of the glistening white piano, hands folded, eyes calm and quiet on his. He thought it the most ridiculous thing, but knew he was very close to falling in love. "Hannah—"

He'd taken no more than two steps toward her when Reeve walked into the room. "Bennett, excuse me, but your father would like to see you before dinner."

Duty and desire. Bennett wondered if he would ever find a full merging of the two. "Thank you, Reeve."

"I'll take Lady Hannah back in."

"All right." Still, he paused and looked at her again. "I'd like to talk with you later."

"Of course." She would move heaven and earth to avoid it.

She remained where she was when he left. Reeve glanced over his shoulder before he came closer. "Is there a problem, Lady Hannah?"

"No." She drew a deep breath, but didn't relax. "Why should there be?"

"Bennett can be…distracting."

This time when her eyes met his, she made certain they were slightly amused. A layer, the thinnest of the layers of her outer covering was dismissed. "I'm not easily distracted, particularly when I'm working."

"So I've been told," Reeve said easily enough. He was still looking for flaws and was afraid he might have found the first in the way she had looked at Bennett. "But you've never worked on an assignment quite like this one."

"As a senior agent for the ISS, I'm capable of handling any assignment." Her voice was brisk again, not the voice of a woman who'd been moved, almost unbearably, by a kiss. "You'll have my report by tomorrow. Now I think we'd better join the others."

She started by, but he took her arm and stopped her. "There's a great deal riding on this. On you."

Hannah only nodded. "I'm aware of that. You requested the best, and I am."

"Maybe." But the closer it came, the more he worried. "You've got a hell of a reputation, Hannah, but you've never come up against anyone like Deboque before."

"Nor he anyone like me." She glanced toward the hallway again, then lowered her voice. "I'm an established member of his organization now. It's taken me two years to get this close. I saved him two and a half million by seeing that that munitions deal wasn't botched six months ago. A man like Deboque appreciates initiative. In the last few months, I've been planting the seeds that will discredit his second in command."

"Or get your throat cut."

"That's for me to worry about. In a matter of weeks, I'll be his right hand. Then I'll serve him to you on a platter."

"Confidence is an excellent weapon, if it isn't overdone."

"I don't overdo." She thought of Bennett and strengthened her resolve. "I've never failed with an assignment, Reeve. I don't intend to begin with this one."

"Just make sure you keep in contact. I'm sure you'll understand when I say I don't trust anyone."

"I understand perfectly, because neither do I. Shall we go?"

Chapter 4

Hannah's plans to avoid driving with Bennett to Le Havre were neatly demolished. She'd justified her decision by convincing herself she could detail more useful information by concentrating on the palace. In order to remain behind, she'd come up with the credible, if unoriginal excuse of a headache.

Hannah had deliberately waited until Alexander had finished breakfasting with his family so that she could speak to Eve alone. It took Eve less than ten minutes to turn it on her.

"It's no wonder you're not feeling yourself." Eve sipped tea in the sunny nursery while she looked over her schedule. "I've kept you cooped up ever since you arrived."

"Don't be silly. The palace is the size of a small town. I've hardly been cooped up."

"However big it is, it still has walls. A nice drive along the coast is just what you need. Bernadette." She glanced up at the young nurse who was preparing to take Marissa for her morning walk. "Would you see that Princess Marissa has a hat? It's a bit breezy out."

"Yes, ma'am."

Eve held out her arms for her daughter. "Have a nice time, darling."

"Flowers," Marissa said, and laughed at her own voice.

"Yes, pick some flowers. We'll put them right here in your room." She kissed both of Marissa's cheeks then let her go. "I hate not being able to take her for a walk this morning, but I have a meeting at the Center in an hour."

"You're a wonderful mother, Eve," Hannah murmured when she saw the concern in Eve's eyes.

"I love her so much." With a long sigh, she picked up her tea again. "I know it's foolish, but when I'm not with her I think of dozens of things that might happen, that could happen."

"I'd say it was normal."

"Maybe. Being who we are, what we are, just magnifies everything." Unconsciously, she rested her hand where even now her second child slept. "I want so badly to give her a sense of normalcy, and yet..." Eve shook her head. "There's a price for everything."

Hannah remembered Alexander saying almost the same thing in referring to his wife.

"Eve, Marissa is a lovely, healthy and happy child. I'm not sure they get any more normal than that."

Eve stared at her a moment, then dropped her chin on her open palm. "Oh, Hannah, I'm not sure how I got through the last two years without you. Which brings me right back to where we were." Briskly, Eve refilled Hannah's cup. "You came here to visit and so far I haven't given you a moment's free time unless you were hand-cuffed to me. That makes me feel very selfish."

"The reason I'm here is to be with you," Hannah reminded Eve, as she felt herself rapidly losing ground.

"The reason you're here is because we're friends. As a favor, take the day, relax, enjoy the sea air. I promise you Ben can be wonderful company. I guarantee that five minutes after you're in the car, your headache will disappear."

"Someone have a headache?" Ben asked as he strode in. He was wearing the white dress uniform with the red insignia that stated his rank as officer in the Cordinian Navy. On the left breast pocket was the royal seal that proclaimed him prince. Hannah had always considered the opinion that women fell for men in uniform nonsense. Until now.

He looked so…dashing, she admitted, though her practical side searched for a less dramatic word. The snowy-white jacket accented his tan and the dark contrast of his hair. He grinned at her, making Hannah aware that he understood his effect. Automatically she rose to dip into a curtsy.

"Bennett, I'd forgotten what a heartbreaker you are in dress whites." Eve tipped her face up for a kiss. "Maybe I should tell Hannah to take an aspirin and stay behind after all."

"I think Lady Hannah can take care of herself. Can't you, *chérie*?"

Hannah decided then and there that if she had to fence with him, she would wield her foil well. "It's always been the case."

"You are a bit pale." He touched a finger to her cheek. "Are you really not well?"

"It's nothing." She wondered if he could feel her blood stir at the casual contact. "And Eve assures me that a drive along the sea is exactly the right prescription."

"Good. I'll bring her back with roses in her cheeks."

"If you'll give me a moment, I need to get my bag."

"Bennett." Eve stopped him before he could follow Hannah out. "Am I wrong, or did I see something just now?"

He didn't pretend to misunderstand her. "I'm not sure."

"Hannah's lived a very sheltered life. I suppose I don't have to tell you to be…well, careful?"

Though the sunlight streamed in behind him, his eyes cooled. "No, I don't have to be reminded who a man in my position can and can't have an affair with."

"I didn't say that to annoy you." Instantly Eve was on her feet, taking his hands. "We were friends long before we were family, Ben. I only ask because I'm fond of her and I know how irresistible you can be."

He softened, as he always did with Eve. "You always managed to resist."

"You always treated me like a sister." Eve hesitated again, torn between two loyalties. "Would I be pushing if I said she's not your usual type?"

"No, she's not. Perhaps that's what baffles me. Stop worrying." He bent to kiss her brow. "I won't damage your proper British friend."

"It could be I'm just as concerned about you."

"Then don't be." Giving her cheek a careless stroke,

he walked to the door. "Tell Marissa I'll bring her some seashells."

Calm and resigned to her decision, Hannah met him at the top of the stairs. "I hope I didn't keep you waiting."

"We've plenty of time. I can promise the drive will be worth the pomp and speeches on the other end."

"I don't object to pomp and speeches."

"Then we're fortunate. Claude." Bennett nodded to the tall, sturdy man who waited beside the main doors.

"Good morning, Your Highness. Lady Hannah. Your car is ready, sir."

"Thank you, Claude." Bennett steered Hannah through the doors knowing the simple statement meant that the road between Cordina and Le Havre had been secured.

Hannah saw the car the moment they stepped outside. The zippy little French convertible sat at the foot of the steps flanked by two solid sedans.

"Do you drive that?"

"Looks like I should wind it up, doesn't it?" Bennett touched the shiny red hood with affection. "Handles like a dream. I've had her up to one-twenty on a straight."

She thought of how it would feel, speeding beside the sea with the wind on her face. Hannah pushed aside such wishes and tried for an uneasy look. "I hope you don't intend to try to break your record today."

With a laugh, he opened the door for her himself. "For you, I'll drive like a grandfather."

Hannah slipped into the seat and nearly sighed with pleasure. "It is rather small."

"Big enough for two." Bennett rounded the hood. Claude already had his door opened.

"But surely you don't travel without your security or an assistant."

"Whenever possible. My secretary will be in the car behind us. Let's give them a run, shall we?" He switched on the ignition. From the rich sound under the hood, Hannah decided it was filled with engine. Before she could draw a breath, Bennett sent the car speeding down the long, sedate drive. He drove the way he rode a stallion. Full speed.

"They're muttering already, I imagine." He gave the guards at the gates an easy salute. "If Claude had his way, I'd never go over thirty kilometers. I'd also be closed up in a bulletproof limo wearing a suit of armor."

"It's his job to protect you."

"A pity he has so little humor about it." Bennett downshifted, then sent the car squeaking around a curve.

"Did your grandfather live a long and fruitful life?"

"What?"

"Your grandfather," Hannah repeated as she folded her hands neatly in her lap. "I wondered if he lived a long life. It seems unlikely if he drove like this."

The wind was blowing his hair around his face as he turned his head to grin at her. "Trust me, *ma belle*, I know the roads."

She didn't want him to slow down. It was the first time she'd felt true freedom in months. She'd nearly forgotten how sweet it tasted. The sea shimmered blue and white beside the road as they traveled down from the heights of the capital. Palms twisted their way toward the sky, bending and swaying in the stiff breeze. Lush red flowers burst out of bushes that grew helter-skelter along the roadside. The air smelled of sea and perpetual spring.

"Do you ski?" Bennett asked her as he noticed her watching a man glide over the water behind a low-slung boat.

"I never have." It looked wonderful. "I'm sure you have to be fairly athletic. I'm more at home in libraries."

"One can't read all the time."

She watched the skier take a somersaulting tumble into the water. "I think perhaps I can."

Bennett grinned and roared through a lazy S-turn. "Life's hardly worth the trouble without a few spills. Don't you ever have the urge for adventure, Hannah?"

She thought of the past ten years of her life, of the assignments that had taken her from castles to ghettos and everywhere in between. French alleys. Italian waterfronts. She thought of the small-caliber pistol she carried in her bag and the pencil-slim stiletto tucked like a lover against her thigh.

"I suppose I've always preferred my adventures vicariously, through books."

"No secret dreams?"

"Some of us are exactly what we seem." Suddenly uncomfortable, she shifted away from the topic. "I didn't realize you were a naval officer." Another lie, she thought. But her profession was built on them.

"I served a couple of years. At this point, it's more of an honorary rank. Second sons are traditionally bound for the military."

"So you chose the navy."

"Cordina's surrounded by the sea. Our fleet is smaller than yours, certainly, but it's strong."

"And these are uneasy times."

Something came and went in his eyes. "In Cordina we've learned that all times are uneasy times. We're a peaceful country, and because we want to remain so, we're prepared always for war."

She thought of the pretty white palace with its exotic gardens and fairy-tale turrets. Inaccessible by sea, with a cliff-top view that scanned miles with the naked eye. She sat back as the sea rolled by. Nothing ever was as simple as it seemed.

Le Havre was charming. Nestled at the base of a long hill, it clustered together with small whitewashed buildings and clapboard cottages. Fishing and sailboats swayed quietly at neat docks at one curve of the harbor. Around the seawall of old stone, hardy blue flowers pushed their way through cracks. There were lobster traps and nets spread and drying in the sun. The scent of fish was heady and oddly pleasant in the early-morning air.

At a glance, it could have been taken for any tidy fishing town that survived on and with the sea. But as they rounded the harbor the docks became more expansive, the buildings larger. Cargo ships with men hauling freight down gangplanks flanked an ocean liner. Like much of Cordina, Le Havre was more than it seemed. Through location and the skill of its people, it was one of the finest ports of call in the Mediterranean. It was also the center of Cordina's naval base.

Negotiating the narrow, winding streets, Bennett drove through a set of gates. He slowed only long enough to be acknowledged by the guards with snappy salutes. There were bungalows here painted a faded pink that reminded Hannah of the inside of a seashell. Palms and flowers grew in profusion, but she recognized the structure and order of a military facility. Moments later, Bennett drew up in front of a stucco building where seamen in whites stood at attention.

"For the next few hours," he murmured to Hannah, "we're official." Bennett reached in the back and picked up his hat. Even as he set it on his wind-ruffled hair, one of the seamen reached the door to open it for him. With the brim shading his eyes, Bennett returned the salutes. He knew the sedan had already pulled up behind him, but didn't look back as he guided Hannah into the building.

"First, we have a few formalities," he warned her, tucking his hat under his arm.

The formalities were a group of officers, from admiral down, and their wives and attachés who were waiting to greet and be greeted by His Royal Highness.

Hannah acknowledged the introductions and pretended not to see the looks of speculation. *Not the prince's type.* She could read it easily in every eye that met hers. She fully agreed.

They were given tea and a tour of the building—for her sake. Hannah feigned an ignorance of the equipment shown her, asking the proper questions and looking properly polite at the simplistic answers. She could hardly mention that the radar and communication systems were as familiar to her as they were to the trained operators. In a pinch, she could have rigged the equipment to contact the ISS base outside London or Deboque's headquarters in Athens.

She walked by display cases, listening with apparent fascination as an admiral explained to her the difference between a destroyer and an aircraft carrier.

The pomp and circumstance continued as they were escorted outside to await the docking of the *Indépendance*. The band, their white uniforms blinding in the sun, struck up a rousing march as Bennett stepped onto the dock. Crowds of people cheered from behind the military barricade. Babies and small children were held up so that they could catch a glimpse of the prince.

Hannah counted off a dozen security people mingled with the crowd in addition to the two men who were never more than an arm's span from Bennett's elbow.

Deboque is out, she thought. Everything is a risk.

The battle-gray destroyer maneuvered into position while the crowd applauded and the band continued to play. Seamen on the dock stood at attention as did seamen on deck. After six months at sea, the *Indépendance* was home.

The gangplank came ponderously down. The pipes were sounded. The captain strode down to salute the officers and bow to his prince.

"Welcome home, Captain." Bennett offered his hand, and the crowd cheered again.

There was, as there always was on such occasions, a speech to be made. Hannah kept her face attentive while she slowly scanned the crowd.

It was no surprise to find him there. The small, slightly stoop-shouldered man was on the edge of the crowd holding a small Cordinian flag. In his plain work clothes and quiet face, he would never be noticed or remembered. He was one of Deboque's best.

There would be no move on Prince Bennett today, she thought, though the back of her neck itched. Her successful planting at the palace had been one of her highest contributions to Deboque's organization. The working order now was for care and cleverness rather than a rash assassination attempt.

In any case, she knew Deboque wasn't as interested in Bennett as he was in Alexander, and in Alexander not so much as in Armand. He wouldn't settle for the second in line to the throne after so long a wait.

Still, she closed her hand over the handle of her bag. She shifted, only a matter of inches, but Bennett's body was now more than half shielded by hers.

Had the man been sent with a message for her? Hannah wondered. Or had he simply been ordered to stay close and watch? Instinct told her it was the second. Casually, she swept the crowd again. Her eyes met his and held for only a fraction of a second. There was an acknowledgement, but no signal. Hannah let her gaze move on, knowing they'd meet within a few days at the museum.

The pretty ceremony with its brisk military music and banners continued with a tour of the ship and an inspection of the crew. Hannah walked with the admiral's wife as Bennett was led down the line of officers and seamen. Now and then he stopped to comment or ask a personal estion of one of the men. More, she saw that he listened he answers. Even a casual observer could have seen he was given more than respect due his rank by the

men he greeted. There was love, the kind Hannah was
aware only men could give men.

Though she was certain Bennett had seen enough of
ships to last a lifetime, he toured the bridge, the officers' quarters and the galleys with apparent fascination.
The ship was as neat as a parlor, utilitarian certainly, but
freshly scrubbed and without a sign of peeling paint or
rust.

Bennett moved quickly through the ship, without seeming to hurry over the decks. There were questions that had
to be asked, compliments that were deserved, but he knew
duffel bags were packed and waiting. He clasped hands
with the captain again, aware that the man had every right
to be proud of his ship and his men. As he started down
the gangplank, the cheers rose up again. Bennett had to
wonder if they were for him or because the ceremonies
were finally over and the men could go ashore.

Protocol demanded that he be escorted back through
headquarters. It was here that Hannah began to sense
his impatience to be off. Still, he was gracious, shaking hands, kissing hands, exchanging a last pleasantry.
It wasn't until he was seated in his own car again that he
let out a low oath.

"I beg your pardon, sir?"

Bennett merely patted Hannah's hand before he started
the engine. "Four hours was a long time to keep you on
your feet. Thank you for bearing with me."

"On the contrary, I found it fascinating." Nothing
had ever seemed more wonderful than the wind blowing on her face again as the convertible picked up speed.
"The tour of the ship was particularly educational. It was

clever, wasn't it, for the ship's cook to frame a recipe for crepes where the flour was measured in pounds rather than cups?"

"Food becomes a priority after a few months at sea." He glanced over, surprised she'd been so well entertained by a ship and several pompous speeches. "If I'd known you were really interested I wouldn't have hurried things along quite so much."

"I suppose it becomes all routine and a bit boring for you after a while."

"I was thinking of the men. All they really wanted was to get ashore to their wives or lovers—or both." He was grinning when he turned his head toward her. "You can't imagine what six months at sea is like when the only woman you see is in a glossy photo with staple marks in the middle."

Her lips twitched, but she managed to hold the smile to a bare acknowledgement. "No, I'm sure I can't. But I think you enjoyed your time at sea, Bennett. It showed in the way you spoke with the men and looked at the ship."

He said nothing for a moment, surprised and not displeased that she had understood that so quickly. "I was more of an officer and less of a prince then. I can't say I have the sea in my blood the way Captain Dumont does, but it isn't something I'll forget."

"What is it you remember best?" she asked before she caught herself.

"Watching the sun rise at sea or better, riding out a .m. God, we went through one off Crete. The waves a fifty-foot wall. The wind was like the wrath of o loud, so enormous that you could shout in someone's ear and not be heard. No sky, only water, wall after wall of it. An experience like that changes you."

"How?"

"It makes you realize that no matter who you are, what you are, there's something bigger, greater. Nature's a powerful equalizer, Hannah. Look at her now." With one hand he gestured toward the sea as he negotiated another curve. "Calm, almost impossibly beautiful. A hurricane doesn't make her less beautiful, only more dangerous."

"It sounds as though you prefer the danger." She understood that, perhaps too well.

"At times. Danger's its own seduction."

She could say nothing to that. It was something she had learned herself years before.

With the briefest of signals to the car behind him, Bennett pulled over. "At the moment I prefer the calm." He got out of the convertible, ignoring the guard who stood anxiously by the hood of the trailing car. "Walk with me on the beach, Hannah." He opened her door and held out a hand. "I promised Marissa some shells."

"Your security doesn't look pleased." Nor was she when she noticed how open they were.

"They'd only be pleased if I were sitting in a bulletproof globe. Come now, Hannah, didn't you tell me sea air was good for the constitution?"

"Yes." She laid her hand in his. He was safe, after all, as long as she played her part and played it well. "You'll have to find shells big enough that they can't be swallowed. At Marissa's age, children tend to eat the oddest things."

"Always practical." With an easy laugh, he lifted her by the waist over the low seawall. He saw her gaze focus over his shoulder and knew a guard would be following at a discreet distance. "You should take your shoes off, Hannah. You'll only get sand in them."

It was the practical thing to do, of course. The logical thing. Hannah tried to tell herself she wasn't shedding part of her cover along with the pumps. "You must have some fascinating coral formations in these waters."

"Do you scuba?"

"No," she lied. "I'm not a very strong swimmer. I went to a marine exhibit in London a few years ago. Until then, I had no idea what an incredible variety of shells there were, or how valuable they can be."

"Lucky for me Marissa has simple tastes." With his hand on hers, he walked to the sea edge. "A couple of clam shells, and she'll be delighted."

"It's kind of you to think of her." He *was* kind, she thought. That itself was one of the most difficult things to overlook. "You seem to be a great favorite among your nieces and nephews."

"Oh, I suppose that's because I don't mind making a fool of myself now and then in a game. How about this one?" Bending, he picked up a long spiral that had broken off a larger shell and been worn smooth by the ebb and flow of the sea. At the top of the curve was a peaked cap that looked almost like a crown.

"Very suitable," Hannah commented when he handed it to her.

"Marissa doesn't care for suitable. She prefers pretty."

"is pretty." With a smile, Hannah ran a finger along rve that went from pale amber to polished pink. uld have it in her windowsill where the sun would hit it. Oh look." Forgetting herself, she stepped into the surf and pried out an unbroken scallop shell. It was shaped like a fan, bone-white on one side, opalescent pink inside its shallow bowl. "You could tell her that fairies take their biscuits in it when they have tea."

"So Hannah believes in fairies," he murmured.

Caught up short, she handed him the shell. "No, but I think Marissa might."

Bennett slipped the shell into his pocket. "Your feet are wet."

"They'll dry quickly enough." She started to step back. He took her hand again, holding her in the shallow, foaming surf.

"Since we're here, we ought to try for a couple more." Without waiting for a response he began to walk along the shoreline.

The water was warm and soft on her feet and ankles, but no warmer, no softer, than the air that blew in over it. Through the crystal water she could see the bed of white sand and the glittering sparkles of shells that had been crushed by waves. The surf was quiet here, all sighs and whispers.

There was nothing romantic in it, Hannah warned herself. She couldn't allow there to be. The line she walked was thinner and sharper than any she'd walked before. One misstep could mean tragedy at least, war at the worst. Determined to keep her place, she concentrated on the guards a few yards at their back.

"The ceremony today was lovely. I'm grateful you asked me to come."

"My reasons were purely selfish. I wanted your company."

Struggling not to be touched, she tried again. "In England there's often satire and criticism of the Royal Family, but beneath it all is a very real affection. I see that same kind of love and respect for your family here."

"My father would tell you that we serve as well as govern. He gives them solidity and confidence. Alex gives them the hope for the future. A continuation of tradition. In Brie they have glamour and intelligence as well as humanity."

"And in you?"

"Entertainment."

It annoyed her. She couldn't say why but his careless dismissal of himself made her stop and frown at him. "You underestimate yourself."

Surprised, Bennett cocked his head and studied her. It was there again, that something, that indefinable something in her eyes that had attracted him all along. "Not really. I'm well aware that I do my duty. My father raised all of us to understand that we didn't simply inherit a title or position. We had to earn it." He drew her back a bit so that the spray from the surf didn't dampen her skirt. "I won't rule. Thank God. That's for Alex and then for the son I continue to hope Eve gives us all this time around. Because I won't, I don't have to take myself as seriously ʌt that doesn't mean I take Cordina or my re- es to it lightly."

ʌean to criticize."

ink you did. I only meant that above my of- ı official position, I give the people something—someone to talk about over a glass of wine or an evening meal. I've been haunted by the title of Playboy Prince since I was in my teens." He grinned then and tucked a stray hair behind her ear. "I can't say I didn't do everything possible to earn it."

"I prefer literature to gossip," Hannah said primly as she started to walk on.

"Gossip has its place." Amused, Bennett stopped her. "Apparently you enjoy it."

"No." His eyes darkened as he looked beyond her and out to sea. "I'm just accustomed to it. It's difficult, when you're twenty, to know that every time you look more than casually at a woman it's going to be splashed somewhere in bold print, pictures included. I like women." This time he smiled and looked back at her. "Since I didn't want to change that aspect of my personality, I decided to live with public speculation. If I've sinned, it was in lack of discretion."

"Some might say it was the quantity."

There was only the shortest of hesitations before he threw his head back and roared with laughter. "Oh, Hannah, what a gem you are. So you *have* whiled away some time with something besides Yeats."

"I may have skimmed a few headlines."

Laughing again, he swung her in a circle before she could prevent it. "Priceless. Absolutely priceless." His eyes were glowing as he set her back down. "I adore how you cut me down to size so skillfully."

Automatically, Hannah smoothed down her skirt. "I'm sure you've mistaken my intent."

"The devil I have. That's what delights me about you."

The frustrated look she gave him had nothing to do with the role she was playing. Delighting him had never been part of the plan. She was there to observe, to cement her position and to carry out a plan that was years in the making. Never before had the proper Lady Hannah had to worry about piquing a man's interest. Even as she calculated how to cancel it out again, he was reaching for her.

"Your hair's falling down." In a casual move he plucked a loose pin that was dangling near her shoulder. "My fault for not putting the top up."

"I must look as though I've been through a hurricane." She reached up to put the practical hairstyle back in place. Pins fell out in her hand, loosened by wind and weight. Even as she swore silently, her hair tumbled free, waterfalling past her shoulders to her waist.

"Mon Dieu." Before she could twist her hair back, Bennett had filled both hands with it. Twined around his fingers it was deep, honey blond and soft as silk. He stared, thunderstruck, by the transformation. It waved wild and free around her face, accenting the slash of cheekbones that only looked hard and angular without the framing. Her face no longer seemed thin and bony, but exotic. *"C'est magnifique. C'est la chevelure d'un ange."*

With her heart pounding, she tried to ignore what she saw in his eyes. It wasn't innocent delight or casual attraction now. Now there was desire, man for woman, basic, strong and as dangerous as the sea in a storm. She couldn't move back from him for his hands were buried in her hair. She couldn't deny the lunge of her own needs as he kept her close.

It wasn't supposed to happen. Even now she could tell

herself it couldn't happen. Yet she wanted to be held by him, to be comforted, to be, though the words sounded foolish in her mind, cherished. Desired, needed, loved. All of those things were against the rules, but she found it hard to pull back.

"Angel hair," Bennett repeated in a whisper. "Why does a woman bind beauty up and hide it?"

No, she couldn't deny what was happening inside her, but she could, as she'd been trained, deny herself. "It's more practical worn up." She lifted her hands to scoop it from his and met resistance.

Yes, he'd been right all along. There was more, much more to her than she allowed to show on the surface. Perhaps it was that which continued to draw him in, make him want, make him need in a way he never had before. If it had been possible, he would have pulled her to him then. It wasn't the guards that stopped him, but the trace of anxiety he saw in her eyes.

"If that was true, my most practical Hannah, why haven't you simply cut it off?"

How many times had she nearly done so then pulled back at the last minute? Drawing a deep breath she offered the simple truth because truth was often the best cover of all. "Even I have some vanity."

"It makes you beautiful." He dragged his hands through her hair again, hardly able to believe it had been hidden by a handful of pins.

"Only different." Her smile hid the tension that was pulling her in two directions.

"Any man would approve of such a difference." She was stiff beneath his hands. With reluctance he acknowledged it and released her. "But then, you don't look for a man's approval, do you?"

"I've never found it necessary." With a few expert twists, she had her hair at the base of her neck again. The pins were pushed in until it was secure. She could almost, just almost feel secure herself. "We should be getting back. Eve may need me."

With a nod, Bennett began to walk back to the car with her. There would be another time and another place. He found in himself something he experienced rarely, particularly when it had to do with a woman. Patience.

"You can pin it up, Hannah. But now that I know what it looks like down, I'll see it that way whenever I look at you." When they reached the seawall, he again lifted her over, but this time stood, his hands around her waist and the wall between them. "Knowing this one secret makes me wonder how many others you have, and how soon I'll find them."

Anxiety and desire were a powerful combination. She felt her heart thud with both. "I'm afraid you'll be disappointed, Bennett. I have no interesting secrets."

"We'll see," he said, before he vaulted easily over the seawall.

Chapter 5

It wasn't often Hannah yearned to be beautiful. Her work had given her a fine appreciation for the beauty of being unremarkable, even forgettable. Over the years, she'd experienced a twinge now and then, but only a twinge when she thought of soft colors and filmy dresses. It had always been possible to release the urge when she was off duty and out of the country. Then her appearance could be changed with a more discerning choice of color and cut and a few clever strokes with a makeup brush.

There could be no release now, and no yearning.

Hannah knew everyone would look wonderful for Eve's dinner party. An affair at the palace was meant to be elegant, even extravagant. Hannah had no doubt every woman who attended would strive to live up to the occasion. Every woman, of course, except her.

She'd already seen Eve's glittery black dress with its swirls of material from waist to ankle and its daring draping back. Gabriella would no doubt wear something delicate that would accent her fragile, feminine looks.

Then there was Chantel O'Hurley. Hannah was certain the actress would be stunning whether she chose silk or sackcloth. Remembering how Bennett had looked at her as he'd started down the stairs in the Center took no effort at all.

It shouldn't have mattered.

It mattered too much.

Lecturing herself, Hannah chose the best of the worst in a pale lavender gown with a fussy bodice that played down her curves. With her hair unpinned, it gave her the look of a wanton puritan. An image, she knew, that wouldn't go unnoticed. With only the smallest of sighs, she drew her hair back to begin the laborious job of braiding it into submission.

When it was neatly coiled at her neck, Hannah was satisfied that all traces of sexuality were tamed. She looked presentable, perfectly proper and sexless.

There could be no regrets, Hannah told herself as she slipped her pistol into her evening bag. Duty came above personal desire, and certainly far ahead of vanity.

He'd been waiting for her. The guests were being entertained in the Salle des Miroirs where they were served aperitifs by short-coated waiters. Both the cast and the crew of Eve's production had been invited so that conversation was a babble of noise underlaid with excitement.

Though impatient and distracted, Bennett performed his duty without a ripple. There were always polite questions to be asked, a hand to kiss and a joke to laugh at.

Under usual circumstances, the party would have amused and entertained him, but...

Where was she? He found himself straining against the evening clothes he usually wore without a thought. All around him women glittered. Their scents mingled and mixed into one exotic fragrance that did nothing to tempt him. He wanted a moment alone with Hannah. He hadn't the least idea why it was so important, but he wanted it desperately.

He kept one eye on the doorway while he spoke with the wardrobe mistress. His gaze paused briefly on the ormolu clock while he listened to the director expound on the potential of Eve's play.

"Looking for me?" The sultry voice sounded in his ear just ahead of a cloud of scent.

"Chantel." Bennett kissed both her cheeks before drawing her back for a survey. "Stunning, as always."

"I do what I'm best at." Smiling, she accepted a glass from a passing waiter. Shimmering white left her shoulders bare, then dipped low enough to be tantalizing before it closely followed the subtle, feminine curves. "Your home is everything it's rumored to be." She lifted the wine to her lips as her gaze passed over the dozens of antique mirrors that graced the walls. "And how clever of you to choose such a room to entertain a group of narcissistic actors."

"We have our moments." He looked beyond her for a moment, but still saw no sign of Hannah. "I saw your last movie. You were extraordinary."

A woman who was accustomed to absorbing all of a man's attention knew instinctively when she had only a part of it. Still, Chantel only smiled and speculated. "I'm still waiting for you to come back to Hollywood."

"You seem to be keeping busy in the meantime." He reached in his pocket for a box of matches to light her cigarette. "How do you manage to divide your time among tennis stars, oilmen and producers?"

Chantel tilted her head as she blew out a thin stream of smoke. "Oh, much the same way I imagine you divide yours among countesses, marchesas and—was it a barmaid in Chelsea?"

Laughing, Bennett dropped the matches back in his pocket. "*Ma chére amie,* if either of us enjoyed all the incredible and innumerable affairs the press gifts us with, we'd be hospitalized."

With the true affection she felt for few men, Chantel touched a hand to his cheek. "To anyone else, I'd say speak for yourself. However, since we've never been lovers, regardless of the headlines to the contrary, I'll ask you how things are for you, romantically speaking."

"Confusing." At that moment, in the oval glass over Chantel's shoulder, he saw Hannah slip into the room. She looked like a dove lost in a group of peacocks. "Very confusing. Excuse me a moment, will you, love?"

"Of course." She'd seen which direction his attention had taken. "*Bonne chance,* Bennett."

A lifetime of experience allowed him to slip through the groups of people, exchanging a quick word, a smile or a murmured excuse without leaving any offense behind. Less than a minute after Hannah had settled into a corner, he was beside her.

"*Bonsoir,* Lady Hannah."

"Your Highness." She used his title and curtsied as protocol demanded. He caught her hands as she straightened, negating the formality.

"It's usual, when a woman is late, that she makes an entrance rather than slip into a corner."

Damn him for making her pulse skittish. Even as she tried to calm it again, she noted that more than one head was turned in their direction. So much for going unnoticed. "I prefer watching to being watched, sir."

"I prefer watching you." He signaled a waiter, then took a glass from the tray for her himself. "You move well, Hannah, as though you wouldn't make a sound in an empty room."

That had as much to do with her training in tae kwon do as her childhood lessons in ballet. "I was raised not to make disturbances." She accepted the glass because it freed one of her hands. "Thank you. This is a lovely room." She said it casually, as casual as the glance she sent sweeping over the guests. Her reflection was thrown back at her a dozen times. Hers, and Bennett's, close together.

"I've always been partial to it." Now that she was here, he was content. He'd almost heard the click of things falling into their proper place when he'd taken her hand in his. "As it happens it was another Bennett, some generations back, who started the collection. It seems he was miserably vain without much cause and continued to buy mirrors in hopes one would tell him a different story."

She had to laugh. For a moment she felt almost as though she belonged there with the gowns and the glass and the glamour. "I'd say you made that up, but it sounds foolish enough to be true."

"You have the most alluring laugh," he murmured. "It's a laugh that reminds me how you look with your hair down and your eyes dark."

She couldn't allow this. Hannah told herself she was foolish to be moved when she knew how clever he was with women. She was more foolish to be caught off guard when she knew what a dangerous game was being played. This time her voice was cool and formal.

"Shouldn't you see to your guests?"

"I have been." He passed his thumb gently over her knuckles. It was a small gesture and an intimate one that made her wish once again she could have been lovely for him. That she could, very simply, have been for him. "While I was waiting for you." He stepped closer. Because she was already wedged into a corner, there was no place to go. "You smell wonderful."

"Bennett, please." She almost lifted a hand to his chest before she remembered eyes were on them. In defense she lifted her glass instead.

"Hannah, I can't tell you how it pleases me to see you become unnerved. The only time you become at all unsure of yourself is when I'm just a bit too close."

It was true, and a bitter pill to swallow for a woman who survived by being sure of herself. "People are watching."

"Then walk in the gardens with me later, when we can be alone."

"I don't think that would be wise."

"Are you afraid I'd seduce you?"

There was both amusement and arrogance in his tone, but when Hannah looked back at him, she saw desire as well. She sipped again to moisten a throat that had gone bone-dry. "Not afraid. Uncomfortable seems a better word."

"It would give me great pleasure to make you uncomfortable, Hannah." His voice was low, a caress to accompany the brush of his lips over her knuckles. "I want to make love with you in some dark, quiet place. Very slowly and very gently."

The need sprinted inside of her until she had to fight off a shudder of anticipation. It could be like that, with him, it could be. If only...

There could be no "ifs" in her life. They meant uncertainty and uncertainty was lethal. Hannah, pulling herself steady by nerve ends, looked at him. He meant it. There was desire in his eyes—but more a kindness, a sweetness that was almost her undoing. She could marvel at the fact that he felt something real for her, that somehow, he'd looked beyond the surface and cared.

She could want it, but she couldn't accept it. There was only one way to stop what should never have started. She had to hurt him, and she had to do it now.

"I'm sure I should be flattered." Her voice was cool and calm again. "But if you'll forgive me, sir, I'm aware that your tastes are not very selective."

He stiffened his fingers on hers before he released her hand. She saw by his eyes that the arrow had hit its mark. "I'd appreciate an explanation for that, Hannah."

"The explanation seems obvious. Please let me pass, you'll cause a scene."

"I've caused one before." There was something new in his voice now. It was anger, certainly, but a reckless, heedless anger. Hannah knew that if she didn't play her game exactly right now, she'd find her name splashed in headlines for battling with Bennett in public.

"Very well." Setting her glass down on a nearby table, she folded her hands in her usual fashion. "I'm a woman, and therefore of some passing interest. To be blunt, the interest isn't returned."

"That's a lie."

"No." Firmer now, she cut him off. "Though it might be difficult for a man like you to understand, I'm a simple woman with simple values. As you told me yourself, your reputation precedes you." She paused just long enough to see him wince.

Oh, Bennett, I'm sorry. So sorry.

"I didn't come to Cordina to amuse you," she murmured as she took a step to the side.

He suddenly lifted his hand to stop her, and she waited. "You don't amuse me, Hannah."

"Then I must beg your pardon." Knowing it would be more insult than courtesy, she dipped into a curtsy. "If you'll excuse me now, sir, I'd like to speak with Eve."

He held her another moment. Hannah could feel his fury sear through his fingertips and burn her flesh. Then, in an instant, there was ice. "I won't keep you. Enjoy the evening."

"Thank you."

Despising herself, Hannah moved into the crowd. The lights were so brilliant, she told herself. That was why her eyes hurt.

"Lady Hannah, good evening." Reeve stepped beside her and took her arm. "Would you care for some wine?"

"Yes, thank you." Falling into step beside him, she accepted the glass he held out.

"Have you seen this collection of mirrors? I've always found these three particularly impressive. Are you all right?" he added in an undertone.

"Yes, they are lovely. I'm fine."

He cupped his hand around the end of a cigarette, glancing around casually to be certain no one was within earshot. "It looked as though you were having some trouble with Bennett."

"He's persistent." She sipped her wine, amazed that her nerves had yet to calm. "Surely this is eighteenth-century."

"Hannah." He pointed out another glass as they walked, but his voice softened. "I worked with your father when I first got my feet wet with the ISS. That makes me feel almost like family. Are you all right?"

"I will be." She drew a deep breath and smiled as if he'd said something amusing. "I caused him pain just now. I didn't enjoy it."

Reeve brushed a hand over hers in the most casual of gestures. The touch was as reassuring as a hug. "It's rare to get through an assignment without hurting someone."

"Yes, I know—the end justifies the means. Don't worry, I'll do my job."

"I wasn't worried."

"It would help a great deal if you'd see that Bennett was kept busy over the next week or so. Things should be coming to a head and I don't need him…"

"Distracting you?"

"Interfering," Hannah corrected. She glanced in one of the mirrors and saw him across the room with Chantel. "Though I may very well have taken care of that myself. Excuse me."

He drove the horse hard, but still didn't find the level of release he'd been seeking. Swearing, Bennett plunged down the winding path, but neither joy nor excitement rode with him. Fury left little room.

He ached for her. He damned her to the devil and still ached for her. In the days that had passed since she'd turned him aside, the wanting hadn't eased. Now it was coated with self-derision and anger, but it hadn't eased.

He told himself she was a cold, insensitive prude with no generosity or heart. He saw her as she had been on the beach, with a shell in her hand, her eyes rich with laughter as the wind pulled pins from her hair.

He told himself she was hard as stone and just as unfeeling. Then he remembered how soft, how sweet her lips had been when his own had tasted them.

So he cursed her and rode harder.

The skies threatened rain, but he ignored them. It was the first time in days he'd been able to get away from obligations long enough to take Dracula out for more than cursory exercise. The wind whistled in off the sea and set waves dancing high.

He wanted the storm. By God, he wanted the wind and the rain and the thunder.

He wanted Hannah.

Imbécile! Only a fool wanted a woman when there

was nothing returned. Only a madman thought of ways to have what had already been denied. He'd told himself all this before, but still he caught himself dreaming of ways he could gather her up and take her somewhere until he found the right way to show her.... Show her what? Bennett asked himself. Show her that it was different with her?

What woman would believe it?

Dozens, he thought, and his own laughter echoed bitterly behind him. He could certainly attest to that. But now when it was true, when it mattered the most, this woman wouldn't believe.

Because he'd acted like an idiot. Drawing the stallion to a halt, he stopped at a precipice over the sea and looked out. He'd pushed, too hard, too fast. It was humbling to admit he might have done so because he'd never met with a great deal of resistance before.

Women were drawn to him—because of the title and position. He wasn't so vain or so foolish not to know it. But they were also drawn to him because he enjoyed them. He liked their softness, their humor, their vulnerabilities. It was also true that he hadn't been intimate with as many as his reputation allowed, but there'd been enough women in his life for him to understand and appreciate that romance was a two-way street.

Hannah was young, inexperienced, sheltered. The term "Lady" wasn't merely a title, but a way of life. As far as men were concerned, it was doubtful she'd taken herself away from her books long enough to form any strong relationships.

With another oath, Bennett dragged a hand through his

wind-tossed hair. And what had he done? He'd tried to seduce her at a dinner party. How could he have expected a woman of her breeding and sensitivity to be anything less than insulted? It had been the clumsiest, and perhaps the crudest of propositions.

Dracula danced impatiently, but Bennett held him steady another moment as he watched the storm roll slowly from the horizon toward the shore.

He hadn't told her, had never attempted to tell her what it was she did to him inside, to his heart. Just talking with her, watching that solemn face and quiet manner excited him in a way the most exotic or flamboyant woman never had. It was something deeper, and so much richer. He'd never said that with her, he was on the edge of finding the love he hadn't been sure would ever be there for him.

He could hardly do all of that now that he'd alienated and insulted her. But he could do something else. His smile began as the first drops of water hit the sea. He could start at the beginning.

Bennett wheeled the horse around. As the first streak of lightning split the sky, they were racing for home.

Within an hour, in dry clothes and dripping hair, Bennett made his way up to the nursery. Bernadette barred him at the door.

"Your pardon, Your Highness, but it's Princess Marissa's nap time. Her Highness is resting with the baby."

"I'm looking for Lady Hannah." He leaned into the room, but Bernadette stood her ground.

"Lady Hannah isn't here, sir. I believe she went to the museum this afternoon."

"The museum." Bennett calculated a moment. "Thank you, Bernadette."

Before she could finish her curtsy, he was gone.

Le Musée d'Art was small and lovely as was the rest of Cordina. It was like a miniature palace itself with its marble floors and carved columns. In the main lobby was a high, domed ceiling of stained glass and a circling balcony that gave the illusion of space.

Rooms ran off this circular hub like spokes of a wheel. On the floor below was a moderately priced restaurant where diners could enjoy a view of the gardens through a wide glass wall.

Hannah had arrived early to take inventory of the entire building. Security was tight but people who rested on the benches near the exhibits were largely ignored. Groups of school children were led by, most of them more impressed with an afternoon away from classes than they were with the paintings and sculptures. Tourists, brochures in hands, muddled through with a weaving of French, Italian, British, and American accents.

On a rainy weekday afternoon, the museum was a pleasant pastime. A healthy number of people flowed in and out. Hannah decided she couldn't have planned it better.

At the time she'd requested in her message, she strolled toward a Monet seascape. She loitered there long enough to read the plaque and study the brushwork. Whoever she was going to meet was probably there, making his own study of the building, and of her. In a leisurely pattern, she moved from painting to painting.

Then she saw the watercolor and both heart and mind raced back to the music room, and Bennett.

The plaque read Her Serene Highness, Princess Louisa de Cordina, but in small letters in the corner of the painting was the signature. Louisa Bisset.

She'd titled it simply *La Mer*. It was indeed the sea, but from a view Hannah had yet to see in Cordina. There was a jagged fall of cliffs that gave way to a sheer incline and ended in a jumble of rocks. From there, the beach spread white to the blue verge of water. But it wasn't peaceful. In this painting, the artist had looked for and captured the power and the danger. The spray rose high, and on the horizon a storm was brewing.

He found this stored in a trunk, Hannah thought and had to resist the urge to touch the frame as he might have done. He'd found it, she thought again, and perhaps had seen part of himself in it.

"An interesting subject."

The voice beside her was French, brusquely accented. Contact was made.

"Yes, the artist is very skillful." Hannah dropped her brochures. As she bent to pick them up she glanced around and was satisfied that no one was close enough to hear or even notice them. "I have information."

"You are to pass it through me."

She turned to smile at him as though they were exchanging a few pleasant remarks about the painting. He was of medium height, dark complexion with no scars. She gauged his age at fifty, though he might have been younger. Certain professions tend to age people quickly.

He was not French by birth. The Germanic tone was faint, but she caught it and filed it away.

"There are certain aspects to some of my information that I feel must be given directly to the man who pays me."

"That is against the organization's policy."

"So I was told. However, I'm aware of what nearly happened six months ago because of policy. It wasn't looked on unfavorably when I used my own initiative and saved the organization, shall we say, certain embarrassments."

"*Mademoiselle*, I'm only here to receive your information."

"Then my information is this." Before speaking again, she moved toward another painting. Again, she took her time studying it. She lifted a hand as if to show her companion a certain combination of colors. "I have unlimited access to the palace. Neither my person nor my possessions are searched. I have already compiled the complete statistics on the security system both there, and at the Fine Arts Center."

"That will be most useful."

"And will be given to the man who pays me. That is *my* policy, *monsieur*."

"You are paid by the organization."

"And the organization is run by men. I know who I work for and why." She turned to him then, her smile very cool, very calm. They might have been discussing the weather. "I am not a fool. The...organization has certain goals. So do I. I am more than happy to have them merge to our mutual satisfaction. I will meet and speak with the highest authority. See that it's soon."

"Some people take a step and find themselves falling from a cliff."

"I'm sure-footed. Pass this on, *s'il vous plaît*. What I know is worth a great deal. What I can find out is worth even more. You'll find enough to prove it in here." Hannah let her brochure fall to her feet, but this time she left it there. *"Bonjour, monsieur."*

She turned, knowing that such demands would either take her to the next stage, or end in her being summarily disposed of. Nerves tingling, she began to wander toward the exit. Her heart stopped when Bennett walked in.

A dozen thoughts ran through her mind in a matter of seconds. Had she been set up? Had they used her to get him out in the open at a certain time and place? Had he come for her because Deboque had already struck somewhere else?

It took her only seconds more to dismiss them all as irrational. It was simply coincidence and bad luck that he should show up now on the tail of her meeting.

"I hope you don't mind company," Bennett said before she could think of a plausible opening.

"Of course not." She didn't dare look behind her yet to see if her contact was still there. She smiled, not quite sure how to behave since both she and Bennett had done an excellent job of avoiding each other for days. "The museum is even more beautiful than I'd been told."

"Have you seen everything? I'd be glad to show you around." He took her hand in a casual, friendly way that she realized could only cement her position if Deboque's man was watching.

She let her fingers curl into his, hating herself for using

Bennett's generosity against him. "I could spend days looking, but I'm a bit tired."

She saw him then. He'd moved into her peripheral vision. The brochure she'd passed him was in his hand, and though his back was to them, she knew he was listening.

Bennett didn't notice the man, but only her. "Let me give you coffee up in my office. I'd like to talk with you."

She felt the unexpected prick of tears. Everything he said, and the way he said it, only made her claims more plausible. "I'd love some coffee." Hannah let him take her arm and lead her out, knowing every detail would be reported back to Deboque.

With a silent and stone-faced bodyguard, they stepped into an elevator. Bennett used a key to send them up to the third floor.

They crossed pale gray carpet, past uniformed guards to a suite of rooms. Two secretaries, one manning a bank of phones, the other working on a state-of-the-art computer, rose as Bennett entered.

"Janine, could we have some coffee, please?"

"Yes, Your Highness. Right away."

With his hand still on Hannah's arm, Bennett opened a door. The moment it shut behind them, the whispers started. His Highness had never brought a woman to his office before.

It was a room that reflected a man who loved beautiful things. Grays and blues blended softly with ivory walls. Deep-cushioned chairs invited long stays and easy conversation while an ornamental lemon tree thrived in a corner. Glass shelves held small treasures, a china bowl, a T'ang horse, a handful of shells she imagined he'd gathered himself and a chipped demitasse cup that might have been picked up in a flea market.

Though there was a very businesslike antique desk and chair, the essence of the room was relaxation. Hannah wondered if he came here when he needed to escape the palace and his title.

"Sit down, Hannah. If you've gone through the whole museum, you've been on your feet for hours."

"Yes, but I loved it." She chose a chair rather than the cozy lounge and folded her hands over each other on her lap. "I've always loved the Louvre, but this is so much more personal."

"The Board of Directors and the Chamber of Commerce will be delighted to hear it." He remained standing, his hands in his pockets, wondering just how to begin. "If you'd let me know you were coming today, I'd have enjoyed showing you through myself."

"I didn't want to disturb you. In any case, I rather liked just wandering."

Why, he's nervous, she realized. It might have pleased her in some secret place if she hadn't discovered she was nervous herself. It was the meeting, she told herself. No, it was Bennett. It was foolish to deny it.

"Do you work here often?"

"When necessary. It's often more convenient to work out of my office at home." He didn't want to talk about the museum. Bennett dug his hands deeper in his pockets. Since when had he had trouble talking to a woman? Since Hannah, he thought wryly, and tried again. "Hannah—"

The knock on the door had him biting off an oath. Bennett opened the door for Janine and the coffee tray. The pot was silver, Hannah noted, while the cups were violet bone china edged in gold.

"Yes, just set it down there, Janine. I'll see to it."

"Yes, sir." She set it down on the table in front of the lounge then curtsied.

Aware he'd been terse, Bennett smiled at her. "Thank you, Janine. It smells wonderful."

"You're welcome, sir." The door closed behind her with a discreet click.

"Looks like we're in luck." Bennett lifted the pot and poured. "These little pastries are from the restaurant downstairs. They're wonderful. Cream?"

"Yes, thank you. No sugar." How polite we are, she thought as the tension began to spread from her neck to her shoulders. Like two strangers on a blind date.

"Will you come sit over here if I promise to behave?"

Though he said it lightly, Hannah heard the strain. She lowered her gaze to her hands. He couldn't know it was shame and not shyness. "Of course." Rising, she moved over and joined him on the lounge. She lifted her coffee while he left his alone.

"Hannah, I apologize for my behavior the other night. It's no wonder you were offended."

"Oh, please, don't." With a distress even her training couldn't smother, she set her cup down and started to rise. His hand reached for hers and held her still. "I don't want an apology." Fighting for control, she forced herself to look at him. "I wasn't offended, really. I was just—"

"Frightened then? That's just as inexcusable."

"No—yes." Which answer was the right one? In the

end, she gave up. "Bennett, the truest thing I can say to you is that no one has ever confused me so well."

"Thank you."

"That wasn't a compliment, but a complaint."

"Hannah, thank God you're back." Laughing, he pulled both her hands to his lips. When she stiffened, he released them but continued to smile.

"Friends?"

Still wary, she nodded. "I'd like to be."

"Then friends it is." Satisfied the first hurdle was successfully negotiated, Bennett sat back. He would wait and be a great deal more cautious before attempting the second. "What did you like best about the museum?"

She didn't trust him. No, Hannah was far too good at game playing not to know when one was afoot. "The airy, unrestricted atmosphere, I think. Too often museums are solemn, serious places. Oh, I did see another of your ancestor's paintings. The one of the sea. It was stunning."

"One of my favorites." He was careful not to touch her again. "I was tempted to keep it locked in my room, all to myself, but…" With a shrug he picked up his cup. "It didn't seem fair."

"And you are fair," she murmured, knowing she'd used him.

"I try to be," he returned, knowing he would use fair means or foul to win her. "Hannah, you ride, don't you?"

"Yes."

"Ride with me tomorrow morning. It has to be early as the rest of my day is full, but it's been a long time since I had any company on a ride."

"I'm not sure I can. Eve—"

"Will be busy with Marissa until ten," Bennett finished.

How she would love a ride. An hour of freedom and movement. "Yes, but I've promised to go with her to the Center. She has appointments there at eleven."

"We'll be back by then if you're willing to start out early." He wasn't willing to lose the opportunity. In her eyes he saw hesitation and pressed his advantage. "Come, Cordina's at its best in the morning on horseback."

"All right then." It was impulse, she knew, but she could use an hour of relaxation.

In a matter of days, she would meet with Deboque. Hannah lifted her coffee again and sipped. Or she would be dead.

Chapter 6

He hadn't lied. Hannah had already thought Cordina beautiful, but in the early morning it was exquisite. With the dawn light, Cordina reminded Hannah of a young girl dressing for her first ball. The colors were soft, shimmering. Pinks and roses and misty blues still gathered to the east as they got mounted.

Settling into her own saddle, Hannah eyed Bennett's Dracula with a mixture of envy and anxiety. Her father's stables included some of the finest horseflesh in Britain, but he had nothing to compare with the black stallion. He looked fast and reckless and just a bit angry. Even as she imagined herself on his back, she could also picture Bennett being thrown.

"A mount like that would have a mind of his own," she commented when the old groom stepped back from the prince.

"Of course." Bennett steadied the stallion as he side-stepped. Then, misunderstanding her, he smiled in reassurance. "Your Quixote's strong, but quite the gentleman. Brie often rides him when she's here."

Hannah only lifted a brow, recognizing the soothing words for what they were. "Thank you, sir. It eases my mind to know you've given me a lady's mount."

He thought he caught a trace of sarcasm, but when he looked at her he saw only calm eyes and a polite smile. "I thought we'd ride to the sea."

"I'd like that."

With a nod, Bennett turned his horse and started off at a gentle trot. "Are you comfortable?"

"Yes, thank you." As she settled into the easy rhythm, Hannah tried not to yearn for a wild gallop. "It was kind of you to invite me. I'm told your morning rides are sacred."

He grinned at her, pleased that she sat the horse well and confidently. "It's often true that I need an hour on horseback before I can be civil. Still, there are times I prefer company."

That hadn't been true lately. Since Deboque's release he felt he could never stretch his arms out without bumping a guard. And still nothing. His eyes clouded, as much with impatience as with anger. He wanted Deboque to move. He relished the thought of being able to deal with him personally, and finally. Instinctively he touched a hand to his shoulder where a bullet had entered. Yes, he would relish it.

The look in his eyes made her uneasy. There was something to watch for and defend against there. The man beside her was not the easygoing, easy-loving prince she'd come to expect. Whatever, whoever he thought of seemed to communicate itself to his mount for Dracula shied nervously. She saw how easily he controlled the stallion, only a flexing of muscle. He could be kind or harsh, gentle or rough. Her own palm grew damp on the reins.

"Is something wrong?"

"What?" He glanced over. For an instant the look was still there, hard and dark enough to make her tense. Then it was gone and he was smiling again. There was no Deboque this morning, Bennett told himself. He was sick of having every aspect of his life and his family's lives clouded by one name. "No, nothing. Tell me what you do at home, Hannah. I can't picture you there."

"We live quietly in London." It was partially the truth. She wondered why she thought of it as partially a lie. "I do a great deal of my work at home, which makes it convenient for me to keep house for my father."

"Your work," he repeated. "Your essays?" He was leading her along the easiest route, where the incline was gentle.

"Yes." Again, there was a twinge of discomfort. "I hope to have them ready for publication in a year or two."

"I'd like to read them."

She shot him a look of surprise, then almost immediately felt her muscles tighten. It had nothing to do with fear. Even if he'd demanded to see her work, she had enough that would satisfy him. No, it wasn't fear but a certainty that if she had to continue to lie to him much longer, she would be physically ill.

"You're welcome to, of course, but I don't think my writing would be of great interest to you."

"You're wrong. You're of great interest to me."

She looked down, but not in the shyness he thought he saw. Once again it was shame. "It's lovely here," she managed after a moment. "Do you ride this way often?"

She wouldn't allow him to get too close. Bennett fought back frustration and reminded himself he was in for the long haul. "No, actually I haven't been this way in quite a while." When they reached the top of a rise, he stopped. Her gelding was content to busy himself with the grass alongside the path. Beside her, Dracula nearly shivered with energy. She thought she felt the same impatience from Bennett.

"A little distance changes things," he murmured.

Following his gaze, she looked back at the palace. From here it looked like an exquisite child's toy, a magnificent dollhouse a pampered child might find near the tree on Christmas morning. To the east was the sea, still hidden from view by the cliffs and trees and barely heard. Like the palace, it hardly seemed real.

"Do you need to get away from it so badly?" Hannah asked him quietly.

"Sometimes." It no longer surprised him that she read his moods. With a hand firm on the reins, he controlled the stallion and continued to look at his home. "I had my time at Oxford, and at sea. When I was away, I missed Cordina so badly it was like an ache. In the past six months, past year, I've felt a restlessness, a waiting for something to happen."

They both thought of Deboque.

"Often in England, especially at this time of year, I'll complain about the cold and the damp." She shifted in the saddle, then smiled as she thought of her home. "I'll look out the window and think I'd almost sell my soul for a week of warm, sunny days. Then, when I'm away, I begin to miss the fog and the mists and the smells of London."

They began to walk the horses again while she cast her mind back to England. "There's a man who sells roasted chestnuts just around the corner from our house. You can buy a little bag and warm your hands on them and smell them, just smell them long before you ever eat them." Remembering made her smile again, but she had no idea how wistfully. "Sometimes I'd wonder how it could be Christmastime anywhere without roasted chestnuts."

"I didn't know you missed England so much."

Nor had she until that moment. "One always misses home. Our hearts are always there." And what she was, all that she had done, had always been for England first.

"I've often wondered how difficult it was for Reeve," Bennett said. The sounds of the sea became louder as they moved their way east. "Although he and Brie spend nearly six months every year at their farm in America. I know for Brie it's as much home as Cordina is."

"For many, real contentment comes with acclimation." Hadn't it been so for her, all of her adult life?

"It's a great deal harder for Eve. She has only a few weeks with her family in America."

"Some loves are greater than others. Some needs stronger." She was just beginning to truly understand it. "Eve would live anywhere as long as Alexander was with her. And I think the same is true for your brother-in-law."

Yes, it was true. Perhaps that was a part of the restlessness in him. Over the last few years he'd seen how beautiful, how strong, real commitment, real feelings could be. Somehow they always seemed so remote from him, so unattainable. Now there was Hannah.

"For love, could you turn your back on England?"

Hannah caught her first glimpse of the sea as they climbed higher. She concentrated on that, but saw, in her mind's eyes, the twisting charm of the Thames.

Could she? So much of her life, so much of her duty was bound with England. Even her current assignment had been as much to protect her country from Deboque as it had been to insure the safety of the Royal Family of Cordina.

"I don't know. You especially would understand how strong some ties can be."

The trees thinned. Those that remained were bent and battered from the wind that swept in from the sea. The path grew rougher so that Bennett put himself between the edge and Hannah. Her mouth twitched at the move, but she said nothing. He could hardly know that she was capable of riding down the path pell-mell without saddle or reins. Besides, she found herself savoring the unaccustomed feeling of being protected.

Without the trees to break its power, the wind swirled from the sea to the top of the rise, carrying traces of salt. Even Hannah's tightly pinned hair couldn't resist it completely. Wispy tendrils escaped to dance around her cheeks. As she watched, a gull caught the current and glided peacefully up on a stream of air. Another, far below, skimmed the water looking for food.

"It's breathtaking." She relaxed enough to sigh.

He saw what was always in her heart, but which showed so rarely in her eyes. Her love of adventure, of power and of risk. It made her beautiful, arousing, mysterious. The need to reach out for her was so strong, he had to tighten his fingers on the reins to keep them still.

"I wanted to bring you here, but I worried that the height might bother you."

"No, I love it." Her horse shied a bit and she controlled him with the ease of long experience. "There are so many beautiful places in the world, but so few special ones. This is a special one. I think I could…" She trailed off as the full impact struck her. "This is the scene from the painting. There's no storm brewing, but this is it, isn't it?"

"Yes." He had no idea that her recognition of it would mean so much. Nor did he know what to do with the sudden, inescapable realization that he was in love with her. Completely. Unalterably.

He tossed his head back as the wind blew his hair into his eyes. He wanted a clear look at her, at this, perhaps the most important moment in his life.

She sat straight in the saddle, her eyes dark with appreciation of the scene spread out before and below them. Her profile was sharp, sculpted. The plain brown riding shirt and pants did nothing to enhance her pale skin. But when he looked at her, he saw the most beautiful, the most precious thing he'd ever found. And for the first time in his life, he had no words to tell her.

"Hannah." He reached out a hand and waited.

She turned. He was the most magnificent man she'd ever seen. More breathtaking than the view, more dangerous than a plunge to the rocks below. He sat on the huge stallion, straight as a soldier, as heartbreaking as a poet. In his eyes she saw both passion and compassion, both need and generosity.

Her heart betrayed her and was lost to him even before she could tell herself it couldn't be. As duty warred with emotion, she let her hand join with his.

"I know what you think I am."

"Bennett—"

"No." His fingers tightened on hers. "You're not far wrong. I could lie to you and promise to change, but I won't lie or promise."

Before she could stop herself, she softened. Only for this moment, she promised herself. There was magic, if only for the moment.

"Bennett, I don't want you to change."

"I meant what I said, though I said it badly the other night. I do want you, Hannah." Like her, he looked out to sea. "I also understand that it would be difficult for you to believe that I've never said that to another woman and meant it in the same way."

But she did believe him. It was thrilling, terrifying and forbidden, but she did. For one glorious moment, she let herself hope. Then she remembered who she was. Duty was first. Always.

"Please, believe me, if I could give you what you want, I would. It's just not possible." She drew her hand away because the contact was making her weak, making her dream.

"I've always believed anything is possible if you work hard enough for it."

"No, some things remain out of reach." She turned her horse away from the sea. "We should get back."

Before she could move, he'd backed up enough to cover the hands on her reins with his own. His arm brushed her arm, his leg, her leg. His face was close, too close, as their mounts stood in opposite directions.

"Tell me what you feel," he demanded. The patience was gone, dissolved in need and frustration. "Give me that much, dammit."

"Regret." As she spoke, the word shimmered with it.

He released her hands only to cup the back of her neck. "Tell me again how you feel," he murmured, then leaned toward her.

The kiss was like a whisper, soft, seductive, sultry. Hannah tightened her hands on the reins, then let them go limp as emotion swamped her. It wasn't supposed to be like this, so encompassing, so heady, so right. The wind ribboned around them. The sea crashed below. For a moment, just one moment, all rational thought fled, leaving only desires behind.

"Bennett." She only murmured his name as she started to draw away. He held her, firm, insistent.

"Another moment."

He needed it. He needed every scrap she would throw him. Never had he felt the desire to beg for what a woman could give or withhold. It wasn't just the passion he wanted; it was more than the physical. He wanted her heart with a desperation he'd never felt before.

It was that desperation that made him keep the kiss gentle, that made him draw back long before his craving for her was satisfied. If he wanted her heart, he would have to move slowly. His Hannah was delicate and shy.

"No regrets, Hannah," he said quietly, then smiled. "I

won't hurt you, or push you further than you're ready for. Trust me. That's really all I want for now."

She wanted to weep. He was giving her a kindness, a sensitivity she didn't deserve. Lies were all she'd given him. Lies were all she would continue to give. To keep him alive, she reminded herself as the tears burned at the back of her eyes. To keep him and the people he loved safe and unharmed.

"No regrets," she told him, letting the words echo through her mind for herself. Tossing her head, she pressed her heels to the gelding's sides and took off in a gallop.

Bennett's first reaction was surprise. He hadn't expected her to ride so well or so forcefully. He took a moment to watch her race down the rise before he grinned and let Dracula have his head. Though she'd taken a good lead, Hannah heard them gaining ground behind her. Delighted, she bent lower over the gelding's neck as she urged him on.

"We can't beat them head-to-head," she called to her mount. "But we might outwit them."

The challenge was enough. Spurred by it, Hannah swung off the track and into the trees. The path here was narrow and rough, but what she sacrificed in speed, she gained in maneuverability. Bennett was hard on her heels, but she kept to the center giving him no room to pass. She burst through the trees and onto a field less than two lengths ahead. Instinct had her veering to the left and pounding up another rise so that Bennett had to check his momentum at the unexpected maneuver. Still, he continued to gain so that when the stables came into view they were nearly neck and neck. Laughing, she veered left again and headed for a hedge.

He felt an instant's panic as he imagined her flying off her mount onto the ground. Then they were sailing over, side by side. Heels down, knees snug, they thundered toward the stables.

Pipit stood with his hands on his hips. He'd watched them since they'd barreled over the rise with the gelding in the lead. Since they'd taken the jump, the stallion had pulled ahead with smooth, easy strides. To be expected, Pipit thought as he rubbed his hands on the thighs of his pants. There wasn't another horse in Cordina—or in Europe as far as he was concerned—that could match the stallion.

But he thought as he watched the woman keep the distance close that Prince Bennett had at last met his match.

Bennett reined in and slid from the horse's back with excitement still drumming in his head. She was only seconds behind him. Her laughter was low and a bit breathless as she started to swing down. Bennett was there to take her by the waist and turn her to him before her feet hit the ground.

"How did you learn to ride like that?"

She lifted her hands to his chest, as much to keep the distance as her balance. "It's the one thing I excel at other than literature. I'd forgotten how much I've missed it these last few months."

He couldn't take his eyes off her. It was pure desire now, basic, vital. The ride they could have together would be as wild, as reckless as the ride they'd just completed. Somehow he knew it, could almost taste it. For reasons he couldn't name, he felt that he was holding two women.

One calm, one passionate. He wasn't sure which one drew him more.

"Ride with me tomorrow."

Once had been a risk and a delight. Twice, Hannah knew, would be a foolish mistake. "I don't think that's possible. With Eve's play about to open, there's so much to be done at the theater."

He wouldn't push. He'd promised himself that he would give her the time to become accustomed to having him with her. From the moment on the rise when he'd realized just what that meant to him, he'd been more determined than ever to court her properly.

A first for the Royal Rake, he thought as he stepped back to kiss her hand.

"The stables are at your disposal whenever you find the time to use them."

"I appreciate that." She reached up a hand to her hair to be certain her pins were in place. "I enjoyed this, Bennett, very much."

"So did I."

"Well, Eve will be waiting for me."

"Go ahead. Pipit and I will see to them."

"Thank you." She was stalling. The moment she realized it, Hannah drew herself in. "Goodbye, Bennett."

"Hannah." He nodded, then watched her walk back toward the palace. A smile tugged at his mouth as he patted his horse's neck. "I'm getting to her, *mon ami*," he murmured. "It's just going to take a bit of time."

Time moved so quickly. Locked in her room, Hannah held the letter from Sussex. Inside, she would find Deboque's answer to the demand she'd made only days before in the museum. Her hands were steady as she sat at her desk. With the ivory-handled letter opener provided her, she slit through the envelope. Inside was a casual, even uninspired letter from an acquaintance in England. It took Hannah less than fifteen minutes to decode it.

Request granted. December third, 23:30. Café du Dauphin. Alone. Contact will ask for the time, in English, then comment, in French, on the weather. Be certain your information warrants the exception to procedure.

Tonight. The next step would be taken tonight. Hannah folded the letter back into the envelope, but left it in plain view on her desk. Beside it was a single white rose Bennett had sent to her that morning. Hannah hesitated, then gave herself the pleasure of touching the petals.

If only life were as sweet and as simple.

Moments later, she was knocking on Prince Armand's office door.

It was opened by his secretary who bowed stiffly to her before announcing her to the prince. Armand stood behind his desk as he gave permission to admit her.

"Your Highness." Hannah made a deep curtsy. "I apologize for disturbing you."

"Not at all, Hannah."

"But you're busy." She stood just inside of the door, hands folded. "I only wished to ask your advice on something. If it's convenient, I'll come back later."

"It's convenient now. Please come in and sit. Michel, if you would see to those few matters now, I'll have a private word with Lady Hannah."

"Of course, Your Highness." Michel bowed his way out

of the room. When the door was closed, Hannah dropped her hands to her sides. Her stride firm, she walked to the desk. "We've gotten a break. You'll have to call Reeve immediately."

"I'm not easy about this," Armand said some time later when his son-in-law sat across from him. "How can we be sure Deboque will be fooled by the information Hannah will feed him?"

"Because it's so nearly the truth." Reeve downed his second cup of coffee. "Unless Hannah can give him something important, something he has no other way of getting, she'll never get close to him."

"But will he believe her?"

"It's my job to make sure he does," Hannah said quietly. "Your Highness, I know you've had objections to this operation all along, but up to this point it's worked exactly as we've wanted."

"To this point," Armand agreed, and rose. He gestured them both back into their seats so that he could pace in peace. "Now I'm in the position of asking a woman, a woman who both my family and myself have become very fond of, to go alone to meet a man who kills as much for pleasure as for profit."

"She won't be alone."

At Reeve's announcement, Hannah sat straight up. "I have to be. If Deboque or one of his men have the slightest clue that I'm not, the whole operation goes up in smoke. I won't have it." Now, she rose as well. "I've given this two years of my life."

"And I intend to see that you live a bit longer," Reeve

said mildly. "We suspect that Deboque has his headquarters in a small villa about five miles from here. We'll have men watching it."

"And they'll have Deboque's men watching them."

"Leave that part to me, Hannah, and do your job. You have the blueprints and the specs on the security systems?"

"Yes, of course." Annoyed, she sat again. "And I know I'm to give them to no one but Deboque."

"You also know that at the first sign that things are going wrong, you're to pull out."

She nodded, though she had no intention of doing so. "Yes."

"There'll be two men stationed at the café."

"Why don't you just send up a flare?" Hannah tossed back.

He understood her frustration, but merely poured a third cup of coffee. "It's a choice between that or wiring you."

"The last agent who attempted to get a wire into Deboque's organization was sent back to the ISS in three boxes."

Reeve moved his shoulders. "Your choice."

Again, Hannah rose. "I'm not used to being second-guessed, Reeve." When he said nothing, she set her teeth. "I realize that you're my superior on this assignment, so I don't believe I have much of a choice."

"As long as we understand each other." He rose then, and took her hand. "Hannah, I'm aware of your reputation. Why don't we just say I don't want to take any chances on losing one of the best?" Releasing her, he turned back to the prince. "I have a few things to put into motion. I'll keep in touch."

Armand waited until the door was closed again. "Another moment, please," he said to Hannah. "If you'd sit?"

She wanted to be alone, to plan each detail out carefully. There was only a matter of hours left. Breeding was as strong as training, so she sat. "Would you like me to go over things with you again, sir?"

"No." His lips curved, just slightly. "I believe I grasp the situation well enough. I have a personal question, Hannah, and I ask you beforehand not to be offended." He sat across from her, militarily straight. "Am I mistaken, or has my son become fond of you?"

She linked her hands together immediately as her whole body went on alert. "If you mean Prince Bennett, sir, he's been very kind."

"Hannah, for my sake, please dispense with the evasions and the manners. Too often duty has interfered with the time I can spend with my family, but that doesn't mean I don't know my children and know them well. I believe Bennett is in love with you."

She went pale instantly. "No." She had to swallow, but the word came out a second time just as strongly. "No, he's not. Perhaps he's a bit intrigued, but only because I'm not the kind of woman he's used to spending time with."

"Hannah." Armand held up a hand before she could continue her rambling denial. "I don't ask in order to upset you. When I began to suspect this, it made me uncomfortable only because Bennett is unaware of your true purpose here."

"I understand."

"I'm not sure you do. Bennett is more like his mother than my other children. So...kindhearted. His temper has more of a lash, but his feelings are more easily reached. I only ask you this because if the answer to my next question is no, I must request that you tread softly. Do you love him, Hannah?"

Everything she felt was in her eyes. She knew it, and lowered her gaze quickly. "Whatever I feel for Bennett, for your family, won't interfere with my job."

"I know enough to recognize a person who will do what has to be done." He felt a stirring for her, a grave kind of pity that twined with empathy. "But you didn't answer me. Do you love my son?"

"I can't." This time her voice wasn't strong and there were tears chasing behind it. "I've lied to him since the first, and I'll go on doing so. You can't love and lie. Please excuse me, Your Highness."

Armand let her go. For a moment, he sat back in the chair and closed his eyes. For the next few hours, he could do nothing more than pray for her.

The café wasn't one of the pretty little tourist spots in Cordina. It was a local waterfront bar that catered to the crews from the fishing and cargo boats. Inside it was cramped with tables, many empty, and smoke and the smell of liquor. Not as rough as they came, Hannah thought as she slipped inside, but neither was it a place where a woman alone would wander unless she was looking for trouble.

Still, she didn't cause much of a stir as she came in. In her plain gray sweater and slacks, she nearly blended into the walls. The handful of women who were already there were more interesting fare. If she could get this over with quickly, she might not have to discourage any of the locals.

Hannah chose a bar stool and ordered a bourbon, neat. By the time it was served, she had sized up the room. If Reeve had indeed planted two agents here, they were certainly good ones. It was a rare thing when Hannah couldn't spot one of her own.

She'd been drinking silently for ten minutes when one of the men stood from a table and wandered in her direction. Hannah continued to drink while every muscle tensed. When he spoke, it was in French and thickened by whiskey.

"It's a sad thing for a woman to drink alone."

Hannah relaxed only enough to be annoyed. She used her primmest British tones. "It's a sadder thing for a woman not to remain alone when she chooses to."

"When one is so plain, she shouldn't be so picky," he grumbled, but moved away again. Hannah nearly smiled, then another man came through the doors.

He was dressed in seaman's clothes, with his cap pulled low. Beneath it his face was deeply tanned and gaunt. This time she tensed because she was certain.

Still, she idly lifted her drink as he moved to sit beside her at the bar.

"You have the time, *mademoiselle?*"

"Yes, it's quarter to twelve."

"Thank you." He signaled for a drink. Another minute passed as he toyed with it. *"Il fait chaud ce soir."*

"Oui, un peu."

They didn't speak again. Behind them a group began to sing a song, in French and off-key. The wine was flowing freely and the night was still young. He finished his drink and left the bar. Hannah waited only a moment, then got up to follow.

He waited for her at the edge of the dock. There was little lighting here so that he was more shadow than man. Hannah moved toward him, knowing it could be the beginning or the end for her.

"You have the information." Again he spoke in English. It was bland and unaccented, just as his French had been. Deboque chose well, she thought and only nodded.

"We go by boat." He indicated the small open runabout.

Hannah knew she had no choice. She could refuse, or she could go on. Though she knew she would have no backup on the sea, she never even considered the first. Deboque was the destination. That was the bottom line.

Without hesitation, she lowered herself into the boat and took a seat at the stern. In silence, her contact got in beside her, cast off, and started the engine. It sounded like thunder on the open water.

Hannah took a deep breath. She was on her way.

Chapter 7

Reeve would be furious. Hannah rested a hand on the
seat for balance as the boat picked up speed. He could
afford to be, she thought, but she had to keep her head.

So Deboque wasn't on land in the villa as they'd expected. He was, unless the boat made a sudden and dramatic change in direction, at sea. No, there would be
no backup now. Hannah drew another deep breath and
watched the water wake behind them. She preferred working alone in any case.

Tonight, she would meet Deboque. She could feel
it. Her pulse was slow and steady, her breathing even.
The spray the boat kicked up teased her skin as she kept
her expression placid. Nerves, what there were of them,
couldn't be allowed to show. Her midnight cruise across
the Mediterranean was bringing her closer to the goal
she'd worked toward for just over twenty-four months.

Excitement, not fear, was building inside of her. Even
that had to be controlled. Anything that made the pulse

beat too fast or tempted the mind to swing too far ahead was dangerous. She couldn't make a mistake. Over the past two years she'd worked her way up in Deboque's organization, relying for the most part on her own skill. With the backing of the ISS she'd seen several jobs through to completion. Arms sold, diamonds liberated, drugs delivered.

The end justifies the means.

Rungs on the ladder, she thought. If she could continue to climb, it wouldn't be long before Deboque's kingdom of misery would come tumbling down on his own shoulders.

The trickiest rung had been making the well-placed Bouffe look incompetent. Deboque's senior lieutenant wasn't a fool and it'd taken a lot of guile and some risk to see that several of his assignments over the last few months had fallen through, without throwing suspicion back on herself. The biggest of these had been the arms deal with a terrorist group known for their lack of patience.

It had been sticky, but the timing had been perfect. Hannah had managed to make it seem as though Bouffe had nearly botched the deal before she had slipped in to make things right.

The terrorists had their arms—she had to leave the ISS to deal with that. And Deboque had his five million francs. It would be her pleasure to deal with that. And soon.

She saw the sleek white yacht anchored majestically in dark water. A thrill of anticipation moved through her. At the wheel, her contact signaled with an electric lantern. There was an answering flash from the ship. The engine was cut, throwing the night into silence as they drifted alongside the yacht.

Hannah reached out for the ladder and found the metal cool and hard. She knew she would be the same. Without a backward glance, she climbed up, and into the unknown.

"Lady Hannah."

There was a tall, dark-skinned man waiting for her. He took her hand and bowed over it. She recognized him from her last briefing, though she would have placed his accent as Jamaican in any case. He was Ricardo Batemen, a twenty-six-year-old islander, an Ivy League graduate with a degree in medicine. He still used a scalpel, but he preferred to wield it on the healthy and unanesthetized.

He had become a favorite of Deboque's.

"I'm Ricardo." His young, smooth face spread into a smile. "Welcome to the *Invincible*."

"Thank you, Ricardo." She gave a casual look around and counted five more men and one woman on deck. The men were dressed in dark suits and carried machine guns. The woman had a sarong draped over a bikini and looked bored. "Might I have a drink?"

"Of course." His eyes, she noted, were pale, an almost translucent green that never seemed to blink. His voice was like rich cream over hot coffee. "But first, you must excuse our precautions. Your bag, Lady Hannah."

She lifted a brow and met his eyes straight on. "I'll depend on you to see that everything in it is returned to me."

"You have my word." He bowed as she handed it to him. "Now, if you would go with Carmine. She will take you to your cabin. You may like to freshen up after she makes certain no one has planted any electronic devices on you."

A strip search, Hannah thought resignedly. "No one plants anything on me, Ricardo. But I admire a cautious man." Hannah crossed the deck to Carmine as though she was going to tea.

Moments later, Ricardo set Hannah's black alligator bag on a gleaming mahogany desk. "Carmine is seeing to her. She has a small-caliber pistol, her passport and identification and about three thousand francs along with a few cosmetics. There is an envelope, sealed."

"Thank you, Ricardo." The voice was deep and smoky with its traces of France. "You may bring her to me in ten minutes. Then we won't be disturbed."

"Oui, monsieur."

"Ricardo, your impressions?"

"Attractive enough, more so than her photograph. And cool, very cool. Her hand was dry and steady."

"Good." There was a trace of amusement in the voice now. "Ten minutes, Ricardo." He picked up the envelope and broke the seal.

A short time later, Hannah adjusted her sweater. She'd found the search more annoying than humiliating. Carmine had taken her stiletto, but she'd expected that. Ricardo had her pistol. For now, she was alone and unarmed in the middle of the sea. She still had her wits.

Hannah stood in the center of the cabin when Ricardo opened the door. "My apologies again for the inconvenience, Lady Hannah."

"A small annoyance, Ricardo." He hadn't brought back

her bag, but she said nothing of it. "I hope there won't be too many more."

"None at all. If you'd just come with me."

Hannah followed him, walking easily as the boat swayed in the current. It was the size of a small hotel, she'd noted. And there were escape routes if it became necessary. The carpet they walked on was rich red. In the cabin where she'd been searched had been an antique mirror with beveled glass and a bedspread in velvet. There had also been a porthole big enough for a child, or a slender woman to work their way through.

Ricardo stopped by a glossy oak door and knocked twice. Without waiting for an answer, he turned the knob and gestured her inside. Hannah stepped through and heard the door click shut at her back.

It was opulent, elegant, even fanciful. Eighteenth-century France seemed to come alive. Now the carpet was the deep shimmering blue of kings and the paneled walls were polished to a mirrorlike gleam. Two delicate, glittering chandeliers sprinkled light over the antique wood and plush upholstery. Brocade had been used lavishly to drape over and around a bed fit for a king. All the colors were vivid, almost shocking.

There was a scent of something floral and something old that merged together into one strangely compelling and oddly uneasy fragrance. With the gentle sway of the ship, a collection of crystal animals shuddered with life.

It only took Hannah seconds to absorb this. As grand and extravagant as the room was, the man who sat behind the Louis XVI desk dominated. She didn't feel the evil she'd expected to. With the truly wicked, Hannah knew you often experienced a chill or a dread. What she saw was a slender and attractive man in his fifties, with steel-gray hair flowing back in a mane from a chiseled, aristocratic face. He wore black. It seemed to accent his almost poetically pale skin. His eyes were black, too, like a raven's. They studied her now as his full, rather beautiful mouth curved into a smile.

She'd seen pictures of him, of course. She'd studied every scrap of information that had been gathered on him in the last twenty years. And yet... And yet she hadn't been prepared for the shock of sensuality which seemed to emanate from him.

He was a man women had died for. And now she understood it. He was a man who other men had killed for without question. She understood that, too, as she stood ten feet away and felt the power.

"Lady Hannah." He rose, slowly, gracefully. His body was trim, almost delicate. His hand, as he offered it to her, was narrow and beautiful with a trio of diamonds on long fingers.

She couldn't hesitate, though she felt if her hand touched his she would be pulled out of what she knew into something foreign and frightening.

Hannah smiled and stepped forward. "Monsieur Deboque." She was glad to see his slight surprise at her use of his name. "It's a pleasure."

"Please sit. Will you have brandy?"

"Yes, thank you." She chose a soft high-backed chair that faced the desk. There was music playing through hidden speakers. Chopin. She listened to the notes as Deboque crossed to an enameled cabinet and withdrew a decanter. "Your ship is exquisite, *monsieur*." There was a painting behind his desk. One of six she knew had been stolen from a private collection only the year before. She herself had helped execute the theft.

"I appreciate beauty." He offered the brandy, then instead of going behind the desk again, sat beside her. "To your health, *mademoiselle*."

"And yours." She smiled at him again before she sipped.

"Perhaps you will tell me how you became aware of my name."

"I make it a habit of knowing who I work for, Monsieur Deboque." She shook her head as he drew out a cigarette case and offered her one. "I must congratulate you on your security and your staff. Discovering who, shall we say, reigned, was hardly an easy matter."

He drew in the smoke slowly, as a man who appreciated fine tastes. "Most have found it impossible."

Her eyes were cool and amused on his. "I find little impossible."

"Others have found it fatal." When she only smiled, he let it pass. She was, as Ricardo had said, very cool. "My reports on you are very flattering, Lady Hannah."

"Of course."

It was his turn to smile. "I admire confidence."

"And I."

"It appears I'm in your debt for smoothing over an exchange with our Mediterranean neighbors a few months ago. I would have been, to say the least, annoyed to have lost that contract."

"It was my pleasure. It would seem, *monsieur*, that you have a few weak links in the chain."

"It would seem," he murmured. He'd already debated handing Bouffe over to Ricardo for disposal. A pity, Deboque thought. Bouffe had been a loyal and valued employee for over a decade. "You are enjoying your stay in Cordina?"

Her heart drummed lightly but she sipped again. "The palace is quite lovely." She moved her shoulders as she let her gaze roam around the room. "I, too, appreciate beauty. It helps compensate for the fact that the Bissets are a bit boring."

"You're not impressed with the Royal Family, Lady Hannah?"

"I'm not easily impressed. They are certainly very pretty people, but so...devoted." She tinted her voice with derision, lightly. "I prefer devoting myself to something more tangible than honor and duty."

"And loyalty, Lady Hannah?"

She turned to him again. He was looking deep, trying to see inside, trying to see beyond. "I can be loyal." She touched her tongue to the rim of her snifter. "As long as it's profitable."

It was a chance, she knew. Disloyalty in Deboque's organization was punishable by death. She waited, outwardly cool while a single line of sweat beaded down her back. He studied her a moment, then threw his lion's head back and laughed. Hannah felt each individual muscle in her body sing with relief.

"An honest woman. I admire that. Yes, I admire that a great deal more than sworn oaths." He drew in the rich French smoke then exhaled again. "It would seem to my advantage to continue to make it profitable for someone of your skills and ambitions."

"I was hoping you'd see it that way. I prefer the executive branch, if you comprehend, Monsieur Deboque, but I'm willing to work my way to it. Delegation, organization, is so much more rewarding than execution, don't you think?"

"Indeed, yes." He studied her again, considering. She appeared to be a mild, well-bred young woman of some means. He preferred a quiet, unassuming outer shell in a woman. He thought briefly of Janet Smithers who he'd used and discarded nearly a decade before. Lady Hannah, he thought, might prove to be a great deal more interesting, and more competent. "You've been with us two years now?"

"Yes."

"And in those two years, you've proven yourself to be very useful." He rose now and retrieved the envelope on his desk. "You brought this to me, I assume?"

"I did." She swirled her brandy. "Though I found the method with which it was delivered irksome."

"My apologies. This information is interesting, Lady Hannah, but I fear, incomplete."

She crossed her legs and relaxed back in the chair. "A woman who writes everything she knows on paper loses her value quickly. What isn't there, is in here." She laid a finger against her temple.

"I see." He admired an employee who knew her own worth, and guarded it. "If we say I'm interested in the security systems of the Royal Palace, the Fine Arts Center, the museum, for the purpose of emulating such systems for my own use, you would be able to fill in the blanks?"

"Of course."

"And if I asked how you came by such information?"

"This was the purpose of my visit to Cordina."

"One of them." Intrigued, he tapped the envelope on his palm. "It was fortunate that you were able to become close to Princess Eve."

"Fortunate, but not difficult. She was lonely for female companionship. I'm accommodating. I fuss over her daughter, listen to her fears and complaints. By easing some of her workload, I also earn the gratitude of Prince Alexander. He worries that his wife will tire herself while carrying his child."

"And you are trusted?"

"Implicitly. And why not?" she added. "My family is well respected, my breeding without mark. Prince Armand sees me as a young cousin of his dead wife. Your pardon, *monsieur,* but aren't these the reasons you enlisted me to find a place at the palace?"

"Yes, they are." He sat back. She pleased him, but he was a long way from giving her his full confidence. "I have word that the young prince is interested in you."

Something inside her froze at that. "Your network of information is admirable." Hannah glanced at her empty snifter, then tilted it in question. Deboque rose immediately to refill her glass. It was just enough time to regain her composure.

"Bennett is, as I'm sure you're aware, invariably interested in the female closest at hand." She gave a low laugh and tried not to hate herself. "He's really only a boy, and spoiled at that. I've found the simplest way to handle him is to act disinterested."

Deboque nodded slowly. "Then he pursues."

"Such men are always more—accommodating under those circumstances."

"I beg your pardon if I seem to be getting too personal, my dear, but how accommodating?"

"He's a bit bored, a bit reckless. His weakness for women should have its uses. I believe with a certain— flair—information can be drawn out of him. It was he, you see, who took me through the Center, and through the naval base at Le Havre." She sipped again, lingering over it. Deboque would already know about her tête-à-tête with Bennett at the museum. So, she would use his knowledge and twist the truth.

"It was a simple matter to ask questions and express interest in how the museum guards its treasures. With that, I was shown the setup, alarms, monitors, sensors." She paused again to let it sink in. "The more a woman pretends ignorance, the more she learns."

Deboque warmed the brandy in his hands. "Hypothetically, you understand, can the security at the palace be broken?"

At last, she thought, they were homing in. "Hypothetically, any security can be broken. I will say that Reeve MacGee has designed an admirable system, but not an invincible one."

"Interesting." He picked up a small china figure of a hawk and began to study it. The room fell into silence long enough for her to be sure he was trying to unnerve her. "And do you have a theory on how this system can be undermined?"

"From inside." She sipped her brandy again. "It's always cleaner from the inside."

"And the Center?"

"Much the same."

"This play the princess wrote, it opens in a few days. It would be amusing to cause a small disturbance."

"Of what nature?"

He only smiled. "Oh, I'm just speaking in theory, you understand. It seems to me that the Royal Family would be uncomfortable if something disrupted the evening. I should hate to miss it. You'll be there?"

"I'm expected." She needed to push him, push him into something definite. "I prefer knowing which door to walk into, *monsieur*."

"Then you might be wise to remain in the audience. I wouldn't want to lose you now that we've become close."

She acknowledged this, but realizing he would demand the rest of the stats then dismiss her, Hannah changed gears. "As a matter of personal curiosity may I ask why you have such interest in the Royal Family? It intrigues me because I see you much as I see myself, as a person most interested in profit and personal gain."

"Profit is always desirable." He set the hawk down. He had hands that might have played a violin or written sonnets. They rarely killed, only gestured for others to do so. "Personal gain can have a multitude of variables, *n'est-ce pas?*"

"As long as it satisfies," she agreed. "Using the kidnapping of the Princess Gabriella or the threats on the Bissets as a lever to gain your release from prison was one thing. You're no longer in prison." Again she looked with admiration around the room. "I would think you would move on to more profitable waters."

"All business needs a completion." She saw emotion for the first time as his fingers tightened around his glass. "All debts require payment. The interest of ten years is dear, very dear. Do you agree?"

"Yes. Revenge, or retribution if you prefer. This I understand is as sweet as diamonds." And looking at him, she knew he would stop at nothing to collect. "*Monsieur*, you have arranged for me to be in the palace. I intend to continue to remain there until you alter the order, but I prefer to do so with some direction." She gestured casually, palm up. "The revenge, after all, is yours, not mine. I've never worked well blindfolded."

"A man who puts all of his cards on the table loses his edge."

"Agreed. So does a man who doesn't sharpen his tools and use them where they're best suited. I'm in, *monsieur*. Having a map of some sort would be useful."

He intended to use her, and well. Sitting back again, Deboque steepled his hands. His diamonds shot out violent light. He had failed, twice before he had failed to use the Bissets for his own purposes. He had failed to bring Armand to his knees. Whatever had to be done, whomever had to be used, he wouldn't fail this time. In Hannah, he thought he'd found the instrument.

"Let me ask you this. If one man wishes to destroy another, what does he do?"

"The simplest is to end his life."

Deboque smiled, and now Hannah saw the evil. It was coated with class, pampered with elegance, but very real. "I'm not a simple man. Death is so final, and even when it is slow, it's soon over. To destroy a man, the soul, the heart, requires more than a bullet in the brain."

He was speaking of Armand, she knew. It wasn't time to demand he name names and reveal his plan. He would tell her nothing and trust her less. Hannah set down her glass and tried to think as he did. "To truly destroy, you take away what is most valuable." Her heart began to beat in the back of her throat, clogging a wave of nausea. Still, when she spoke it was with cool admiration. "His children?"

"You are intelligent as well as lovely." Leaning over he placed his hand on hers. She felt it from him, the vile, dark movement of death. "To make a man suffer, to destroy his soul, you deprive him of what he loves best and leave him to live with it. His children and grandchildren dead, his country in chaos, a man would have nothing left but misery. And a country without an heir becomes unstable—and profitable—if one is shrewd."

"All of them," Hannah murmured. She thought of little Marissa, so pretty and soft, and Dorian with his smudged face and bright grin. Fear for them was suddenly so strong, so vital, she thought it had to show in her eyes. She kept them down, looking at his hand as it lay over hers and the cold, hard glint of the diamonds.

"All of them, *monsieur?*" When she thought she could trust herself again, she looked back at his face. He was smiling. In the fragile light of the chandeliers he looked wan as a ghost and infinitely more frightening. "Not an easy task, even for someone of your power."

"Nothing worthwhile is simple, my dear. But as you said, nothing is impossible—particularly when one is trusted and close."

Her brow lifted. She didn't shudder or draw away. Business, she told herself. Lady Hannah was all business. She was being offered a job, the most vital one Deboque had to offer.

"You were carefully chosen, Lady Hannah. For more than ten years, I've had one dream. I believe you are the instrument to see it to fruition."

She pursed her lips as if considering while her mind raced ahead. He was giving her a contract, a royal one. As she said nothing, his fingers played lightly over her knuckles. Like a spider, she thought, a handsome and very clever spider.

"Such a responsibility is weighty for someone in my position in your organization."

"That can be seen to. Bouffe is—retiring," he said softly. "I will be looking for a replacement."

She let her hand lie under his as she touched her tongue to her top lip. "A guarantee, *monsieur*."

"My word."

She smiled a little. *"Monsieur."*

With a nod of acknowledgement, he rose and pressed a button on his desk. Within seconds Ricardo appeared. "Lady Hannah will be replacing Bouffe. See to the arrangements, Ricardo. Discreetly."

"Of course." The pale green eyes half closed as if with pleasure.

Hannah waited for the door to shut again. A man's life was over. "The day may come when you decide to replace me as casually."

"Not if you continue to please me." He lifted her hand again and kissed it. "I have a feeling you will."

"I must tell you, *monsieur,* I have a distaste for killing children." His fingers tightened, very slightly on hers, but she didn't fidget. "I believe it will take five million American dollars to overcome this distaste."

She saw it in his eyes. He would break her fingers as easily as he would kiss them. Hannah kept her gaze steady on his and hoped she hadn't pushed her luck too far.

"Is it money that seduces you, *ma petite?*"

"Not seduces, pleases. I like to be pleased."

"You have two weeks to please me, Lady Hannah. Then I shall return the favor." He kept her hand in his as he drew her to her feet. "Now, as a show of faith, you will tell me what you failed to note down here."

Hannah walked over to the specs and prepared to lie to him.

She was exhausted. In a decade of assignments, nothing had left her feeling so empty and soiled. As she drove through the palace gates, she could only think about a long hot shower where she could scrub off whatever traces remained of Deboque's cologne. Reeve was standing a hundred feet beyond the gates. Hannah stopped the car and waited for him to slide in beside her.

"You were gone a long time." He gave her a long, thorough study. "It wasn't in the plans for you to be out of contact for over an hour."

"It was in the plans for me to get to Deboque."

"And you did?"

She rolled down her window a bit farther. "I met him on a yacht, the *Invincible*. It's anchored about five miles northwest. He has at least six armed guards, double that by a guess. He has the information we wanted him to have. I'm replacing Bouffe."

Reeve's brow lifted. "You must have impressed him."

"That was the idea." She wondered how soon she could wash the taste of his brandy from her mouth. "He's planning something for the opening of Eve's play." When Reeve stiffened beside her, she went on. "I don't believe it's going to be anything directly against the family. He seemed to think it would be entertaining to confuse matters. He's very careful how he phrases things. Nothing too direct. Even if I testified against him, it would be difficult to actually convict him of conspiracy. He hypothesizes, theorizes."

"Did he give you an idea where he intends to make his move?"

She listened for a moment to a bird that was singing its heart out. "He seemed most interested in the palace. It's the biggest challenge. We have two weeks."

"He moves in two weeks?"

"That's how long he gave me to murder your family." She turned to him then and saw his face was pale and set. "All of you but Armand, Reeve. The children, everyone. He wants to destroy Armand's soul and leave Cordina without an heir. If you trust my judgment, he wants this done as much for personal satisfaction as for the profit he might make when Cordina is thrown into chaos."

Reeve drew out a cigarette but didn't light it. "I trust your judgment."

"We have two weeks to stop him, or to convince him that I've done what he wants."

It was his family, his heart, yet he knew he had to think as coolly as she did. "Is he setting you up?"

She thought for a moment, then shook her head. "I don't think so. It's certainly possible that he'd dispose of me after I've finished the job, but I think it's more likely he'd continue to use me. We did a good job of planting information about me, and over the past two years I've saved him a bit of trouble and money. If he believes I can give him this, he'll sit back and wait."

"Armand will have to be told."

"I know." But not Bennett. Armand and only Armand.

"For now, just go on as usual." He indicated that she should drive ahead. "We'll need some time."

"Eve's opening is in a few days."

"We'll handle it. You get some sleep. As soon as we have a direction, I'll let you know."

Hannah got out of the car, then as Reeve stood on the other side she stopped. "I want him. I want him for myself. I know it's unprofessional and stupid. But if I have the chance, if I find the way, I'm going to take him out myself."

Reeve said nothing as she walked up the steps. He'd already vowed the same thing.

Chapter 8

"**I** don't want you to go tonight."

"You know I have to." Eve stood, grim and stubborn, facing her husband. "It's my play, my troupe, my production. I don't have a choice, Alex."

"Excuses can be made." He looked at her, dressed in midnight blue that skimmed her shoulders and swirled to her ankles. Her hair was caught up in the back so that it fell over one shoulder like ebony. Even after all the years he'd known her, just looking at her made his pulse race. "You know how dangerous it could be. With the information we have now, we can be sure there'll be an incident tonight. I don't want you involved."

"I am involved." She was frightened. Ever since Reeve had told them that he'd received a tip that there would be trouble at the theater on opening night, her nerves had been stretched tight. Yes, she was frightened, but she was no less determined. She crossed to the beveled mirror above the bureau as if checking the arrangement of her hair was of some importance. "I wrote the play, I produced it, and more important than either of those," she continued before he could interrupt, "I belong at the theater tonight because I'm your wife."

The fact that her arguments were valid meant nothing. He wanted her in the palace, safe, untouchable. His heart would rest easy if he knew she was here, in the suite of rooms she'd decorated, tucked high in the palace that had been his family home for generations. Nothing could happen to her here. Anything could happen outside.

"My love, Reeve is rarely wrong. If he says there'll be trouble tonight, I want you well away from it. The fact that you're carrying a child is a very simple reason for you to be excused. I know the play is important to you, but—"

"Yes, it is," she interrupted. "But you're more important."

"Then do this for me, and stay home tonight."

She tilted her head, holding on to both her nerves and her temper. "Alexander, would you stay behind with me?"

"If it was possible, of course." Impatience had him dragging a hand through his hair. It was a ploy she'd used before, and one there was little argument against. "I can't close myself up every time there's a rumble from Deboque."

"For Cordina," she said quietly. "And Cordina is now my country, too."

"Eve." He thought he loved her as much as it was possible to love. Every day he learned there could be more. "You are the most precious thing in the world to me. I almost lost you once."

She crossed to him then, knowing the first step, the

first touch should be hers. When both of his hands were in hers, she looked up into his eyes. "And I you, Alex. I'm going to sit in the Royal Box beside you, where I belong."

From outside the door, Hannah heard the conversation clearly enough. It was moments like this that made it difficult to think of what she was doing, what she had yet to do, as merely another assignment. There were people beyond the door who she'd come to care about. The Bissets were no longer names or symbols, but friends. After ten years of playing dangerous games, she knew how risky it could be to make friends.

She closed her eyes and drew her breath deep before she knocked.

"Entrez." It was Alexander who answered, the impatience in his voice ripe. Hannah opened the door but didn't cross the threshold.

"I'm sorry. I'm disturbing you."

"Of course not." With the warmth that was so much a part of her, Eve smiled and gestured her inside. "I see you're ready for the evening." She felt a little twinge of regret at Hannah's severe beige dress and hairstyle. She'd hoped with a little time she could urge Hannah to soften her image. Tonight, however, there were more immediate matters of concern. "We were just about to come down ourselves."

Hannah saw Eve take Alexander's hand again. "I thought you might need some help."

"No, there's nothing." But the cloud of concern didn't leave Eve's eyes. "Hannah, I don't want you to feel obligated to go with the family. Knowing there's a possibility of an—incident," she began. "Well, it might be more comfortable for you here at home."

"Of course I'm going." With the hated secret tucked inside of her, she shifted the wrap on her arms. "And I really believe everything's going to be fine. If you don't need me then, I'll just go down."

"Please, let's not talk about it anymore," Eve said when Hannah shut the door behind her. "Let's go say good-night to Marissa before we leave."

"Eve." Alexander gathered her close. He could feel the slight swell where another child lay. "I love you."

"Talk's cheap," she murmured, and tried for a laugh. "Promise to show me later, after the play."

He let his cheek rest on her hair. "You have my word."

Bennett was already waiting in the main hall. Even with the distance separating them, Hannah could feel the impatience coming from him. Impatience, she thought, mixed with a recklessness that the elegant evening clothes couldn't disguise. He was looking for trouble, Hannah realized. More, he was hoping for it.

"There you are." Though he smiled up at her, his mind was already on the evening ahead. Instinctively he took her hand, holding it as she reached the bottom of the stairs. "You don't have to go tonight, Hannah. I'd be happier if you didn't."

Guilt came so quickly that she had squeezed his hand in reassurance before she could stop herself. "Now even you sound like Eve," she said lightly. "I want to be there. A vague tip from an anonymous source is a foolish reason to miss a night at the theater."

He touched the pearl cluster at her ear. "Is that what we call British pluck?"

"It's what we call common sense."

"Whatever it's called I want you to stay close. There'll be enough guards to smother us, but I prefer to keep an eye on you myself." Before she could stop him, he was leading her toward the doors.

"Eve and Alexander are nearly ready. I said I'd wait for them."

"Security feels better splitting us up." He acknowledged Claude with a brief nod. "You'll ride with me. Father will come along after Alexander and Eve."

"All right." She walked out into the star-studded night, calmly holding the .22 that lay within her beaded evening bag.

The theater was sold out. Long before the first curtain, the seats were filled so that the babble of conversation rose up to the Royal Box. There was thunderous applause when the Bissets entered. From the background as bows were made, Hannah held her breath and studied the sea of faces.

If Deboque had been there, she knew she would have found him.

"The Center's been swept twice," Reeve murmured in her ear. "There's nothing here."

She nodded and took her seat as the curtain rose.

The play was everything Eve had hoped for, though Hannah doubted anyone in the box had their full attention on the drama and pathos onstage. More than once, she cast a sidelong look at Bennett to find him studying the audience.

Deboque wasn't there. Hannah hadn't expected him. Whatever happened, whenever it happened, he would be far away with an alibi as solid as Cordinian rock.

So they would wait. And watch.

When the lights came up for intermission, Hannah could almost feel Eve relax. A false alarm? No. Though she preferred Eve believing it was so, Hannah knew better. There was an itch between her shoulder blades, vague but persistent. Some called it a hunch. Others called it instinct. Hannah had been in the game long enough to know when to wait and when to go with it.

"Would you like something to drink?"

She turned to Bennett, set to refuse. For personal reasons, she wanted him close at hand. "Yes," she heard herself saying, knowing this would be just one more deception. "I'd love something cool."

The moment he was through the doors behind them, Hannah leaned toward Reeve. "I'm going to look around."

"I'd stay close—I have a feeling." With him it was in the gut. He'd yet to let Gabriella move more than an arm's span away.

"I do too. Deboque said something about me staying in the audience. I want to take a walk backstage."

He started to object, but Gabriella took his hand and gave Hannah the few seconds she needed to slip out. She made her way toward the ladies' lounge until she was certain no one was watching. With the ease of long experience, she slipped into a stairway and began moving down.

She had ten minutes, Hannah thought as she checked her watch, before anyone would miss her.

There were costume changes and stretched nerves backstage when Hannah crossed the corridor. Most of the actors were too wound up to spare her a glance. Nothing out of place. Nothing out of synch. And yet, the itch between her shoulder blades persisted.

Chantel's dressing room door was half-open. The actress caught a glimpse of Hannah, hesitated, then called out. "Lady Hannah."

Because she saw no choice, Hannah stopped at the doorway. "Miss O'Hurley. Her Highness wasn't able to come down, but you should know she's delighted with your performance."

"Thank you." Chantel set down the grease pencil she'd been using to touch up her eyes. "And what do you think of the play?"

"It's gripping. Your interpretation of Julia is breathtaking."

With a nod, Chantel moved toward her. The exaggerated stage makeup only made her look more exotic. "You know, I was born into show business. It's in the blood, if you get my drift. And I've always thought one inveterate actor easily recognizes another."

Very cool, almost smiling, Hannah met her eyes. "I suppose that's true."

"Perhaps that's why while I'm still not sure if I like you, I know I don't trust you." Chantel adjusted the cuff of the dress she'd wear in the next scene. "I've always been very fond of Bennett. A woman like myself has few men she can call real friends."

There was something strong, something honest in the woman who faced her. Hannah gave as much as she could. "I can tell you that Bennett is a special man, and one I care for very much."

Chantel was silent a moment, weighing, considering. "I'm not sure why, but I believe you." She shook her head. "I can't figure out why you're playing Jane Eyre, but I imagine you have your reasons."

"Places, Miss O'Hurley."

Chantel turned to give herself one last check in a full-length mirror. She lifted her chin to a different angle and became Julia. Her voice took on the slightest of drawls, an echo of the American South, as she turned back to walk past Hannah. "Darling," she said in character. "You must know beige is the worst possible color for you." Then she winked and walked to the wings.

Hannah let out a long breath. She'd seen nothing out of place, seen no one who didn't belong and had learned a lesson. Her cover wasn't as foolproof as she'd always thought.

She walked back down the corridor, turned into the stairway and started up. She heard the applause as the curtain came up. Then came the distant sound, the rumble and boom, of an explosion. The lights went out.

There were scattered screams as the theater plunged into darkness. From here, the warning rumble couldn't be heard. In the Royal Box, guards closed in like a wedge. Guns were drawn and held ready.

"Stay where you are," Reeve ordered. He gave Gabriella's hand a quick, reassuring squeeze. "Two of you come with me." He moved into the hallway with two guards.

"We'll need a light." Swearing, he dug in his pocket for a lighter. "We'll need someone to go over the PA and keep the audience from panicking." Even as he flicked the lighter on, throwing dull and shadowy light off his face, Chantel's voice came cool and clear through the speakers.

"*Mesdames and messieurs,* if you would stay seated for a moment or two. We seem to be having some difficulties with the lights. If you'd like to take advantage of the opportunity by getting to know your neighbor better..."

"Good girl," Reeve murmured as he heard the nervous laughter. "Let's get down to the main breakers."

Hannah hadn't come back. The words kept echoing over in Bennett's mind as he heard Alexander murmuring reassurances to Eve. She was out there somewhere, alone in the dark. Without hesitation, he was moving toward the door.

"Your Highness." The looming figure of a guard inched toward him. "If you would please remain seated."

"Let me pass."

"Bennett." His father's voice cut through the dark. "Please sit. This should be over in moments."

"Hannah's not here."

There was the briefest of silences. "Reeve will handle things."

There was duty, and the honor he'd never questioned. Now there was love. Bennett shoved his way through the door and went to find her.

Hannah had the gun in her hand as she stood in the stairwell. She didn't move, barely breathed, as she debated whether to go up and check on the Bissets, or whether to go down and check the power. If there had been one bomb, there could all too easily be another.

Her head told her that the Bissets were well guarded and her job was to find the source of the trouble. Her heart wanted only to see if Bennett was well and safe. Following it, Hannah started up the stairs. She'd climbed no more than three when she heard the sound of a door closing on the landing below.

With her finger wrapped around the trigger, she pointed the barrel of the gun up and started down again. She saw the beam of the flashlight before she heard the footsteps. Cautious ones. Quiet ones. Like a shadow, Hannah melted into a corner and waited.

She recognized him from the museum. He was dressed now in the dark blue uniform of the maintenance crew and carried a small toolbox. She almost nodded in approval. Anyone seeing him would simply assume he was assigned to fix whatever had gone wrong. The beam skimmed past the toes of her shoes before she stepped out and pressed the gun at his side.

"Be easy," she said in undertones. "I apologize for greeting you this way, but I didn't want a hole in my head before you recognized me."

"Mademoiselle." She heard the tightly controlled fury in his voice. No man liked to be caught unaware. "I was told you would remain out of the way this evening."

Hannah drew the gun back but kept it steady. "I prefer a firsthand look at what's going on. A dramatic distraction," she complimented him. "Are there other plans for tonight?" He was prepared to kill, she was certain. But was he armed? She knew if she detained him too long or pressed too hard, her cover would be in jeopardy.

"Only if the opportunity arises. You will excuse me?"

"Certainly." Her only thought now was to see him out of the theater and away before any opportunity arose. The theater was packed with people, the Royal Family was present. Now wasn't the time for a confrontation. "Can I assist you in making a discreet exit?"

"It's been seen to."

"Very well. Tell our employer that I won't be as dramatic, but I'll be effective." She turned toward the stairs when she heard the door above open.

"Hannah?"

At the sound of Bennett's voice her blood froze. Even as the man beside her made a move, she clamped a hand over his arm. She knew without seeing that he reached for a weapon.

"Don't be a fool," she hissed. "In this light you could too easily miss and ruin everything. Turn off that beam and let me handle it." She felt his resistance, but turned quickly and started up the stairs. "Bennett." She didn't have to fake the fear in her voice. He was hardly more than a shadow at the doorway but she put her arms around him and let her body block his.

"What are you doing down here?" he began.

"I lost my way when the lights went off."

"For God's sake, Hannah. How did you manage to get all the way down here?"

"I—I'm not sure. Please, let's go back."

"You could've broken your neck on these stairs." When

he gave her a slight shake and started to draw her back she shifted to block him more thoroughly.

"Kiss me," she ordered in a whisper.

Almost amused now that he'd found her safe, Bennett tilted up her chin. In the dim light he could only make out the vague outline of her face and the glint of her eyes. "If you insist."

Even as he closed his mouth over hers, she gripped the door handle behind him, prepared to shove him through.

Then his fingers spread over her face, gently. His lips coaxed and comforted and asked so little in return. On the handle her fingers tightened as much in response to him as in fear for him. One hand settled at the small of her back, again to soothe. Hannah felt her heart tear. She loved him, yet knew she couldn't. She wanted the kiss to be no more than what it was, a merging of lips, a symbol of caring. But what it was, what it had to be was a tool to give the man below them the time to escape.

Then Bennett would be safe. For seconds only, she put her heart into the kiss. He would be safe, and she could breathe again.

He felt the change and his heart thudded with it. He had imagined her lost in the dark, alone and in need of comfort and physical contact. So thinking, he had buried his own needs and had kissed her as a friend might, with affection and understanding. Her response was thunder and lightning. His fingers tightened on her face as he murmured her name.

The lights came on in a flash.

It happened very quickly then, but Bennett would re-member, for a lifetime, each movement, each sound.

There was no time for fear, only for surprise, then disillusionment.

When the lights went on, he stiffened. She knew in that moment that Deboque's man had not made his escape as she had hoped, but was waiting to take advantage of the opportunity that had presented itself. Without hesitation she whirled out of Bennett's arms and half shoved him through the door. The man's gun was drawn, but so was hers. And she was very fast.

Bennett had seen the man, and his weapon. He had pushed himself off the door to shield her even as she'd fired. For a moment, he simply stared, stunned at seeing the man fall and lay still. Then he saw the pistol in Hannah's hand. Surprise came and went. His face became very impassive. When he spoke, his voice was neutral.

"What game are you playing, and for whom?"

She'd never killed before. She'd been trained to, of course, but had never actually ended a life by her own hand. As she stood looking down, the gun felt foreign and slimy in her hand. Her face was very pale, her eyes very dark when she turned to Bennett. "I'll have to explain, but there isn't time." She heard the sound of running feet and struggled to pull herself together. "Please trust me."

"That's an interesting request at this point." He started to brush by her to go to the man below.

"Bennett, please." Grabbing his arm, she drew up beside him. "I'll tell you whatever I can later. You can verify it all with Reeve or your father."

She felt his muscles tense. "My father?"

"Please, for his sake, the sake of your family, play this out with me." She pushed the gun into his hand just as

Reeve arrived with five guards on his heels. Now she
let reaction set it. Again, truth was often the best cover.

"He tried to shoot the prince." Hannah let her voice
shake and leaned heavily against Bennett. "He was going
to kill him. If Bennett hadn't…" Trailing off, she buried
her face against Bennett's shoulder.

He didn't move, though he didn't contradict her, there
was no comforting hand now, no murmured reassurances.
Reeve bent over the body, then lifted his gaze and met
Bennett's. "It's fortunate you were quick—and accurate."
The .45 lying beside the body hadn't been fired. His eyes
shifted over briefly to rest on Hannah. "We'll handle this
quietly."

Bennett's lips curved, but it wasn't a smile. "Of course."

"If you'll go back to your box." Reeve signaled two of
the guards to accompany him. "We'll say nothing of this
to the family until we can be private." With a pencil, he
lifted the .45 automatic by the trigger guard. "The police
will come in the back way."

Bennett brushed the guards aside with a gesture. It was
the first time Hannah had seen him use true royal arrogance. "I want to talk to you. Alone. Now."

"All right." He'd seen too much, Reeve knew. It had to
be handled quickly. "Eve's office then. If you'd give me
a few minutes to deal with this first."

"You have ten," Bennett said, and turned his back on
all of them.

"I'd like to go back to the palace." Hannah stood on
the steps, alone now. Her hands, white at the knuckles,
clutched her bag. "I'm not feeling well."

"See to a car and driver," Reeve ordered one of the

guards. To another he gave the dead man's weapon before he climbed the stairs to slip an arm around Hannah. "I'll walk you out." The moment they were out of earshot, his voice became curt and professional. "What happened?"

Her knees were shaking, but she schooled her voice to the same tone. Briefly, she gave him her report. "The entire thing couldn't have taken more than five minutes." It had seemed like hours.

"It was just bad luck all around that Bennett found you. Still, the story will hold. He has a reputation for being an excellent shot. All I have to do is calm him down." Reeve let out a long breath at that. He knew his brother-in-law well, just as he knew all the Bissets. Once their temper was lost, it wasn't easily regained. "We'll go over this in the morning so that the story you pass on to Deboque is the most advantageous one."

"He'll never forgive me."

Reeve was intuitive enough to know she wasn't speaking of Deboque now. "Bennett is neither unjust nor hardhearted. He'll be angry at being kept in the dark, but he won't blame you."

"Won't he?" Hannah walked through the doors and into the night air without looking back.

She sat by the window looking out at the garden. An hour had passed, then two while she watched the moonlight. The palace was quiet. Perhaps the others had come back, but she wouldn't have heard because her rooms faced the back. Guests were always given the loveliest views and the quietest spots.

She could imagine all too well how Bennett would have

reacted to Reeve's explanations. But it wouldn't be Reeve he would blame. Hannah knew the blame would be hers and had accepted it. In the morning he would probably demand to speak with her privately.

She wouldn't apologize. Hannah lifted her chin a fraction higher. She would accept his anger and his coldness, but she wouldn't apologize for being who and what she was.

She loved him. He would hardly believe her now if she had the right to tell him. She would have died for him tonight, not only for duty, not only for honor, but so much more for love. He would never understand or believe that now. Perhaps it was best. If her feelings for him had gotten beyond her control, it was wiser, and safer, if his for her had deadened.

She still had an assignment to complete and two years of work to finish.

Hannah laid her head on the windowsill and wished she were in London where the night would be cold and damp and smell of the river.

He didn't knock. The time for manners, formalities and small kindnesses had passed. She was curled on the window seat with her arms folded on the sill and her head resting on them. She'd loosened her hair so that it fell over the shoulders and down the back of a plain white robe. A man could almost believe she was a woman lost in the night. Bennett no longer believed what he saw and little that he felt. When he shut the door behind him, she was up and standing quickly.

She hadn't expected him that night. Looking at his face,

Hannah saw that she should have. Because she knew the worst when she faced it, she braced.

"You spoke with Reeve?"

"Yes."

"And your father?"

His brow lifted. Though he had discarded his formal jacket, he could be very much the prince when he chose. "We talk tomorrow, though that doesn't concern you."

She acknowledged this with a slight nod. "Only inasmuch as it affects my position at the moment."

"Although you're obviously unaware of it, I'm not a fool. Your position remains." He took the small pistol from his pocket. After crossing to the stand beside her bed, he set it down. "Your property."

No, she would not be forgiven. She'd thought she'd been ready to accept it. She'd been wrong. "Thank you." As coolly as he, she walked to the stand, then placed the pistol in the drawer.

"You're an excellent shot, Lady Hannah."

The drawer shut again with the slightest of slams. "I've been well trained."

He caught her chin then, not gently. "Yes, by God, you have. What other talents do you have, I wonder? Deceit is certainly the sharpest. How many women can you be?"

"However many it takes to do my job. If you'd excuse me, I'm very tired."

"Oh, no." With his other hand, he gathered up her hair. He thought of what she'd put him through in one evening. Anxiety, outright terror and betrayal. "I'm afraid I won't fall for that again. With me, at any rate, the quiet, well-bred English lady is quite done. Cards on the table, Hannah."

It was fear, she realized, that had her stomach heaving. Not fear that he would hurt her physically, not fear that he would do something in temper that would jeopardize the operation, but fear, deadly and cold, that he would always look at her the way he was now.

"I doubt there's much I can tell you that Reeve hasn't. The operation was put in effect just over two years ago. The ISS needed an agent on the inside, so—"

"I've been apprised of the basic details." He let her go, dropping his hands to his sides. There, they balled into fists. "A bit late, but the information seems fairly complete. After establishing yourself with Deboque's organization, you pretended an affection for Eve so you could gain access to the palace." He saw the flicker of emotion cross her face at that but wasn't ready to interpret it. "In this way, Deboque would be deceived into believing he had one of his own on the inside. By playing both ends, you would be privy to his plans, and once he makes a move, the authorities would be able to close in and destroy his organization. I'm told I should be grateful you're so good at what you do."

"I don't need gratitude, just cooperation."

"Then perhaps you should have asked for it from the beginning."

She lifted her head. No, there would be no apologies. "I had orders, Bennett. You're no stranger to duty."

"No, but neither am I a stranger to honor. You played me." Anger broke through the ice so that he held both of her arms. "You used my feelings for you."

"You weren't supposed to have any," she snapped back.

"We can't always choose what we feel. But there are other choices. Did you need to use how I felt for you, Hannah?"

"I had a job to do." Her voice wasn't steady now because she couldn't be sure if she'd done what she'd done coolly or because of her own needs. "I tried to discourage you."

"You knew I cared, that I wanted you."

"I didn't want you to."

"You still lie."

"No." She yanked, but he held her firm. "I did nothing to attract you. Then again, perhaps a woman only has to exist for you to be attracted." She saw the fury bloom but ignored it. "Perhaps by refusing to sleep with you, I became more of a challenge. There are a lot of women who would gladly sleep with royalty."

"Do you believe if all I had wanted was you in bed that you wouldn't have been there a half a dozen times already?"

"I go nowhere I don't take myself." She tossed her head back. His voice had been too low, too precise, but she was past caring. "If you're angry because I'm not what you thought I was, it's because your ego's been bruised."

The rest of her words and her breath were knocked away as she fell under him on the bed. Before she could counter the move, her arms were pinned at her sides. She'd been warned about his temper. There had even been some documentation of it in his dossier. But none of that was nearly as awesome as seeing it firsthand.

"Ego?" He gritted out with his face only inches from

hers. "So to you I'm still only what you've read, only what you've been told." It hurt, how it hurt. He could feel it shimmer inside of him until the only recourse was to turn it into anger. "I won't disappoint you then."

She scissored her legs and nearly succeeded in rocking him off. He shifted until her body was pressed flat against his. One hand rested dangerously on her throat. It gave him grim pleasure to feel her pulse flutter rapidly beneath his fingers.

"This won't prove anything." She managed to free one arm, but he caught it at the wrist. Her pulse beat there as well, fast, uneven. "You'll only demean both of us."

It didn't matter. He'd gone beyond right and wrong, truth and lies. "There was a time when I believed you to be shy and precious. That was a woman I only wanted to show tenderness to. For her I had such patience, such sweet feelings. But for you, we can dispense with such things, can't we?"

"Bennett, don't do this." She said it quietly, knowing it was already too late.

"Why not?" The recklessness was back, in full force, driven by betrayal. "It's a night for lies and passions."

She prepared to do battle, for herself and for him. "You won't rape me."

"No, I won't. But I will have you."

Chapter 9

It would be a battle of wits, a contest for control. Somehow it was easier for Hannah to think of that when Bennett's lips pressed down on hers. He didn't want to make love with her, but to punish, even to conquer. It was anger, not desire that had brought them here. She couldn't afford to forget it, not even for an instant.

Yet the kiss wasn't cruel. Hot and hard he moved his mouth over hers, more taunting than insistent. The hand on her throat didn't so much threaten as control. The callused fingers reminded her of the strength in his hands even as they stroked to arouse and seduce.

She made her body lie still and limp beneath his, waiting not just for a chance to fight back, but for a chance to fight and win.

But her blood was already beginning to stir.

He knew it. He was a man who understood passions, desires, vulnerabilities and how one would feed on the others. He'd used such things before, all in good humor, to give as much as to take. Now he would use them to wound as deeply as he had been wounded.

Women had frustrated him, amused him, baffled him and fascinated him. But no woman had ever hurt him before Hannah. That she'd done so not inadvertently, not in a fit of temper, but coolly, passionlessly, made the sin unforgivable. For the first time in his life he held a woman in his arms with the sole intention of bringing her pain.

Or so he told himself.

There was only flesh beneath the robe. He knew it before he drew the material down her bare shoulder. There was strength there. He'd felt it once before. Now he felt the softness as well. Both moved him, just as, he discovered, his touch moved her. As she began her first struggles, he shifted so that her loosened robe parted for him.

She knew better than to panic, but her heart and her needs betrayed her. The moment he'd stroked his palm down her bare skin the flare of pleasure had opened the door to fear. To excitement. To passion. Her struggles took them rolling over the bed, locked in combat. His lean build and easygoing manner made the steely strength she discovered both a surprise and an arousal. Muscles bunched under his shirt as he countered her moves and took her where he wanted her to go. Hannah found herself trapped beneath him again with her arms pinned by the robe that had slipped down her back.

Breathless, she stared up at him. She was beaten, but far from ready to submit. Moonlight slanted in over her face so that her skin was milky pale, her eyes dark and glowing. The fear in them had turned to condemnation.

In a mass of confusion, her hair spread over the bed, making him think of mermaids and witches.

"I'll despise you."

Something ripped quietly inside him. His heart or perhaps his soul. He ignored it and fixed on the need to punish her for making him love an illusion.

He lowered his mouth again, but she turned her head away. A small defense, and an unwise one as his lips found the soft, vulnerable curve of her throat. Her breath caught, then expelled again on a moan. The sound had his heart drumming as he found her taste as unique and as dangerous as his feelings for her.

He wanted to love her, and to hate her. He needed to comfort and to punish. He sought to hurt and to give pleasure. In the midst of his confusion, he forgot everything but Hannah.

Hardened from work, gentle by nature, his hands moved over her. With the tip of his tongue, he traced patterns, tormenting, tempting patterns over her skin. He could feel it heat beneath him so that the flavor and the softness seemed to intensify. She twisted one way under him, then the other so that her agitated movements only served to arouse them both.

All at once her body became very still, almost as if even breathing had stopped. Then the trembling began.

She'd never been more aware of herself, more distanced from rational thought. She wanted to remember why he was with her, why it was wrong for both of them, but could only feel. Reasons no longer mattered, consequences were forgotten. He wanted. She wanted. Right and wrong were for the sane.

When he brought his mouth back to hers again, she was waiting. He didn't find pliancy or panic, but the passion she had ruthlessly strapped down most of her life. For him it was free, and she had a fleeting moment to realize it would never fully be disguised again.

Impatience. Desperation. Together they rolled over the bed again but in a far different kind of combat. Her robe was lost so that her arms were free to capture him. In a move that might have told him everything, she locked him to her.

Stay with me. Love me. Understand me.

Then even that was lost in a torrent of heat that left them both gasping.

Once before he'd sensed a volcano inside of her. Now as it erupted around him, he was rocked by the power, the dark violence of it. The breeze that fluttered the curtains was cool and temperate. In the center of the bed was a furnace each of them stoked higher and higher.

Frantic for more of him, Hannah pulled his shirt open, scattering buttons over the mattress and floor. When her laugh came, it was low and sultry as he'd heard it before, but now it had an edge of something that might have been triumph. Then it was a sigh as she ran her hands up his chest. Her kiss was hot and hungry on his as naked flesh met naked flesh.

Something snapped inside him. As a lover he'd always been clever, considerate, caring. Love had never been a game to him, nor had it been a contest. Always, it had been a result of affection, a natural culmination of needs.

But he'd never needed like this.

Tenderness was forgotten as completely as revenge as

he dove his hands into her hair and dragged her against him. His teeth nipped into her lower lip, sending dizzying sparks of pleasure through her. Then he began to move swiftly, leaving her lips unsatisfied while his kisses tortured and tamed wherever they reached.

There was panic again, but so twined with excitement she could recognize neither. Afraid, aroused, she tried to draw him back when with a suddenness that left her gasping, he drove her up and over. Her body contracted, almost in defense, then filled with a rush of heat that had her blood burning. Release came on a flood, on a cry of his name, and with the knowledge that no one would ever take her there but him.

She was weak and shuddering. The hands that had clutched the bedclothes went lax. For a moment, she began to float. Then he fanned the flames again.

This is what he'd wanted for her, from her. Her skin was damp and soft under his hands. Her muscles were limber as she began to move with him again. In the moonlight, he saw her face, dazed with passion, flushed with pleasure. Cupping her hips in his hands, he started a lingering line of kisses up her body. He could feel the moment the strength poured back into her.

Still shuddering, still breathless, she tugged at his slacks. She'd had a sample, a taste, and wanted more. She wanted all. As she pulled his clothes from him, he skimmed his fingertips over her inner thighs, hampering her progress, arousing her unbearably. He watched her eyes fly open with the shock of the fresh climax as her body arched up and strained toward the power. Then even as her muscles went lax, his mouth was on hers again and urging her along the next journey.

He was a drug. Her arms felt like lead as she tried to lift them for him. Her head was spinning from the flood of sensations. The ripe scent of passion covered both of them so that their skin was slick and hot. She could hear her own breath come in sighs and moans as she struggled to focus on his face.

His eyes were tawny, like a cat's before it springs. She remembered how he'd looked on the stallion, daring, dangerous. She shuddered once, then surrendered. With her eyes open and her heart willing, she gathered him close.

She opened. He filled.

The ride was fast and rough. Locked together, they raced. Without slackening pace, they plunged headlong over the cliff.

Silence seemed to last forever. Hannah curled herself into it and waited for him to leave her. Though her mind wasn't cool, some sanity had returned. Covered by the dark, she could admit to herself that she would never be the same. He'd broken through that carefully polished veneer and had conquered the inner woman, the woman he hated. She couldn't tell him that she loved, that she already mourned the loss of what she never really had and would spend the rest of her life wishing for it.

He wanted to reach out to her, to gather her close and stroke her hair in the moonlight. It wouldn't be possible to touch her again. He'd taken in anger what he'd once dreamed of taking in tenderness. The guilt was there, real and ripe even as the sense of betrayal crept back.

The woman he'd fallen in love with didn't exist. She'd been a lie even more than an illusion. Now he'd done what even in his wildest moments he'd avoided. He'd made love with a stranger. And God help him, he'd fallen just as deeply in love with her.

Had he hurt her? He wanted to ask, but held himself back. He couldn't afford to feel remorse or he would end up making a fool of himself over this new Hannah as well. Pride followed honor. Since he'd sacrificed one to temper and pain, he would hold firm to the other.

As he rose, he dragged a hand through his hair. How could he love her when he didn't even know her? How could he still love the woman he knew had never existed?

He dressed in silence while Hannah lay still as a stone on the bed.

"Now it seems we've used each other," he murmured.

She opened her eyes then. There were no tears in them. Thank God she still had the strength for that much. He was standing by the bed, naked from the waist up with the ruined shirt balled in his hand. "We can consider ourselves even."

"Can we?" His fingers went white on his shirt. He'd nearly taken a step toward her before he made himself turn and leave her alone.

Hannah lay and listened to the silence until dawn.

"You have questions," Armand began as he faced his youngest son. The morning light was strong through the open windows and showed, all too clearly, the marks of a sleepless night on both faces. "I prefer it if you wait to ask them until after I've finished."

He'd been prepared to demand and to rage. The lines of strain and weariness made his father look suddenly old and much too vulnerable. Again, it was love rather than duty that guided him. "All right." Because he needed it, Bennett poured coffee and left it black.

"Will you sit?"

"No."

Armand's gaze sharpened at the tone. Then he, too, let love hold sway. "I shall." Once seated, he set his untouched coffee aside. "Two years ago, I sat in this office with Reeve and Malori. You and Alexander were also present. You remember?"

Bennett paced to the window and looked out. "Yes. We were speaking of Deboque and what could and should be done."

"Then you remember that Reeve, even then, had an operative in mind to infiltrate the organization."

"I remember, too, that it was decided that the name be kept from Alex and me." The trace of resentment he had felt then had grown to true bitterness in one night. "And that Malori was not completely satisfied with Reeve's choice."

"Malori has always been one of the most trusted members of the security staff in Cordina. But he's old-fashioned." Armand saw no need to add that he, too, had had his doubts. "He was concerned with using a woman."

Bennett downed half his coffee. "I felt then, as I feel now, that Alexander and I had a right to know what was being done. More, all of us had the right to know that the woman we accepted as friend was an ISS agent."

"I felt then as I feel now—" Armand's voice, though

quiet, held the whip of authority "—that neither of you had a need to know. If I had become ill, Alex, of course, would have been apprised. However—"

"Do you think because I won't rule, Cordina is of less importance to me?" Bennett whirled on his father. The fury on his face was lethal. "All of my life I've been the younger brother. Alex was born to rule Cordina after you. He was molded for it, just as his son will be. Do you think because of that I cared less, loved less or would have offered less?"

Armand said nothing for a moment, knowing the words had to be chosen with care, even as they came from the heart. "Bennett, I've watched you grow from child to man and have waited for a sign, for a hint that you resented your position. You have been sometimes wild, always reckless and too often indiscreet, but never have I seen anything in you but love and devotion for your country and your family."

"Then why, when something threatens both, do you keep your plans from me?"

There was a headache drumming behind Armand's temple. He closed his eyes a moment, but didn't lift a hand to soothe it. "Two years ago, Lady Hannah Rothchild was chosen out of a half dozen highly qualified operatives to infiltrate and destroy Deboque's organization. We were aware, as she was, of the risks involved, and the time and skill it would take to succeed."

"Why her?" Bennett found he didn't want to think beyond that for a moment. It was an answer he had to have before he could deal with the others.

"Reeve felt Hannah's talents were uniquely suited to the operation. She's been with the ISS for ten years."

"Ten years?" Bennett roamed the room again as he tried to take it in. "How is that possible? She's so young."

"She's second generation," Armand said mildly. "Her father trained her himself while she was still in school. Lord Rothchild, though semiretired now, is one of the most valued agents in the ISS. He had some part in Reeve's early training, which was another reason Reeve leaned toward Hannah for this assignment."

"Ten years," Bennett repeated. How many women had she been? How many lies had she told?

"Apparently she had a natural aptitude for this kind of work." He saw his son's jaw set, but went on. "After reading Reeve's report on her, I had to agree that she was best suited for what we had in mind."

"Deboque often uses women," Bennett murmured.

"He feels they can be more cunning, even more cruel, than men." Armand remembered Janet Smithers and the bullet that had been dug out of his son's flesh. "His preference runs to a certain type, quiet, well-bred, spotless pedigrees."

"Hannah."

"Yes. It was those qualities in her which weighed the decision in her favor. With the cooperation of the ISS a deep background was created for her. The credentials she was given made it possible for her to slip into Deboque's company. In two years, she's moved from messenger to the top of the organization."

"The top?" The fear started then, like something foul in the back of his throat. "What do you mean?"

"She's met with Deboque himself, and by managing to discredit one of his top men, is now filling that position herself. Reeve explained to you that as far as Deboque knows, she's here at the palace as his instrument."

Bitterness was more palatable than fear. He concentrated on it. "She plays the game very well."

"An agent in her position plays the game well or loses her life. You know firsthand that Deboque doesn't hesitate to kill. Her name and the operation itself were kept in strictest confidence not to protect you or the rest of the family, Bennett, but to protect her."

Bennett set his cup down and stopped pacing. "In what way?"

"Three other agents have been killed trying to do what Hannah has nearly succeeded in doing. The last was butchered." He watched Bennett's face pale. He would have spared his son this, as a father. Now, as prince, he could spare him nothing. "By bringing her here in this way, letting you, all of you, believe what Deboque wanted you to believe, Hannah had the only protection we could offer. If she's discovered, even the ISS can't protect her. Now that you know all that you know, her risk is greater than ever."

In silence, Bennett crossed the room to sit across from his father. Though the turmoil was building all too quickly inside, his face was calm. "I'm in love with her."

"Yes." Armand sat back. "I was afraid you were."

"I will not stand still and watch Deboque hurt someone else I love."

"Bennett, there are times, too many times, when our personal feelings can't influence our actions."

"For you." Bennett's voice was still calm, but slightly colder. "Perhaps for Alex as well, but not for me. I prefer to kill him myself."

Armand felt a ripple of fear, a tingle of pride and controlled both. "If you do anything to interfere with the operation at this point, you could be responsible for Hannah's death, not Deboque's."

Pushed to his limit, Bennett leaned forward. "Do you understand, I'm in love with her? If you were in my position, could you do nothing?"

Armand studied his son's face and remembered the only woman he'd ever loved. "I can only say that I would do whatever was necessary to keep her safe. Even if that meant doing nothing." He rose and went to his desk. "Read these." He lifted a small stack of files that carried the stamp of highest security. "These contain background information on Hannah, some of her own reports concerning certain assignments and most recently, her progress with Deboque. I'll leave you so that you can read them here. They mustn't leave this room."

Bennett rose to accept the files. "Where is she now?"

He had hoped the question wouldn't be asked. "She received a message early this morning. She's gone to Deboque."

She had to play this one very carefully. Hannah sat with her hands folded on her lap in the elegant salon of Deboque's rented villa. Though the meeting was on land this time, she knew if her cover hadn't held up, she was just as much alone as she had been on the yacht.

If he had a hint of the part she'd played in the events

of the evening before, her throat would be slit before she could voice a denial. A risk every agent takes, she reminded herself. To test herself, she lifted the small china pot on the table in front of her and poured coffee. Her hand was steady.

It was imperative that her mind stay sharp and focused on the assignment.

Every other thought in her mind was of Bennett.

"Lady Hannah." Deboque walked into the salon, then shut the double doors at his back. "How delightful to see you again."

She added a careful dollop of cream. "The message I received this morning left little option."

"Ah, I was brusque." He crossed to her, taking her hand and brushing his lips over it. "My apologies. The events of last night caused me some distress."

"And me." She drew her hand away. Instinct told her annoyance was the wisest course. "I find myself wondering if I've chosen wisely."

Deboque chose the seat beside hers, then taking his time, chose a cigarette from a crystal holder. He wore emeralds today. "Meaning?"

"Only months ago, I found myself in the position of having to clean up for another of your employees." She sipped coffee. It was hot and Turkish. "Last night, another of them nearly ruined every carefully laid step I've taken toward the Bissets."

"May I remind you, *mademoiselle,* you were advised to stay out of the way?"

"I'll remind you, *monsieur,* that I haven't reached my current position by not looking toward my own interests.

If I hadn't followed Bennett, you and I might even now be sitting in less agreeable quarters."

Deboque blew out smoke. "Explain."

"Bennett was a bit bored with the play and thought to wait in the American actress's dressing room until the curtain. Because I was aware that there were plans of some sort in the works, I decided it best to keep close. When the lights went out, I had to decide whether to go back or keep Bennett within reach. If I'd gone back, *monsieur,* the prince might indeed be dead."

"And for that you wish my gratitude?"

"He might be dead," Hannah repeated, "and a member of your organization would even now be in custody. Shall I pour you some coffee?"

"Merci." He waited patiently while she filled a second cup. At his nod, she added cream.

Hannah sat back again and folded her ringless hands. "MacGee and the guards were already on their way. I spotted your man." She made a look of disgust. "He was bumbling his way around with a flashlight. I managed to distract Bennett by playing the hysterical female, but the idiot didn't take the opportunity to make good his escape. The lights came up again. Bennett saw him and his weapon. You should be flattered that since your release the prince has carried a small-caliber pistol with him. He used it, and for personal reasons, I'm grateful he used it well. Dead men can't name names." Playing up the role, she rose. "I ask you now, was the man under orders to kill one of the Bissets? Do you or do you not trust me to complete the contract?"

Say it! she ordered silently. Say it out loud, say it plainly so that this can be over.

Smoke curled up in a column toward the ceiling as he tapped the cigarette into an ashtray. "Please, my dear, be calm. The man you speak of may have been told to use initiative, but was never given a specific request. I have confidence in you, of course."

"We agreed. I would dispose of the Bissets in return for five million dollars."

He smiled, like a generous uncle. "We agreed that if such a thing were to happen, there would be some compensation."

"I'm tired of playing games." As if to prove it, Hannah picked up her bag. "If you won't speak frankly, if you won't honor our arrangement, there's no reason to go on with this."

"Sit." The order came sharp and clear as she walked to the door. Hannah stopped, turned, but didn't walk back. "You forget yourself. No one who works for me leaves until they are dismissed."

She knew there would be men outside the door, to detain or dispose of her at Deboque's whim. She gambled that he would respect audacity. "Perhaps it's best if I find other employment then. I'm not accustomed to being dealt only half the cards."

"Remember that I hold them. I ask you again, sit."

This time she obeyed. She let the impatience shimmer, but only enough to let him see her control. "Very well."

"Tell me how the Bissets cope this morning."

"With dignity, of course." She pretended to be amused. "Bennett's pleased with himself. Armand is worried. Eve is confined to bed for the day. Gabriella stays with her. MacGee is closeted with Malori—you know the name?"

"Yes."

"I would guess that they are trying to see what purpose the disturbance last night had. Your man did an excellent job on the main power, though I think the explosive was a bit overstated." She shrugged as though it had been a hat with one too many feathers. "In any case, they ran on auxiliary for the rest of the evening and have a crew in the Center this morning for repairs. It's their belief that the power was blown so that the assassin could break his way into the Royal Box."

"A natural assumption," Deboque said as he went back to his coffee. And exactly the one he'd hoped for. "Though such a move would have been messy and unstylish. And you, my dear? How do you cope after witnessing a killing?"

"I've chosen to be shocked and weakened by the events. But brave, naturally. We British are, you know."

"I've always admired the quality." He smiled at her again. "I have to congratulate you on the depth of your skill. You look as though you didn't close your eyes all night."

It was a mistake to remember, to think even for an instant, of Bennett. "I drank enough coffee to keep me awake until dawn," she said easily as her stomach tied itself in knots. "At the moment I'm supposedly out for a walk to clear my head." To take his attention from that, she added the last of what she and Reeve had discussed. "Are you aware that the entire Royal Family will gather at the palace for the Christmas Ball?"

"So is tradition."

"With Eve being a bit delicate, the Princess Gabriella brings her family to stay for several days during the preparations. The MacGees share a wing with Alexander and Eve so that they can be close to the children."

"Interesting."

"And obliging. I'll require the makings for three plastic explosives."

Deboque only nodded. "The younger prince doesn't reside in the same wing."

"The younger prince will be fatally injured while trying to save the rest of his family. Leave it to me. Just make sure the five million is waiting." She rose again, then inclined her head as if waiting for his permission to leave. Deboque stood as well, then surprised her by taking both of her hands.

"I had thought that some time after the holiday I would take a long vacation. I have an urge to sail, to be in the sun. Vacations can be very dull without companionship."

Her stomach turned over. She prayed the revulsion wouldn't show, even for an instant. "I've always been fond of the sun." She didn't object when he stepped closer, but smiled. "You have a reputation for discarding women as easily as you collect them."

"When they bore me." He cupped a hand around her neck. His fingers were light, smooth, and still made her think of spiders. "I have a feeling you won't. I'm not attracted to looks, but brains and ambitions. Together, I believe we could be very comfortable."

If his lips touched hers, she would retch. Knowing it,

Hannah tilted her head back just an inch. "Perhaps—after our business is completed."

The fingers on her neck tightened, then released. The marks they had left wouldn't fade for several minutes. "You're a cautious woman, Hannah."

"Cautious enough to want the five million before I sleep with you. Now if you'll excuse me, I should get back before I cause any concern."

"Of course."

She walked to the door. "I'll need those supplies by the end of the week."

"Expect a Christmas present from your aunt in Brighton."

With a nod, she swung easily through the door.

Deboque took his chair again and decided he'd become quite fond of her. It was a shame she'd have to die.

Chapter 10

It was midafternoon before Bennett went to find her. He'd read every word in the files Armand had given him. Though some had fascinated him, some had frightened him and some had angered him, he still wasn't sure he knew the woman.

Now he, too, was part of the deception, he thought as he made his way up to Eve's rooms. Nothing he'd read, nothing he'd been told could be confided to his brother. He couldn't comfort his sister or Eve with the fact that every move Deboque made was being monitored. He had, as he was coming to understand Hannah had, no choice but to play the game through. So he went to find her, knowing it was long past time they talked calmly.

He found Eve and Gabriella together at a table with piles of lists and a pot of tea.

"Bennett." Gabriella reached a hand out. "Just in time. We need a man's viewpoint on the Christmas Ball."

"Make sure there's plenty of wine." He bent to kiss both

of her cheeks. Though she'd smiled at him, he'd recognized the signs of strain, just as he recognized them in Eve. "Hannah's not with you?"

"No." Eve set her pencil down as she lifted her face for Bennett's kiss. "I told her I wanted her to rest today. Last night..." She tightened her fingers on his. "Last night must have been dreadful for her. And you."

He shrugged, remembering too clearly the way he'd left her—curled into a silent ball on the bed. "It wasn't a dull evening in any case."

"Don't joke, Ben. You could have been killed. All I can think is that it's the second time in the theater. The second time one of my plays—"

Keeping Eve's hand in his, he crouched down. "I wasn't hurt, and I don't want you letting that fertile imagination go. I'd be very annoyed if my nephew were born with worry lines. Where's Marissa?"

"Napping."

He rubbed a thumb under her eyes. "You should do the same."

Annoyance replaced the strain, as he'd hoped. "Now you sound like Alex."

"God forbid. Where is he, anyway?"

"Meetings." She nervously traced her fingers over the papers. "Most of the day. Everything's been switched to his offices here because of—because security prefers it."

"Then you should relax." He covered her hand with his. "You should know by now the Bissets are indestructible. At the least you should be grateful he's tied up for a while, otherwise he'd be in here hovering over you."

She managed to smile. "You do have a point."

Rising, he grinned down at Gabriella. "I suppose we can trust you to keep her in line—though you're not looking your best, either."

"Chivalry is never dead with you around."

"What are brothers for?" He wanted to gather them both close and tell them that nothing and no one would ever hurt them again. Instead, he gave his sister's hair a tug. "Now I'll let you two get back to what I'm sure is fascinating work." He'd gotten no farther than the head of the stairs when Gabriella caught up with him. "Ben."

He turned, and though he was ready with a smile, her expression stopped it.

Gabriella looked back over her shoulder to be certain they were far enough away from Eve's office, then laid a hand over his on the banister. "Reeve tells me little about certain matters." A trace of temper came into her eyes, then was dismissed. "That's something I have to live with. But particularly since I once lost everything, I have very good instincts when it comes to my family."

"I know you're worried," he began. "All of us are."

"It's more than that, though everything comes back to Deboque and his obsession with destroying us. I still have dreams, even after all these years." She could remember a cabin, and the dark, and the fear.

"Brie." He laid a hand on her cheek. "Nothing like that is ever going to happen again."

She closed her fingers lightly over his wrist. "And I remember seeing you shot and bleeding on the terrace floor. I remember sitting in the hospital while Eve hung between life and death. Deboque." Her face was very pale, but there was strength in it and in the hand that lay on his. "It's all been Deboque. And he isn't finished."

"He will be." Something dangerous came into his voice, into his eyes. "That I promise you."

"I want you to be careful, Bennett."

He smiled, so that the look vanished. "How can I be otherwise with a dozen guards smothering me?"

"Very careful," she repeated. "I've never known you to carry a pistol to the theater."

She knew it was a lie. He didn't have to hear her say it, only to look in her eyes. She knew, but didn't understand. And because she was Gabriella, she wouldn't stop until she did.

"Leave it for now."

"So Reeve told me," she said with an impatient gesture. "It's my family. How can I?"

"I only know it's going to be over soon. In the meantime we have to stand together. Something's being done, Brie. Hold on to that."

"I have been." She knew it was unfair to push, so she released him. "I want you to promise you won't do anything rash."

"What is this reputation I carry with me?"

"Ben, please."

"All right, you have it." He kissed her again. "I adore you, even if you did bring Dorian into the world to pester me." He gave her hand a final pat before he started down the stairs. *"A bientôt."*

She watched him go, but the worry stayed with her. *"A bientôt."*

Hannah wasn't in her rooms. Bennett found himself

frustrated yet again when he entered and found them empty. Had she gone out again? he wondered. Was she even now putting herself in danger to protect his family?

He hated it. The thought of her risking her life, of blocking his body with her own as she had done last night was impossible to accept. Whether it was family, friend or country, he protected. How could he do less for the woman he loved?

Wandering in her rooms, he moved to her dresser. There was a small enameled box with a peacock on the lid. He ran a finger over it, wondering where she had come by it. A gift? From whom? A purchase in some little shop in London? He needed to know even those inconsequential details about her. Couldn't she understand that in order to resolve his feelings he had to know the woman he'd given them to?

He looked up, and reflected in the mirror was the bed where they'd fought, and loved, the night before. If he stood very still, he could almost feel the echoes of passion and discovery in the air. Would she hate him for that? Even though the loving had been as intense and as stunning for her as for him, would she forgive him for forcing her to set the barriers aside?

He'd been rough.... Bennett looked down at his own hands, turning them over, spreading his fingers. And he hadn't cared. All of his life he'd taken such pains never to hurt a woman. Now, when he'd found the only woman, he'd set out to do just so.

Walking to the window he stared out and tried to sort out his feelings. He still resented her. No matter what his brain told him, his heart was still bruised by the deception. More, he couldn't shake off the feeling that he'd fallen in love with two women and could trust neither.

Then he saw her in the gardens below.

She needed some time, Hannah told herself. Just an hour alone to clear her mind and calm her nerves. She knew she'd handled Deboque as smoothly as possible that morning. If nothing went wrong, they would close the trap on him in a week. Then she would have succeeded. In her file would go another favorable report. A two-year assignment successfully tied up could very well mean a promotion. She was, she knew, only inches away from a captaincy. Why didn't it excite her as it once had?

Time, Hannah told herself again. She just needed some time.

She would take a much needed and well-earned vacation. Perhaps at last she would go to America—New York, San Francisco. Wouldn't it be possible to lose herself in such places for a while?

Or perhaps she would go back to England. She could spend time in Cornwall walking the moors or riding by the sea. In England she couldn't lose herself, but perhaps she could find herself again.

Wherever she went, she would be leaving Cordina. And Bennett.

Wisteria rose up in an arch, sheltering a bench and inviting long, lazy contemplations. She sat, and closing her eyes, tried to bring her troubled mind to rest.

Who was she? For the first time in years she was forced to ask herself and admit she didn't know the answer. A part of her was the quiet woman who enjoyed a long afternoon with a book, who liked to talk of literature and art. A part of her was the woman who kept a weapon within reach and listened to footsteps behind her.

The fact that she could be both had always been a benefit before, never, as it was now, a painful puzzle to solve. She wished she could talk with her father, even for an hour. He understood what it was to live two lives and find contentment and challenge in each.

But she couldn't risk even that. In this, as in the assignment that had brought her here, she was alone.

He detested her. It was Bennett who had caused the ache and the doubts. It was Bennett who had forced her to question what she'd always taken for granted. Last night he'd taken her mind and heart and body, only because he'd wanted to humiliate her. And he had. No one, no one had ever shown her how much there could be, how much she could give. No one had ever left her so empty and alone.

He wouldn't know how much he'd hurt her. He couldn't know, she thought as the tears she'd held off throughout the night began to fall. Because he would never know how strong her feelings were for him, and how hopeless.

She had chosen her path, Hannah reminded herself, and she would live with it. In a matter of days it would no longer cross his.

He would be safe. His family would be safe. And she would be gone.

He found her sitting on the bench, her hands folded neatly in her lap, her eyes closed and her face wet with tears. So many feelings tumbled into him that he couldn't separate them. Regret, confusion, love, guilt.

She'd want to be left alone. He thought he understood

her that well. There was still enough bitterness in him to want to leave her alone. He could no more have left her there than he could have left a wounded dog on the side of the road.

As he went closer, Hannah sprang up from the bench. He saw the shock and humiliation run across her face. For a moment, he thought she would turn and run. But she held her ground.

"I thought I was alone." Her voice was cold as she fought anger and embarrassment.

He took out a handkerchief and offered it. At the moment it was the only comfort he could give, or she accept. "I'm sorry I disturbed you." His voice was as stiff as hers. "I think we need to talk."

"Haven't we?" She dried her face then crumpled the linen in her hands.

"Would you like to sit?"

"No, thank you."

He slipped his hands into his pockets. She hadn't slept, he thought as he saw the shadows under her eyes. Neither had he. So perhaps there they were even. "I spoke with my father this morning. You've met with Deboque already today."

She started to cut him off, but relented. The garden was as secure as the palace—for the moment. "I don't report to you on those matters, Your Highness."

Temper narrowed his eyes and balled his hands into fists, but he spoke evenly. "No, but I'm now fully aware of the situation. I read your files."

Her breath came out on a huff of air. Was nothing she was or had done hers alone any longer? "Very well then, your questions have been answered, your curiosity satisfied. You know everything there is to know about me—I hope you were entertained."

"I didn't read it to be entertained," he tossed back. "Dammit, Hannah, I have a right to know."

"You have no rights where I'm concerned. I'm neither servant or subject."

"You're the woman I took to bed last night."

"That's best forgotten. Don't." Her body went rigid as he started forward. "Don't you ever touch me again."

"Very well." He stiffened even as she did. "But we both know certain things can't be forgotten."

"Mistakes can," she countered. "I'm here as an agent of the ISS to protect you and your family, to stop Deboque's plans to ruin Cordina and avoid the repercussions in Europe. Whatever has to be done to assure that, I'll do, but I will *not* let you humiliate me again." The tears started again, blinding her. "Oh, damn you, can't you leave me alone? Wasn't last night enough retribution for you?"

That snapped the very tenuous control he had on his own temper. He grabbed her arm, closing his fingers over the firm muscle. "Is that all it meant to you? Retribution? Can you stand here now and tell me you felt nothing, feel nothing? How accomplished a liar are you?"

"It doesn't matter what I felt. You wanted to punish me, and you did."

"I wanted to love you, and I did."

"Stop." That hurt, more than she was able to stand. She pushed him away only to be caught closer. The movement sent wisteria blossoms raining. "Do you think I couldn't see how much you hated me? You looked at me and made me feel vile. For ten years I've been proud of what I do, and you took even that away from me."

"And what of you?" He kept his voice low, but the anger was just as potent. "Can you tell me you didn't know I was in love with you?" She started to shake her head in denial, but he tightened his fingers. "You knew I was in love with a woman who didn't even exist. A quiet, shy and honest woman to whom I only wanted to show tenderness and patience. For the first time in my life there was a woman I could give my heart and my trust to, and she was nothing but a mirage."

"I don't believe you." But she wanted to and her heart began to race. "You were restless, even bored. I entertained you."

"I loved you." He lifted his hand and held her face very still, very close. She saw his eyes as she had the night before, tawny with passion. "You'll have to live with that."

"Bennett—"

"And when I came to your room last night, I found another woman, one who had lied and used me." He dragged the hand up, raking through her hair so that pins scattered. "One who looked like a witch," he murmured as her hair fell heavily over his hands. "And I wanted her just as badly, but without those tender, those sweet feelings. God help me, I still want her."

When his mouth came down on hers, she didn't protest. She'd also seen the truth in his eyes. He had loved her. Or he had loved the pretense of her. If desire was all he could give her now, she would take it. For duty she had sacrificed love, but even for duty, she wouldn't sacrifice the crumbs she had left.

She wrapped her arms around him. Perhaps if she could give him the passion, someday he would forgive her the rest.

How easily he could lose himself in her. The passion was edgy and achy but it didn't seem to matter. Her mouth was warm, her body slender and straining. If it wasn't love she felt for him, at least there was need. He'd settled for no more than that before.

"Tell me you want me," he demanded as he moved his mouth desperately over her face.

"Yes, I want you." She hadn't known it possible to feel triumph and defeat at the same time.

"Come with me now."

"Bennett, I have no right to this." She turned her face into his throat, wanting to draw just a little more of him into her. "I'm here only because—"

With his hands on her shoulders he drew her away before she could finish the denial. "For today, for one day, we'll put your duty and mine aside."

"And tomorrow?"

"Tomorrow comes whether we want it to or not. Give me a few hours, Hannah."

She would have given him her life, and somehow knew that would be easier than what he was asking now. Still, she put her hand in his.

They went on horseback. As Hannah cantered beside him, she could see that Bennett knew the route to their destination well. They turned into the woods where they'd raced once before, and he took the lead. Each time doubts rose up to plague her, she beat them back. She would take the few hours she was being offered.

She heard the stream before she saw it. It was a simple, musical sound that suited the leafy shade and towering trees. When Bennett came to it, he turned his horse south. For a quarter of a mile they rode along the bank in silence.

The stream curved and twisted, then widened at a point where a trio of willows draped over it. Bennett stopped there and swung from the saddle.

"What a lovely spot." Hannah reined in, but found herself not quite courageous enough to dismount. "Every time I think I've seen the most beautiful place in Cordina, I find another. Do you often come here?"

"Not often enough." He'd secured his horse and now walked to her. Saying nothing, he held up a hand.

Here was the choice he'd refused to give her the night before. Perhaps he gave it to her now because he knew the decision had already been made. Hannah curled her fingers into his, held a moment, then dismounted. The silence continued while she tethered her horse beside his.

"I came here when my mother died." He didn't know why it seemed important that he tell her. "Not to grieve really, but because she always loved places like this. See the little white flowers along the bank?" His hand was on hers again as they moved closer to the stream. "She called them angel wings. They're sure to have a complicated Latin name, but angel wings seemed right."

Bending, he plucked one. It was no bigger than his thumb with thin petals cupped around a tiny blue center. "Every summer, before I'd have to go back to Oxford, I'd come here. For some reason it made leaving easier." He tucked the flower into her hair. "When I was a child, I thought the fairies lived here. I used to look for them in the clover and under toadstools."

She smiled and touched a hand to his cheek. "Did you ever find one?"

"No." With his hand on her wrist, he turned his head to press his lips to her palm. "But I think they're still here. That's why this place is magic. That's why I want to make love with you here."

Their lips were still an inch apart as they lowered to the grass. They remained a breath apart as they began to undress each other. Kneeling, gazes locked, they unfastened buttons. Sunlight dappled over skin as material was pushed aside. Their lips brushed, then clung.

He couldn't stop the rush of power, the flood of need. In seconds they were rolling over the grass. He caressed her everywhere, seeking, finding, exploiting until her moans shuddered into his mouth. The need to take her quickly, fiercely, couldn't be fought down, especially when her fingers were already tugging at the clasp of his jeans.

They waited only until all barriers were removed, then joined in a rocketing, furious journey that left them both sated.

Naked, with the grass tickling her back, Hannah looked up at the sunlight filtering through the leaves overhead. It had been moonlight before and she'd experienced a range of feelings from anger, shame, ecstasy and back to shame again. Today, in the sunlight, she no longer felt the shame.

What was between them could be, for this short time, between the man and the woman. Tomorrow they would be prince and agent again.

"What are you thinking?"

She was able to smile and turn her head toward him. "That this is a beautiful spot."

He'd wanted to bring her there before. He'd imagined it. How he would slowly, patiently, show her the pleasures of loving. Shaking off the mood, he drew her closer. This was a different day, and a different woman. "Are you warm enough?"

"Hmmm. But I..." she trailed off, knowing she'd sound foolish.

"But?"

"Well, I've never—" How to phrase it? "I've never lain naked in the grass under the sun before."

He laughed, not even realizing that the tone and the feeling behind it had come from the woman he'd first known. "Life should always include new experiences."

"I'm sure you've found yourself naked in all manner of unusual places."

The dry voice delighted him. Rolling over, he pressed a kiss to her mouth then drew back just to look at her. Her hair was fanned out over the dark grass. The tiny white flower was tangled in it as though it had grown there. Bruising shadows under her eyes made her look both wanton and delicate, as though she were a virgin who'd just spent a night being initiated into womanhood.

This was how he had once imagined her, how he had once wanted, how he had once loved.

"You're so beautiful."

She smiled, relaxed enough to be amused. "Now *that* I've never been."

He traced a fingertip along her cheekbone. "How unobservant of you, Hannah. Or how foolish. Making yourself look less attractive doesn't change the truth. Flawless skin." He traced his lips over it as if to taste. "These elegant bones that make a man wonder if you're made of flesh and bone or glass. Those calm, intelligent eyes that drove me mad wondering how they might darken and cloud if I could find the right way to touch you. And this." He rubbed a finger over her lips. "So soft, so generous." He lowered his head but only traced the shape with his tongue. "Do you remember the first time I kissed you?"

Her breath was already shaking, her eyes already closing. "Yes. I remember."

"I wondered how it was that such a quiet woman could make my knees weak with just a taste."

"Kiss me now," she demanded and drew him down to her.

It wasn't what she expected. There was tenderness instead of passion, patience rather than urgency. She murmured against his mouth in confusion. Bennett only stroked his fingers over her face and waited for her to relax. More, he waited for her to accept. Even when he deepened the kiss it remained gentle. The fire was there but smoldering rather than blazing.

He was making love to the Hannah he'd understood, she realized and wanted to weep. There was lust for one, affection for the other. How could she fight another woman when the woman was herself?

On a trembling sigh, she let her mind empty. She would give him whatever it was he needed today.

He felt the change—the slow, almost fluid surrender. With a murmured approval, he pressed his lips to her throat. He wanted to show her there could be more than flash and speed. If they only had a few hours, then he would use them to give her whatever sweetness she would accept from him.

Lightly he stroked the smoothness of her body. What he'd demanded from her the night before, he now requested, coaxed, offered. He took the time to watch her arousal grow as the sun filtered down on her face and the stream rushed by beside them. He murmured to her as he kissed her throat. There were promises, endearments, reassurances. She answered him in words so fragile they almost dissolved in the air.

She'd never been loved like this before—as though she was precious, as though she was special. Even with her mind fogging over, she could hear the gentle hiss of water running over rock. She could smell the grass and the wild sweet flowers scattered through it. With her eyes half-opened, the sunlight seemed gold and bountiful over her lover's skin. She ran her hand over it, finding it smooth and taut and warm.

Her lover. Hannah brought his mouth back to hers and gave him everything that was in her heart. If the place was magic, then so was the moment. Dreams hadn't been a part of her life for too long to remember, but she opened herself to them now.

She was so giving, so pliant. He'd wanted too badly to feel this kind of emotion from her. It went far beyond heat, far above desire. She touched him as though she'd been waiting for him all of her life. She kissed him as though he were her first and only lover. The more she gave, the more he found in himself to give back. The shadows shifted and lengthened over them as they stroked and offered and discovered.

Even when he slipped into her, it was slow and easy. The passion that had built was still harnessed by stronger emotions. They moved together in a harmony that seemed almost painful in its perfection while she framed his face with her hands and his lips met hers.

They glided over the top and settled softly.

"You wanted to see me, Monsieur Deboque?"

"Yes, Ricardo." Deboque lifted his teapot and poured. He admired the British habit of tea in the late afternoon. It was so civilized. "I have a little shopping list for you." With one hand he gestured toward the desk by the window. "I'd like you to supervise it personally."

"Of course." Always pleased to be given trust, Ricardo picked up the list written on heavy cream-colored paper. His brow lifted only a fraction. "Shall I requisition this from within the company?"

"Please." Deboque added cream to his tea. "I prefer to keep this at home, so to speak. The delivery should be set up with Lady Hannah on... Thursday, I'd say. It's no use passing the merchandise along to her too soon."

"She risks much, smuggling such a—volatile package into the palace."

"I have implicit trust in our British friend, Ricardo." He remembered the way she'd sat across from him that morning. Trim, tidy and cultured. It gave his plans such a pleasant touch when they were carried out by delicate hands. "She has a certain style, wouldn't you say?"

"Class, even when so quietly cloaked, is still class, *monsieur*."

"Precisely." Deboque smiled and sipped at his tea. "I have no doubt she will carry out her objective with class." He sipped his tea again and sighed. "I do admire the British, Ricardo. So traditional, so resilient. Not as passionate as the French, but so wonderfully pragmatic. In any case, see that the merchandise is shipped from the address on that list. I don't wish it to come through my hands."

"Of course."

"I'm preparing an itinerary, Ricardo. We'll be sailing the end of next week. I'll see Lady Hannah once more. You'll see to the details?"

"As you wish."

"Thank you, Ricardo. Oh, by the way, did you see that a wreath was sent to Bouffe's funeral?"

"Roses as you requested, *monsieur*."

"Excellent." Deboque chose one of the little sugared biscuits from the Wedgwood plate. "You're very dependable."

"I try, *monsieur*."

"Have a pleasant evening then, Ricardo. Do let me know if we get any further word on the accident at the theater. I'm very uncomfortable with the current report."

"I will. Good evening, *monsieur*."

Deboque sat back, nibbling on the cookie. Ricardo continued to please him a great deal. An intelligent man with sociopathic tendencies was an excellent addition to his staff. Deboque was certain Ricardo would be very grateful to have the assignment of dealing with Hannah

when her job was completed. It was tempting, but Deboque discarded it.

He would deal with Hannah himself. After all, the least
he could do after she'd given him his fondest wish was to
see she died as painlessly as possible.

Chapter 11

Hannah appeared very calm as she sipped tea in the library. She listened to Reeve give an updated report to Malori, filling in occasionally when requested to, then lapsing back into silence.

Bennett had started to show her the library once. Then they'd detoured into the music room. And he'd kissed her. Was that when her life had really begun to change? she wondered. Had it been then, or the day on the beach when he'd given her a shell? Perhaps it had been that first night in the gardens.

"Do you agree, Hannah?"

She snapped back, cursing herself for letting her mind wander at such a crucial time. They had only thirty minutes for the briefing, half of which was already gone. Even within the walls of the palace it was dangerous for them to meet.

"I'm sorry. Could you repeat that?"

Armand had been watching her, wondering if her

shoulders were strong enough to hold the fate of so much. "The last few days have been a strain." There wasn't criticism in his voice but concern. Hannah would have preferred the first.

"The last two years have been a strain, Your Highness." Then she lifted her shoulders in a gesture that was more acceptance than dismissal.

"If you're beginning to wear under it," Malori said in his clipped, no-nonsense voice, "it's best we know now."

"I don't wear." Her eyes met his without wavering. "I believe my record shows that."

Before Malori could speak again, Reeve cut in. She was wearing, he knew, but he had to gamble she'd hold out for a few more days. "If we could backtrack? We can assume that Deboque has already ordered the supplies you requested. An educated guess on where he'd procure them?"

"Athens," she said immediately. "I feel strongly that he'd draw from within his own organization. He feels totally secure, invulnerable if it comes to that. He wouldn't want to risk ordering from outside sources. From my other reports, we know that he keeps a warehouse in Athens. He has others, of course, but I think he'd go there because of its proximity to Cordina."

"We'll check our contact there and see if there's news of any explosives being moved." Malori noted it down. "With luck we'll close down his Athens branch once we have him here."

"The ISS won't move on Athens, Paris, London or Bonn until we have an airtight case on Deboque here." Hannah set down her tea. "That's a button I push, *monsieur*."

"Bien." Malori obviously didn't like it, but nodded.

"Will the case be strong enough when Hannah receives the explosives?" Armand glanced at Hannah, then at Reeve. "Hannah has taken the contract, requested the supplies. Once they are delivered, can that be the end of it?"

Hannah started to speak, then subsided. She would let Reeve explain. He was family. "We would have enough for an arrest, possibly for an arraignment. Even with the supplies being traced back to Athens or another of Deboque's companies, it wouldn't be enough for a conspiracy conviction. He's careful enough to divorce himself from business dealings of this kind."

Business dealings, Armand thought as he drummed his fingers on the arm of the chair. "And his request that Hannah assassinate my family?"

"His hypothetical theory of what might happen if such a thing occurred," Reeve corrected. "Your Highness, I'm aware, very aware, of the frustration of not being able to close in on the evidence we have now. We had him once for over a decade, and it didn't stop him. If we want to crush Deboque once and for all, sever all these strings and hack away his control in Europe, we have to have solid and indisputable evidence of murder and conspiracy. Hannah will give us that in a matter of days."

Armand drew out a cigarette and shifted his gaze to Hannah. "How?"

"The payoff." She felt herself on solid ground again. It helped to have Malori there, sharp-eyed and just a bit disapproving. "When Deboque is convinced I've completed the job, he'll pay me off. As soon as money changes hands, we've got him."

"He's not a fool. You agree?"

"No, Your Highness, he's not a fool."

"But you will convince him you have murdered my family."

"Yes. If you would look at this diagram, sir?" She rose and waited for him to accompany her to a table. With Reeve's help, she stretched out a long roll of paper. "The blueprints I smuggled to Deboque show this wing as occupied by Prince Alexander and his family. I gave Deboque the information that Princess Gabriella and her family would also be staying here during the days before the Christmas Ball."

"I see. In truth, my son's family's wing is here." He skimmed his finger to the opposite side of the drawing.

"The night before the ball, I'll set some charges here, and here." She laid a fingertip on the areas. "They'll be much smaller than what Deboque assumes, but with Reeve's special effects added, it should be quite a show. There will be some damage, sir, but it will appear much worse, particularly from the outside, than it really is. You'll need to do some replastering and painting."

He lifted a brow, but she couldn't tell if he was amused. "There are areas of the palace that could do with some redecorating."

"It will be imperative, of course, to clear this wing. Discreetly."

"Of course."

"Ten minutes before the explosion, I will leave to meet with Deboque or his agent. The payment will be made after he considers the job done."

"Have you considered that he would want to have the deaths verified before he pays you?"

"Yes." Hannah straightened away from the diagram. "To some extent we'll use the press. In addition, I'm making it clear that payment must be made that night, as well as arrangements for my passage out of the country. Deboque has invited me to sail with him. I shall accept." She pressed her lips together as Malori grumbled. "The money will change hands because he'll believe I'll be easily accessible if anything has gone wrong."

"And will you be?"

"I'll be with him."

"The ISS will be covering both Deboque's villa and his yacht," Reeve cut in. "The moment we have Hannah's signal, we move."

"There is no other way?"

Again there was concern. This time Hannah found herself laying a hand on the prince's arm. On the arm of Bennett's father. "We could perhaps tie him to other crimes. With the information I've been able to dig up in the last two years, we would have something, but it would take months, even years and we would have no guarantee. This is the only way, Your Highness, to stop him once and for all."

With a nod, the prince looked over at Reeve. "You agree?"

"Yes."

"Malori?"

"It is more dramatic, and certainly more risky than one would like, but yes, Your Highness."

"Then I will presume that you two will see to whatever details have yet to be seen to. I will expect reports every four hours."

Recognizing dismissal Malori bowed. Even as Reeve rolled up the diagram again, Hannah was preparing to curtsy.

"Hannah, I'd like another moment, please."

"Yes, Your Highness." She stood by the table, stiff and tense as the two other men left them alone. He would know of her feelings for Bennett, Hannah thought. Even in the brief time she'd been in Cordina, she'd learned that Armand was both astute and observant. He didn't merely rule from a throne, but behind a desk and in boardrooms. If his country was at peace and prosperous, it was largely because he knew how to govern, how to make choices and how to remain objective.

Yes, he would know, she thought again. And he would not approve. She was European. She was an aristocrat. But she was by choice and by profession a spy.

"You're uncomfortable," Armand began. "Sit, please."

In silence she took a seat and waited.

She looked like a dove, he thought. A small gray dove who expected and accepted the fact that she was about to be mauled by a fox. Studying her, he had difficulty believing she would be the one to end the turmoil that had haunted his family for more than a decade.

"Reeve has confidence in you."

"I can promise it's not misplaced, Your Highness." She nearly relaxed. It wasn't about Bennett, but Deboque.

"Why did you agree to take this assignment?"

Her brow lifted because it seemed such a simple question with such a simple answer. "I was asked."

"And had the right to refuse?"

"Yes, sir. In such matters an agent always has a choice."

A prince didn't. He understood the difference, yet still didn't envy her. "You took the assignment because your superiors requested it."

"Yes, and because what Deboque does here has affected and could continue to affect my country and the rest of Europe. A terrorist, in whatever garb he chooses, remains a terrorist. England wants Deboque's hands tied, tightly."

"Your first consideration is country."

"It always has been."

He nodded again, knowing this could bring both joy and misery. "Did you choose your profession because you looked for adventure?"

Now she relaxed completely and laughed. The moment she did, Armand saw what had captivated his son. "Pardon, sir, I realize that the word 'spy' conjures up all sorts of glamorous images: foggy docks, Parisian alleyways, nickel-plated revolvers and fast cars. In truth, it's often tedious. In the past two years, I've done more work on telephones and computers than the average secretary."

"You wouldn't deny the danger involved."

"No." She sighed a little. "No. But for every hour of danger, there's a year of legwork and preparation. As for Deboque—Reeve, Malori, the ISS, have taken this plan step-by-step."

"Still, in the end, you'll be alone."

"That's my job. I'm good at it."

"Of that I have no doubt. Under normal circumstances, I would worry less."

"Your Highness, I assure you everything that can be done is being done."

He was aware of the truth of it and that, for the moment, his hands were tied. "And if a mistake is made, how will I comfort my son?"

She locked her fingers together. "I know, I promise you whatever happens, Deboque will be punished. If you—"

"I'm not speaking of Deboque now, but of you, and of Bennett." He held up a hand before she could speak again. "It is a rare thing for me to be able to speak as only a father. I ask you to allow me that luxury now, here in this room."

She drew in a breath and tried to be clear. "I realize Bennett is angry and upset because he wasn't told the reasons for my being here. I believe he feels a certain responsibility toward me because I'm here to protect his family."

"He's in love with you."

"No." The panic set in again, along with the shame and the desperate desire for it to be true. "That is, he thought, before when he believed me to be... At one time he began to feel a certain affection, but when he learned who—what I was, that changed."

Armand settled his hands on the arms of his chair. The ring of his office glinted in the lamplight. "My dear, are you any more clear on your feelings for him?"

She looked up. The dark eyes that watched her were kinder than they had been. Hard yes, he could be hard. But she could see now why his family and his country loved and trusted him. "Your confidence, sir?"

"You have it, of course."

"I love him more than I've ever loved anything or anyone. If I could change things, if I could go back and be what he thought I was, and only that, I swear to you I would." There were no tears. She had shed them once and had sworn not to do so again. Instead she looked down at her hands. "Of course, I can't."

"No, we can't change what we are. When we love, and love deeply, we can accept a great deal. Bennett's heart is very generous."

"I know. I promise you, I won't hurt him again."

His lips curved. She was so young, so valiant. "I have no fear of that. When this is done, I ask that you remain in Cordina for a few more days."

"Your Highness, I think it would be best if I returned to England immediately."

"We wish you to remain," he said again, and he no longer spoke as a father. He rose then, extending a hand. "You may want to rest before dinner."

Left without a choice, Hannah stood and curtsied. "Thank you, Your Highness."

Dinner was long and formal. Hannah was introduced to the Minister of State and his wife, as well as a German businessman who had interests in shipping and an ancient Frenchwoman who was some vague connection of the Bissets' and was visiting Cordina for the holidays. The Frenchwoman spoke in a husky grumble that kept Hannah straining to hear enough to make polite answers. The German spoke in short, loud blasts and was obviously delighted to have an invitation to the Royal Palace. Hannah was grateful that he was across the table so that she could avoid direct conversation with him.

Bennett wasn't there at all. A late board meeting at the museum had edged into a dinner for the Equestrian Society. Hannah tried to remember that Claude had been joined by two more guards who would keep Bennett annoyed and protected throughout the evening.

As the Frenchwoman hissed in her ear again, Hannah could only think Bennett the fortunate one.

Across the table, Eve sipped sparkling water and listened with apparent fascination as the German regaled her with stories of his business. Only when she turned to pick up her dessert spoon did her eyes meet Hannah's long enough for the humor to come through. Answering a question in low, polite tones, she rolled her eyes once, quickly, in a gesture that said everything. Then she was smiling at the German again and making him feel fascinating.

Hannah had to lift her glass to hide the grin. The royal were human after all. Not the same, not ordinary, but human. The child Eve carried might one day rule, but he would also laugh and cry and feel and dream.

She herself had loved a prince. Hannah picked up her spoon and began to toy with the elegant chocolate and cream concoction in front of her. She'd given her heart to a man who was second in line to one of the few remaining thrones in Europe. In a few days, she could very likely give her life for him.

For that was the truth of the matter, she thought as the woman beside her droned on. It might have started as duty, to her country and to the organization she had chosen, but when it ended, what she did would be for Bennett.

It would never be possible to tell him, just as it hadn't

been possible to say as much to his father earlier that evening. If she admitted what she felt to a superior, even with all the planning, all the time lost, she could very well be pulled out.

So she would say nothing, but she would feel. And feeling as she did, she would see Deboque finished, if she lived.... And then, Hannah admitted, it would be a choice between her captaincy and retirement. Fieldwork would be all but out of the question now. She didn't believe that she could ever maintain the pose of quiet, unassuming Lady Hannah again. Not now that she had loved and been loved by a prince.

It was nearly midnight before escape could be politely made. Hannah deliberated over a hot bath or quick oblivion in bed as she stepped into her room. Eve was insistent about returning to the Center the next day, so she would have no choice but to go along. Would the message come the next day, or would Deboque take her right down to the wire?

She'd walked into the center of the bedroom when the warning signals began to throb at the base of her neck. There was no one in the room. A quick glance showed her nothing had been disturbed. But...

Hannah took a cautious step back and opened the drawer of the bedside table. She took out her weapon. The light was low and at her back as she began to move toward the adjoining room. The door was slightly ajar, but that could have been done by one of the maids. Her feet were silent on the carpet as she crossed to it. With one hand she pressed on the panel so that it opened slowly and without sound.

There was nothing in the room beyond—nothing except the neat sitting room that smelled of the gardenias that lay moist and lovely in a bowl.

So it had been a maid, she thought, relaxing gradually. One of them had set fresh flowers in the sitting room, and—

It was then she heard a sound, material against material, and tensed again. Keeping the gun secure in her hand, she slid against the wall and into the room.

The little settee faced away from the door so she didn't see him until she was fully inside. Bennett lay sprawled on it, his tie unknotted and hanging, his shoes off and his face buried in a blue velvet pillow.

Hannah swore, but softly, as she lowered the pistol. He looked exhausted, and very much at home, she thought as she lifted a brow. Her first instinct was to tuck a cover around him, but there was still enough of the proper Lady Hannah in her to know that it would never do for Bennett of Cordina to be found snoozing in her sitting room. She started to bend down to him, then remembered the gun in her hand.

Almost curiously, she turned it over in her hand. It looked like a toy, but had already proven itself lethal. A part of her job, she thought. A part of her life. Yet she knew it was a part Bennett would find unpalatable. Moving back into her bedroom she secured it. She had to wake him and send him on his way, but she didn't have to keep a physical reminder of their differences close at hand.

She went back to him, and kneeling by the settee put

a hand to his shoulder. "Bennett." She shook gently and received a mumbled response. Her lips curved. She had to resist the urge to brush at the hair tumbling over his forehead. In sleep, the energy, the amusement and the temper were put to rest. He looked as though he would be perfectly content to cuddle there, half on, half off the little sofa for days. Hannah bent closer and raising her voice gave him a quick, brisk shove. "Bennett, wake up."

He half opened his eyes, but Hannah noted that they focused quickly. Reaching up, he grabbed her earlobe. "Haven't you any respect for a dead man?"

"Ow!" She grabbed his wrist in defense, but she was already several inches closer. "If it's respect you want, I'll call a couple of the servants and have them carry you out, in state. Meanwhile, let go or I'll have to show you how easy it is to cause unconsciousness by applying pressure to certain nerves."

"Hannah, you've got to learn not to be so flighty and romantic."

"It's in the blood." She sat back on her heels to massage her ear. "Bennett, why are you sleeping on my settee instead of in your own bed?"

"I don't know who designed this thing. Another foot longer and a man could be comfortable." He dragged himself up a bit so that his feet dangled over the arm. "I wanted to talk to you." He rubbed both hands over his face. "When I got in, I saw that we still had guests. I took the coward's way and used the back stairs."

"I see. And Madame Beaulieu spoke so highly of you."

"Madame Beaulieu doesn't speak, she hisses."

"I know. I sat next to her at dinner."

"Better you than me."

"How gallant."

"You want gallant?" With one swing, he had her off the floor and stretched on top of him. He cupped the back of her neck with his hand, pressing as his mouth took hers quickly, completely.

"What does that have to do with gallantry?" she managed after a moment.

He smiled and ran a finger down her nose. "All the other women I've known have been impressed by it."

Hannah drew back another inch. Smiling, she ran a finger down his throat, then up again. "About those nerves I mentioned."

He caught one wrist, then the other. "All right then, tomorrow I'll look for a puddle to toss a cape over."

"A safe enough promise since it hasn't rained in days." She started to shift, but he brought her close again.

"Stay. I haven't seen you at all today." His lips were warm and coaxing against her cheek. "Do you know, Hannah, a man has to have you in his arms, has to have his lips against your skin before he catches your scent. Do you do that on purpose?"

She wore no perfume. It had to do with leaving no traces behind. "You said you…" He moved his lips to her ear. "You wanted to talk to me."

"I lied." His teeth closed gently over her earlobe. "I wanted to make love with you. In fact, I had a devil of a time keeping my mind off that thought throughout a long and frustrating board meeting and a noisy dinner." He drew down the zipper at the back of her dress. "I had to give a speech." He found silk, thin, fragile silk, beneath the linen. "It was difficult not to babble when I kept imagining myself here, with you."

"I don't want to interfere with your official duties." With her eyes closed, she pressed her lips to his neck and let herself enjoy the gentle stroking of his hands.

"But you do, *mon amie*. I sat listening to the huffing and puffing of ten stuffy men who are more interested in paintings than people, and I imagined you sitting there with your hands neatly folded and your eyes solemn. And you were wearing nothing but your hair."

She'd slipped off his tie, but paused now on the third button of his shirt. "In the boardroom?"

"In the boardroom." Would he ever stop being fascinated by that dry, serious tone and those dark eyes? "You can see why I had such a problem concentrating." He didn't tell her he'd also dealt with unexpected tingles of fear as he'd pictured her with Deboque, at his mercy, helpless, alone. It was an image he hadn't been able to drown out in innumerable cups of coffee or glasses of wine. "So I came in here to wait for you."

"And fell asleep."

"I'd hoped you'd see the irony and reverse the fairy tale. Wake the sleeping prince with a kiss. Instead I got a shove."

With her hands framing his face, she drew his head up. "Let me make up for it now then."

She touched her lips to his, brushed, retreated, teased then touched again. She felt him tense his fingers at her back as she toyed with his mouth. Her tongue traced, her teeth nipped as heat built to a flash point. She didn't object when he pressed her head closer, when his mouth closed hungrily over hers. If he had longed for her through the day, his need had been no sharper than her own. They would take the night hours together.

She had his shirt unbuttoned and open. Her dress had slipped down, revealing the shimmer of honey-colored lace beneath. Bennett let his fingertips play over it while he absorbed the contrasts and delights that were his Hannah. He drew the pins out of her hair so that it flowed over her shoulders and his. The scent of it was as light and elusive as the scent of her skin. What witchery she had was an innate part of her rather than something that came from bottles and pots.

Fresh, real, his. Delirious from her, he tugged the dress down her body and let it fall to the rug.

And his fingers slid over the stiletto strapped to her thigh.

She stiffened, remembering the weapon the instant he discovered it. Passion cooled so swiftly, she shivered. When she drew away he didn't stop her.

"Bennett, I'm sorry." She'd forgotten there could be no apologies, no regret. His eyes were on hers, blank and flat, as he sat up. Because there was nothing for her to say, no way for her to remove the barrier, she lapsed into silence.

Her hair was a riot of honey-toned waves that fell over her shoulders and the silk that echoed the color. Her eyes, darkly, richly green, were solemn now as she waited for him to speak. Or to leave.

Fighting the first stirrings of anger, he let his gaze pass over her, the milk-pale skin, the slender curves, the delicate silk. She was what she'd convinced herself she was not—beautiful, stunning, desirable. On one long slim thigh strapped by thin strong leather, was a knife associated with dark alleys and smoky bars. Saying nothing, Bennett reached for it. She automatically caught his wrist.

"Bennett—"

"Be quiet." His voice was as flat and cool as his eyes. Hannah let her fingers fall away. Slowly, he drew the weapon from its sheath. It was warmed from her skin, small enough to fit into the palm of his hand. Until he pushed the button and the thin blade slid silently, lethally out. It caught the lamplight and glistened silver.

She wore it intimately, he thought. He wanted to ask her if she'd used it, but a part of him knew it was best to keep the question to himself for now. It weighed nothing, but sat heavy as lead in his hand.

"Why do you need this in the palace?"

She pushed a strap back onto her shoulder, then rubbed the skin there that was growing colder and colder. "I'm expecting word from Deboque. I can't be sure when or where it will come from. Because I may have to respond to it immediately, it's best to be prepared."

"What kind of word?"

"I think you should ask—"

"I'm asking you." His voice carried a lash he used rarely, but effectively. "What kind of word, Hannah?"

Hannah drew her knees up to her chest, wrapped her arms around them and told him everything. There could be no objection now, she reminded herself. He already knew too much.

"So we sacrifice a part of the east wing. Camouflage." He twisted the blade under the light. He knew, without doubt, he could have plunged it into Deboque's heart.

"The more genuine things seem, the more easily De-boque will be convinced. He won't part with five million dollars until he's sure Cordina is left without an heir."

"He would kill the children," Bennett murmured. "Even Alexander's unborn child. All for what? Revenge, power, money?"

"For all three. He would have his revenge on your father, his own power would grow from the chaos, and money would follow. It's his greed that will topple him this time, Bennett. I promise you."

It was the passion in her voice that had him looking at her again. Her eyes were wide and dry, but the emotion almost leapt from them. To protect his family, he thought as he tightened his hand on the handle of the stiletto. To protect herself. As suddenly as he'd fallen in love, he realized the full truth. Whatever she did, whatever she used didn't matter, as long as she kept herself safe.

He pressed the release and sent the blade back home. And he would see to that himself. After setting the knife aside, he reached over to unsnap the strap from her thigh. Her skin had gone cold, he discovered, though the room was warm. It stirred something in him that he recognized again as a need to protect. She didn't move, didn't speak and flinched only slightly when he rose. She was waiting for him to reject her, to dismiss her, to leave her.

He felt both her surprise and her doubt as he gathered her up into his arms. "You should trust me more, Hannah," he said quietly.

When she relaxed against him, when she let her head rest on his shoulder, he carried her to bed.

Chapter 12

The package was delivered in the most pedestrian of ways. It was carried by Dartmouth Shippers, one of Deboque's less profitable but most useful tentacles. It was marked with the return address of Hannah's aunt in England and stamped FRAGILE.

The only difficulty came from the fact that Eve was present when it was delivered.

"Oh, what fun!" Eve hovered around the package. "It's a Christmas present, isn't it? Why don't you open it?"

"It isn't Christmas," Hannah said mildly, and set the package on the shelf in her closet. She would turn it over to Reeve at the first opportunity.

"Hannah, how can you be so casual about it?" With nerves just below the surface, Eve poked around the room. "Didn't you ever search under beds and in closets for packages at this time of year?"

"No." Hannah smiled and went back to arranging the

flowers Eve had brought her. "I never wanted to spoil Christmas morning."

"It doesn't spoil it, it only adds to the excitement." Eve glanced back at the closet. "Couldn't we just peek?"

"Absolutely not, though I can tell you the package probably contains five dozen homemade cookies—as hard as bricks. Aunt Honoria is nothing if not predictable."

"It doesn't feel like Christmas." Moody, Eve wandered to the window. She laid one hand protectively over the swell of her belly and fidgeted nervously at the curtain with the other. "The ballroom's being scrubbed and polished for the holiday, the tree's already trimmed. If I walk by the kitchens there are the most glorious scents, but it just doesn't feel like Christmas."

"Are you homesick, Eve?"

"Homesick?" Puzzled for a moment, she turned around, then smiled. "Oh, no. Alex and Marissa are here. I do hope my sister manages to get away from her art gallery for a week or two, but I don't miss the States really. It's just that everyone tries to pamper me, protect me by hiding things." Sighing, she moved to Hannah's dresser to toy with the little enameled box Bennett had admired. "I know how tense and worried Alex is, no matter how hard he tries to pretend everything's fine. Even when I talk to Bennett, his mind only seems to be half with me. It has to stop, Hannah. I can't bear to see the people I love torn apart this way."

She too would pamper, and protect by hiding things, but it was the only comfort Hannah could allow herself to give. "It's this Deboque, isn't it?"

Eve set the box down again. "How can one man bear

so much hate? How can one man cause so much pain? I know, though after years I still can't really understand, I know that he won't be satisfied until he's destroyed us."

"It isn't possible for most of us to understand real evil," Hannah began, though she could and did understand it. "But I think we only add to it when we let our lives be affected so strongly."

"You're right, of course." Eve held out both hands. "Do you know how grateful I am that you're here? Without you I'm afraid I'd be moody and brooding all of the time. Brie's coming later today with all the children. We still have florists and musicians to deal with." She squeezed Hannah's hands as she drew a deep breath. "I hate being helpless. What I'd like to do is to go up and spit in Deboque's eye, but if all I can do is make things easier here, then I'll have to be content with that."

Hannah vowed, at the first opportunity, to spit in Deboque's eye for her. "Why don't you take me up to the ballroom and show me what's been done? I'd like to help." She wanted to help—and she wanted Eve away from the package that sat on the shelf in the closet.

"All right, but I want you to come to my room first. I have a present for you."

"Presents are for Christmas," Hannah reminded her as they walked to the door.

"This one can't wait." She had to get her mind off the undercurrents that were pressing on them all. Dr. Franco had already warned her that her tension could affect the child. "Pregnant princesses must be indulged."

"How clever of you to use that to your advantage when it suits you." They climbed a short flight of stairs and crossed to the next wing. "You said Gabriella would be here soon. Is the whole family coming today?"

"In force, this afternoon."

Hannah relaxed a little. It would be easy to transfer the package to Reeve and continue on with the plan. "Has Bennett put his treasure in the vault?"

"Treasure? Oh, his yo-yo." With her first easy laugh of the day, Eve entered her bedroom. "He adores that child, you know. I've never known anyone quite as good with children as Bennett. He puts an enormous amount of time into the Aid for Handicapped Children even though it takes away from his free days with his horses." She walked into the adjoining dressing room as she spoke. "Another reason I suppose I've been moody is that I know Bennett should be on top of the world right now, and he looks as though he rarely closes his eyes."

"On top of the world?"

"It's taken him six months and a lot of frustration to get approval for the children's wing in the museum. He finally pushed it over the top at the board meeting the other night, but not without a lot of work and fast talking. He didn't mention it to you?"

"No," she said slowly. "No, he didn't mention it."

"It's been his pet project for a couple of years. It took him months to find the right architect, one who'd mesh practicality with the essence of what Bennett wanted to do. Then, because the board wouldn't give an inch, he had the plans drawn up at his own expense. They're wonderful." Eve came back into the room carrying a long box. "You should ask him to see them sometime. He wanted it open, lots of windows so that the kids wouldn't feel closed in. The board mumbled and grumbled when he talked of sculptures the children could make contact with and illustrations from storybooks instead of Rubenses and Renoirs and Rodins under glass."

"I didn't realize he was so…involved."

"Whatever Bennett does he does with total involvement. His idea was to introduce children to art through media they could understand and enjoy. Then there's a section that's reserved for paintings and models the children make themselves."

Eve set the box on the bed and smiled. "I'm surprised he didn't tell you about it. Usually no one's safe. It's taken him two years of planning and six months of fighting to get this project off the ground."

"It sounds lovely." She felt her heart twist and expand and fill with more love. "One often thinks of him as a man only interested in horses and the next party."

"He enjoys the image, but there's more to Bennett than that. I thought that the two of you had gotten quite close."

"Bennett's very kind."

"Hannah, don't disappoint me." A little tired, Eve sat on the edge of the bed. "He watches you walk out of a room and waits for you to come into one."

"He does?"

"Yes." Now she grinned. "He does. With all the anxiety and all the tension of the last weeks, at least I've had the pleasure of seeing Bennett fall in love. You do care, don't you?"

"Yes." It was almost over. Some deceptions were no longer necessary. "I've never known anyone like him."

"There isn't anyone like him."

"Eve, I don't want you to think, or to hope, for something that isn't going to happen."

"I'm entitled to think and hope as I choose." She lay a hand on the box beside her and patted the lid. "But for now, open your present."

"Is this a royal command or a request?"

"Whatever it takes to get you to open it. Please, I'm dying to see if you like it."

"Well, it's against my principles to open a present before Christmas, but…" Giving in, Hannah lifted the lid. She pushed aside the layers of tissue paper, then stood staring.

It glittered like a jewel and shimmered like fire. The dress was the rich, luscious green of emeralds with thousands and thousands of tiny beads that caught the afternoon light.

"Take it out," Eve insisted, then too impatient for Hannah, drew it out of the box herself.

The silk swayed, whispered and settled. It was cut straight, with a high neck that glistened with its beaded band at the throat. The arms would be bare well onto the shoulders as would the back before the material draped again and followed a long line to the floor. It was a dress made to glitter under chandeliers and shimmer under moonlight.

"Tell me you like it. I've driven the dressmaker crazy for a month."

"It's beautiful." Tentatively Hannah reached out. The dress shivered with life at the barest touch. "Eve, it's the most beautiful thing I've ever seen. I don't know what to say."

"Say you'll wear it to the Christmas Ball." Delighted with herself Eve turned Hannah toward the mirror and held the dress in front of her. "Look what it does to your eyes! I knew it." Laughing, she pushed the dress into Hannah's hands so she could step back and take it in. "Yes, I was sure of it. With that skin of yours... Oh yes," she said as she tapped a finger to her lips. "Bennett's going to take one look and babble like an idiot. I can't wait to see it."

"I don't think I should—"

"Of course you should, and you will because I refuse to take no for an answer." She stepped forward, eyes narrowed to pull free a lock of Hannah's hair. "My hairdresser's going to have a whack at you, too."

"That sounds a little ominous." As much as she longed to, she couldn't let herself go. The plain and proper Lady Hannah Rothchild wouldn't have had the nerve to wear such a dress. "Eve, it's lovely, you're lovely, but I don't think I'm made for a dress like this."

"I'm never wrong." Eve brushed off denials with a careless flick of her wrist. She may have been a princess for only two years, but she'd always been determined. "I've spent too long in the theater not to know what suits and what doesn't. Trust me, and if that's too much, do me a favor as a friend."

They *had* become friends, no matter what the initial reasons were or the ultimate goal. What harm would it do to accept? It was very possible that she wouldn't even be in Cordina for the ball. "I'll feel like Cinderella," she murmured, and wished it could be so.

"Good. And you should remember the clock doesn't always strike twelve."

* * *

But it did. Hannah remembered Eve's words as she and Reeve moved silently through the palace. The game was almost up, and so was her time.

The package had contained the explosives she'd requested and a coded message. She was to make her move that night and meet Deboque's agent at the docks at one a.m. The payoff would come then.

"This has to work," Hannah muttered as she carefully set the first charge. The equipment she used now was ISS-approved. The package she'd received was already being traced. Deboque would soon lose Athens and very much more.

"From outside the walls, it'll look as though the fire's burning out of control," Reeve said, working as quickly and competently as she. "The blasts are rigged for more noise than power. We'll blow out a few windows and put on a hell of a show while Malori and his men will remain here to bank it if necessary."

"Is the prince with them now?"

"Yes, Armand is filling the rest of the family in. Malori objects, but I think you're right. No harm can come from them knowing what's under way at this point, and a lot of anxiety can be relieved." He thought of Gabriella. After tonight, perhaps even the nightmares would fade.

"I couldn't bear to think of Eve waking up to the explosion and thinking it Deboque's doing. And Bennett? He's safe in the family wing?"

"Bennett's safe," he said, and left it at that. "I'm giving you ten minutes. That's enough time for you to get off the grounds. The dock's secure, so that if anything goes down there, we'll be on top of you. I'll be on the boat that has Deboque's yacht under surveillance. We'll move in the moment we have your signal. Hannah, I know the wire's risky. If you're searched—"

"If I'm searched, I'll deal with it." The mike was an ISS masterpiece that resembled an intricately worked locket that rested inches below the pulse in Hannah's throat.

"If he sees through this, he'll move fast."

"I'll move faster." She laid a hand on his when he started to speak again. "Reeve, I have a stake in this too. I don't want to die."

He looked at her for a moment as a woman. "I have a reputation for keeping my partners alive."

She was grateful he could make her smile. "I'm counting on it. But if something goes wrong, would you give Bennett a message for me?"

"Of course."

"Tell him…" She hesitated, unused to trusting her feelings to anyone. The clock struck the hour, midnight, and she prayed the magic would hold. "Tell him I loved him, both parts of me loved him. And there are no regrets."

She left through the main door and drove slowly toward the gates. In minutes, the guards who'd not been informed of the camouflage would react in precisely the way it was expected. Anyone watching the palace would see the shock and the action. For now, she passed through the gates with only the briefest of checks.

She kept an eye on her watch as she drove, hearing the minutes tick off and thinking of Bennett. He would be safe now. Whatever happened that night, he and his family would be safe. If Deboque paid her, he would be arrested for conspiracy. If he killed her, he would be arrested for the murder of an ISS agent. The end justified the means.

Hannah stopped the car, waited and heard the explosion. Malori had promised loud, and had delivered. She opened the door and stood beside the car a moment. The palace was a dim white blur against the night sky, but the east wing was lit like day. The fire was impressive from here, and knowing that none of Deboque's men could get much closer, she was satisfied. Within twenty minutes one of Malori's men would leak word that the Royal Family, save Armand, had perished in the explosion.

By the time she arrived, the docks were deserted. Word of trouble had already spread this far. Hannah parked her car in the shadows, then left it behind to wait in the light. She made an excellent target.

The boat anchored off the coast appeared to be a small, expensive pleasure yacht. Several times during the day, a dark-haired woman had appeared on deck, to sun, to read. From time to time, she'd been joined by a man, bare chested, young, bronzed. They'd sipped wine, cuddled, slept. The watch on the *Invincible* had kept it under surveillance, and had taken bets as to whether the two lovers would have sex under the sun. They'd been disappointed.

Belowdeck, the ISS had everything from television monitors to grenade launchers. Eight men and three women crowded into the hulled-out cabin and waited.

Bennett had been confined to the cabin since an hour after dawn. For the past three hours, he'd swallowed nothing but coffee and impatience. He'd watched the monitor until his eyes had blurred. Not once had Deboque appeared in the focus of the long-range camera. He wanted to see him. By God, he wanted to look into his eyes as the trap snapped shut. But more, so much more, he wanted to hear over the transmitter that it was done, and Hannah was safe.

"MacGee's boarding." The man with the headphones spoke, and continued to smoke. Seconds later, Reeve slipped into the already crowded cabin. He was dressed in black from head to foot. Even his face and hands were smeared with it. He took off his sailor's cap and tossed it aside.

"First stage is finished." He nodded toward Bennett. "From beyond the gates, it looks as though the east wing is devastated. The ISS is theatrical."

"The family?" Bennett asked as he looked back to the monitor.

"Safe."

He reached for the bitter, cooling coffee beside him. "Hannah?"

"Word should be coming in within minutes. Some of our best men are on the docks as backup."

Bennett shot him a look that held for a long moment. He'd wanted to be at the docks, as close by as possible. He'd run into the stone wall of his father, Reeve and Malori on that, and eventually had had to concede. If he'd been spotted, the entire operation would have been put in jeopardy.

Now it was only Hannah, he thought, only Hannah who risked it all.

"Deboque hasn't been seen all day."

"He's there." Reeve lit a cigarette and prepared to wait. "He wouldn't want to be too far away tonight."

"Contact." An agent on the port side of the cabin lifted a hand to his headphones. "She's made contact."

The breeze off the water was cool and the night was clear. Hannah recognized the man who approached her as the one who had come into the smoky little bar. He came alone and empty-handed.

"Mademoiselle."

"My part of the bargain is met, *monsieur*. You have the compensation?"

"It's a nice night for a ride on the water."

The yacht. She felt a ripple that was both unease and excitement. "You understand I'm no longer in a position to return to Cordina?"

"This is understood." He gestured toward a small motorboat. "Your needs will be seen to."

As before, she had a choice. She could draw her weapon now and take him in. If luck was with them, he would trade his own freedom for Deboque's. She couldn't risk Bennett's safety to luck. Without a word, she stepped into the boat and sat.

Her life was in her own hands now, Hannah thought, and folded them. However the night turned out, Deboque would be ruined.

Her contact didn't speak again, but his gaze shifted back and forth over the dark water. They were all waiting and watching now. Because the night was clear, Deboque's yacht stood out white and stark on the sea. She could see three men on deck, Ricardo and two others. It was Ricardo who assisted her onto the yacht.

"Lady Hannah, it's a pleasure to see you again."

There was something in his eyes, something smirking and self-satisfied. She knew then, as surely as if he'd held a knife to her throat, that she wasn't meant to leave the *Invincible.* Her voice was cool and calm when she spoke, and she hoped, clearly received across the span of water.

"Thank you, Ricardo. I hope this won't take long. I'm forced to admit I'm uneasy in Cordinian waters."

"We sail in an hour."

"For?"

"A more comfortable climate. The radio has announced the tragic deaths of several members of the Royal Family. Prince Armand is grieving in seclusion."

"Of course. Cordina is left without its heart, and without its heir. Monsieur Deboque has been informed?"

"He waits for you in his cabin." Ricardo reached out a hand for Hannah's bag.

"Are employees always searched, Ricardo?"

"We can dispense with that, Lady Hannah, if you will allow me to hold your weapons." He drew out her pistol and pocketed it. "And your knife?"

With a shrug, Hannah lifted her skirt to her thigh. She watched Ricardo's gaze dip and hold there as she drew out the knife. She pushed the release. On either side of her guns clicked.

"An admirable weapon," she said mildly as she held the blade up to the light. "Quiet, stylish, utilitarian." She smiled and sent the blade sliding back into place. "And one I would hardly use on the man who is about to give me five million American dollars." She dropped the knife into Ricardo's palm, knowing she had only her wits as defense now. "Shall we go? I enjoy the smell of money when it's still warm."

He took her arm in his surgeon's hand and with considerable panache, led her belowdeck to Deboque's cabin.

"Lady Hannah." The cabin was lit with a dozen candles. It was a Beethoven sonata this time that poured gently through the speakers. He wore a burgundy jacket and rubies. Blood colors. A magnum of champagne sat nestled in a silver bucket. "How prompt you are. You may leave us, Ricardo."

Hannah heard the door shut behind her. She didn't have to be told Ricardo would be stationed outside it.

"A pleasant ambience," she stated. "Most business isn't transacted in candlelight."

"There's no need for formalities between us now, Hannah." He was smiling as he moved to the champagne. "The announcements from Cordina are a bit hysterical and tragic." The cork rushed out. Wine bubbled to the lip. "I felt a small, tasteful celebration was in order."

"I rarely refuse champagne, *monsieur,* but its taste goes down so much more smoothly when I have money in my hand."

"Patience, my dear." He filled two tulip glasses and offered one. His face was marble pale in the dim light, his eyes almost black and full of pleasure. "To a job well done and a rich, rich future."

She touched her glass to his then sipped. "An excellent vintage."

"I've come to understand you prefer the excellent, and the expensive."

"Precisely. *Monsieur,* I hope you won't be offended if

I say while I appreciate the wine and soft light, I would appreciate them more after our business is completed."

"So mercenary." He ran his fingers down her cheek. The candlelight flattered her, he thought. In time she would bloom under his hands. A pity he couldn't take the risk and keep her with him for a few months. He had only an hour for her. But much could be accomplished in an hour. "You'll forgive me, but my mood is very light. I find myself wanting to celebrate your success, our success."

His hand roamed down her throat, within inches of the microphone. She caught it at the wrist and smiled. "You set the mood, *monsieur,* first by taking my weapons. Do you prefer defenseless women?"

"I prefer amenable women." He lifted his hand to her hair, digging his fingers into its richness. Hannah steeled herself for the kiss. She could show resistance, but not revulsion. "You're strong," he murmured and brought his mouth to hers again. "I prefer that as well. When I take you to bed, you'll give me a fight."

"I'll give you more than that. After I've seen the money."

He tightened his fingers, bringing pain quickly enough so that she gasped. Then they relaxed with his laugh. "Very well, *mon amie cupide.* You will see your money, and then you'll give me something in return."

When he turned his back to reveal a hidden safe, Hannah scrubbed her lips with the back of her hand. "I've already given payment for payment."

"The lives of the Royal Family." He spun the dial as Hannah's heart began to drum. "Five million dollars to assassinate the Bissets. Five million dollars to give me a full plate of revenge and the sweet dessert of power. Do you think it so much?" His eyes glittered as he turned back to her with a large case. "My dear child, you could have asked ten times as much. For over ten years I've plotted, and twice very nearly succeeded in killing a member of the Royal Family. Now, for the paltry sum of five million dollars, you have disposed of them all for me."

"That's it," Reeve announced as Deboque's voice came over the receiver. "Move in. Slowly."

Bennett's hand closed over his brother-in-law's. "I board with you."

"It's out of the question."

"I board with you," Bennett repeated in a hard, icy voice. Moment by moment, he had listened and sweated as Hannah stood alone with Deboque. As Deboque put his hands on her. As Deboque prepared to pay her for the murder of everything and everyone he loved. "Give me a weapon, Reeve, or I go unarmed."

"My orders are to keep you here."

"If it were Brie?" Bennett's eyes were hot and reckless. "If it were Brie, would you stay behind and let others protect her?"

Reeve looked down at the hand closed over his. It was strong and capable. And young. Then he looked into the eyes that were darker than his wife's but that held the same passions. Rising, he took a .45 automatic from the arsenal.

They would move now, Hannah thought and struggled to keep her voice impassive. "Do you tell me this now so I can regret?" She laughed and walked to the desk. "Five million will do me nicely. I plan to invest and to live quietly in Rio for the next few years."

He kept his eyes on hers as he unlocked the case. The money was there, but would be for his own uses. "You have no desire to continue in my employment?"

"Unfortunately, that would be risky for both of us after the events of tonight."

"Yes." His thoughts exactly. But he opened the lid so that she would at least have the pleasure of seeing the money before he killed her.

"Lovely." Clinging to the role, Hannah stepped forward and lifted a thick stack of crisp hundreds. "Do you know how sensual new money smells?" She fanned the stack.

"Indeed." He slid the top drawer of his desk open. Inside was an elegant pearl-handled revolver. He thought it just to kill her with style. He closed his fingers over it when the first shots were heard from above.

Hannah swung toward the door, hoping he would take excitement for alarm. "What game is this?" she demanded. She slammed the lid on the case, and taking the money headed for the door. Her hand closed over the knob.

"Remain still." Deboque warned. The gun was in his hand now and pointed at her heart. A fine film of sweat pearled over his brow as the sound of running feet pounded over their heads. He held the trigger lightly, but didn't press home. Whatever trouble was on deck, he didn't want to draw it down to him. "The case, Hannah."

"A double cross?" Her eyes narrowed as she calculated how much time she dared stall him. "Yes, you would easily have paid me ten times this if you never intended to pay me at all."

"The case." He started toward her, slowly. Fear was blossoming inside him, not of death, not of defeat, but of prison. He would never survive behind bars again.

Hannah waited until he was two feet away, then with both hands on the handle, swung the heavy case at his gun arm.

Deboque's men, whether in loyalty or fear, fought madly. Gunfire exploded back and forth from the two boats. A spray of bullets from a machine gun smashed in the wood above Bennett's head and sent splinters raining down his back. He watched a man fall over the rail of the yacht and into the water below.

Already the firing from Deboque's side was coming more sporadically, but time was speeding by. And Hannah was still with Deboque. Alive, Bennett told himself as he aimed and fired. She was alive. He'd know if it was otherwise because his heart would have stopped. But there was an urgency churning in him, more than the wild night and the scent of blood. Moving with it, he worked his way to stern and slipped into the water.

The night was rent with shooting and the shouts of men. He saw a man dive from Deboque's yacht and swim frantically toward a shore that was ten miles off. His hand brushed a body that floated facedown. ISS or the enemy, he didn't know. While the fighting raged, he swam silently around the yacht.

Because it was nearly over, Reeve signaled for his men

to close in. It was then he noticed that Bennett was no longer beside him.

"The prince." His throat went dry with panic. "Where is Prince Bennett?"

"There." One of the men spotted Bennett just before he disappeared around the stern of Deboque's yacht.

"In the name of God," Reeve breathed. "Move in fast. Prepare to board."

There was no one on the starboard side as Bennett dragged himself on deck. There was the occasional blast and rip of bullets, but the shouting had died. He'd spent an hour during that long, endless day belowdeck studying Hannah's diagram of Deboque's yacht. He went to find her.

She'd managed to knock the gun across the room, but he was faster and stronger than he appeared. Even as she dove after it, Deboque was on top of her. One hand closed over her throat, shutting off her air. Hannah freed one arm and brought her fist into his windpipe. Then both of them were gasping. She reached forward and her fingers scrabbled over the handle of the gun. She swore in both pain and fury as he dragged her back by the hair. For thirty grim and exhausting seconds, they struggled on the cabin floor. Her blouse tore at the seam. Beneath, bruises were already forming. She bloodied his mouth but was frustrated, unable to land a disabling injury.

Wrapped like lovers they rolled toward the gun again. She reached again, nearly grasping it. Out of the corner of her eye, she saw the fist coming and dodged. The blow was glancing, but strong enough to send her reeling. Then she was looking into the barrel of his gun.

She'd prepared herself to die. Struggling for breath, she braced. If she could do nothing else, she could fulfill her vow to spit in his eyes. "I'm an ISS agent. The Bissets are safe, and you've nowhere to run."

She saw the fury come into his eyes. She smiled at him and waited for the bullet.

When Bennett broke into the room, he saw Deboque crouched over Hannah, pointing a gun at her head. It happened in flashes, so quick that immediately afterward he couldn't be sure who had fired first.

Deboque's head swung around. Their eyes met. As the gun swiveled from Hannah's head toward Bennett's, she screamed and swung out. Two triggers were pressed. Two bullets exploded.

Bennett felt one whiz by him, so close that his skin shuddered and heated from it. He saw the blood bloom on Deboque's chest an instant before he crumpled onto Hannah.

She started shaking then. All the years of training dissolved as she lay trembling under the dead man. She'd prepared for her own death. That was duty. But she'd seen the bullet smash into the wood less than an inch from Bennett's face.

Even when he came to her, pushing what had been Deboque aside and gathering her close, the trembling didn't pass. "It's over, Hannah." He cradled her, rocked her, pressed kisses to her hair. "It's over now." Instead of the satisfaction, even the glory he'd expected to feel there was only relief. She was safe. And he was going to see that she stayed that way.

"You might have been killed. Damn you, Bennett, you were supposed to be home."

"Yes." He glanced up as Reeve rushed into the room. "We'll both go there soon."

There were tears on her cheeks. Brushing them aside, Hannah struggled to stand. She faced Reeve, but had to draw several breaths. "I'm ready to make my report."

"The hell with that." Bennett swept her into his arms. "I'm taking her home."

Epilogue

She'd slept around the clock. It wasn't until over twenty-four hours had passed that Hannah realized that Dr. Franco, the Bissets' personal physician, had given her a sedative.

She'd woken rested and resentful. And though she'd hated to admit it, aching.

The doctor had fussed for another full day, murmuring over her bumps and bruises in his kind but implacable tones. Because his orders to keep her in bed had come from His Royal Highness, neither doctor nor patient had a choice but to obey.

She complained. Even though visitors came often, she fidgeted at the inactivity. Word was delivered through Reeve from ISS headquarters, word that should have delighted her. Deboque's operation had crumbled. She'd been given her promotion. Hannah sulked in bed and wished for escape.

It was Eve who ultimately provided it on the night of the Christmas Ball.

"You're awake. Wonderful."

"Of course I'm awake." Cranky from two days in bed, Hannah shifted. The fact that her ribs were still sore to the touch only made it worse. "I'm going crazy."

"I'm sure you are." Smiling, Eve sat on the edge of the bed. "And I'm not going to embarrass you by going on again about how grateful we all are for everything you did. What I'm going to do is give you Dr. Franco's latest orders."

"Oh, spare me."

"Which are, to get up, get dressed and dance until dawn."

"What?" Hannah pushed herself up, wincing only a little. "I can get up? Do you mean it?"

"Absolutely. Now here." Rising, she lifted Hannah's robe. "Put this on. My hairdresser's expected any minute and she's going to do her magic on you first."

"Magic." With a sigh, Hannah lifted a hand to her hair. "More like a miracle at this point. Eve, as much as I want to get up and be doing, I don't think the ball is the best idea."

"It's the perfect idea." After helping Hannah into her robe, she leaned over to smell the clutch of gardenias by the bedside. "From Bennett?"

"Yes." Hannah gave in enough to touch the waxy leaves with her fingertips. "He brought them this morning. I haven't seen a great deal of him." Shaking off the mood, she tied the belt of the robe. "I know how busy you've all been, with the press conferences and public statements to clear up the entire mess."

Eve lifted a brow. She decided against telling Hannah that Bennett hadn't moved from her bedside throughout the first night. There was enough romance in her for her to want them to discover each other for themselves.

"Speaking of messes, you should see the east wing. Mostly glass. It'll take the maids weeks to get it all. Hannah." On a long breath, Eve took both her shoulders. "I'm going to embarrass you. I know it was an assignment, but whatever reasons brought you to us, you've given us peace. There's nothing I can say or do that can repay that. My child..." She smiled a little. "Marissa and this one are safe. I know what Deboque had planned to do."

"It's over now, Eve."

"Yes." Solemn, Eve kissed both of Hannah's cheeks. "I owe you my life, and the lives of all of my loved ones. If there's anything I can ever do, and I speak as your friend and as the wife of the heir of Cordina, you have only to ask."

"Put it behind you, and me. Eve, I've never been able to make and keep friends. I'd like to feel that's changed."

Eve studied the woman she was just beginning to know. "I have two sisters, the one I was born with and the one I was given by Alexander." She held out a hand. "I'd like to have three."

"Your Highness." One of the young maids hovered at the doorway. "I beg your pardon, but Madame Frissoutte is here."

"Wonderful." Eve hooked her arm through Hannah's. "Prepare to be transformed."

It was a transformation, Hannah thought as she studied herself in the glass. Her hair, curled wild as a gypsy's down her back, was caught away from her face with two glittering combs. The dress sparkled and shimmered as it draped from her throat to her ankles. She was clever enough with makeup to have covered the bruises on her arms and face.

All she needed were glass slippers, she thought with a half laugh. More illusion. But if this was to be her last night with Bennett, she would take it. There would be no regret when the clock struck twelve.

There was already music in the ballroom. Hannah slipped in, as was her habit, and absorbed the brilliance. Mirrors were polished to reflect the glitter and glamour of gowns and jewels. Chandeliers shone like stars. It was all shimmering silver and icy blue with draping garlands and shiny balls. On a tree that towered to twenty feet were a thousand crystal angels that caught the light.

He'd been watching for her. Waiting. When he saw her the breath simply left his body. The couple he'd been chatting with fell silent, brows lifting as he walked away without a word.

He caught both her hands even as she dipped into a curtsy. "My God, Hannah." For the first time in his life his tongue tied itself into knots. "You're exquisite."

"It's Eve's doing." He wore dress whites, with the insignia of his rank and a sword at his side. However many ways she remembered him, and she knew there would be many, she would never forget how he looked just now. "Everything is so beautiful."

"It is now." His hand slipped around her waist as he swirled her into the waltz.

It was magic, she thought. The music, the lights, the

mirrors. For hours they danced together, spinning around and around the room, leaving the food and the wine for others. When he circled her out to the terrace, she didn't object. There were still a few minutes until midnight.

Drawing away, she went to the rail to look out at Cordina. Lights glowed in festive colors for the holiday. The breeze held a springtime warmth and scent.

"Do you ever tire of looking at it?"

"No." He stood beside her. "I think it means even more now."

She understood, but wanted to keep even Deboque's ghost at bay. "In England, it would be cold, sleeting. There might be snow by morning, or we'd have gray, heavy skies. All the fires would be lit and the rum warmed. The cooks would have all the puddings and turkeys cooking so that you'd smell Christmas everywhere."

"We can't give you snow." He lifted her hand and kissed it. "But we could offer the fire and warm rum."

"It doesn't matter." She drew a deep breath. "When I'm home, I'll remember standing here with Christmas almost upon us. I'll remember it smelled like roses and jasmine."

"Would you wait here a moment?"

"All right."

"Just here," he said, and kissed her hand again. "I'll only be a minute."

When he was gone, she turned back to look out again at the lights and the sea. She would be home in a few days, and in time, perhaps Cordina would seem like a dream. Cordina, she thought, but never Bennett. She lifted her face to a star but didn't dare wish.

"I have something for you."

With a half smile, she turned, then caught the scent. "Oh, chestnuts!" With a laugh, she took the bag he offered. "And they're warm."

"I wanted to give you something from home."

She looked up. There was so much to say, and nothing that could be said. Instead, she rose on her toes to kiss him. "Thank you."

He brushed his fingers over her cheek. "I'd thought you'd share."

Hannah opened the bag and with her eyes closed, drew in the scent. "Isn't it wonderful? Now it feels like Christmas."

"If Cordina can be enough like home, perhaps you'll stay."

She opened her eyes, then lowered them quickly to the bag. "I have orders to return at the end of the week."

"Orders." He started to reach for her, but held himself back. "Your position in the ISS is important to you." He couldn't prevent the trace of resentment. "I'm told you received a promotion."

"A captaincy." She bit her bottom lip. "I'll be working behind a desk for a good while. Giving orders." She managed to smile.

"Have you ever considered giving it up?"

"Giving it up?"

It was the blank, puzzled look that worried him. Was it possible she could think of nothing else but her duty to her organization? "If you had something to replace it. Is it the excitement that pulls you?" He cupped her face in his hand, turning it toward the light so that the bruise Deboque had put there showed in a shadow.

"It's simply what I do." She drew a breath. "Bennett, we never talked about what happened on the yacht. I never thanked you for saving my life. I suppose it's because I've been used to taking care of myself."

"I would have killed him for this alone," he murmured as he traced the bruise on her cheek. She started to step back, but a look from him stopped her. "Don't back away from me. I haven't spoken before this because Franco was concerned with keeping you quiet and undisturbed. But dammit, I'll speak of it now."

He stepped closer so she could feel it, the recklessness, the barely controlled fury. "I had to sit and wait and listen to you deal with that man. I had to stay where I was, helpless while you were alone with him. And when I broke into that cabin and saw him holding a gun at your head, I had one hideous flash of what life would be like if you weren't in it. So don't back away from me now, Hannah."

"I won't." She steadied her breathing then lay a calming hand on his. "It's over, Bennett. The best thing for everyone is to put it aside. Cordina is safe. Your family is safe. And so am I."

"I won't accept your risking your life again for anyone."

"Bennett—"

"I won't." He caught her hair in his hands and kissed her, but this time with a force and power that left her breathless. He dragged himself away, reminding himself he had a plan and meant to see it through. "Are you going to try those chestnuts or just stand there smelling them?"

"What?" She had the bag locked in a viselike grip. She swallowed and opened it again. "I'm sure they're wonderful," she began, knowing she was going to babble. "It was so thoughtful of you to..." She broke off when she reached in and touched a small box. Puzzled, she drew it out.

"There's an American tradition. A box of candied popcorn with a prize in it. I had an urge to give you your Christmas present early."

"I've always been very strict about waiting until Christmas morning."

"I could make it a command, Hannah." He touched her cheek again. "I'd rather not."

"Well, since it *is* the Christmas Ball." She opened the lid and for the first time in her life felt faint.

"It was my grandmother's. I had it reset but it meant more to me to give you this than to choose another from a jeweler." He touched her hair, just the ends of it with his fingertips. "She was British, like you."

It was an emerald, fiery, stunning, made only more brilliant by the symphony of diamonds that circled it. Just looking at it made her light-headed. "Bennett, I couldn't take something like this. It belongs in your family."

"Don't be thickheaded." He took the bag from her to set it on the wall. The scent of chestnuts mixed with the summer fragrance of roses. "You know very well I'm asking you to marry me."

"You—you're carried away," she began, and this time did step back from him. "It's everything that's happened. You're not thinking clearly."

"My mind's never been more clear." He took the box from her, slipped the ring out and tossed the container aside. "We'll do it my way then." Taking her hand, he pushed the ring on. "Now, I can drag you back inside and announce our engagement—or we can talk about it reasonably first."

"Reasonably." How was it she needed to laugh and cry at the same time? "Bennett, you're being anything but reasonable."

"I love you—unreasonably then." He pulled her into his arms and covered her mouth with his. He could feel her heart thud, hear her breath shudder, taste both need and fear. "I'm not letting you go, Hannah, not now, not tomorrow, not ever. You'll have to exchange captain for princess. Believe me, it can be every bit as wearing."

Was it magic, or was it a dream come true? Her head was still spinning as she tried to get a grip on common sense. "You know I'm not the woman you cared for. Please, Bennett, listen to me."

"Do you think I'm a fool?" He spoke so mildly she was deceived into thinking him calm.

"Of course I don't. I only mean that—"

"Shut up." He caught her face in his hands, and she saw by his eyes he was anything but calm. "I thought the woman I first fell in love with was an illusion." He gentled as he brushed his lips over her cheeks. "I was wrong, because she's right here. There was another woman who made my mouth dry every time I looked." His kisses were more urgent now, more possessive. "She's here as well. It's not every man who can love two women and have them both. And I will have you, Hannah."

"You already have me." She was almost ready to believe it could be real, and true and lasting. "But even you can't command a marriage."

He lifted his brow, arrogant, confident. "Don't be too sure. You told me once you wanted me. Was it a lie?"

"No." She steadied herself with two hands on his chest. She was crossing a line in her life, one that allowed for no deceptions. He was offering her a chance to be herself, to love openly and honestly. "No, it wasn't a lie."

"I ask you now if you love me."

She couldn't speak. From deep within the palace the clock began to strike. Midnight. She counted off the gongs and waited for the illusion to fade. Then there was silence and she was still in his arms. Looking down, she saw the ring glow against her finger. A promise. A lifetime.

"I love you, and nothing's ever been more true."

"Share my home." He caught her ring hand in his and pressed his lips to the palm.

"Yes."

"And my family."

She twined her fingers with his. "Yes."

"And my duty."

"From this moment."

She wrapped her arms around him. She lifted her face for his kiss. Below and as far as eyes could see, Cordina spread out before them and prepared to sleep.

* * * * *

Charmed

To everyone who believes in happy endings

Prologue

Magic exists. Who can doubt it, when there are rainbows and wildflowers, the music of the wind and the silence of the stars? Anyone who has loved has been touched by magic. It is such a simple and such an extraordinary part of the lives we live.

There are those who have been given more, who have been chosen to carry on a legacy handed down through endless ages. Their forebears were Merlin the enchanter, Ninian the sorceress, the faerie princess Rhiannon, the Wegewarte of Germany and the jinns of Arabia. Through their blood ran the power of Finn of the Celts, the ambitious Morgan le Fay, and others whose names were whispered only in shadows and in secret.

When the world was young and magic as common as a raindrop, faeries danced in the deep forests, and— sometimes for mischief, sometimes for love—mixed with mortals.

And they do still.

Her bloodline was old. Her power was ancient. Even as a child she had understood, had been taught, that such gifts were not without price. The loving parents who treasured her could not lower the cost, or pay it themselves, but could only love, instruct and watch the young girl grow to womanhood. They could only stand and hope as she experienced the pains and the joys of that most fascinating of journeys.

And, because she felt more than others, because her gift demanded that she feel more, she learned to court peace.

As a woman, she preferred a quiet life, and was often alone without the pain of loneliness.

As a witch, she accepted her gift, and never forgot the responsibility it entailed.

Perhaps she yearned, as mortals and others have yearned since the beginning, for a true and abiding love. For she knew better than most that there was no power, no enchantment, no sorcery, greater than the gift of an open and accepting heart.

Chapter 1

When she saw the little girl peek through the fairy roses, Anastasia had no idea the child would change her life. She'd been humming to herself, as she often did when she gardened, enjoying the scent and the feel of earth. The warm September sun was golden, and the gentle whoosh of the sea on the rocks below her sloping yard was a lovely background to the buzzing of bees and the piping of bird-song. Her long gray cat was stretched out beside her, his tail twitching in time with some feline dream.

A butterfly landed soundlessly on her hand, and she stroked the edge of its pale blue wings with a fingertip. As it fluttered off, she heard the rustling. Glancing over, she saw a small face peeping through the hedge of fairy roses.

Ana's smile came quickly, naturally. The face was charming, with its little pointed chin and its pert nose, its big blue eyes mirroring the color of the sky. A pixie cap of glossy brown hair completed the picture.

The girl smiled back, those summer-sky eyes full of curiosity and mischief.

"Hello," Ana said, as if she always found little girls in her rosebushes.

"Hi." The girl's voice was bright, and a little breathless. "Can you catch butterflies? I never got to pet one like that before."

"I suppose. But it seems rude to try unless one invites you." She brushed the hair from her brow with her forearm and sat back on her heels. Ana had noticed a moving van unloading the day before, and she concluded she was meeting one of her new neighbors. "Have you moved into the house next door?"

"Uh-huh. We're going to live here now. I like it, 'cause I get to look right out my bedroom window and see the water. I saw a seal, too. In Indiana you only see them in the zoo. Can I come over?"

"Of course you can." Ana set her garden spade aside as the girl stepped through the rosebushes. In her arms was a wriggling puppy. "And who do we have here?"

"This is Daisy." The child pressed a loving kiss to the top of the puppy's head. "She's a golden retriever. I got to pick her out myself right before we left Indiana. She got to fly in the plane with us, and we were hardly scared at all. I have to take good care of her and give her food and water and brush her and everything, 'cause she's my responsibility."

"She's very beautiful," Ana said soberly. And very heavy, she imagined, for a little girl of five or six. She held out her arms. "May I?"

"Do you like dogs?" The little girl kept chattering as

she passed Daisy over. "I do. I like dogs and cats and everything. Even the hamsters Billy Walker has. Someday I'm going to have a horse, too. We'll have to see about that. That's what my daddy says. We'll have to see about that."

Utterly charmed, Ana stroked the puppy as she sniffed and licked at her. The child was as sweet as sunshine. "I'm very fond of dogs and cats and everything," Ana told her. "My cousin has horses. Two big ones and a brand-new baby."

"Really?" The child squatted down and began to pet the sleeping cat. "Can I see them?"

"He doesn't live far, so perhaps one day. We'll have to ask your parents."

"My mommy went to heaven. She's an angel now."

Ana's heart broke a little. Reaching out, she touched the shiny hair and opened herself. There was no pain here, and that was a relief. The memories were good ones. At the touch, the child looked up and smiled.

"I'm Jessica," she said. "But you can call me Jessie."

"I'm Anastasia." Because it was too much to resist, Ana bent down and kissed the pert nose. "But you can call me Ana."

Introductions over, Jessie settled down to bombard Ana with questions, filtering information about herself through the bright chatter. She'd just had a birthday and was six. She would be starting first grade in her brand-new school on Tuesday. Her favorite color was purple, and she hated lima beans more than anything.

Could Ana show her how to plant flowers? Did her cat have a name? Did she have any little girls? Why not?

So they sat in the sunshine, a bright pixie of a girl in pink rompers and a woman with garden dirt smearing her shorts and her lightly tanned legs, while Quigley the cat ignored the playful attentions of Daisy the dog.

Ana's long, wheat-colored hair was tied carelessly back, and the occasional wisp worked free of the band to dance in the wind around her face. She wore no cosmetics. Her fragile, heartbreaking beauty was as natural as her power, a combination of Celtic bones, smoky eyes, the wide, poetically sculptured Donovan mouth—and something more nebulous. Her face was the mirror of a giving heart.

The pup marched over to sniff at the herbs in her rockery. Ana laughed at something Jessica said.

"Jessie!" The voice swept over the hedge of roses, deeply male, and touched with exasperation and concern. "Jessica Alice Sawyer!"

"Uh-oh. He used my whole name." But Jessie's eyes were twinkling as she jumped to her feet. There was obviously little fear of reprisals.

"Over here! Daddy, I'm right over here with Ana! Come and see!"

A moment later, there was a man towering over the fairy roses. No gift was needed to detect waves of frustration, relief and annoyance. Ana blinked once, surprised that this rough-and-ready male was the father of the little sprite currently bouncing beside her.

Maybe it was the day or two's growth of beard that made him look so dangerous, she thought. But she doubted it. Beneath that dusky shadow was a sharp-featured face of planes and angles, a full mouth set in grim lines. Only the eyes were like his daughter's, a clear, brilliant blue, marred now by an expression of impatience. The sun brought out glints of red in his dark, tousled hair as he dragged a hand through it.

From her perch on the ground, he looked enormous. Athletically fit and disconcertingly strong, in a ripped T-shirt and faded jeans sprung at the seams.

He cast one long, annoyed and unmistakably distrustful glance at Ana before giving his attention to his daughter.

"Jessica. Didn't I tell you to stay in the yard?"

"I guess." She smiled winningly. "Daisy and I heard Ana singing, and when we looked, she had this butterfly right on her hand. And she said we could come over. She has a cat, see? And her cousin has horses, and her other cousin has a cat *and* a dog."

Obviously used to Jessie's rambling, her father waited it out. "When I tell you to stay in the yard, and then you're not there, I'm going to worry."

It was a simple statement, made in even tones. Ana had to respect the fact that the man didn't have to raise his voice or spout ultimatums to get his point across. She felt every bit as chastened as Jessie.

"I'm sorry, Daddy," Jessie murmured over a pouting lower lip.

"I should apologize, Mr. Sawyer." Ana rose to lay a hand on Jessie's shoulder. After all, it looked as if they were in this together. "I did invite her over, and I was enjoying her company so much that it didn't occur to me that you wouldn't be able to see where she was."

He said nothing for a moment, just stared at her with those water-clear eyes until she had to fight the urge to squirm. When he flicked his gaze down to his daughter again, Ana realized she'd been holding her breath.

"You should take Daisy over and feed her."

"Okay." Jessie hauled the reluctant pup into her arms, then stopped when her father inclined his head.

"And thank Mrs…?"

"Miss," Ana supplied. "Donovan. Anastasia Donovan."

"Thank Miss Donovan for putting up with you."

"Thank you for putting up with me, Ana," Jessie said with singsong politeness, sending Ana a conspirator's grin. "Can I come back?"

"I hope you will."

As she stepped through the bushes, Jessie offered her father a sunny smile. "I didn't mean to make you worry, Daddy. Honest."

He bent down and tweaked her nose. "Brat." Ana heard the wealth of love behind the exasperation.

With a giggle, Jessie ran across the yard, the puppy wriggling in her arms. Ana's smile faded the moment those cool blue eyes turned back to her.

"She's an absolutely delightful child," Ana began, amazed that she had to wipe damp palms on her shorts. "I do apologize for not making certain you knew where she was, but I hope you'll let her come back to visit me again."

"It wasn't your responsibility." His voice was cool, neither friendly nor unfriendly. Ana had the uncomfortable certainty that she was being weighed, from the top of her head to the bottom of her grass-stained sneakers. "Jessie is naturally curious and friendly. Sometimes too much of both. It doesn't occur to her that there are people in the world who might take advantage of that."

Equally cool now, Ana inclined her head. "Point taken, Mr. Sawyer. Though I can assure you I rarely gobble up young girls for breakfast."

He smiled, a slow curving of the lips that erased the harshness from his face and replaced it with a devastating appeal. "You certainly don't fit my perception of an ogre, Miss Donovan. Now I'll have to apologize for being so abrupt. She gave me a scare. I hadn't even unpacked yet, and I'd lost her."

"Misplaced." Ana tried another cautious smile. She looked beyond him to the two-story redwood house next door, with its wide band of windows and its curvy deck. Though she was content in her privacy, she was glad it hadn't remained empty long. "It's nice to have a child nearby, especially one as entertaining as Jessie. I hope you'll let her come back."

"I often wonder if I *let* her do anything." He flicked a finger over a tiny pink rose. "Unless you replace these with a ten-foot wall, she'll be back." And at least he'd know where to look if she disappeared again. "Don't be afraid to send her home when she overstays her welcome." He tucked his hands in his pockets. "I'd better go make sure she doesn't feed Daisy our dinner."

"Mr. Sawyer?" Ana said as he turned away. "Enjoy Monterey."

"Thanks." His long strides carried him over the lawn, onto the deck and into the house.

Ana stood where she was for another moment. She couldn't remember the last time the air here had sizzled with so much energy. Letting out a long breath, she bent to pick up her gardening tools, while Quigley wound himself around her legs.

She certainly couldn't remember the last time her palms had gone damp just because a man had looked at her.

Then again, she couldn't recall ever being looked at in quite that way before. Looked at, looked into, looked through, all at once. A very neat trick, she mused as she carried the tools into her greenhouse.

An intriguing pair, father and daughter. Gazing through the sparkling glass wall of the greenhouse, she studied the house centered in the next yard. As their closest neighbor, she thought, it was only natural that she should wonder about them. Ana was also wise enough—and had learned through painful experience—to be careful not to let her wondering lead to any involvement beyond a natural friendliness.

There were precious few who could accept what was not of the common world. The price of her gift was a vulnerable heart that had already suffered miserably at the cold hand of rejection.

But she didn't dwell on that. In fact, as she thought of the man, and of the child, she smiled. What would he have done, she wondered with a little laugh, if she had told him that, while she wasn't an ogre—no, indeed—she was most definitely a witch.

In the sunny and painfully disorganized kitchen, Boone Sawyer dug through a packing box until he unearthed a skillet. He knew the move to California had been a good one—he'd convinced himself of that—but he'd certainly underestimated the time, the trouble and the general inconvenience of packing up a home and plopping it down somewhere else.

What to take, what to leave behind. Hiring movers, having his car shipped, transporting the puppy that Jessie had fallen in love with. Justifying his decision to her worried grandparents, school registration—school shopping. Lord, was he going to have to repeat that nightmare every fall for the next eleven years?

At least the worst was behind him. He hoped. All he had to do now was unpack, find a place for everything and make a home out of a strange house.

Jessie was happy. That was, and always had been, the most important thing. Then again, he mused as he browned some beef for chili, Jessie was happy anywhere. Her sunny disposition and her remarkable capacity to make friends were both a blessing and a bafflement. It was astonishing to Boone that a child who had lost her mother at the tender age of two could be unaffected, so resilient, so completely normal.

And he knew that if not for Jessie he would surely have gone quietly mad after Alice's death.

He didn't often think of Alice now, and that fact sometimes brought him a rush of guilt. He had loved her—God, he had loved her—and the child they'd made together was a living, breathing testament to that love. But he'd been without her now longer than he'd been with her. Though he had tried to hang on to the grief, as a kind of proof of that love, it had faded under the demands and pressures of day-to-day living.

Alice was gone, Jessie was not. It was because of both of them that he'd made the difficult decision to move to Monterey. In Indiana, in the home he and Alice had bought while she was carrying Jessie, there had been too many ties to the past. Both his parents and Alice's had been a ten-minute drive away. As the only grandchild on both sides, Jessie had been the center of attention, and the object of subtle competition.

For himself, Boone had wearied of the constant advice, the gentle—and not-so-gentle—criticism of his parenting. And, of course, the matchmaking. The child needs a mother. A man needs a wife. His mother had decided to make it her life's work to find the perfect woman to fit both bills.

Because that had begun to infuriate him, and because he'd realized how easy it would be to stay in the house and wallow in the memories it held, he'd chosen to move.

He could work anywhere. Monterey had been the final choice because of the climate, the life-style, the schools. And, he could admit privately, because some internal voice had told him this was the place. For both of them.

He liked being able to look out of the window and see the water, or those fascinatingly sculptured cypress trees. He certainly liked the fact that he wasn't crowded in by neighbors. It was Alice who had enjoyed being surrounded by people. He also appreciated the fact that the distance from the road was enough to muffle the sound of traffic.

It just felt right. Jessie was already making her mark. True, it had given him a moment of gut-clutching fear when he'd looked outside and hadn't seen her anywhere.

But he should have known she would find someone to talk to, someone to charm.

And the woman.

Frowning, Boone settled the top on the skillet to let the chili simmer. That had been odd, he thought as he poured a cup of coffee to take out on the deck. He'd looked down at her and known instantly that Jessie was safe. There had been nothing but kindness in those smoky eyes. It was his reaction, his very personal, very basic reaction, that had tightened his muscles and roughened his voice.

Desire. Very swift, very painful, and totally inappropriate. He hadn't felt that kind of response to a woman since... He grinned to himself. Since never. With Alice it had been a quiet kind of rightness, a sweet and inevitable coming together that he would always treasure.

This had been like being dragged by an undertow when you were fighting to get to shore.

Well, it had been a long time, he reminded himself as he watched a gull glide toward the water. A healthy reaction to a beautiful woman was easily justified and explained. And beautiful she'd been, in a calm, classic manner that was the direct opposite of his violent response to her. He couldn't help but resent it. He didn't have the time or inclination for any kind of reaction to any kind of woman.

There was Jessie to think of.

Reaching in his pocket, he took out a cigarette, lit it, hardly aware he was staring across the lawn at the hedge of delicate roses.

Anastasia, he thought. The name certainly suited her. It was old-fashioned, elegant, unusual.

"Daddy!"

Boone jolted, as guilty as a teenager caught smoking in the boys' room by the high school principal. He cleared his throat and gave his pouting daughter a sheepish grin.

"Give your old man a break, Jess. I'm down to half a pack a day."

She folded her arms. "They're bad for you. They make your lungs dirty."

"I know." He tamped the cigarette out, unable to take even a last drag when those wise little eyes were judging him. "I'm giving them up. Really."

She smiled—it was a disconcertingly adult sure-you-are smile—and he jammed his hands in his pockets. "Give me a break, Warden," he said in a passable James Cagney imitation. "You ain't putting me in solitary for snitching one drag."

Giggling, already forgiving him for the lapse, she came over to hug him. "You're silly."

"Yeah." He cupped his hands under her elbows and lifted her up for a hearty kiss. "And you're short."

"One day I'm going to be big as you." She wrapped her legs around his waist and leaned back until she was upside down. It was one of her favorite pastimes.

"Fat chance." He held her steady as her hair brushed the deck. "I'm always going to be bigger." He pulled her up again, lifting her high and making her squeal with laughter. "And smarter, and stronger." He rubbed the stubble of his beard against her while she wriggled and shrieked. "And better-looking."

"And ticklish!" she shouted in triumph, digging her fingers into his ribs.

She had him there. He collapsed on the bench with her. "Okay, okay! Uncle!" He caught his breath, and caught her close. "You'll always be trickier."

Pink-cheeked, bright-eyed, she bounced on his lap. "I like our new house."

"Yeah?" He smoothed her hair, as always enjoying the texture of it under his palm. "Me too."

"After dinner, can we go down to the beach and look for seals?"

"Sure."

"Daisy, too?"

"Daisy, too." Already experienced with puddles on the rug and chewed-up socks, he glanced around. "Where is she?"

"She's taking a nap." Jessie rested her head against her father's chest. "She was very tired."

"I bet. It's been a big day." Smiling, he kissed the top of Jessie's head, felt her yawn and settle.

"My favorite day. I got to meet Ana." Because her eyes were heavy, she closed them, lulled by the beating of her father's heart. "She's nice. She's going to show me how to plant flowers."

"Hmm."

"She knows all their names." Jessie yawned again, and when she spoke again her voice was thick with sleep. "Daisy licked her face and she didn't even mind. She just laughed. It sounded pretty when she did. Like a fairy," Jessie murmured as she drifted off.

Boone smiled again. His daughter's imagination. His gift to her, he liked to think. He held her gently while she slept.

* * *

Restless, Ana thought as she strolled along the rocky beach at twilight. She simply wasn't able to stay inside, working with her plants and herbs, when she was dogged by this feeling of restlessness.

The breeze would blow it out of her, she decided, lifting her face to the moist wind. A nice long walk and she'd find that contentment again, that peace that was as much a part of her as breathing.

Under different circumstances she would have called one of her cousins and suggested a night out. But she imagined Morgana was cozily settled in with Nash for the evening. And at this stage of her pregnancy, she needed rest. Sebastian wasn't back from his honeymoon yet.

Still, it had never bothered her to be alone. She enjoyed the solitude of the long, curved beach, the sound of water against rock, the laughing of the gulls.

Just as she had enjoyed the sound of the child's laughter, and the man's, drifting to her that afternoon. It had been a good sound, one she didn't have to be a part of to appreciate.

Now, as the sun melted, spilling color over the western sky, she felt the restlessness fading. How could she be anything but content to be here, alone, watching the magic of a day at rest?

She climbed up to stand on a driftwood log, close enough to the water that the spray cooled her face and dampened her shirt. Absently she took a stone out of her pocket, rubbing it between her fingers as she watched the sun drop into the flaming sea.

The stone warmed in her hand. Ana looked down at

the small, waterlike gem, its pearly sheen glinting dully in the lowering light. Moonstone, she thought, amused at herself. Moon magic. A protection for the night traveler, an aid to self-analysis. And, of course, a talisman, often used to promote love.

Which was she looking for tonight?

Even as she laughed at herself and slipped the stone back into her pocket, she heard her name called.

There was Jessie, racing down the beach with the fat puppy nipping at her heels. And her father, walking several yards behind, as if reluctant to close the distance. Ana took a moment to wonder if the child's natural exuberance made the man appear all the more aloof.

She stepped down from the log and, because it was natural, even automatic, caught Jessie up in a swing and a hug. "Hello again, sunshine. Are you and Daisy out hunting for fairy shells?"

Jessie's eyes widened. "Fairy shells? What do they look like?"

"Just as you'd suppose. Sunset or sunrise—that's the only time to find them."

"My daddy says fairies live in the forest, and usually hide because people don't always know how to treat them."

"Quite right." She laughed and set the girl on her feet. "But they like the water, too, and the hills."

"I'd like to meet one, but Daddy says they hardly ever talk to people like they used to 'cause nobody really believes in them but kids."

"That's because children are very close to magic." She looked up as she spoke. Boone had reached them, and the sun setting at his back cast shadows over his face that were both dangerous and appealing. "We were discussing fairies," she told him.

"I heard." He laid a hand on Jessie's shoulder. Though the gesture was subtle, the meaning was crystal-clear. *Mine*.

"Ana says there are fairy shells on the beach, and you can only find them at sunrise or sunset. Can you write a story about them?"

"Who knows?" His smile was soft and loving for his daughter. When his gaze snapped back to hers, Ana felt a shudder down her spine. "We've interrupted your walk."

"No." Exasperated, Ana shrugged. She understood that he meant she had interrupted theirs. "I was just taking a moment to watch the water before I went in. It's getting chilly."

"We had chili for dinner," Jessie said, grinning at her own joke. "And it was *hot!* Will you help me look for fairy shells?"

"Sometime, maybe." When her father wasn't around to stare holes through her. "But it's getting too dark now, and I have to go in." She flicked a finger down Jessie's nose. "Good night." She gave a cool nod to her father.

Boone watched Ana walk away. She might not have gotten chilled so quickly, he thought, if she'd worn something to cover her legs. Her smooth, shapely legs. He let out a long, impatient breath.

"Come on, Jess. Race you back."

Chapter 2

"I'd like to meet him."

Ana glanced up from the dried petals she was arranging for potpourri and frowned at Morgana. "Who?"

"The father of this little girl you're so enchanted with." More fatigued than she cared to admit, Morgana stroked her hand in a circular motion over her very round belly. "You're just chock-full of information on the girl, and very suspiciously lacking when it comes to Papa."

"Because he doesn't interest me as much," Ana said lightly. To a bowl filled with fragrant leaves and petals she added lemon for zest and balsam for health. She knew very well how weary Morgana was. "He's every bit as standoffish as Jessie is friendly. If it wasn't obvious that he's devoted to her, I'd probably dislike him instead of being merely ambivalent."

"Is he attractive?"

Ana lifted a brow. "As compared to?"

"A toad." Morgana laughed and leaned forward. "Come on, Ana. Give."

"Well, he isn't ugly." Setting the bowl aside, she began to look through the cupboard for the right oil to mix through the potpourri. "I guess you'd say he has that hollow-cheeked, dangerous look. Athletic build. Not like a weight lifter." She frowned, trying to decide between two oils. "More like a…a long-distance runner, I suppose. Rangy, and intimidatingly fit."

Grinning, Morgana cupped her chin in her hands. "More."

"This from a married woman about to give birth to twins?"

"You bet."

Ana laughed, chose an oil of rose to add elegance. "Well, if I have to say something nice, he does have wonderful eyes. Very clear, very blue. When they look at Jessie, they're gorgeous. When they look at me, suspicious."

"What in the world for?"

"I haven't a clue."

Morgana shook her head and rolled her eyes. "Anastasia, surely you've wondered enough to find out. All you'd have to do is peek."

With a deft and expert hand, Ana added drops of fragrant oil to the mixture in the bowl. "You know I don't like to intrude."

"Oh, really."

"And if I was curious," she added, fighting a smile at Morgana's frustration, "I don't believe I'd care to see what was rolling around inside Mr. Sawyer's heart. I have a feeling it would be very uncomfortable to be linked with him, even for a few minutes."

"You're the empath," Morgana said with a shrug. "If Sebastian was back, he'd find out what's in this guy's mind anyway." She sipped more of the soothing elixir Ana had mixed for her. "I could do it for you if you like. I haven't had cause to use the scrying mirror or crystal for weeks. I may be getting stale."

"No." Ana leaned forward and kissed her cousin's cheek. "Thank you. Now, I want you to keep a bag of this with you," she said as she spooned the potpourri into a net bag. "And put the rest in bowls around the house and the shop. You're only working two days a week now, right?"

"Two or three." She smiled at Ana's concern, even as she waved it off. "I'm not overdoing, darling, I promise. Nash won't let me."

With an absent nod, Ana tied the bag securely. "Are you drinking the tea I made up for you?"

"Every day. And, yes, I'm using the oils religiously. I'm carrying rhyolite to alleviate emotional stress, topaz against external stresses, zircon for a positive attitude and amber to lift my spirits." She gave Ana's hand a quick squeeze. "I've got all the bases covered."

"I'm entitled to fuss." She set the bag of potpourri down by Morgana's purse, then changed her mind and opened the purse herself to slip it inside. "It's our first baby."

"Babies," Morgana corrected.

"All the more reason to fuss. Twins come early."

Indulging in a single sigh, Morgana closed her eyes. "I certainly hope these do. It's getting to the point where I can hardly get up and down without a crane."

"More rest," Ana prescribed, "and very gentle exercise. Which does not include hauling around shipping boxes or being on your feet all day waiting on customers."

"Yes, ma'am."

"Now let's have a look." Gently she laid her hands on her cousin's belly, spreading her fingers slowly, opening herself to the miracle of what lay within.

Instantly Morgana felt her fatigue drain away and a physical and emotional well-being take its place. Through her half-closed eyes she saw Ana's darken to the color of pewter and fix on a vision only Ana could see.

As she moved her hands over her cousin's heavy belly and linked with her, Ana felt the weight within her and, for one incredibly vivid moment, the lives that pulsed inside the womb. The draining fatigue, yes, and the nagging discomfort, but she also felt the quiet satisfaction, the burgeoning excitement, and the simple wonder of carrying those lives. Her body ached, her heart swelled. Her lips curved.

Then she *was* those lives—first one, then the other. Swimming dreamlessly in that warm, dark womb, nourished by the mother, held safe and fast until the moment when the outside would be faced. Two healthy hearts beating steady and close, beneath a mother's heart. Tiny fingers flexing, a lazy kick. The rippling of life.

Ana came back to herself, came back alone. "You're well. All of you."

"I know." Morgana twined her fingers with Ana's. "But I feel better when you tell me. Just as I feel safe knowing you'll be there when it's time."

"You know I wouldn't be anywhere else." She brought

their joined hands to her cheek. "But is Nash content with me as midwife?"

"He trusts you—as much as I do."

Ana's gaze softened. "You're lucky, Morgana, to have found a man who accepts, understands, even appreciates, what you are."

"I know. To have found love was precious enough. But to have found love with him." Then her smile faded. "Ana, darling, Robert was a long time ago."

"I don't think of him. At least not really of him, but of a wrong turn on a particularly slippery road."

Indignation sharpened Morgana's eyes. "He was a fool, and not in the least worthy of you."

Rather than sadness Ana felt a chuckle bubble out of her. "You never liked him. Not from the first."

"No, I didn't." Frowning, Morgana gestured with her glass. "And neither did Sebastian, if you recall."

"I do. As I recall Sebastian was quite suspicious of Nash, too."

"That was entirely different. It *was*," she insisted as Ana grinned. "With Nash, he was just being protective of me. As for Robert, Sebastian tolerated him with the most insulting sort of politeness."

"I remember." Ana shrugged. "Which, of course, put my back up. Well, I was young," she said with a careless gesture. "And naive enough to believe that if I was in love I must be loved back equally. Foolish enough to be honest. And foolish enough to be devastated when that honesty was rewarded with disbelief, then outright rejection."

"I know you were hurt, but there's little doubt you could do better."

"None at all," Ana agreed, for she wasn't without pride. "But there are some of us that aren't meant to mix with outsiders."

Now there was frustration, as well as indignation. "There have been plenty of men, with elfin blood and without, who've been interested in you, cousin."

"A pity I haven't been interested in them." Ana laughed. "I'm miserably choosy, Morgana. And I like my life just as it is."

"If I didn't know that to be true, I'd be tempted to work up a nice little love spell. Nothing binding, mind," she said with a glint in her eye. "Just something to give you some entertainment."

"I can find my own entertainment, thanks."

"I know that, too. Just as I know you'd be furious if I dared to interfere." She pushed away from the table and rose, regretting for a moment her loss of grace. "Let's take a walk outside before I head home."

"If you promise to put your feet up for an hour when you get there."

"Done."

The sun was warm, the breeze balmy. Both of which, Ana thought, would do her cousin as much good as the long nap she imagined Nash would insist his wife take when she returned home.

They admired the late-blooming larkspur, the starry asters and the big, bold zinnias. Both had a deep love of nature that had come through the blood and through upbringing.

"Do you have any plans for All Hallows' Eve?" Morgana asked.

"Nothing specific."

"We were hoping you'd come by, at least for part of the evening. Nash is going all out for the trick-or-treaters."

With an appreciative laugh, Ana clipped some mums to take inside. "When a man writes horror films for a living, he's duty bound to pull out the stops for Halloween. I wouldn't miss it."

"Good. Perhaps Sebastian will join you and me for a quiet celebration afterward." Morgana was bending awkwardly over the thyme and verbena when she spotted the child and dog skipping through the hedge of roses.

She straightened. "We have company."

"Jessie." Pleased but wary, Ana glanced over to the house beyond. "Does your father know where you are?"

"He said I could come over if I saw you outside and you weren't busy. You aren't busy, are you?"

"No." Unable to resist, Ana bent down to kiss Jessie's cheek. "This is my cousin, Morgana. I've told her you're my brand-new neighbor."

"You have a dog and a cat. Ana told me." Jessie's interest was immediately piqued. Then her gaze focused, fascinated, on the bulge of Morgana's belly. "Do you have a baby in there?"

"I certainly do. In fact, I have two babies in there."

"Two?" Jessie's eyes popped wide. "How do you know?"

"Because Ana told me." With a laugh, she laid a hand on her heavy stomach. "And because they kick and squirm too much to be only one."

"My friend Missy's mommy, Mrs. Lopez, had one baby in her tummy, and she got so fat she could hardly walk."

Out of brilliant blue eyes, Jessie shot Morgana a hopeful glance. "She let me feel it kick."

Charmed, Morgana took Jessie's hand and brought it to her while Ana discouraged Daisy from digging in the impatiens. "Feel that?"

Giggling at the movement beneath her hand, Jessie nodded. "Uh-huh! It went pow! Does it hurt?"

"No."

"Do you think they'll come out soon?"

"I'm hoping."

"Daddy says babies know when to come out because an angel whispers in their ear."

Sawyer might be aloof, Morgana thought, but he was also very clever, and very sweet. "That sounds exactly right to me."

"And that's their special angel, forever and ever," she went on, pressing her cheek to Morgana's belly in the hope that she could hear something from inside. "If you turn around really quick, you maybe could get just a tiny glimpse of your angel. I try sometimes, but I'm not fast enough." She peered up at Morgana. "Angels are shy, you know."

"So I've heard."

"I'm not." She pressed a kiss to Morgana's belly before she danced away. "There's not a shy bone in my body. That's what Grandma Sawyer always says."

"An observant woman, Grandma Sawyer," Ana commented while wrestling Daisy into her arms to prevent her from disturbing Quigley's afternoon nap.

Both women enjoyed the energetic company as they walked among the flowers—or rather as they walked and Jessie skipped, hopped, ran and tumbled.

Jessie reached for Ana's hand as they started toward the front of the house and Morgana's car. "I don't have any cousins. Is it nice?"

"Yes, it's very nice. Morgana and Sebastian and I practically grew up together, kind of like brothers and sisters do."

"I know how to get brothers and sisters, 'cause my daddy told me. How do you get cousins?"

"Well, if your mother or father have brothers or sisters, and they have children, those children are your cousins."

Jessie digested this information with a frown of concentration. "Which are you?"

"It's complicated," Morgana said with a laugh, opting to rest against her car for a moment before getting in. "Ana's and Sebastian's and my father are all brothers. And our mothers are sisters. So we're kind of double cousins."

"That's neat. If I can't have cousins, maybe I can have a brother or sister. But my daddy says I'm a handful all by myself."

"I'm sure he's right," Morgana agreed as Ana chuckled. Brushing her hair back, Morgana glanced up. There, framed in one of the wide windows on the second floor of the house next door, was a man. Undoubtedly Jessie's father.

Ana had described him well enough, Morgana mused. Though he was more attractive, and certainly sexier, than her cousin had let on. That very simple omission made her smile. Morgana lifted a hand in a friendly wave. After a moment's hesitation, Boone returned the salute.

"That's my daddy." Jessie pinwheeled her arms in

greeting. "He works up there, but we haven't unpacked all the boxes yet."

"What does he do?" Morgana asked, since it was clear Ana wasn't going to.

"Oh, he tells stories. Really good stories, about witches and fairy princesses and dragons and magic fountains. I get to help sometimes. I have to go because tomorrow's my first day of school and he said I wasn't supposed to stay too long. Did I?"

"No." Ana bent down to kiss her cheek. "You can come back anytime."

"Bye!" And she was off, gamboling across the lawn, with the dog racing behind her.

"I've never been more charmed, or more worn out," Morgana said as she climbed into her car. "The girl's a delightful whirlwind." Smiling out at Ana, she jiggled her keys. "And the father is certainly no slouch."

"I imagine it's difficult, a man raising a little girl alone."

"From the one glimpse I had, he looked up to it." She gunned the engine. "Interesting that he writes stories. About witches and dragons and such. Sawyer, you said?"

"Yes." Ana blew tousled hair out of her eyes. "I guess he must be Boone Sawyer."

"It might intrigue him to know you're Bryna Donovan's niece—seeing as they're in the same line of work. That is, if you wanted to intrigue him."

"I don't," Ana said firmly.

"Ah, well, perhaps you already have." Morgana put the car in Reverse. "Blessed be, cousin."

Ana struggled with a frown as Morgana backed out of the drive.

* * *

After driving to Sebastian's to give his horses their morning feeding and grooming, Ana spent most of the next morning delivering her potpourris, her scented oils, her medicinal herbs and potions. Others were boxed and packaged for shipping. Though she had several local customers for her wares, including Morgana's shop, Wicca, a great portion of her clientele was outside the area.

Anastasia's was successful enough to suit her. The business she'd started six years before satisfied her needs and ambitions and allowed her the luxury of working at home. It wasn't for money. The Donovan fortune, and the Donovan legacy, kept both her and her family comfortably off. But, like Morgana with her shop and Sebastian with his many businesses, Ana needed to be productive.

She was a healer. But it was impossible to heal everyone. Long ago she had learned it was destructive to attempt to take on the ills and pains of the world. Part of the price of her power was knowing there was pain she could not alleviate. She did not reject her gift. She used it as she thought best.

Herbalism had always fascinated her, and she accepted the fact that she had the touch. Centuries before, she might have been the village wise woman—and that never failed to amuse her. In today's world, she was a businesswoman who could mix a bath oil or an elixir with equal skill.

If she added a touch of magic, it was hers to add.

And she was happy, happy with the destiny that had been thrust on her and with the life she had made from it.

Even if she'd been miserable, she thought, this day would have lifted her spirits. The beckoning sun, the caressing breeze, the faintest taste of rain in the air, rain that would not fall for hours—and then would fall gently.

Wanting to take advantage of the day, she decided to work outside, starting some herbs from seed.

He was watching her again. Bad habit, Boone thought with a grimace as he glanced down at the cigarette between his fingers. He wasn't having much luck with breaking bad habits. Nor was he getting a hell of a lot of work done since he'd looked out of the window and seen her outside.

She always looked so...elegant, he decided. A kind of inner elegance that wasn't the least diminished by the grass-stained cutoffs and short-sleeved T-shirt she wore.

It was in the way she moved, as if the air were wine that she drank lightly from as she passed through it.

Getting lyrical, he mused, and reminded himself to save it for his books.

Maybe it was because she was the fairy-princess type he so often wrote about. There was that ethereal, otherworldly air about her. And the quiet strength in her eyes. Boone had never believed that fairy princesses were pushovers.

But there was still this delicacy about her body—a body he sincerely wished he hadn't begun to dwell upon. Not a frailty, but a serene kind of femininity that he imagined would baffle and allure any male who was still breathing.

Boone Sawyer was definitely breathing.

Now what was she doing? he wondered, crushing out his cigarette impatiently and moving closer to the window. She'd gone into the garden shed and had come out again with her arms piled high with pots.

Wasn't it just like a woman to try to carry more than she should?

Even as he was thinking it, and indulging in a spot of male superiority, he saw Daisy streak across her lawn, chasing the sleek gray cat.

He had a hand on the window, prepared to shoot it up and call off the dog. Before he could make the move, he saw it was already too late.

In slow motion, it might have been an interesting and well-choreographed dance. The cat streaked like gray smoke between Ana's legs. She swayed. The clay pots in her arms teetered. Boone swore, then let out a sigh of relief when she righted them, and herself, again. Before the breath was out, Daisy plowed through, destroying the temporary balance. This time Ana's feet were knocked completely out from under her. She went down, and the pots went up.

Though he was already swearing, Boone heard the crash as he leapt through the terrace doors and down the steps to the lower deck.

She was muttering what sounded to him like exotic curses when he reached her. And he could hardly blame her. Her cat was up a tree, spitting down on the yipping dog. The pots she'd been carrying were little more than shards scattered over the grass and the edge of the patio where the impact had taken place.

Boone winced, cleared his throat. "Ah, are you all right?"

She was on her hands and knees, and her hair was over

her eyes. But she tossed it back and shot him a long look through the blond wisps. "Dandy."

"I was at the window." This certainly wasn't the time to admit he'd been watching her. "Passing by the window," he corrected. "I saw the chase and collision." Crouching down, he began to help her pick up the pieces. "I'm really sorry about Daisy. We've only had her a few days, and we haven't had any luck with training."

"She's a baby yet. No point in blaming a dog for doing what comes naturally."

"I'll replace the pots," he said, feeling miserably awkward.

"I have more." Because the barking and spitting were getting desperate, Ana sat back on her heels. "Daisy!" The command was quiet but firm, and it was answered instantly. Tail wagging furiously, the pup scrambled over to lick at her face and arms. Refusing to be charmed, Ana cupped the dog's face in her hands. "Sit," she ordered, and the puppy plopped her rump down obligingly. "Now behave yourself." With a little whine of repentance, Daisy settled down with her head on her paws.

Almost as impressed as he was baffled, Boone shook his head. "How'd you do that?"

"Magic," she said shortly, then relented with a faint smile. "You could say I've always had a way with animals. She's just happy and excited and roaring to play. You have to make her understand that some activities are inappropriate." Ana patted Daisy's head and earned an adoring canine glance.

"I've been trying bribery."

"That's good, too." She stretched out under a trellis

of scarlet clematis, looking for more broken crockery. It was then that Boone noticed the long scratch on her arm.

"You're bleeding."

She glanced down. There were nicks on her thighs, too. "Hard to avoid, with pots raining down on me."

He was on his feet in a blink and hauling Ana to hers. "Damn it, I asked you if you were all right."

"Well, really, I—"

"We'll have to clean it up." He saw there was more blood trickling down her legs, and he reacted exactly as he would if it were Jessie. He panicked. "Oh, Lord." He scooped an amazed Ana into his arms and hurried toward the closest door.

"Honestly, there's absolutely no need—"

"It's going to be fine, baby. We'll take care of it."

Half amused, half annoyed, Ana huffed out a breath as he pushed his way into the kitchen. "In that case, I'll cancel the ambulance. If you'd just put me—" He dropped her into one of the padded ice-cream chairs at her kitchen table. "Down."

Nerves jittering, Boone raced to the sink for a cloth. Efficiency, speed and cheer were the watchwords in such cases, he knew. As he dampened the cloth and squirted it with soap, he took several long breaths to calm himself.

"It won't look so bad when we get it cleaned up. You'll see." After pasting a smile on his face, he walked back to kneel in front of her. "I'm not going to hurt you." Gently he began to dab at the thin line of blood that had dripped down her calf. "We're going to fix it right up. Just close your eyes and relax." He took another long breath. "I knew this man once," he began, improvising a story as he always did for his daughter. "He lived in a place called Briarwood, where there was an enchanted castle behind a high stone wall."

Ana, who had been on the point of firmly telling him she could tend to herself, stopped and did indeed relax.

"Growing over the wall were thick vines with big, razor-sharp thorns. No one had been to the castle in more than a hundred years, because no one was brave enough to climb that wall and risk being scraped and pricked. But the man, who was very poor and lived alone, was curious, and day after day he would walk from his house to the wall and stand on the tips of his toes to see the sun gleam on the topmost towers and turrets of the castle."

Boone turned the cloth over and dabbed at the cuts. "He couldn't explain to anyone what he felt inside his heart whenever he stood there. He wanted desperately to climb over. Sometimes at night in his bed he would imagine it. Fear of those thick, sharp thorns stopped him, until one day in high summer, when the scent of flowers was so strong you couldn't take a breath without drinking it in, that glimpse of the topmost towers wasn't enough. Something in his heart told him that what he wanted most in the world lay just beyond that thorn-covered wall. So he began to climb it. Again and again he fell to the ground, with his hands and arms pricked and bleeding. And again and again he pushed himself up."

His voice was soothing, and his touch—his touch was anything but. As gentle as he was with the cool cloth, an ache began to spread, slow and warm, from the center of her body outward. He was stroking her thighs now, where the sharp edge of a shard had nicked the flesh. Ana closed her hand into a fist, the twin of which clenched in her stomach.

She needed him to stop. She wanted him to go on. And on.

"It took all of that day," Boone continued in that rich, mesmerizing storyteller's voice. "And the heat mixed sweat with the blood, but he didn't give up. Couldn't give up, because he knew, as he'd never known anything before, that his heart's desire, his future and his destiny, lay on the other side. So, with his hands raw and bleeding, he used those thorny vines and dragged himself to the top. Exhausted, filled with pain, he stumbled and fell down and down, to the thick, soft grass that flowed from the wall to the enchanted castle.

"The moon was up when he awoke, dazed and disoriented. With the last of his strength, he limped across the lawn, over the drawbridge and into the great hall of the castle that had haunted his dreams since childhood. When he crossed the threshold, the lights of a thousand torches flared. In that same instant, all his cuts and scrapes and bruises vanished. In that circle of flame that cast shadow and light up the white marble walls stood the most beautiful woman he had ever seen. Her hair was like sunlight, and her eyes like smoke. Even before she spoke, even before her lovely mouth curved in a welcoming smile, he knew that it was she he had risked his life to find. She stepped forward, offered her hand to him, and said only 'I have been waiting for you.'"

As he spoke the last words, Boone lifted his gaze to Ana's. He was as dazed and disoriented as the man in the story he had conjured up. When had his heart begun to pound like this? he wondered. How could he think when the blood was swimming in his head and throbbing in his loins? While he struggled for balance, he stared at her.

Hair like sunlight. Eyes like smoke.

And he realized he was kneeling between her legs, one hand resting intimately high on her thigh, and the other on the verge of reaching out to touch that sunlight hair.

Boone rose so quickly that he nearly overbalanced the table. "I beg your pardon," he said, for lack of anything better. When she only continued to stare at him, the pulse in her throat beating visibly, he tried again. "I got carried away when I saw you were bleeding. I've never been able to take Jessie's cuts and scrapes in stride." Struggling not to babble, he thrust the cloth at her. "I imagine you'd rather handle it yourself."

She accepted the cloth. She needed a moment before she dared speak. How was it possible that a man could stir her so desperately with doctoring and a fairy tale, then leave her fighting to find a slippery hold on her composure when he apologized?

Her own fault, Ana thought as she scrubbed—with more force than was really necessary—at the scrape on her arm. It was her gift and her curse that she would feel too much.

"You look like you should be the one sitting down," she told him briskly, then rose to go to the cupboard for one of her own medications. "Would you like something cold to drink?"

"No... Yes, actually." Though he doubted that a gallon of ice water would dampen the fire in his gut. "Blood always makes me panic."

"Panicked or not, you were certainly efficient." She poured him a glass of lemonade from the fat pitcher she fetched from the refrigerator. "And it was a very nice story." She was smiling now, more at ease.

"A story usually serves to calm both Jessie and me during a session with iodine and bandages."

"Iodine stings." She expertly dabbed a tobacco-brown liquid from a small apothecary jar onto her cleaned cuts. "I can give you something that won't, if you like. For your next emergency."

"What is it?" Suspicious, he sniffed at the jar. "Smells like flowers." And so did she.

"For the most part it is. Herbs, flowers, a dash of this and that." She set the bottle aside, capped it. "It's what you might call a natural antiseptic. I'm an herbalist."

"Oh."

She laughed at the skeptical look on his face. "That's all right. The majority of people only trust healing aids they can buy at the drugstore. They forget that people healed themselves quite well through nature for hundreds of years."

"They also died of lockjaw from a nick from a rusty nail."

"True enough," she agreed. "If they didn't have access to a reputable healer." Since she had no intention of trying to convert him, Ana changed the subject. "Did Jessie get off for her first day of school?"

"Yeah, she was raring to go. I was the one with the nervous stomach." His smile came and went. "I want to thank you for being so tolerant of her. I know she has a tendency to latch on to people. It doesn't cross her mind that they might not want to entertain her."

"Oh, but she entertains me." In an automatic gesture of courtesy, she took out a plate and lined it with cookies. "She's very welcome here. She's very sweet, unaffected and bright, and she doesn't forget her manners. You're doing a marvelous job raising her."

He accepted a cookie, watching her warily. "Jessie makes it easy."

"As delightful as she is, it can't be easy raising a child on your own. I doubt it's a snap even with two parents when the child is as energetic as Jessie. And as bright." Ana selected a cookie for herself and missed the narrowing of his eyes. "She must get her imagination from you. It must be delightful for her to have a father who writes such lovely stories."

His eyes sharpened. "How do you know what I do?"

The suspicion surprised her, but she smiled again. "I'm a fan—actually, an avid fan—of Boone Sawyer's."

"I don't recall telling you my first name."

"No, I don't believe you did," Ana said agreeably. "Are you always so suspicious of a compliment, Mr. Sawyer?"

"I had my reasons for settling quietly here." He set the half-empty glass down on the counter with a little clink. "I don't care for the idea of my neighbor interrogating my daughter, or digging into my business."

"Interrogating?" She nearly choked on the word. "Interrogating Jessie? Why would I?"

"To get to know a little more about the rich widower in the next house."

For one throbbing moment, she could only gape. "How

unbelievably arrogant! Believe me, I enjoy Jessie's company, and I don't find it necessary to bring you into the conversation."

What he considered her painfully transparent astonishment made him sneer. He'd handled her type before, but it was a disappointment, a damned disappointment, for Jessie. "Then it's odd that you'd know my name, that I'm a single parent, and my line of work, isn't it?"

She wasn't often angry. It simply wasn't her nature. But now she fought a short, vicious war with temper. "You know, I doubt very much you're worth an explanation, but I'm going to give you one, just to see how difficult it is for you to talk when you have to shove your other foot in your mouth." She turned. "Come with me."

"I don't want—"

"I said come with me." She strode out of the kitchen, fully certain he would follow.

Though annoyed and reluctant, he did. They moved through an archway and into a sun-drenched great room dotted with the charm of white wicker furniture and chintz. There were clusters of glinting crystals, charming statues of elves and sorcerers and faeries. Through another archway and into a cozy library with a small Adam fireplace and more mystical statuary.

There was a deep cushioned sofa in raspberry that would welcome an afternoon napper, daintily feminine lace curtains dancing in the breeze that teased through an arching window, and the good smell of books mixed with the airy fragrance of flowers.

Ana walked directly to a shelf, rising automatically to her toes to reach the desired volumes. *"The Milkmaid's*

Wish," she recited as she pulled out one book after another. *"The Frog, the Owl and the Fox. A Third Wish for Miranda."* She tossed a look over her shoulder, though tossing one of the books would have been more satisfactory. "It's a shame I have to tell you how much I enjoy your work."

Uncomfortable, he tucked his hands in his pockets. He was already certain he'd taken a wrong turn, and he was wondering if he could find a suitable way to backtrack. "It isn't often grown women read fairy tales for pleasure."

"What a pity. Though you hardly deserve the praise, I'll tell you that your work is lyrical and valuable, on both a child's and an adult's level." Far from mollified, she shoved two of the books back into place. "Then again, perhaps such things are in my blood. I was very often lulled to sleep by one of my aunt's stories. Bryna Donovan," she said, and had the pleasure of seeing his eyes widen. "I imagine you've heard of her."

Thoroughly chastised, Boone let out a long breath. "Your aunt." He flicked his gaze over the shelf and saw several of Bryna's stories of magic and enchanted lands alongside his. "We've actually corresponded a few times. I've admired her work for years."

"So have I. And when Jessie mentioned that her father wrote stories about fairy princesses and dragons, I concluded the Sawyer next door was Boone Sawyer. Grilling a six-year-old wasn't necessary."

"I'm sorry." No, actually, he was much more embarrassed than sorry, but that would have to do. "I had an… uncomfortable experience not long before we moved, and it's made me overly sensitive." He picked up a small, fluidly sculpted statue of an enchantress, turning it in his fingers as he spoke. "Jessie's kindergarten teacher...she pumped all sorts of information out of the kid. Which isn't too hard, really, since Jessie's pump's always primed."

He set the statue down again, all the more embarrassed that he felt this obligation to explain. "But she manipulated Jessie's feelings, her natural need for a mother figure, gave her all sorts of extra attention, requested several conferences to discuss Jessie's unusual potential, even going so far as to arrange a one-on-one with me over dinner where she... Suffice it to say she was more interested in an unattached male with a nice portfolio than she was in Jessie's feelings or her welfare. Jessie was very hurt by it."

Ana tapped a finger on the edge of one of his books before replacing it. "I imagine it was a difficult experience for both of you. But let me assure you, I'm not in the market for a husband. And, if I were, I wouldn't resort to manipulations and maneuvers. I'm afraid happy-ever-after has been too well indoctrinated in me for that."

"I'm sorry. After I get those feet out of my mouth, I'll try to come up with a better apology."

The way she lifted her brow told him he wasn't out of the woods yet. "I think the fact that we understand each other will do. Now I'm sure you want to get back to work, and so do I." She walked past him into a tiled foyer and opened the front door. "Tell Jessie to be sure to drop by and let me know how she likes school."

Here's your hat, what's your hurry, Boone thought as he stepped out. "I will. Take care of those scratches," he added, but she was already closing the door in his face.

Chapter 3

Good going, Sawyer. Shaking his head, Boone sat down in front of his word processor. First his dog knocks her down in her own yard, then our blundering hero barges into her house uninvited to play with her legs. To cap it, he insults her integrity and insinuates that she's using his daughter to try to trap him.

All in one fun-filled afternoon, he thought in disgust. It was a wonder she hadn't pitched him bodily out of her house rather than simply slamming the door in his face.

And why had he acted so stupidly? Past experience, true. But that wasn't the root of it, and he knew it.

Hormones, he decided with a half laugh. The kind of raging hormones better suited to a teenager than a grown man.

He'd looked up at her face in that sun-washed kitchen, feeling her skin warm under his hand, smelling that serenely seductive scent she exuded, and he'd wanted. He'd craved. For one blinding moment, he'd imagined with perfect clarity what it would be like to drag her off that curvy little chair, to feel that quick jerk-shudder of reaction as he devoured that incredibly soft-looking mouth.

That instant edge of desire had been so sharp, he'd needed to believe there was some outside force, some ploy or plot or plan to jumble his system so thoroughly.

Safest course, he realized with a sigh. Blame her.

Of course, he might have been able to dismiss the whole thing if it hadn't been for the fact that at that moment he'd looked up into her eyes and seen the same dreamy hunger he was feeling. And he'd felt the power, the mystery, the titanic sexuality, of a woman on the point of yielding.

His imagination had a great deal of punch, he knew. But what he'd seen, what he'd felt, had been utterly real.

For a moment, for just a moment, the tensions and needs had had that room humming like a harp string. Then he'd pulled back—as he should. A man had no business seducing his neighbor in her kitchen.

Now he'd very likely destroyed any chance of getting to know her better—just when he'd realized he very much wanted to get to know Miss Anastasia Donovan.

Pulling out a cigarette, Boone ran his fingers over it while he thought through various methods of redemption. When the light dawned, it was so simple he laughed out loud. If he'd been looking for a way into the fair maiden's heart—which he wasn't, exactly—it couldn't have been more perfect.

Pleased with himself, he settled down to work until it was time to pick up Jessie at school.

Conceited jerk. Ana worked off her temper with mortar and pestle. It was very satisfying to grind something—

even if it was only some innocent herbs—into a powder. Imagine. *Imagine* him having the idea that she was...on the make, she decided, sneering. As if she'd found him irresistible. As if she'd been pining away behind some glass wall waiting for her prince to come. So that she could snare him.

The gall of the man.

At least she'd had the satisfaction of thumbing her nose at him. And if closing a door in anyone's face was out of character for her, well, it had felt wonderful at the time.

So wonderful, in fact, that she wouldn't mind doing it again.

It was a damn shame he was so talented. And it couldn't be denied that he was a wonderful father. They were traits she couldn't help but admire. There was no denying he was attractive, magnetically sexual, with just a dash of shyness tossed in for sweetness, along with the wild tang of untamed male.

And those eyes, those incredible eyes that just about stopped your breath when they focused on you.

Ana scowled and tightened her grip on the pestle. Not that she was interested in any of that.

There might have been a moment in the kitchen, when he was stroking her flesh so gently and his voice blocked out all other sound, that she found herself drawn to him.

All right, aroused by him, she admitted. It wasn't a crime.

But he'd certainly shut that switch off quickly enough, and that was fine by her.

Beginning this instant, and from now on, she would think of him only as Jessica's father. She would be aloof if it killed her, friendly only to the point where it eased her relationship with the child.

She enjoyed having Jessie in her life, and she wasn't about to sacrifice that pleasure because of a basic and very well justified dislike of Jessie's father.

"Hi!"

There was that pixie face peeping through Ana's screen door. Even the dregs of temper were difficult to hold on to when she was faced with those big smiling eyes.

Ana set the mortar and pestle aside and smiled back. She supposed she had to be grateful that Boone hadn't let the altercation that afternoon influence him to keep Jessie away.

"Well, it looks like you survived your first day of school. Did school survive you?"

"Uh-huh. My teacher's name is Mrs. Farrell. She has gray hair and big feet, but she's nice, too. And I met Marcie and Tod and Lydia and Frankie, and lots of others. In the morning we—"

"Whoa." With a laugh, Ana held up both hands. "Maybe you should come in and sit down before you give me the day's events."

"I can't open the door, 'cause my hands are full."

"Oh." Ana obligingly pushed open the screen. "What have you got there?"

"Presents." On a huff of breath, Jessie dropped a package on the table. Then she held up a large crayon drawing. "We got to draw pictures today, and I made two. One for Daddy and one for you."

"For me?" Touched, Ana accepted the colorful drawing

on the thick beige paper that brought back some of her own school memories. "It's beautiful, sunshine."

"See, this is you." Jessie pointed out a figure with yellow hair. "And Quigley." Here a childish, but undeniably clever, depiction of a cat. "And all the flowers. The roses and the daisies and the lark things."

"Larkspur," Ana murmured, misty-eyed.

"Uh-huh. And all the others," Jessie continued. "I couldn't remember all the names. But you said you'd teach me."

"Yes, I will. It's just lovely, Jessie."

"I drew Daddy one of our new house with him standing out on the deck, because he likes to stand there best. He put it on the refrigerator."

"An excellent idea." Ana walked over to center the picture on the refrigerator door, anchoring it with magnets.

"I like to draw. My daddy draws real good, and he said my mommy drew even better. So I come by it naturally." Jessie slipped her hand into Ana's. "Are you mad at me?"

"No, sweetheart. Why would I be?"

"Daddy said Daisy knocked you down and broke your pots, and you got hurt." She studied the scratch on Ana's arm, then kissed it solemnly. "I'm sorry."

"It's all right. Daisy didn't mean it."

"She didn't mean to chew up Daddy's shoes, either, and make him say swear words."

Ana bit her lip. "I'm sure she didn't."

"Daddy yelled, and Daisy got so nervous she peed right on the rug. Then he chased her around and around the house, and it looked so funny that I couldn't stop laughing. And Daddy laughed, too. He said he was going to build a doghouse outside and put Daisy and me in it."

Ana lost any hope of taking it all seriously, and she laughed as she scooped Jessie up. "I think you and Daisy would have a great time in the doghouse. But if you'd like to save your father's shoes, why don't you let me help you work with her?"

"Do you know how? Can you teach her tricks and everything?"

"Oh, I imagine. Watch." She shifted Jessie to her hip and called Quigley out from his nap beneath the kitchen table. The cat rose reluctantly, stretched his front legs, then his back, then padded out. "Okay, sit." Heaving a feline sigh, he did. "Up." Resigned, Quigley rose on his haunches and pawed the air like a circus tiger. "Now, if you do your flip, I might just open a can of tuna fish later, for your dinner."

The cat seemed to be debating with himself. Then— perhaps because the trick was small potatoes compared to tuna—he leapt up, arching his back and flipping over to land lightly on his feet. While Jessie crowed with laughter and applauded, Quigley modestly cleaned his paws.

"I didn't know cats could do tricks."

"Quigley's a very special cat." Ana set Jessie down to give Quigley a stroking. He purred like a freight train, nuzzling his face against her knee. "His family's in Ireland, like most of mine."

"Does he get lonely?"

Smiling, Ana scratched under Quigley's jaw. "We have each other. Now, would you like a snack while you tell me about the rest of your day?"

Jessie hesitated, tempted. "I don't think I can, 'cause it's close to dinner, and Daddy— Oh, I almost forgot." She rushed back to the table to pick up a package wrapped in candy-striped paper. "This is for you, from Daddy."

"From..." Unconsciously Ana linked her hands behind her back. "What is it?"

"I know." Jessie grinned, her eyes snapping with excitement. "But I can't tell. Telling spoils the surprise. You have to open it." Jessie picked it up and thrust it at Ana. "Don't you like presents?" Jessie asked when Ana kept her hands clasped tight behind her back. "I like them best of anything, and Daddy always gives really good ones."

"I'm sure he does, but I—"

"Don't you like Daddy?" Jessie's lower lip poked out. "Are you mad at him because Daisy broke your pots?"

"No, no, I'm not mad at him." Not for the broken pots, anyway. "It wasn't his fault. And, yes, of course I like him— That is, I don't know him very well, and I..." Caught, Ana decided, and she worked up a smile. "I'm just surprised to get a present when it's not my birthday." To please the child, Ana took the gift and shook it. "Doesn't rattle," she said, and Jessie clapped and giggled.

"Guess! Guess what it is!"

"Ah...a trombone?"

"No, no, trombones are too big." Excitement had her bouncing. "Open it. Open it and see."

It was the child's reaction that had her own heart beating a shade too fast, Ana assured herself. To please Jessie, she ripped the paper with a flourish. "Oh."

It was a book, a child's oversize book with a snowy white cover. On the front was a beautiful illustration of a golden-haired woman wearing a sparkling crown and flowing blue robes.

"The Faerie Queen," Ana read. "By Boone Sawyer."

"It's brand-new," Jessie told her. "You can't even buy it yet, but Daddy gets his copies early." She ran a hand gently over the picture. "I told him she looks like you."

"It's a lovely gift," Ana said with a sigh. And a sneaky one. How was she supposed to stay irritated with him now?

"He wrote something inside for you." Too impatient to wait, Jessie opened the cover herself. "See, right there."

To Anastasia, with hopes that a magic tale works as well as a white flag. Boone.

Her lips curved. It was impossible to prevent it. How could anyone refuse a truce so charmingly requested?

Which was, of course, what Boone was counting on. As he shoved a packing box out of his way with his foot, he glanced through the window toward the house next door. Not a peep.

He imagined it might take a few days for Ana to calm down, but he thought he'd made a giant stride in the right direction. After all, he didn't want any antagonism between himself and Jessie's new friend.

Turning back to the stove, he lowered the heat on the boneless chicken breasts he had simmering, then deftly began to mash potatoes.

Jessie's number one favorite, he thought, as he sent the beaters whirling. They could have mashed potatoes every night for a year and the kid wouldn't complain. Of course, it was up to him to vary the menu, to make sure she got a healthy meal every night.

Boone poured in more milk and grimaced. He had to admit, if there was one part of parenting he would cheerfully give up, it was the pressure of deciding what they were to eat night after night.

He didn't mind cooking it so much, it was that daily decision between pot roast, baked chicken, pork chops and all the others. Plus what to serve with it. Out of desperation, he'd begun to clip recipes—secretly—in hopes of adding some variety.

At one time he'd seriously considered hiring a housekeeper. Both his mother and his mother-in-law had urged him to, and then they'd gone into one of their competitive huddles on how to choose the proper woman to fit the bill. But the idea of having someone in the house, someone who might gradually take over the rearing of his daughter, had deterred him.

Jessie was his. One hundred percent his. Despite dinner decisions and grocery shopping, that was the way he liked it.

As he added a generous slice of butter to the creamy potatoes, he heard her footsteps racing across the deck.

"Good timing, frog face. I was just about to give you a whistle." He turned, licking potatoes from his finger and saw Ana standing in the doorway, one hand on Jessie's shoulder. The muscles in his stomach tightened so quickly that he nearly winced. "Well, hello."

"I didn't mean to interrupt your cooking," Ana began. "I just wanted to thank you for the book. It was very nice of you to send it over."

"I'm glad you like it." He realized he had a dishcloth tucked in his jeans and hastily tugged it out. "It was the best peace offering I could think of."

"It worked." She smiled, charmed by the sight of him hovering busily over a hot stove. "Thanks for thinking of me. Now, I'd better get out of your way so you can finish cooking your dinner."

"She can come in, can't she?" Jessie was already tugging on Ana's hand. "Can't she, Daddy?"

"Sure. Please." He shoved a box out of her way. "We haven't finished unpacking yet. It's taking longer than I thought it would."

Out of politeness, and curiosity, Ana stepped inside. There were no curtains on the window as yet, and a few packing boxes littered the stone-colored floor tiles. But ranged along the royal blue countertop there was a glossy ceramic cookie jar in the shape of Alice's white rabbit, a teapot of the mad hatter, and a dormouse sugar bowl. Pot holders, obviously hooked by a child's hand, hung on little brass hooks. The refrigerator's art gallery was crowded with Jessie's drawings, and the puppy was snoozing in the corner.

Unpacked and tidy, no, she thought. But this was already a home.

"It's a great house," she commented. "I wasn't surprised when it sold quickly."

"You want to see my room?" Jessie tugged on Ana's hand again. "I have a bed with a roof on it, and lots of stuffed animals."

"You can take Ana up later," Boone put in. "Now you should go wash your hands."

"Okay." She looked imploringly at Ana. "Don't go."

"How about a glass of wine?" Boone offered when his daughter raced off. "A good way to seal a truce."

"All right." Drawings rustled as he opened the fridge. "Jessie's quite an artist. It was awfully sweet of her to draw a picture for me."

"Careful, or you'll have to start papering the walls with them." He hesitated, the bottle in his hand, wondering where he'd put the wineglasses, or if he'd unpacked them at all. A quick search through cupboards made it clear that he hadn't. "Can you handle chardonnay in a Bugs Bunny glass?"

She laughed. "Absolutely." She waited for him to pour hers, and his—Elmer Fudd. "Welcome to Monterey," she said, raising Bugs in a toast.

"Thanks." When she lifted the glass to her lips and smiled at him over the rim, he lost his train of thought. "I... Have you lived here long?"

"All my life, on and off." The scent of simmering chicken and the cheerful disarray of the kitchen were so homey that she relaxed. "My parents had a home here, and one in Ireland. They're based in Ireland for the most part now, but my cousins and I settled here. Morgana was born in the house she lives in, on Seventeen Mile Drive. Sebastian and I were born in Ireland, in Castle Donovan."

"Castle Donovan."

She laughed a little. "It sounds pretentious. But it actually is a castle, quite old, quite lovely, and quite remote. It's been in the Donovan family for centuries."

"Born in an Irish castle," he mused. "Maybe that explains why the first time I saw you I thought, well, there's the faerie queen, right next door in the rosebushes." His smiled faded, and he spoke without thinking. "You took my breath away."

The glass stopped halfway to her lips. Those lips parted in surprised confusion. "I…" She drank to give herself a moment to think. "I suppose part of your gift would be imagining faeries under bushes, elves in the garden, wizards in the treetops."

"I suppose." She smelled as lovely as the breeze that brought traces of her garden and hints of the sea through his windows. He stepped closer, surprised and not entirely displeased to see the alarm in her eyes. "How's that scratch? Neighbor." Gently he cupped his hand around her arm, skimmed his thumb up until he felt the pulse inside her elbow skitter. Whatever was affecting him was damn well doing the same to her. His lips curved. "Hurt?"

"No." Her voice thickened, baffling her, arousing him. "No, of course it doesn't."

"You still smell of flowers."

"The salve—"

"No." The knuckles of his free hand skimmed just under her chin. "You always smell of flowers. Wildflowers and sea foam."

How had she come to be backed against the counter, his body brushing hers, his mouth so close, so temptingly close, that she could all but taste it?

And she wanted that taste, wanted it with a sudden staggering force that wiped every other thought out of her head. Slowly, her eyes on his, she brought her hand to his chest, spread it over his heart where the beat was strong. Strong and wild.

And so would the kiss be, she thought. Strong and wild, from the first instant.

As if to assure her of that, he grabbed a fistful of her hair, tangling his fingers in it. It was warm, as he'd known it would be, warm as the sunlight it took its shade from. For a moment, his entire being was focused on the kiss to come, the reckless pleasure of it. His mouth was a breath from hers, and her sigh was already filling him, when he heard his daughter's feet clattering on the stairs.

Boone jolted back as if she'd burned him. Speechless, they stared at each other, both of them stunned by what had nearly happened and by the force behind it.

What was he doing? Boone asked himself. Grabbing a woman in his kitchen when there was chicken on the stove, potatoes going cold on the counter and his little girl about to skip into the room?

"I should go." Ana set down her glass before it could slip out of her trembling hand. "I really only meant to stay a minute."

"Ana." He shifted, blocking the way in case she sprinted for the door. "I have a feeling what just happened here was out of character for both of us. That's interesting, don't you think?"

She lifted those solemn gray eyes to his. "I don't know your character."

"Well, I don't make a habit of seducing women in the kitchen when my daughter's upstairs. And I certainly don't make a habit out of wanting the hell out of a woman the minute I lay eyes on her."

She wished she hadn't set the wine down. Her throat

was bone dry. "I suppose you want me to say I'll take your word for it. But I won't."

Both anger and challenge sparkled in his eyes. "Then I'll have to prove it to you, won't I?"

"No, you—"

"My hands are clean, clean, clean." Blissfully unaware of the tension shimmering in the air, Jessie danced into the kitchen, palms held out for inspection. "How come they have to be clean when I don't eat with my fingers anyway?"

Effortfully, he pulled himself back and tweaked his daughter's nose. "Because germs like to sneak off little girls' hands and into their mashed potatoes."

"Yuck." She made a face, then grinned. "Daddy makes the best mashed potatoes in the whole wide world. Don't you want some? She can stay for dinner, can't she, Daddy?"

"Really, I—"

"Of course she can." Mirroring his daughter's grin— but with something a great deal more dangerous in his eyes—Boone studied Ana. "We'd love to have you. We have plenty. And I think it would be a good idea for us to get to know each other. Before."

She didn't have to ask before what. That was crystal-clear. But, no matter how she tried, she couldn't make her temper overtake the quick panicked excitement. "It's very nice of you to ask," she said with admirable calm. "I wish I could, but—" She smiled down at Jessie's sound of disappointment. "I have to drive out to my cousin's and take care of his horses."

"Will you take me with you sometime, so I can see them?"

"If your father says it's all right." She bent down and kissed Jessie's sulky lips. "Thank you for my picture, sunshine. It's beautiful." Taking a cautious step away, she looked at Boone. "And the book. I know I'll enjoy it. Good night."

Ana didn't run out of the house, though she freely admitted she wasn't leaving so much as escaping. Back home, she went through the motions, giving Quigley his promised tuna, then changing into jeans and a denim shirt for the drive to Sebastian's house.

She was going to have to do some thinking, she decided as she pulled on her boots. Some serious thinking. Weigh the pros and cons, consider the consequences. She had to laugh, thinking how Morgana would roll her eyes and accuse her of being impossibly Libran.

Perhaps her birth sign was partially responsible for the fact that Ana could always see and sympathize with both sides of an argument. It complicated matters as often as it solved them. But in this case she was quite certain that a clear head and calm deliberation were the order of the day.

Maybe she was unusually attracted to Boone. And the physical aspect of it was completely unprecedented. Certainly she'd felt desire for a man before, but never this quick, sharp edge of it. And a sharp edge usually meant a deep wound to follow.

That was certainly something to consider. Frowning, she grabbed a jean jacket and started downstairs.

Of course, she was an adult, unattached, unencumbered, and perfectly free to entertain the thought of a relationship with an equally free adult man.

Then again, she knew just how devastating relationships could be when people were unable to accept others for what they were.

Still debating, she swung out of the house. She certainly didn't owe Boone any explanations. She was under no obligation to try to make him understand her heritage, as she had tried to do years before with Robert. Even if they became involved, she wouldn't have to tell him.

Ana got into her car and backed out of the drive, her thoughts shifting back and forth.

It wasn't deception to hold part of yourself back. It was self-preservation—as she'd learned through hard experience. And it was foolish even to be considering that angle when she hadn't decided if she wanted to be involved.

No, that wasn't quite true. She wanted. It was more a matter of deciding if she could afford to become involved.

He was, after all, her neighbor. A relationship gone sour would make it very uncomfortable when they lived in such close proximity.

And there was Jessie to consider. She was half in love with the girl already. She wouldn't want to risk that friendship and affection by indulging her own needs. Purely physical needs, Ana told herself as she followed the winding road along the coast.

True, Boone would be able to offer her some physical pleasure. She didn't doubt that for a moment. But the emotional cost would just be too steep for everyone involved.

It would be better, much better, for everyone involved

if she remained Jessie's friend while maintaining a wise distance from Jessie's father.

Dinner was over, and the dishes were done. There had been a not-too-successful session with Daisy—though she would sit down if you pushed on her rump. Afterward, there'd been a lot of splashing in the tub, then some horseplay to indulge in with his freshly scrubbed daughter. There was a story to be told, that last glass of water to be fetched.

Once Jessie was asleep and the house was quiet, Boone indulged himself with a brandy out on the deck. There were piles of forms on his desk—a parent's homework—that had to be filled out for Jessie's school files.

He'd do them before he turned in, he decided. But this hour, this dark, quiet hour when the nearly full moon was rising, was his.

He could enjoy the clouds that were drifting overhead, promising rain, the hypnotic sound of the water lapping against rock, the chatter of insects in the grass that he would have to mow very soon, and the scent of night-blooming flowers.

No wonder he had snapped this house up at the very first glimpse. No place he'd ever been had relaxed him more, or given him more of a sense of rightness and peace. And it appealed to his imagination. The mystically shaped cypress, the magical ice plants that covered the banks, those empty and often eerie stretches of night beach.

The ethereally beautiful woman next door.

He smiled to himself. For someone who hadn't felt much more than an occasional twinge for a woman in too long to remember, he was certainly feeling a barrage of them now.

It had taken him a long time to get over Alice. Though he still didn't consider himself part of the dating pool, he hadn't been a monk over the past couple of years. His life wasn't empty, and he'd been able, after a great deal of pain, to accept the fact that he had to live it.

He was sipping his brandy, enjoying it and the simple pleasure of the night, when he heard Ana's car. Not that he'd been waiting for it, Boone assured himself even as he checked his watch. He couldn't quite smother the satisfaction at her being home early, too early to have gone out on a date.

Not that her social life was any of his business.

He couldn't see her driveway, but because the night was calm he heard her shut her car door. Then, a few moments later, he heard her open and close the door to her house.

Propping his bare feet on the rail of the deck, he tried to imagine her progress through the house. Into the kitchen. Yes, the light snapped on, and he could see her move past the window. Brewing tea, perhaps, or pouring herself a glass of wine.

Shortly, the light switched off again, and he let his mind follow her through the house. Up the stairs. More lights, but it looked to Boone like the glow of a candle against the dark glass, rather than a lamp. Moments later, he heard the faint drift of music. Harp strings. Haunting, romantic, and somehow sad.

Briefly, very briefly, she was silhouetted against a window. He could see quite clearly that slim feminine shadow as she stripped out of her shirt.

Hastily he swallowed brandy and looked away. However tempting it might be, he wouldn't lower himself to the level of a Peeping Tom. He did, however, find himself craving a cigarette, and with apologies to his disapproving daughter he pulled one out of his pocket.

Smoke stung the air, soothed his nerves. Boone contented himself with the sound of harpsong.

It was a very long time before he went back into the house and slept, with the sound of a gentle rain falling on the roof and the memory of harpsong drifting across the night breeze.

Chapter 4

Cannery Row was alive with sounds, the chattering of people as they strolled or rushed, the bright ringing of a bell from one of the tourist bikes, the ubiquitous calling of gulls searching for a handout. Ana enjoyed the crowds and the noise as much as she enjoyed the peace and solitude of her own backyard.

Patiently she chugged along with the stream of weekend traffic. On her first pass by Morgana's shop, Ana resigned herself to the fact that the perfect day had brought tourists and locals out in droves. Parking was going to be at a premium. Rather than frustrate herself searching for a spot on the street, she pulled into a lot three blocks from Wicca.

As she climbed out to open her trunk, she heard the whine of a cranky toddler and the frustrated muttering of weary parents.

"If you don't stop that right this minute, you won't get

anything at all. I mean it, Timothy. We've had just about enough. Now get moving."

The child's response to that command was to go limp, sliding in a boneless heap onto the parking lot as his mother tugged uselessly at his watery arms. Ana bit her lip as it curved, but it was obvious the young parents didn't see the humor of it. Their arms were full of packages, and their faces were thunderous.

Timothy, Ana thought, was about to get a tanning—though it was unlikely to make him more cooperative. Daddy shoved his bags at Mommy and, mouth grim, bent down.

It was a small thing, Ana thought. And they all looked so tired and unhappy. She made the link first with the father, felt the love, the anger, and the dark embarrassment. Then with the child—confusion, fatigue, and a deep unhappiness over a big stuffed elephant he'd seen in a shop window and been denied.

Ana closed her eyes. The father's hand swung back as he prepared to administer a sharp slap to the boy's diaper-padded rump. The boy sucked in his breath, ready to emit a piercing wail at the indignity of it.

Suddenly the father sighed, and his hand fell back to his side. Timothy peeked up, his face hot and pink and tear-streaked.

The father crouched down, holding out his arms. "We're tired, aren't we?"

On a hiccuping sob, Timothy bundled into them and rested his heavy head on his daddy's shoulder. "Thirsty."

"Okay, champ." The father's hand went to the child's bottom, but with a soothing pat. He gave his teary-eyed wife an encouraging smile. "Why don't we go have a nice, cold drink? He just needs an n-a-p."

They moved off, tired but relieved.

Smiling to herself, Ana unlocked her trunk. Family vacations, she thought, weren't all fun and frolic. The next time they were ready to snarl at each other, she wouldn't be around to help. She imagined they'd muddle through without her.

After swinging her purse behind her back, she began to unload the boxes she was delivering to Morgana. There were a half dozen of them, filled with sacks of potpourri, bottles of oils and creams, beribboned sachets, satiny sleep pillows and a month's supply of special orders that ran from tonics to personalized perfumes.

Ana considered making two trips, gauged the distance and decided that if she balanced the load carefully she could make it in one.

She stacked, juggled and adjusted, then just managed to shut her trunk with an elbow. She made it across the parking lot and down half a block before she began berating herself.

Why did she always do this? she asked herself. Two comfortable trips were better than one difficult one. It wasn't that the boxes were so heavy—though they were. It was simply that they were awkward and the sidewalk was jammed. And her hair was blowing in her eyes. With a quick, agile dance, she managed, barely, to avoid a collision with a couple of teenage tourists in a surrey.

"Want some help?"

Annoyed with herself and irresponsible drivers, she turned around. There was Boone, looking particularly wonderful in baggy cotton slacks and shirt. Riding atop his shoulders, Jessie was laughing and clapping her hands.

"We had a ride on the carousel and had ice cream and we saw you."

"Looks like you're still overloading," Boone commented.

"They're not heavy."

He patted Jessie's leg and, following the signal, she began to slide down his back. "We'll give you a hand."

"That's all right." She knew it was foolish to reject help when she needed it, but she had managed quite success-fully to avoid Boone for the better part of a week. And had managed—almost as successfully—to avoid think-ing about him. Wondering about him. "I don't want to take you out of your way."

"We're not going any way in particular, are we, Jessie?"

"Uh-uh. We're just wandering today. It's our day off."

Ana couldn't prevent the smile, any more than she could prevent the wariness from creeping into her eyes when she looked back at Boone. He was certainly look-ing at her, she realized, in that disconcertingly thorough way of his. The smile creeping around his mouth had less to do with humor than it did with challenge.

"I don't have to go far," she began, grabbing at a pack-age that was beginning to slide. "I can just—"

"Fine." Overriding her objections, Boone shifted boxes from her arms to his. His eyes stayed on hers. "What are neighbors for?"

"I can carry one." Eager to help, Jessie bounced in her sneakers. "I can."

"Thank you." Ana handed Jessie the lightest box. "I'm going a couple of blocks down to my cousin's shop."

"Has she had her babies?" Jessie asked as they started to walk.

"No, not yet."

"I asked Daddy how come she got to have two in there, and he said sometimes there's twice the love."

How could anyone possibly have a defense against a man like this? Ana wondered. Her eyes were warm when they met his. "Yes, sometimes there is. You always seem to have the right answer," she murmured to Boone.

"Not always." He wasn't certain if he was relieved or annoyed that his hands were full of boxes. If they'd been free, he would have been compelled to touch her. "You just try for the best one at the time. Where have you been hiding, Anastasia?"

"Hiding?" The warmth fled from her eyes.

"I haven't seen you out in your yard in days. You didn't strike me as the type to scare that easily."

Because Jessie was skipping just ahead of them, she bit off a more acid response. "I don't know what you mean. I had work. Quite a bit of it, as a matter of fact." She nodded toward the boxes. "You're carrying some of it now."

"Is that so? Then I'm glad I didn't resort to knocking on your door and pretending I needed to borrow a cup of sugar. I nearly did, but it seemed so obvious."

She slanted him a look. "I appreciate your restraint."

"And so you should."

She merely tossed her hair out of her eyes and called to Jessie. "We'll go down this way, so we can go in the back. Saturdays are usually busy," she explained to Boone. "I don't like going through the shop and distracting the customers."

"What does she sell, anyway?"

"Oh." Ana smiled again. "This and that. I think you'd find her wares particularly interesting. Here we go." She gestured to a little flagstone stoop flanked by pots of bloodred geraniums. "Can you get the door, Jessie?"

"Okay." Anxious as ever to see what was on the other side, Jessie shoved it open, then let out a squeal. "Oh, look. Daddy, look!" Jessie set her package aside on the first available space and made a dive for the big white cat grooming herself on the table.

"Jessica!" Boone's voice was short and firm, stopping his daughter in midstride. "What have I told you about going up to strange animals?"

"But, Daddy, he's so pretty."

"She," Ana corrected as she laid her boxes on the counter. "And your father's quite right. Not all animals like little girls."

Jessie's fingers itched to stroke the thick white fur. "Does she?"

"Sometimes Luna doesn't like anyone." With a laugh, Ana scratched the cat between the ears. "But if you're very polite, and pet her when she gives the royal consent, you'll get along well enough." Ana gave Boone a reassuring smile. "Luna won't scratch her. When she's had enough, she'll just stalk off."

But apparently Luna was in the mood for attention. Walking to the end of the table, she rubbed her head against the hand Jessie had held out. "She likes me!" The smile nearly split her face in two. "See, Daddy, she likes me."

"Yes, I see."

"Morgana usually keeps cold drinks back here." Ana opened the small refrigerator. "Would you like something?"

"Sure." He really wasn't thirsty, but the offer made it easy to linger. He leaned back against the counter of the kitchenette while Ana got out glasses. "The shop through there?"

When he gestured at a door, Ana nodded. "Yes. And through there's the storeroom. A great deal of what Morgana sells is one-of-a-kind, so she doesn't keep a large supply of inventory."

He reached over Ana's shoulder to finger the thin leaves of a rosemary plant on the windowsill. "She into this kind of thing, too?"

Ana tried to ignore the fact that his body was brushing hers. She could smell the sea on him, and imagined he and Jessie had gone down to feed the gulls. "What kind of thing?"

"Herbs and stuff."

"In a manner of speaking." She turned, knowing she'd be entirely too close, and pushed the glass into his chest. "Root beer."

"Terrific." He knew it wasn't particularly fair—and it was probably unwise, as well—but he took the glass and stood precisely where he was. She had to tilt her head back to meet his eyes. "It might be a good hobby for Jessie and me. Maybe you could show us how to grow some."

"It's no different from growing any living thing." It took a great deal of effort to keep her voice even when breathing was so difficult. "Care and attention, and affection. You're very much in my way, Boone."

"I hope so." With his eyes very intense, very focused, he lifted a hand to her cheek. "Anastasia, I really think we need to—"

"A deal's a deal, babe." The smug voice carried through the door as it opened. "Fifteen minutes of sit-down time every two hours."

"You're being ridiculous. For heaven's sake, you act as though I'm the only pregnant woman in the world." Heaving a sigh, Morgana walked into the back room. Her brows lifted when she saw the trio—and particularly when she saw the way Boone Sawyer was caging her cousin at the rear counter.

"You're the only pregnant woman in my world." Nash stopped short. "Hey, Ana, you're just the woman I need to convince Morgana to take it easy. Now that you're here, I can..." He glanced once at the man beside her, then back again to focus. "Boone? Well, I'll be damned. Boone Sawyer, you son of a—" He caught himself, mostly because Morgana shot an elbow into his ribs. There was a little girl, all eyes, standing at the table. "Gun," he finished, and strode across the room to shake Boone's hand and slap his back in a typical male greeting. "What are you doing here?"

"Delivering stock, I think." He grinned, gripping Nash's hand hard in his. "How about you?"

"Trying to keep my wife in line. Lord, what's it been? Four years?"

"Just about."

Morgana folded her hands on her belly. "I take it you two know each other?"

"Sure we do. Boone and I met at a writers' conference. It has to be ten years ago, doesn't it? I haven't seen you since—" Since Alice's funeral, Nash remembered abruptly. And he remembered, too, the devastation, the despair and the disbelief in Boone's eyes as he'd stood beside his wife's grave. "How are you?"

"Okay." Understanding, Boone smiled. "We're okay."

"Good." Nash put a hand on Boone's shoulder and squeezed before he turned to Jessie. "And you're Jessica."

"Uh-huh." She beamed up at him, always interested in meeting someone new. "Who are you?"

"I'm Nash." He crossed to her, crouched down. Except for the eyes, eyes that were all Boone, she was the image of Alice. Bright, pretty, pixielike. He offered her a formal handshake. "It's nice to meet you."

She giggled and shook his hand. "Did you put the babies into Morgana?"

To his credit, he was speechless only for a moment. "Guilty." With a laugh, he picked her up. "But I'm leaving it up to Ana to get them out. So, what are the two of you doing in Monterey?"

"We live here now," Jessie told him. "Right next door to Ana's house."

"No kidding?" Nash grinned over at Boone. "When?"

"A little more than a week. I'd heard you'd moved here, and I figured I'd look you up once we got things together. I didn't realize you were married to my neighbor's cousin."

"A small and fascinating world, isn't it?" Morgana commented. She tilted her head at Ana, well aware that her cousin hadn't said a word since they'd come into the room. "Since no one's going to introduce me, I'm Morgana."

"Sorry," Nash said, jiggling Jessie on his hip. "Sit down."

"I'm perfectly—"

"Sit." This from Ana as she pulled out a chair.

"Outnumbered." Sighing, Morgana sat. "Are you enjoying Monterey?"

"Very much," Boone told her, and his gaze shifted to Ana. "More than I anticipated."

"I always enjoy having more than I anticipated." With a light laugh, she patted her belly. "We'll all have to get together very soon, so you can tell me things Nash doesn't want me to know."

"I'd be glad to."

"Babe, you know I'm an open book." He kissed the top of Morgana's head and winked at Ana. "That the stuff Morgana's been waiting for?"

"Yes, all of it." Anxious to keep her hands busy, Ana turned to the pile of boxes. "I'll unpack it for you. Morgana, I want you to try out this new violet body lotion before you put it out, and I brought extra of the soapwort shampoo."

"Good, I'm completely out." She took the bottle of lotion from Ana and unstopped the bottle. "Nice scent." She dabbed a bit on the back of her hand and rubbed it in. "Good texture."

"Sweet violets, and the Irish moss Da sent me." She glanced up from her unpacking. "Nash, why don't you show Jessie and Boone the shop?"

"Good idea. I think you're going to find a lot of this right up your alley," Nash told Boone as he led the way to the door.

Boone shot a look over his shoulder before he passed through. "Anastasia." He waited until she glanced up from the boxes. "Don't run away."

"My, my, my." Morgana settled back and smiled like a cat with a direct line to Bossy. "Want to fill me in?"

With a little more force than necessary, Ana ripped through packing tape. "On what?"

"On you and your gorgeous neighbor, of course."

"There's nothing to fill in."

"Darling, I know you. When I walked into this room, you were so wrapped up in him I could have called out a tornado and you wouldn't have blinked."

Ana busied herself unpacking bottles. "Don't be ridiculous. You haven't called out a tornado since the first time we saw *The Wizard of Oz.*"

"Ana." Morgana's voice was low and firm. "I love you."

"I know. I love you, too."

"You're never nervous. Perhaps that's why it's so fascinating—and concerning—to me that you're so nervous just now."

"I'm not." She rapped two bottles together and winced. "All right, all right, all right. I have to think about it." She whipped around. "He makes me nervous, and it would be ridiculous to deny it's the fact that I'm very attracted to him that's making me so nervous. I just have to think about it."

"Think about what?"

"How to handle it. Him, I mean. I have no intention of making another mistake, particularly since anything I do that involves Boone also involves Jessie."

"Oh, honey, are you falling in love with him?"

"That's absurd." Ana realized too late that the denial was too forceful to be taken at face value. "I'm just jumpy, that's all. I haven't had a man affect me like this, physically, in…" Ever. Never before, and, she was very much afraid, never again. "In a long time. I just need to think," she repeated.

"Ana." Morgana held out both hands. "Sebastian and Mel will be back in a couple of days from their honeymoon. Why don't you ask him to look? It would relieve your mind if you knew."

Resolute, Ana shook her head. "No…not that I haven't considered it. Whatever happens, however it happens, I want it to be on equal terms. Knowing would give me an unfair advantage over Boone. I have a feeling those equal terms would be important, to both of us."

"You know best. Let me tell you something, as a woman." Her lips curved. "As a witch. Knowing, not knowing, makes no difference with a man, once he touches your heart. No difference at all."

Ana nodded. "Then I'll have to make sure he doesn't touch mine until I'm ready."

"This is incredible," Boone was saying as he surveyed Wicca. "Just incredible."

"I thought so, too, the first time I walked in." Nash picked up a crystal wand tipped at the end with a spear of amethyst. "I guess people in our line of work are suckers for this stuff."

"Fairy tales," Boone agreed, accepting the wand before running a finger over a bronze cast of a snarling wolf. "Or the occult. A fine line between the two. Your last movie chilled my blood even when it made me laugh."

Nash grinned. "The humor in horror."

"Nobody does it better." He glanced over at his daughter. She was staring at a miniature silver castle surrounded by a moat of rainbow glass, her eyes huge, her hands behind her back. "I'll never get out of here empty-handed."

"She's beautiful," Nash said, wondering, as he often did, about the children that would be his before much longer.

"Looks like her mother." He saw the question and the concern in his friend's eyes. "Grief passes, Nash, whether you want it to or not. Alice was a wonderful part of my life, and she gave me the best thing in it. I'm grateful for every moment I had with her." He set the wand down. "Now I'd like to know how you—the world's most determined bachelor—came to be married and expecting twins."

"Research." Nash grinned and rocked back on his heels. "I wanted to get out of L.A., and keep within commuting distance. I'd only been here a short time when I needed to do some research on a script. I walked in here, and there she was."

There was more, of course. A great deal more. But it wasn't Nash's place to tell Boone about the Donovan legacy. Not even if Boone would have believed him.

"When you decide to take the plunge, you take it big."

"You, too. Indiana's a long way from here."

"I didn't want to be able to commute," Boone said with a grimace. "My parents, Alice's parents. Jessie and I were becoming their life's work. And I wanted a change, for both of us."

"Next door to Ana, huh?" Nash narrowed his eyes. "The redwood place, with all the glass and decks?"

"That's the one."

"Good choice." He glanced toward Jessie again. She'd wandered around the shop and had worked her way back to the little castle. She hadn't once asked for it, and that made the naked desire in her eyes all the more effective. "If you don't buy her that, I will."

When Ana came out to restock a few shelves for Morgana, she saw not only the silver castle being rung up on the counter, but the wand, a three-foot sculpture of a winged fairy she'd had her eye on herself, a crystal suncatcher in the shape of a unicorn, a pewter wizard holding a many-faceted ball, and a baseball-sized geode.

"We're weak," Boone said with a quick, sheepish grin as Ana lifted a brow. "No willpower."

"But excellent taste." She ran a fingertip over the fairy wings. "Lovely, isn't she?"

"One of the best I've seen. I figured I'd put her in my office for inspiration."

"Good idea." She bent over a compartment containing tumbling stones. "Malachite, for clear thinking." Her fingers walked through the smooth stones, testing, rejecting, selecting. "Sodalite to relieve mental confusion, moonstone for sensitivity. Amethyst, of course, for intuition."

"Of course."

She ignored him. "A crystal for all-around good things." Tilting her head, she studied him. "Jessie says you're trying to quit smoking."

He shrugged. "I'm cutting down."

She handed him the crystal. "Keep it in your pocket. Tumbling stones are on the house." When she turned away with her colorful bottles, he picked up the crystal and rubbed it with his fingers.

It couldn't hurt.

He didn't believe in magic crystals or stone power— though he did think they had plot possibilities. Boone also had to admit they looked kind of nice in the little bowl on his desk. Atmosphere, he thought, like the geode he'd bought to use as a paperweight.

All in all, the afternoon had had several benefits. He and Jessie had enjoyed themselves thoroughly, riding the carousel at the Emporium, playing video games, just walking down Cannery Row and Fisherman's Wharf. Running into Anastasia had been a plus, he mused as he toyed with the creamy moonstone. And seeing Nash again, discovering that they lived in the same area, was gold.

He'd been missing male companionship. Funny, he hadn't realized it, as busy as his life had been over the past few months, with planning the move, executing the move, adjusting to the move. And Nash, though their friendship had primarily been through correspondence over the years, was exactly the kind of companion Boone preferred. Easygoing, loyal, imaginative.

It would be a kick to be able to pass on a few fatherly hints to Nash once his twins were born.

Oh, yeah, he reflected as he held up the moonstone, watching it gleam in the bright wash of moonlight through his office window, it certainly was a small and fascinating world.

One of his oldest friends, married to the cousin of the woman next door. It would certainly be hard for Anastasia to avoid him now.

And, no matter what she said, that was exactly what she'd been doing. He had a very strong feeling—and he couldn't help being a bit smug about it—that he was making the fair maiden nervous.

He'd nearly forgotten what it was like to approach a woman who reacted with faint blushes, confused eyes and rapid pulses. Most of the women he'd escorted over the past couple of years had been sleek and sophisticated—and safe, he added with a little shrug. He'd enjoyed their companionship, and he'd never lost his basic enjoyment of female company. But there'd been no tug, no mystery, no illusion.

He supposed he was still the kind of man attracted to the old-fashioned type. The roses-and-moonlight type, he thought with a half laugh. Then he saw her, and the laugh caught in his throat.

Down in her garden, walking, almost gliding through the silvery light, with the gray cat slipping in and out of the shadows. Her hair loose, sprinkling gold dust down her back and over the sheer shoulders of a pale blue robe. She carried a basket, and he thought he could hear her singing as she cut flowers and slipped them into it.

She was singing an old chant that had been passed down generation to generation. It was well past midnight, and Ana thought herself alone and unobserved. The first night of the full moon in autumn was the time to harvest, just as the first night of the full moon in spring was the time to sow. She had already cast the circle, purifying the area.

She laid the flowers and herbs in the basket as gently as children.

There was magic in her eyes. In her blood.

"Under the moon, through shadow and light, these blooms I chose by touch, by sight. Spells to weave to ease and free. As I will, so mote it be."

She plucked betony and heliotrope, dug mandrake root and selected tansy and balsam. Blood roses for strength, and sage for wisdom. The basket grew heavy and fragrant.

"Tonight to reap, tomorrow to sow. To take only that which I've caused to grow. Remembering always what is begun. To serve, to aid, an it harm none."

As the charm was cast, she lowered her face to the blooms, drawing in the ripe melody of the fragrance.

"I wondered if you were real."

Her head came up quickly, and she saw him, hardly more than a shadow by the hedge. Then he stepped through, into her garden, and became a man.

The heart that had leapt to her throat gradually settled again. "You startled me."

"I'm sorry." It must be the moonlight, he thought, that made her look so…enchanting. "I was working late, and I looked out and saw you. It seemed late to be picking flowers."

"There's a lot of moonlight." She smiled. He had seen nothing it wasn't safe for him to see. "I would think you'd know that anything picked under the full moon is charmed."

He returned the smile. "Got any rampion?"

The reference to Rapunzel made her laugh. "As a matter of fact, I do. No magic garden is complete without it. I'll pot some for you, if you like."

"I rarely say no to magic." The breeze fluttered her hair. Giving in to the moment, he reached out, took a handful. He watched the smile in her eyes fade. What replaced it had his blood singing.

"You should go in. Jessie's alone."

"She's asleep." He moved closer, as if the hair he'd twined around his finger were a rope and she were drawing him to her. He was within the circle now, within the magic she'd cast. "The windows are open, so I'd hear her if she called for me."

"It's late." Ana gripped the basket so tightly that the wicker dug into her skin. "I need to..."

Gently he took the basket and set it on the ground. "So do I." His other hand moved into her hair, combing it back from her face. "Very much."

As he lowered his mouth toward hers, she shivered and tried one last time to take control. "Boone, starting something like this could complicate things for all of us."

"Maybe I'm tired of things being simple." But he turned his head, just a fraction, so that his lips cruised up her cheek, over her temple. "I'm surprised you don't know that when a man finds a woman picking flowers in the moonlight he has no choice but to kiss her."

She felt her bones melting. Her body was pliant when she slipped into his arms. "And she has no choice but to want him to."

Her head fell back, and she offered. He thought he

would take gently. The night seemed to call for it, with its perfumed breezes and the dreamy music of sea against rock. The woman in his arms was wand-slender, and the thin silk of her robe was cool over the warmth of satin skin.

But as he felt himself sink into that soft, lush mouth, as her fragrance whispered seductively around him, he dragged her hard against him and plundered.

Instantly desperate, instantly greedy. No rational thought could fight its way through the maze of sensations she brought to him. A sharp arrow of hunger pierced him, bringing on a groan that was only part pleasure.

Pain. He felt the aches of a thousand pricks of pain. Yet he couldn't pull himself away from her, couldn't stop his mouth from seeking more of hers. He was afraid, afraid that if he released her she would disappear like smoke— and he would never, never feel this way again.

She couldn't soothe him. Part of her wanted to stroke him and ease him and promise him that it would be all right, for both of them. But she couldn't. He devastated her. Whether it was her own grinding needs, the echo of his need seeping into her, or a mix of both, the result was a complete loss of will.

She had known, yes, she had known that this first meeting would be wild and strong. She'd craved it even as she'd feared it. Now she was beyond fear. Like him, she found the mixture of pain and pleasure irresistible.

Her trembling hands skimmed over his face, into his hair and locked there. Her body, shuddering from the onslaught, pressed urgently to his. When she murmured his name, she was breathless.

But he heard her, heard her through the blood pounding in his head, heard that soft, shaky sound. She was trembling—or he was. The uncertainty about who was more dazed had him slowly, carefully drawing away.

He held her still, his hands on her shoulders, his gaze on her face. In the moonlight, she could see herself there, trapped in that sea of blue. Trapped in him.

"Boone..."

"Not yet." He needed a moment to steady himself. By God, he'd nearly swallowed her whole. "Not just yet." Holding himself back, he touched his lips to hers, lightly, in a long, quiet kiss that wrecked whatever was left of her defenses. "I didn't mean to hurt you."

"You didn't." She pressed her lips together and tried to bring her voice over a whisper. "You didn't hurt me. You staggered me."

"I thought I was ready for this." He ran his hands down her arms before he released her. "I don't know if anyone could be." Because he wasn't sure what would happen if he touched her again, he slipped his hands into his pockets. "Maybe it's the moonlight, maybe it's just you. I have to be straight with you, Anastasia, I don't know quite how to handle this."

"Well." She wrapped her arms tight and cupped her elbows. "That makes two of us."

"If it wasn't for Jessie, you wouldn't go into that house alone tonight. And I don't take intimacy lightly."

Steadier now, she nodded. "If it wasn't for Jessie, I might ask you to stay with me tonight." She took a long breath. She knew it was important to be honest, at least in this. "You would be my first."

"Your—" His hands went limp. Now he felt both a lick of fear and an incredible excitement at the thought of her innocence. "Oh, God."

Her chin came up. "I'm not ashamed of it."

"No, I didn't mean…" Speechless, he dragged a hand through his hair. Innocent. A golden-haired virgin in a thin blue robe with flowers at her feet. And a man was supposed to resist, and walk away alone. "I don't suppose you have any idea what that does to a man."

"Not precisely, since I'm not a man." She bent down for her basket. "But I do know what realizing that you may soon be giving yourself for the first time does to a woman. So it seems to me we should both give this some clear thinking." She smiled, or tried to. "And it's very difficult to think clearly after midnight, when the moon's full and the flowers are ripe. I'll say good-night, Boone."

"Ana." He touched her arm, but didn't hold on. "Nothing will happen until you're ready."

She shook her head. "Yes, it will. But nothing will happen unless it's meant."

With her robe billowing around her, she raced toward the house.

Chapter 5

Sleep had been a long time coming. Boone hadn't tossed and turned so much as lain, staring up at the ceiling. He'd watched the moonlight fade into that final deep darkness before dawn.

Now, with the sun streaming in bright ribbons over the bed, he was facedown, spread out, and fast asleep. In the dream floating through his brain, he scooped Ana into his arms and carried her up a long curved staircase of white marble. At the top, suspended above puffy cotton clouds, was an enormous bed pooled in waterfalls of white satin. Hundreds of long, slender candles burned in a drifting light. He could smell them—the soft tang of vanilla, the mystique of jasmine. And her—that quietly sexy scent that went everywhere with her.

She smiled. Hair like sunlight. Eyes like smoke. When he laid her on the bed, they sank deep, as if into the clouds themselves. There was harpsong, romantic as tears, and a whisper that was nothing more than the clouds themselves breathing.

As her arms lifted, wound around him, they were floating, like ghosts in some fantasy, bound together by needs and knowledge and the unbearable sweetness of that first long, lingering kiss. Her mouth moved under his, yielding as she murmured...

"Daddy!"

Boone came awake with a crash as his daughter landed with a thump on his back. His unintelligible grunt had her giggling and scooting down to smack a kiss on his stubbled cheek.

"Daddy, wake up! I fixed you breakfast!"

"Breakfast." He grumbled into the pillow, struggling to clear the sleep from his throat and the dream from his system. "What time is it?"

"The little hand's on the ten, and the big hand's on the three. I made cinnamon toast and poured orange juice in the little glasses."

He grunted again, rolling over to peer through gritty eyes at Jessie. She looked bright as a sunbeam in her pink cotton blouse and shorts. She'd done the buttons up wrong, but she'd brushed the tangles from her hair. "How long have you been up?"

"Hours and hours and hours. I let Daisy outside and gave her breakfast. And I got dressed all by myself and brushed my teeth and watched cartoons. Then I got hungry, so I fixed breakfast."

"You've been busy."

"Uh-huh. And I was real quiet, too, so you didn't have to wake up early on your sleep-in day."

"You were real quiet," Boone agreed, and reached up to fix her buttons. "I guess you deserve a prize."

Her eyes lit. "What? What do I get?"

"How about a pink belly?" He rolled with her on the bed, wrestling while she squealed and wriggled. He let her win, pretending exhaustion and defeat when she bounced on his back. "Too tough for me."

"That's 'cause I eat my vegetables. You don't."

"I eat some."

"Uh-uh, hardly any."

"When you get to be thirty-three, you won't have to eat your brussels sprouts, either."

"But I like them."

He grinned into the pillow. "That's only because I'm such a good cook. My mother was lousy."

"She doesn't ever cook now." Jessie printed her name with a fingertip on her father's bare back. "Her and Grandpa Sawyer always go out to eat."

"That's because Grandpa Sawyer's no fool." She was having trouble with the letter *S,* Boone noted. They'd have to work on it.

"You said we could call Grandma and Grandpa Sawyer and Nana and Pop today. Can we?"

"Sure, in a couple of hours." He turned over again, studying her. "Do you miss them, baby?"

"Yeah." With her tongue between her teeth, she began to print *Sawyer* on his chest. "It seems funny that they're not here. Will they come to visit us?"

"Sure they will." The guilt that was part and parcel of parenthood worked at him. "Do you wish we'd stayed in Indiana?"

"No way!" Her eyes went huge. "We didn't have the beach there, and the seals and stuff, or the big carousel in town, or Ana living next door. This is the best place in the world."

"I like it here, too." He sat up and kissed her brow. "Now beat it, so I can get dressed."

"You'll come right downstairs for breakfast?" she asked as she slid from the bed.

"Absolutely. I'm so hungry I could eat a whole loaf of cinnamon toast."

Delighted, she rushed for the door. "I'm going to make more, right now."

Knowing she would take him at his word and go through an entire loaf of bread, Boone hurried through his shower, opted not to shave, and pulled on cutoffs and a T-shirt that would probably have done better in the rag pile.

He tried not to dwell on the dream. After all, it was simple enough to interpret. He wanted Ana—no big revelation there. And all that white—white on white—was obviously a symbol of her innocence.

It scared the hell out of him.

He found Jessie in the kitchen, busily slathering butter on another piece of toast. There was a plate heaped with them, more than a few of them burnt. The smell of cinnamon was everywhere.

Boone put on the coffee before he snagged a piece. It was cold, hard, and lumped with sugary cinnamon. Obviously, Jessie had inherited her grandmother's culinary talents.

"It's great," he told her, and swallowed gamely. "My favorite Sunday breakfast."

"Do you think Daisy can have some?"

Boone looked at the pile of toast again, glanced down at the pup, whose tongue was lolling out. With any luck he might be able to pawn off half his Sunday breakfast on the dog. "I think she could." Crouching, Boone held out a second piece of toast close enough for Daisy to sniff. "Sit," he ordered, in the firm, no-nonsense voice the training books had suggested.

Daisy continued to loll her tongue and wag her tail.

"Daisy, sit." He gave her rump a nudge. Daisy went down, then bounded back on all fours to jump at him. "Forget it." He held the toast out of reach and repeated the command. After five frustrating minutes—during which he tried not to remember how simple it had been for Ana—he managed to hold the dog's hindquarters down. Daisy gobbled up the bread, pleased with herself.

"She did it, Daddy."

"Sort of." He rose to pour himself some coffee. "We'll take her outside in a little while and have a real lesson."

"Okay." Jessie munched happily on her toast. "Maybe Ana's company will be gone, and she can help."

"Company?" Boone asked as he reached for a mug.

"I saw her outside with a man. She gave him a big hug and a kiss and everything."

"She—" The mug clattered onto the counter.

"Butterfingers," Jessie said, smiling.

"Yeah." Boone kept his back turned as he righted the mug and poured the coffee. "What, ah, sort of a man?" He thought his voice was casual enough—to fool a six-year-old, anyway.

"A really tall man with black hair. They were laughing and holding hands. Maybe it's her boyfriend."

"Boyfriend," Boone repeated between his teeth.

"What's the matter, Daddy?"

"Nothing. Coffee's hot." He sipped it black. Holding hands, he thought. Kissing. He'd get a look at this guy himself. "Why don't we go out on the deck, Jess? See if we can get Daisy to sit again."

"Okay." Singing the new song she'd learned in school, Jessie gathered up toast. "I like to eat outside. It's nice."

"Yeah, it's nice." Boone didn't sit when they were on the deck, but stood at the rail, the mug in his hand. He didn't see anyone in the next yard, and that was worse. Now he could imagine what Ana and her tall, dark-haired boyfriend might be doing inside.

Alone.

He ate three more pieces of toast, washing them down with black coffee while he fantasized about just what he'd say to Miss Anastasia Donovan the next time he saw her.

If she thought she could kiss him to the point of explosion one night, then dally with some strange guy the next morning, she was very much mistaken.

He'd straighten her out, all right. The minute he got ahold of her he'd—

His thoughts broke off when she came out the kitchen door, calling over her shoulder to someone.

"Ana!" Jessie leapt up on the bench, waving and shouting. "Ana, hi!"

While Boone watched through narrowed eyes, Ana looked in their direction. It seemed to him that her hand hesitated on its way up to return the wave, and her smile was strained.

Sure, he thought as he gulped down more coffee. I'd be nervous, too, if I had some strange man in the house.

"Can I go tell her what Daisy did? Can I, Daddy?"

"Yeah." His smile was grim as he set his empty mug on the rail. "Why don't you do that?"

Snatching up some more toast, she darted down the steps, calling for Daisy to follow and for Ana to wait.

Boone waited himself until he saw the man stroll outside to join Ana. He was tall, all right, Boone noted with some resentment. Several inches over six feet. He drew his own shoulders back. His hair was true black, and long enough to curl over his collar and blow—romantically, Boone imagined a woman would think— in the breeze.

He looked tanned, fit and elegant. And the breath hissed out between Boone's teeth when the stranger slipped an arm around Ana's shoulders as if it belonged there.

We'll see about this, Boone decided, and started down the deck stairs with his hands jammed in his pockets. We'll just see about this.

By the time he reached the hedge of roses, Jessie was already chattering a mile a minute about Daisy, and Ana was laughing, her arms tucked intimately around the stranger's waist.

"I'd sit, too, if someone was going to feed me cinnamon toast," the man said, and winked at Ana.

"You'd sit if anyone was going to feed you anything." Ana gave him a little squeeze before she noticed Boone at the hedge. "Oh." It was useless to curse the faint blush she felt heating her cheeks. "Good morning."

"How's it going?" Boone gave her a slow nod. Then his gaze moved suspiciously to the man beside her. "We didn't mean to interrupt while you have...company."

"No, that's all right, I—" She broke off, both confused and disconcerted by the tension humming in the air. "Sebastian, this is Jessie's father, Boone Sawyer. Boone, my cousin, Sebastian Donovan."

"Cousin?" Boone repeated, and Sebastian didn't bother to control the grin that spread over his face.

"Fortunately you made the introductions quickly, Ana," he said. "I like my nose precisely the way it is." He held out a hand. "Nice to meet you. Ana was telling us she had new neighbors."

"He's the one with horses, Daddy."

"I remember." Boone found Sebastian's grip firm and strong. He might have appreciated it if he hadn't seen the gleam of amusement in the man's eyes. "You're recently married?"

"Indeed I am. My..." He turned when the screen door slammed. "Ah, here she is now. Light of my life."

A tall, slim woman with short, tousled hair strode over in dusty boots. "Cut it out, Donovan."

"My blushing bride." It was obvious they were laughing at each other. He took his wife's hand and kissed it. "Ana's neighbors, Boone and Jessie Sawyer. My own true love, Mary Ellen."

"Mel," she corrected quickly. "Donovan's the only one with the nerve to call me Mary Ellen. Great-looking house," she added, with a nod toward the neighboring building.

"I believe Mr. Sawyer writes fairy tales, children's books, much in the manner of Aunt Bryna."

"Oh, yeah? That's cool." Mel smiled down at Jessie. "I bet you like that."

"He writes the best stories in the world. And this is Daisy. We taught her to sit. Can I come see your horses?"

"Sure." Mel crouched down to ruffle the pup's fur. While Mel engaged Jessie in conversation about horses and dogs, Sebastian looked back at Boone.

"It is a lovely house you have," he said. Actually, he'd toyed with buying it himself. Amusement lit his eyes again. "Excellent location."

"We like it." Boone decided it was foolish to pretend not to understand the meaning behind the words. "We like it very much." Very deliberately, he reached out to trail a fingertip down Ana's cheek. "You're looking a little pale this morning, Anastasia."

"I'm fine." It was easy enough to keep her voice even, but she knew very well how simple it would be for Sebastian to see what she was thinking. Already she could feel his gentle probing, and she was quite certain he was poking his nosy mental fingers into Boone's brain. "If you'll excuse me, I promised Sebastian some hawthorn."

"Didn't you pick any last night?"

Her gaze met his, held it. "I have other uses for that."

"We'll get out of your way. Come on, Jess." He reached for his daughter's hand. "Nice meeting both of you. I'll see you soon, Ana."

Sebastian had the tact to wait until Boone was out of earshot. "Well, well… I go away for a couple of weeks, and look at the trouble you get into."

"Don't be ridiculous." Ana turned her back and started toward an herb bed. "I'm not in any sort of trouble."

"Darling, darling Ana, your friend and neighbor was prepared to rip my throat out until you introduced me as your cousin."

"I'd have protected you," Mel said solemnly.

"My hero."

"Besides," Mel went on, "it looked to me as though he was more in the mood to drag Ana off by the hair than tackle you."

"You're both being absurd." Ana snipped hawthorn without looking up. "He's a very nice man."

"I'm sure," Sebastian murmured. "But, you see, men understand this territorial thing—which is, of course, an obscure concept to the female."

"Oh, please." Mel shoved an elbow in his ribs.

"Facts are facts, my dear Mary Ellen. I had intruded on his territory. Or so he thought. Naturally, I would only think less of him if he had made no effort to defend it."

"Naturally," Mel said dryly.

"Tell me, Ana, just how involved are you?"

"That's none of your business." She straightened, deftly wrapping the stems of the hawthorn. "And I'll thank you to keep out of it, cousin. I know very well you were poking in."

"Which is why you blocked me. Your neighbor wasn't so successful."

"It's rude," she muttered, "unconscionably rude, the way you peek into people's heads at the drop of a hat."

"He likes to show off," Mel said sympathetically.

"Unfair." Disgusted, Sebastian shook his head. "I do

not poke or peek at the drop of a hat. I always have an excellent reason. In this case, being your only male relative on the continent, I feel it's my duty to survey the situation, and the players."

Mel could only roll her eyes as Ana's spine stiffened. "Really?" Eyes bright, Ana jammed a finger into Sebastian's chest. "Then let me set you straight. Just because I'm a woman doesn't mean I need protection or guidance or anything else from a male—relative or otherwise. I've been handling my own life for twenty-six years."

"Twenty-seven next month," Sebastian added helpfully.

"And I can continue to handle it. What's between Boone and me—"

"Ah." He held up a triumphant finger. "So there is something between you."

"Stuff it, Sebastian."

"She only talks like that when she paints herself into a corner," Sebastian told Mel. "Usually she's extremely mild and well-mannered."

"Careful, or I'll give Mel a potion to put in your soup that'll freeze your vocal cords for a week."

"Oh yeah?" Intrigued by the idea, Mel tilted her head. "Can I have it anyway?"

"A lot of good it would do you, since I do all the cooking," Sebastian pointed out. Then he scooped Ana up in a hug. "Come on, darling, don't be angry. I have to worry about you. It's my job."

"There's nothing to worry about." But she was softening.

"Are you in love with him?"

Instantly she stiffened. "Really, Sebastian, I've only known him for a week."

"What difference does that make?" He gave Mel a long look over Ana's head. "It took me less than that to realize the reason Mel irritated me so much was that I was crazy about her. Of course, it took her longer to understand she was madly in love with me. But she has such a hard head."

"I'm getting that potion," Mel decided.

Ignoring the threat, he drew back to consider Ana at arm's length. "I ask because he definitely has more than a neighborly interest in you. As a matter of fact, he—"

"That's enough. Whatever you dug out of his head, you keep to yourself. I mean it, Sebastian," she said before he could interrupt. "I prefer doing things my own way."

"If you insist," he said with a sigh.

"I do. Now take your hawthorn and go home and be newlyweds."

"Now that's the best idea I've heard all day." Taking a firm grip on her husband's arm, Mel tugged him back. "Leave her alone, Donovan. Ana's perfectly capable of handling her own affairs."

"And if she's going to have one, she should know—"

"Out." On a strangled laugh, Ana gave him a shove. "Out of my yard. I have work to do. If I need a psychic, I'll call you."

He relented and gave her a kiss. "See that you do." A new smile began to bloom as he walked away with his wife. "I believe we'll stop by and see Morgana and Nash."

"That's fine." She shot a last glance over her shoulder. "I'd like to hear what they have to say about this guy myself."

Sebastian laughed and hugged her close. "You are a woman after my own heart."

"No, I'm not." She kissed him soundly. "I've already got it."

For the next several days, Ana busied herself indoors. It wasn't that she was avoiding Boone—at least not to any great extent. She simply had a lot to do. Her medicinal supplies had become sadly depleted. Just that day, she'd had a call from a client in Carmel who was out of the elixir for her rheumatism. Ana had had just enough to ship, but that meant she had to make more as soon as possible. Even now she had dried primrose simmering with motherwort on the stove.

In the little room adjoining the kitchen through a wide archway, she had her distilling flasks, condensers, burners and bottles, along with vials and silver bowls and candles, set up for the day. To the casual eye, the room resembled a small chemistry lab. But there was a marked difference between chemistry and alchemy. In alchemy there was ritual, and the meticulous use of astrological timing.

All of the flowers and roots and herbs she had harvested by moonlight had been carefully washed in morning dew. Others, plucked under different phases of the moon, had already been prepared for their specific uses.

There was syrup of poppy to be distilled, and there was hyssop to be dried for cough syrup. She needed some oil of clary for a specialty perfume, and she could combine that with some chamomile for a digestive aid. There were infusions and decoctions to be completed, as well as both oils and incense.

Plenty to do, Ana thought, particularly since she had the touch of magic from the flowers picked in moonlight. And she enjoyed her work, the scents that filled her kitchen and workroom, the pretty pink leaves of the flowering marjoram, the deep purple of foxglove, the sunny touch of the practical marigold.

They were lovely, and she could never resist setting some in vases or bowls around the house. She was testing a dilution of gentian, grimacing at the bitter taste, when Boone knocked on her screen door.

"I really do need sugar this time," he told her with a quick, charming grin that had her heart pumping fast. "I'm homeroom mother this week, and I have to make three dozen cookies for tomorrow."

Tilting her head, she studied him. "You could buy them."

"What homeroom mother worth her salt serves the first grade class store-bought? A cup would do it."

The image of him baking made her smile. "I probably have one. Come on in. Just let me finish this up."

"It smells fabulous in here." He leaned over to peek into the pots simmering on the stove. "What are you doing?"

"Don't!" She warned, just as he was about to dip a finger in a black glass pan cooling on the counter. "That's belladonna. Not for internal consumption in that form."

"Belladonna." His brows drew together. "You're making poison?"

"I'm making a lotion—an anodyne—for neuralgia, rheumatism. And it isn't a poison if it's brewed and dispensed properly. It's a sedative."

Frowning, he looked into the room behind, with its

chemical equipment and its bubbling brews. "Don't you have to have a license or something?"

"I'm a qualified herbal practitioner, with a degree in pharmacognosy, if that relieves you." She batted his hand away from a pot. "And this is not something for the novice."

"Got anything for insomnia—besides belladonna? No offense."

She was instantly concerned. "Are you having trouble sleeping? Are you feverish?" She lifted a hand to his brow, then went still when he took her wrist.

"Yes, to both questions. You could say you're the cause and the cure." He brought her hand from his brow to his lips. "I may be homeroom mother, but I'm still a man, Ana. I can't stop thinking about you." He turned her hand over, pressing those lips to the inside of her wrist, where the pulse was beginning to jerk. "And I can't stop wanting you."

"I'm sorry if I'm giving you restless nights."

His brow quirked. "Are you?"

She couldn't quite suppress the smile. "I'm trying to be. It's hard not to be flattered that thinking about me is keeping you awake. And it's hard to know what to do." She turned away to switch off the heat on the stove. "I've been feeling a little restless myself." Her eyes closed when his hands came down on her shoulders.

"Make love with me." He brushed a kiss on the back of her neck. "I won't hurt you, Ana."

Not purposely, she thought. Never that. There was so much kindness in him. But would they hurt each other if she gave in to what she wanted, needed, from him, and held back that part of herself that made her what she was?

"It's a big step for me, Boone."

"For me, too." Gently he turned her to face him. "There's been no one for me since Alice died. In the past couple of years there was a woman or two, but nothing that meant any more than filling a physical emptiness. No one I've wanted to spend time with, to be with, to talk to. I care about you." He lowered his mouth to hers, very carefully, very softly. "I don't know how I came to care this much, this quickly, but I do. I hope you believe that."

Even without a true link, she couldn't help but feel it. It made things more complicated somehow. "I do believe you."

"I've been thinking. Seeing as I haven't been sleeping, I've had plenty of time for it." Absently he tapped a loosened pin back into her hair. "The other night, I was rushing you, probably scared you."

"No." Then she shrugged and turned back to filter one of her mixtures into a bottle, already labeled. "Yes, actually, I guess you did."

"If I'd known you were... If I'd realized you'd never..."

With a sigh, she capped the bottle. "My virginity is by choice, Boone, and nothing I'm uncomfortable with."

"I didn't mean—" He let out a hissing breath. "I'm doing a great job with this."

She chose another funnel, another bottle, and poured. "You're nervous."

With some chagrin, he noted that her hands were rock-steady when she capped the next bottle. "I think terrified comes closer. I was rough with you, and I shouldn't have been. For a lot of reasons. The fact that you're inexperienced is only one of them."

"You weren't rough." She continued to work to hide her nerves, which were jumping every bit as much as his. As long as she had to concentrate on what she was doing, she could at least pretend to be calm and confident. "You're a passionate man. That's not something to apologize for."

"I'm apologizing for pressuring you. And for coming over here today fully intending to keep things light and easy, and then pressuring you again."

Her lips curved as she walked to the sink to soak her pans. "Is that what you're doing?"

"I told myself I wasn't going to ask you to go to bed with me—even though I want you to. I was going to ask if you'd spend some time with me. Come to dinner, or go out, or whatever people do when they're trying to get to know each other."

"I'd like to come to dinner, or go out, or whatever."

"Good." That hadn't been so hard, he decided. "Maybe this weekend. Friday night. I should be able to find a sitter." His eyes clouded. "Somebody I can trust."

"I thought you were going to cook for me and Jessie."

A weight lifted. "You wouldn't mind?"

"I think I'd enjoy it."

"Okay, then." He framed her face in his hands. "Okay." The kiss was very sweet, and if it felt as if something inside were going to rip in two, he told himself, he could deal with it. "Friday."

It wasn't difficult to smile, even if her system felt as if it had been rocked by a small earthquake. "I'll bring the wine."

"Good." He wanted to kiss her again, but he was afraid he'd scare her off. "I'll see you then."

"Boone." She stopped him before he'd reached the door. "Don't you want your sugar?"

He grinned. "I lied."

Her eyes narrowed. "You're not homeroom mother, and you're not baking cookies?"

"No, that was true. But I have five pounds in the pantry. Hey, it worked." He was whistling as he walked out the door.

Chapter 6

"Why isn't Ana here yet? When is she coming?"

"Soon," Boone answered for the tenth time. Too soon, he was afraid. He was behind in everything. The kitchen was a disaster. He'd used too many pans. Then again, he always did. He could never figure out how anyone cooked without using every pot, pan and bowl available.

The chicken cacciatore smelled pretty good, but he was uncertain of the results. Stupid, he supposed, absolutely stupid to try out a new recipe at such a time, but he'd figured Ana was worth more than their usual Friday-night meatloaf.

Jessie was driving him crazy, which was a rarity. She was overexcited at the thought of having Ana over, and she'd been pestering him without pause ever since he'd brought her home from school.

The dog had chosen that afternoon to chew up Boone's bed pillows, so he'd spent a great deal of valuable time chasing dog and feathers. The washing machine had overflowed, flooding the laundry room. He was much too male to consider calling a repairman, so he'd torn the machine apart and put it back together again.

He was pretty sure he'd fixed it.

His agent had called to tell him that *A Third Wish for Miranda* had been optioned for an animated feature by one of the major studios. That would have been good news at any other time, but now he was expected to fit a trip to L.A. into his schedule.

Jessie had decided she wanted to be a Brownie and had generously volunteered him as a Brownie leader.

The thought of having a group of six-and seven-year-old girls looking to him to teach them how to make jewelry boxes out of egg cartons chilled his blood.

With a lot of ingenuity and plenty of cowardice, he thought, he might be able to ease his way out of it.

"Are you sure she's coming, Daddy? Are you sure?"

"Jessica." The warning note in his voice was enough to make her lower lip poke out. "Do you know what happens to little girls who keep asking the same question?"

"Nuh-uh."

"Keep it up and you'll find out. Go make sure Daisy's not eating the furniture."

"Are you awfully mad at Daisy?"

"Yes. Now go on or you're next." He softened the order with a gentle pat on her bottom. "Beat it, brat, or I'll put you in the pot and have you for dinner."

Two minutes later, he heard the mayhem that meant Jessie had located Daisy, and girl and dog were now wrestling. The high-pitched yelps and happy squeals played hell with the headache pulsing behind his eyes.

Just need an aspirin, he thought, an hour or two of quiet, and a vacation on Maui.

He was on the point of giving a roar that would probably pop his head off his shoulders when Ana knocked.

"Hi. Smells good."

He hoped it did. She looked much better than good. He hadn't seen her in a dress before, and the swirl of watercolor silk did wonderful things for her slim body. Things like showing off those soft white shoulders under thin straps. With it she wore an amulet on a long chain that had the square of engraved gold hanging just below her breasts. Crystals glinted in it, drawing the eye, and were echoed by the tear-shaped drops at her ears.

She smiled. "You did say Friday."

"Yeah. Friday."

"Then are you going to ask me in?"

"Sorry." Lord, he felt like a bumbling teenager. No, he decided as he slid the screen open for her, no teenager had ever been this bumbling. "I'm a little distracted."

Ana's brows lifted as she surveyed the chaos of pots and bowls. "So I see. Would you like some help?"

"I think I've got it under control." He took the bottle she offered, noting that the pale green bottle was etched with symbols and that it carried no label. "Homemade?"

"Yes, my father makes it. He has..." Her eyes lit with secrets and humor. "A magic touch."

"Brewed in the dungeons of Castle Donovan."

"As a matter of fact, yes." She left it at that, and wandered to the stove as he took out some glasses. "No Bugs Bunny this time?"

"I'm afraid Bugs met a fatal accident in the dishwasher." He poured the clear golden wine into the crystal glasses. "It wasn't pretty."

She laughed and lifted her glass in a toast. "To neighbors."

"To neighbors," he agreed, clinking crystal against crystal. "If they all looked like you, I'd be a dead man." He sipped, then lifted a brow. "Next time we'll have to drink to your father. This is incredible."

"One of his many hobbies, you might say."

"What's in it?"

"Apples, honeysuckle, starlight. You can give him your compliments, if you like. He and the rest of my family should be here for All Hallows' Eve. Halloween."

"I know what it is. Jessie's torn between being a fairy princess or a rock star. Your parents travel all the way to the States for Halloween?"

"Usually. It's a kind of family tradition." Unable to resist, she took the lid off the pan and sniffed. "Well, well, I'm impressed."

"That was the idea." Equally unable to resist, he lifted a handful of her hair. "You know that story I told you the day Daisy knocked you down? I find myself compelled to write it. So much so that I've put what I was working on aside."

"It was a lovely story."

"Normally I could have made it wait. But I need to know why the woman was bound inside the castle all those years. Was it a spell, one of her own making? What was the enchantment that made the man climb the wall to find her?"

"That's for you to decide."

"No, that's for me to find out."

"Boone..." She lifted a hand to his, then looked down quickly. "What have you done to yourself?"

"Just rapped my knuckles." He flexed his fingers and shrugged. "Fixing the washing machine."

"You should have come over and let me tend to this." She ran her fingers over the scraped skin, wishing she was in a position to heal it. "It's painful."

He started to deny it, then realized his mistake. "I always kiss Jessie's hurts to make them better."

"A kiss works wonders," she agreed, and obliged him by touching her lips to the wound. Briefly, very briefly, she risked a link to be certain there was no real pain and no chance of infection. She found that, while the knuckles were merely sore, he did have real pain from a tension headache working behind his eyes. That, at least, she could help him with.

With a smile, she brushed the hair from his brow. "You've been working too hard, getting the house in order, writing your story, worrying if you made the right decision to move Jessie."

"I didn't realize I was that transparent."

"It isn't so difficult to see." She laid her fingers on either side of his temples, massaging in small circles. "Now you've gone to all this trouble to cook me dinner."

"I wanted—"

"I know." She held steady as she felt the pain flash behind her own eyes. To distract him, she touched her lips to his as she absorbed the ache and let it slowly fade. "Thank you."

"You're very welcome," he murmured, and deepened the kiss.

Her hands slid away from his temples, lay weakly on his shoulders. It was much more difficult to absorb this ache—this ache that spread so insidiously through her. Pulsing, throbbing. Tempting.

Much too tempting.

"Boone." Wary, she slipped out of his arms. "We're rushing this."

"I told you I wouldn't. That's not going to stop me from kissing you whenever I get the chance." He picked up his wine, then hers, offering her glass to her again. "Nothing goes beyond that until you say so."

"I don't know whether to thank you for that or not. I know I should."

"No. There's no more need to thank me for that than there is to thank me for wanting you. It's just the way it is. Sometimes I think about Jessie growing up. It gives me some bad moments. And I know that if there was any man who pushed or pressured her into doing what she wasn't ready to do I'd just have to kill him." He sipped, and grinned. "And, of course, if she thinks she's going to be ready to do anything of the kind before she's, say, forty, I'll just lock her in her room until the feeling passes."

It made her laugh, and she realized as he stood there, with his back to the cluttered, splattered stove, a dishcloth hanging from the waist of his slacks, that she was very, very close to falling in love with him.

Once she had, she would be ready. And nothing would make the feeling pass.

"Spoken like a true paranoid father."

"Paranoia and fatherhood are synonymous. Take my word for it. Wait until Nash has those twins. He'll start thinking about health insurance and dental hygiene. A sneeze in the middle of the night will send him into a panic."

"Morgana will keep him level. A paranoid father only needs a sensible mother to..." Her words trailed off as she cursed herself. "I'm sorry."

"It's all right. It's easier when people don't feel they have to tiptoe around it. Alice has been gone for four years. Wounds heal, especially if you have good memories." There was a thud from the next room, and the sound of racing feet. "And a six-year-old who keeps you on your toes."

At that moment, Jessie ran in and threw herself at Ana. "You came! I thought you'd never get here."

"Of course I came. I never turn down a dinner invitation from my favorite neighbors."

As Boone watched them, he realized his headache had vanished. Odd, he thought as he switched off the stove and prepared to serve dinner. He'd never gotten around to taking an aspirin.

It wasn't what he would call a quiet, romantic dinner. He had lit candles and clipped flowers in the garden he'd inherited when he'd bought the house. They had the meal in the dining alcove, with its wide, curved window, with music from the sea and birdsong. A perfect setting for romance.

But there were no murmured secrets or whispered promises. Instead, there was laughter and a child's bubbling voice. The talk was not about what the candlelight did to her skin, or how it deepened the pure gray of her eyes. It centered on first grade, on what Daisy had done that day and on the fairy tale still brewing in Boone's mind.

When dinner was over, and Ana had listened to Jessie's exploits at school, along with those of Jessie's new and very best friend, Lydia, she announced that she and the child were assuming kitchen duty.

"No, I'll take care of it later." He was very comfortable in the sunset-washed dining alcove, and he remembered too vividly the mess he'd left behind in the kitchen. "Dirty dishes don't go anywhere."

"You cooked." Ana was already rising to stack the dishes. "When my father cooks, my mother washes up. And vice versa. Donovan rules. Besides, the kitchen's a good place for girl talk, isn't it, Jessie?"

Jessie didn't have any idea, but she was instantly intrigued by the notion. "I can help. I hardly ever break any dishes."

"And men aren't allowed in the kitchen during girl talk." She leaned conspiratorially toward Jessie. "Because they just get in the way." She sent Boone an arch look. "I think you and Daisy could use a walk on the beach."

"I don't..." A walk on the beach. Alone. With no KP. "Really?"

"Really. Take your time. Jessie, when I was in town the other day, I saw the cutest dress. It was blue, just the color of your eyes, and had a big satin bow." Ana stopped, a pile of dishes in her hands, and stared at Boone. "Still here?"

"Just leaving."

As he walked out in the deepening twilight with Daisy romping around him, he could hear the light music of female laughter coming through his windows.

"Daddy said you were born in a castle," Jessie said as she helped Ana load the dishwasher.

"That's right. In Ireland."

"A for-real castle?"

"A real castle, near the sea. It has towers and turrets, secret passageways, and a drawbridge."

"Just like in Daddy's books."

"Very much like. It's a magic palace." Ana listened to the sound of water as she rinsed dishes and thought of the squabbles and laughing voices in that huge kitchen, with a fire going in the hearth and the good, yeasty smell of fresh bread perfuming the air. "My father and his brothers were born there, and his father, and his, and further back than I can say."

"If I were born in a castle, I would always live there." Jessie stood close to Ana while they worked, enjoying without knowing why, the scent of woman, and the lighter timbre of a female voice. "Why did you move away?"

"Oh, it's still home, but sometimes you have to move away, to make your own place. Your own magic."

"Like Daddy and me did."

"Yes." She closed the dishwasher and began to fill the sink with hot, soapy water for the pots and pans. "You like living here in Monterey?"

"I like it a lot. Nana said I might get homesick when the novelty wears off. What's novelty?"

"The newness." Not a very wise thing to suggest to an impressionable child, Ana mused. But she imagined

Nana's nose was out of joint. "If you do get homesick, you should try to remember that the very best place to be is usually where you are."

"I like where Daddy is, even if he took me to Timbuktu."

"Excuse me?"

"Grandma Sawyer said he might as well have moved us to Timbuktu." Jessie accepted the clean pot Ana handed her and began to dry, an expression of deep concentration on her face. "Is that a real place?"

"Um-hmm. But it's also a kind of expression that means far away. Your grandparents are missing you, sunshine. That's all."

"I miss them, too, but I get to talk to them on the phone, and Daddy helped me type a letter on his computer. Do you think you could marry Daddy so Grandma Sawyer would get off his back?"

The pan Ana had been washing plopped into the suds and sent a small tidal wave over the lip of the sink. "I don't think so."

"I heard him telling Grandma Sawyer that she was on his back all the time to find a wife so he wouldn't be lonely and I wouldn't have to grow up without a mother. His voice had that mad sound in it he gets when I do something really wrong, or like when Daisy chewed up his pillow. And he said he'd be damned if he'd tie himself down just to keep the peace."

"I see." Ana pressed her lips hard together to keep the proper seriousness on her face. "I don't think he'd like you to repeat it, Jessie, especially in those words."

"Do you think Daddy's lonely?"

"No. No, I don't. I think he's very happy with you, and with Daisy. If he decided to get married one day, it would be because he found somebody all of you loved very much."

"I love you."

"Oh, sunshine." Soapy hands and all, Ana scooted down to give Jessie a hug and a kiss. "I love you, too."

"Do you love Daddy?"

I wish I knew. "It's different," she said. She knew she was navigating on boggy ground. "When you grow up, love means different things. But I'm very happy that you moved here and we can all be friends."

"Daddy never had a lady over to dinner before."

"Well, you've only been here a couple of weeks."

"I mean ever, at all. Not in Indiana, either. So I thought maybe it meant that you were going to get married and live with us here so Grandma Sawyer would get off his back and I wouldn't be a poor motherless child."

"No." Ana did her best to disguise a chuckle. "It meant that we like each other and wanted to have dinner." She checked the window to make certain Boone wasn't on his way back. "Does he always cook like this?"

"He always makes a really big mess, and sometimes he says those words—you know?"

"I know."

"He says them when he has to clean it up. And today he was in a really bad mood 'cause Daisy ate his pillow and there were feathers all over and the washing machine exploded and he maybe has to go on a business trip."

"That's a lot for one day." She bit her lip. Really, she

didn't want to pump the child, but she was curious. "He's going to take a trip?"

"Maybe to the place where they make movies, 'cause they want to make one out of his book."

"That's wonderful."

"He has to think about it. That's what he says when he doesn't want to say yes but probably he's going to."

This time Ana didn't bother to smother the chuckle. "You certainly have his number."

By the time they'd finished the kitchen, Jessie was yawning. "Will you come up and see my room? I put everything away like Daddy said to when we have company."

"I'd love to see your room."

The packing boxes were gone, Ana noted as they moved from the kitchen into the high-ceilinged living room, with its open balcony and curving stairs. The furniture there looked comfortably lived-in, bold, bright colors in fabrics that appeared tough enough to stand up under the hands and feet of an active child.

It could have used some flowers at the window, she mused. Some scented candles in brass holders on the mantel. Perhaps a few big, plump pillows scattered here and there. Still, there were homey family touches in the framed photographs, the ticking grandfather clock. And clever, whimsical ones, like the brass dragon's-head andirons standing guard on the stone hearth, and the unicorn rocking horse in the corner.

And if there was a little dust on the banister, that only added to the charm.

"I got to pick out my own bed," Jessie was telling her.

"And once everything settles down I can pick out wallpaper if I want to. That's where Daddy sleeps." She pointed to the right, and Ana had a glimpse of a big bed under a jade-colored quilt—sans pillows—a handsome old chest of drawers with a missing pull, and a few stray feathers.

"He has his own bathroom in there, too, with a big tub that has jets and a shower that's all glass and has water coming out of both sides. I get to use the one out here, and it has two sinks and this little thing that isn't a toilet but looks like one."

"A bidet?"

"I guess so. Daddy says it's fancy and mostly for ladies. This is my room."

It was a little girl's fantasy, one provided by a man who obviously understood that childhood was all too short and very precious. All pink and white, the canopy bed sat in the center, a focal point surrounded by shelves of dolls and books and bright toys, a snowy dresser with a curvy mirror, and a child-sized desk littered with colored paper and crayons.

On the walls were lovely framed illustrations from fairy tales. Cinderella rushing down the steps of a silvery castle, a single glass slipper left behind. Rapunzel, her golden hair spilling out of a high tower window while she looked longingly down at her prince. The sly, endearing elf from one of Boone's books, and—a complete surprise to Ana—one of her aunt's prized illustrations.

"This is from *The Golden Ball*."

"The lady who wrote it sent it to Daddy for me when I was just little. Next to Daddy's I like her stories best."

"I had no idea," Ana murmured. As far as she'd known,

her aunt had never parted with one of her drawings except to family.

"Daddy did the elf," Jessie pointed out. "All the rest my mother did."

"They're beautiful." Not just skillful, Ana thought, and perhaps not as clever as Boone's elf or as elegant as her aunt's drawing, but lovely, and as true to the spirit of a fairy tale as magic itself.

"She drew them just for me, when I was a baby. Nana said Daddy should put them away so they wouldn't make me sad. But they don't. I like to look at them."

"You're very lucky to have something so beautiful to remember her by."

Jessie rubbed her sleepy eyes and struggled to hold back a yawn. "I have dolls, too, but I don't play with them much. My grandmothers like to give them to me, but I like the stuffed walrus my daddy got me better. Do you like my room?"

"It's lovely, Jessie."

"I can see the water, and your yard, from the windows." She tucked back the billowing sheer curtains to show off her view. "And that's Daisy's bed, but she likes to sleep with me." Jessie pointed out the wicker dog bed, with its pink cushion.

"Maybe you'd like to lie down until Daisy comes back."

"Maybe." Jessie sent Ana a doubtful look. "But I'm not really tired. Do you know any stories?"

"I could probably think of one." She picked Jessie up to sit her on the bed. "What kind would you like?"

"A magic one."

"The very best kind." She thought for a moment, then

smiled. "Ireland is an old country," she began, slipping an arm around the girl. "And it's filled with secret places, dark hills and green fields, water so blue it hurts the eyes to stare at it for long. There's been magic there for so many centuries, and it's still a safe place for fairies and elves and witches."

"Good witches or bad ones?"

"Both, but there's always been more good than bad, not only in witches, but in everything."

"Good witches are pretty," Jessie said, stroking a hand down Ana's arm. "That's how you know. Is this a story about a good witch?"

"It is indeed. A very good and very beautiful witch. And a very good and very handsome one, too."

"Men aren't witches," Jessie informed her, giggling. "They're wizards."

"Who's telling the story?" Ana kissed the top of Jessie's head. "Now, one day, not so many years ago, a beautiful young witch traveled with her two sisters to visit their old grandfather. He was a very powerful witch—wizard— but had grown cranky and bored in his old age. Not far from the manor where he lived was a castle. And there lived three brothers. They were triplets, and very powerful wizards, as well. For as long as anyone could remember, the old wizard and the family of the three brothers had carried on a feud. No one remembered the why of it any longer, but the feud ran on, as they tend to do. So the families spoke not a word to each other for an entire generation."

Ana shifted Jessie to her lap, stroking the child's hair

as she told the story. She was smiling to herself, unaware that she'd lapsed into her native brogue.

"But the young witch was headstrong, as well as beautiful. And her curiosity was great. And on a fine day in high summer, she slipped out of the manor house and walked through the fields and the meadows toward the castle of her grandfather's enemy. Along the way was a pond, and she paused there to dangle her bare feet in the water and study the castle in the distance. And while she sat, with her feet wet and her hair down around her shoulders, a frog plopped up on the bank and spoke to her.

"'Fair lady,' he said, 'why do you wander on my land?'

"Well, the young witch was not at all surprised to hear a frog speak. After all, she knew too much of magic, and she sensed a trick. 'Your land?' she said. 'Frogs have only the water, and the marsh. I walk where I choose.'

"'But your feet are in my water. So you must pay a forfeit.'

"So she laughed and told him that she owed a common frog nothing at all.

"Well, needless to say, the frog was puzzled by her attitude. After all, it wasn't every day he plopped down and spoke to a beautiful woman, and he had expected at least a shriek or some fearful respect. He was quite fond of playing tricks, and was sorely disappointed that this one wasn't working as he'd hoped. He explained that he was no ordinary frog, and if she didn't agree to pay the forfeit he would have to punish her. And what forfeit did he expect? His answer was a kiss, which was no more and no less than she had expected, for as I said, she was young, but not foolish.

"She said that she doubted very much if he would turn into a handsome prince if she did so, and that she would save her kisses.

"Now the frog was very frustrated, and he plied more magic, whistling up the wind, shaking the leaves in the trees, but she merely yawned at this. At the end of his tether, the frog jumped right into her lap and began to berate her. To teach him a lesson for his forwardness, she plucked him up and tossed him into the water. When he surfaced, he wasn't a frog at all, but a young man, quite wet and furious to have had his joke turned on him. After he swam to shore, they stood on the bank and shouted at each other, threatening spells and curses, sending lightning walking the sky, and shooting the air with thunder. Though she threatened him with the hounds of hell and worse, he said he would have his forfeit regardless, for it was his land, his water, and his right. So he kissed her soundly.

"And it took only that to turn the heat in her heart to warmth, and the fury in his breast to love. For even witches can fall under that most powerful of spells. There and then they pledged to each other, marrying within the month right there on the banks on the pond. And they were happy, then and after, with lives full of love. Still, every year, on a day in high summer, though she is no longer young, she goes to the pond, dangles her feet and waits for an indignant frog to join her."

Ana lifted the sleeping girl. She had told the end of the story only for herself—or so she thought. But as she drew back the cover, Boone's hand closed over hers.

"That was a pretty good story for an amateur. Must be the Irish."

"It's an old family one," she said, thinking how often she had heard how her mother and father had met.

He expertly unlaced his daughter's shoes. "Be careful. I might steal it from you."

As he tucked the covers around Jessie, Daisy took a running leap and landed on the foot of the bed. "Did you enjoy your walk?"

"After I stopped feeling guilty for leaving you with the dishes—which took about ninety seconds." He brushed Jessie's hair from her brow and bent to kiss her good-night. "One of the most enviable things about childhood is being able to drop off to sleep like that."

"Are you still having trouble?"

"I've got a lot on my mind." Taking Ana's hand, he drew her out of the room, leaving the door open, as he always did. "A lot of it's you, but there are a few other things."

"Honest, but not flattering." She paused at the top of the stairs. "Seriously, Boone, I could give you something—" She flushed and chuckled when she saw the light come into his eyes. "A very mild, very safe herbal remedy."

"I'd rather have sex."

Shaking her head, she continued downstairs. "You don't take me seriously."

"On the contrary."

"I mean as an herbalist."

"I don't know anything about that sort of thing, but I don't discount it." He wasn't about to let her dose him, either. "Why'd you get into it?"

"It's always been an interest. There have been healers in my family for generations."

"Doctors?"

"Not exactly."

Boone picked up the wine and two glasses as they walked through the kitchen and out onto the deck. "You didn't want to be a doctor."

"I didn't feel qualified to go into medicine."

"Now that's a very odd thing for a modern, independent woman to say."

"One has nothing to do with the other." She accepted the glass he offered. "It's not possible to heal everyone. And I...have difficulty being around suffering. What I do is my way of satisfying my needs and protecting myself." It was the most she felt she could give him. "And I like working alone."

"I know the feeling. Both my parents thought I was crazy. The writing was okay, but they figured I'd write the great American novel, at the very least. Fairy tales were hard for them to swallow at first."

"They must be proud of you."

"In their way. They're nice people," he said slowly, realizing he'd never discussed them with anyone but Alice. "They've always loved me. God knows they dote on Jessie. But they have a hard time understanding that I might not want what they want. A house in the suburbs, a decent golf game, and a spouse who's devoted to me."

"None of those things are bad."

"No, and I had it once—except for the golf game. I'd rather not spend the rest of my life convincing them that I'm content with the way things are now." He twined a lock of her hair around his fingers. "Don't you get the same sort of business from yours? Anastasia, when are you going to settle down with some nice young man and raise a family?"

"No." She laughed into her wine. "Absolutely not." The very idea of her mother or father saying, even thinking, such a thing made her laugh again. "I suppose you could say my parents are…eccentric." Comfortable, she laid her head back and looked at the stars. "I think they'd both be appalled if I settled for nice. You didn't tell me you had one of Aunt Bryna's illustrations."

"When you made the family connection, you were ready to chew me up and spit me out. It didn't seem appropriate. Then, I guess, it slipped my mind."

"Obviously she thinks highly of you. She only gave one to Nash after the wedding, and he'd been coveting one for years."

"That so? I'll be sure to rub his nose in it the next time I see him." Tipping up her chin with a finger, he turned her face toward his. "It's been a long time since I sat on a porch and necked. I'm wondering if I still have the hang of it."

He brushed his lips over hers, once, twice, a third time, until hers trembled open in invitation. He took the glass from her fingers, set it aside with his as his mouth moved to accept what was offered.

Sweet, so sweet, the taste of her, warming him, soothing him, exciting him. Soft, so soft, the feel of her, tempting him, luring him, charming him. And quiet, so quiet, that quick, catching sigh that sent a streak of lightning zipping up his spine.

But he was no sweaty, fumbling boy groping in the dark. The volcano of needs simmering inside him could be controlled. If he couldn't give her the fullness of his passion, then he could give her the benefit of his experience.

While he filled himself with her, slowly, degree by painful degree, he gave back a care and a tenderness that had her teetering helplessly on that final brink before love.

To be held like this, she thought dimly, with such compassion mixed with the hunger. In all of her imaginings, she had never reached for this. His tongue danced over hers, bringing her all those dark and dusky male flavors. His hands stroked persuasively while the muscles in his arms went taut. When his mouth left hers to cruise down her jaw and over her throat, she arched back, willing, desperately willing, for him to show her more.

It was surrender he felt from her, as clearly as he felt the night breeze against his skin. Knowing it would drive him nearer to the brink, he gave in to the fevered need to touch.

She was small, gloriously soft. Her heart beat frantically under his hand. He could almost taste it, taste that hot satin skin on his lips, on his tongue, deep within his mouth. It was torture not to sample it now, not to drag her dress down to her waist and feast.

The feel of her hardened nipples pressed against the silk had him groaning as he brought his mouth back to hers.

Her mouth was as avid, as desperate. Her hands moved over him as urgently as his over her. She knew, as she gave herself fully to this one moment, that there would be no turning back. They would not love now. It couldn't be now, on the starlit deck, beneath windows where a child might wake and look for her father in the night.

But there was no turning back from being in love. Not for her. She could not change that tidal wave of feeling any more than she could change the blood that coursed through her veins.

And because of it there would come a time, very soon, when she would give to him what she had given to no other.

Overwhelmed, she turned her head, burying her face in his shoulder. "You have no idea what you do to me."

"Then tell me." He caught the lobe of her ear between his teeth, making her shudder. "I want to hear you tell me."

"You make me ache. And yearn." And hope, she thought, squeezing her eyes shut. "No one else has." With a long, shuddering sigh, she drew away. "That's what we're both afraid of."

"I can't deny that." His eyes were like cobalt in the dim light. "And I can't deny that the idea of carrying you upstairs now, taking you into my bed, is something I want as much as I want to go on breathing."

The image had her heart thundering. "Do you believe in the inevitable, Boone?"

"I've had to."

She nodded. "So do I. I believe in destiny, the whims of fate, the tricks of what men used to call the gods. When I look at you, I see the inevitable." She rose, pressed a hand to his shoulder to prevent him from standing with her. "Can you accept that I have secrets I can't tell you, parts of myself I won't share?" She saw both puzzlement and denial in his eyes, and shook her head before he could speak. "Don't answer now.... You need to think it through and be sure. Just as I do."

She leaned down to kiss him, and linked quickly, firmly. She felt his jerk of surprise before she backed away. "Sleep well tonight," she said, knowing that he would now. And that she would not.

Chapter 7

The one gift Ana always gave herself on her birthday was a completely free day. She could be as lazy as she chose, or as industrious. She could get up at dawn and gorge on ice cream for breakfast, or she could laze in bed until noon watching old movies on television.

The single best plan for the one day of the year that belonged only to her was no plan at all.

She did rise early, indulging herself in a long bath scented with her favorite oils and a muslin bag filled with dried herbs chosen for their relaxing properties. To pamper herself, she mixed up a toning face pack of elder flowers, yogurt and kaolin powder, lounging in the tub with harp music and iced juice while it worked its magic.

With her face tingling and her hair silky from its chamomile shampoo, she slicked on her personalized body oil and slipped into a silk robe the color of moonbeams.

As she walked back into the bedroom, she considered crawling back into bed and dozing to complete the morning's indulgence. But in the center of the room, where there had been nothing but an antique prayer rug when she'd gone in to bathe, stood a large wooden chest.

On a quick cry of pleasure, she dashed over to run her hands over the old carved wood, which had been polished to a mirror gleam. It smelled of beeswax and rosemary and felt like silk under her fingers.

It was old, ages old, for it was something she had admired even as a child living in Donovan Castle. A wizard's chest, it was reputed to have resided once in Camelot, commissioned for Merlin by the young Arthur.

With a laughing sigh, she sat back on her heels. They always managed to surprise her, Ana thought. Her parents, her aunts and uncles...so far away, but never out of her heart.

The combined power of six witches had sent the chest from Ireland, winking through the air, through time, through space, by means that were less, and more, than conventional.

Slowly she lifted the lid, and the scent of old visions, ancient spells, endless charms, rose out to her. The fragrance was dry, aromatic as crusted petals ground to dust, tangy with the smoke of the cold fire a sorcerer calls in the night.

She knelt, lifting her arms out, the silk sliding down to her elbows as she cupped her hands, palms facing.

Here was power, to be respected, accepted. The words she spoke were in the old tongue, the language of the Wise Ones. The wind she called whipped the curtains, sent her hair flying around her face. The air sang, a thousand harp strings crying in the breeze, then was silent.

Lowering her arms, Ana reached into the chest. A bloodstone amulet, the inner red of the stone bleeding through the deep green, had her sitting back on her heels once more. She knew it had belonged to her mother's family for generations, a healing stone of enormous worth and mighty power. Tears stung the backs of her eyes when she realized that it was being passed to her, as it was only every half century, to denote her as a healer of the highest order.

Her gift, she thought, running her fingers over a stone smoothed by other fingers in other times. Her legacy.

She gently set it back in the chest and reached for the next gift. She lifted out a globe of chalcedony, its almost transparent surface offering her a glimpse of the universe if she should choose to look. This from Sebastian's parents, she knew, for she felt them as she cupped the globe in her hands. Next was a sheepskin, inscribed with the writing of the old tongue. A fairy story, she noted as she read and smiled. As old as time, as sweet as tomorrow. Aunt Bryna and Uncle Matthew, she thought as she laid it back inside.

Though the amulet had been from her mother, Ana knew there would always be something special from her father, as well. She found it, and she laughed as she took it out. A frog, as small as her thumbnail, intricately carved in jade.

"Looks just like you, Da," she said, and laughed again. Replacing it, she closed the chest, then rose. It would be afternoon in Ireland, she mused, and there were six people who would be expecting a call to see if she'd enjoyed her gifts.

As she started toward the phone, she heard the knock at her back door. Her heart gave one quick, unsteady leap, then settled calmly. Ireland would have to wait.

Boone held the gift behind his back. There was another package at home, one that he and Jessie had chosen together. But he'd wanted to give Ana this one himself. Alone.

He heard her coming and grinned, the greeting on the tip of his tongue. He was lucky he didn't swallow his tongue, as well as the words, when he saw her.

She was glowing, her hair a rain of pale gold down the back of a robe of silver. Her eyes seemed darker, deeper. How could they be as clear as lake water, he wondered, yet seem to hold a thousand secrets? The gloriously female scent that swirled around her nearly brought him to his knees.

When Quigley rushed against his legs in greeting, Boone jolted as if he'd been shot.

"Boone." With a quiet laugh bubbling in her throat, Ana put her hand on the screen. "Are you all right?"

"Yeah, yeah. I... Did I get you up?"

"No." As calm as he was rattled, she opened the door in invitation. "I've been up quite a while. I'm just being lazy." When he continued to stand on the porch, she tilted her head. "Don't you want to come in?"

"Sure." He stepped inside, but kept a careful distance.

He'd been as restrained as could be over the past couple of weeks, resisting the temptation to be alone with her too often, keeping the mood light when they were alone.

He realized now that his control had been as much for his sake as for hers.

She was painful to resist, even when they were standing outside in the sunlight, discussing Jessie or gardening, his work or hers.

But this, standing with her, the house empty and silent around them, the mysterious perfume of a woman's art tormenting his senses, was almost too much to bear.

"Is something wrong?" she asked, but she was smiling, as if she knew.

"No, nothing... Ah, how are you?"

"I'm fine." Her smile widened, softened. "And you?"

"Great." He thought that if he were any more tense he'd turn to stone. "Fine."

"I was going to make some tea. I'm sorry I don't have any coffee, but perhaps you'd like to join me."

"Tea." He let out a quiet breath. "Terrific." He watched her walk to the stove, the cat winding around her legs like gray rope. She put the kettle on, then poured Quigley's breakfast into his bowl. Crouching down, she stroked the cat as he ate. The robe slipped back like water, exposing one creamy leg.

"How's the woodruff coming, and the hyssop?"

"Ah..."

She tossed her hair back as she looked up and smiled. "The herbs I gave you to transplant into your yard."

"Oh, those. They look great."

"I have some basil and some thyme potted in the greenhouse. You might want to take them along, leave them on a windowsill for a while. For cooking." She rose when the kettle began to sputter. "I think you'll find them better than store-bought."

"That'd be great." He was almost relaxed again, he thought. Hoped. It was soothing to watch her brew tea, heating the little china pot, spooning aromatic leaves out of a pale blue jar. He hadn't known a woman could be restful and seductive all at once. "Jessie's been watching those marigold seeds you gave her to plant like a hen watches an egg."

"Just don't let her overwater." Setting the tea to steep, she turned. "Well?"

He blinked. "Well?"

"Boone, are you going to show me what's behind your back or not?"

"Can't fool you, can I?" He held out a box wrapped in bright blue paper. "Happy birthday."

"How did you know it was my birthday?"

"Nash told me. Aren't you going to open it?"

"I certainly am." She tore the paper, revealing a box with the logo of Morgana's shop imprinted on the lid. "Excellent choice," she said. "You couldn't possibly go wrong buying me something from Wicca." She lifted the lid and, with a quiet sigh, drew out a delicate statue of a sorceress carved in amber.

Her head was thrown back and exquisite tendrils of the dark gold hair tumbled down her cloak. Slender arms were raised, bent at the elbows, palms cupped and facing—mirroring the age-old position Ana had assumed over the chest that morning. In one elegant hand she held a small gleaming pearl, in the other a slender silver wand.

"She's beautiful," Ana murmured. "Absolutely beautiful."

"I stopped by the shop last week, and Morgana had just gotten it in. It reminded me of you."

"Thank you." Still holding the statue, she lifted her free hand to his cheek. "You couldn't have found anything more perfect."

She leaned in, rising on her toes to touch her lips to his. She knew exactly what she was doing, just as she knew even as he returned the kiss that he was holding himself on a choke chain of control. Power, as fresh and cool as rainwater, washed into her.

This was what she had been waiting for, this was why she had spent the morning in that ancient female ritual of oils and creams and perfumes.

For him. For her. For their first time together.

There were knots of thorny vines ripping through his stomach, an anvil of need ringing frantically in his head. Though their lips were barely touching, her taste was drugging him, making ideas like restraint and control vague, unimportant concepts. He tried to draw back, but her arms wound silkily around him.

"Ana…"

"Shh." She soothed and excited as her mouth played softly over his. "Just kiss me."

How could he not, when her lips were parting so softly beneath his? He brought his hands to her face, framing it with tensed fingers while he fought a vicious internal war to keep the embrace from going too far.

When the phone rang, he let out a groan that was both frustration and relief. "I'd better go."

"No." She wanted to laugh, but only smiled as she drew out of his arms. Never had she sampled a power more delicious than this. "Please stay. Why don't you pour the tea while I answer that?"

Pour tea, he thought. He'd be lucky if he could lift the pot. System jumbled, he turned blindly to the stove as she took the receiver from the wall phone.

"Mama!" Now she did laugh, and Boone heard the pure joy of it. "Thank you. Thank all of you. Yes, I got it this morning. A wonderful surprise." She laughed again, listening. "Of course. Yes, I'm fine. I'm wonderful. I— Da." She chuckled when her father broke in on the line. "Yes, I know what the frog means. I love it. I love you, too. No, I much prefer it to a real one, thank you." She smiled at Boone when he offered her a cup of tea. "Aunt Bryna? It was a lovely story. Yes, I am. Morgana's very well, so are the twins. Not very much longer now. Yes, you'll be here in time."

Restless, Boone wandered the room, sipping the tea, which was surprisingly good. He wondered what the devil she'd put into it. What the devil she'd put into him. Just listening to her voice was making him ache.

He could handle it, he reminded himself. They'd have a very civilized cup of tea—while he kept his hands off her. Then he'd escape, bury himself in his work for the rest of the day to keep his mind off her, as well.

His story line was all but finished, and he was nearly ready to start on the illustrations. He already knew just what he wanted.

Ana.

With a brisk shake of his head, he gulped more tea. It

sounded as if she were going to carry on a conversation with every relative she had. That was fine, that was dandy. It would give him time to calm himself down.

"Yes, I miss you, too. All of you. I'll see you in a couple of weeks. Blessed be."

She was a little teary-eyed when she hung up, but she smiled at Boone. "My family," she explained.

"I gathered."

"They sent me a chest of gifts this morning, and I hadn't gotten a chance to call and thank them."

"That's nice. Look, I really— This morning?" he said with a slight frown. "I didn't see any delivery truck."

"It came early." She looked away to set her cup down. "Special delivery, you could say. They're all looking forward to visiting at the end of the month."

"You'll be glad to see them."

"Always. They were here briefly over the summer, but with all the excitement about Sebastian and Mel getting engaged and married so quickly, there wasn't much time to just be together." She moved to the door to let Quigley out. "Would you like more tea?"

"No, thanks, really. I should go. Get to work." He was edging toward the door himself. "Happy birthday, Ana."

"Boone." She laid a hand on his arm, felt his muscles quiver. "Every year on my birthday I give myself a gift. It's very simple, really. One day to do whatever I choose. Whatever feels right to me." Hardly seeming to move at all, she pulled the door closed and stood between it and him. "I choose you. If you still want me."

Her words seemed to ring in his ears as he stared down

at her. She appeared so calm, so utterly serene, she might have been discussing the weather. "You know I want you."

"Yes." She smiled. At that moment she was calm, the eye of the hurricane. "Yes, I do." When she took a step forward, he took one in retreat. Was this seduction? she wondered, keeping her eyes on his. "I see that when I look at you, feel it whenever you touch me. You've been very patient, very kind. You kept your word that nothing would happen between us until I decided it should."

"I'm trying." Unsteady, he took another step back. "It isn't easy."

"Nor for me." She stood where she was, the silver robe shimmering around her in the sunlight. "You've only to accept me, to accept that I'm willing to give you everything I can. Take that, and let it be enough."

"What are you asking me?"

"To be my first," she said simply. "To show me what love can be."

He dared to reach out and touch her hair. "Are you sure?"

"I'm very sure." Offering and asking, she held out both hands. "Will you take me to bed and be my lover?"

How could he answer? There were no words to translate what was churning inside him at that moment. So he wasted no words, only lifted her into his arms.

He carried her as if she were as delicate as the amber enchantress he'd given her. Indeed, he thought of her that way, and he felt a thud of panic at the thought that he wouldn't be careful enough, restrained enough. It was so easy to damage delicacy.

When he reached the base of the stairs and started to climb, his pulse was throbbing in anticipation and fear.

For her sake, he wished it could have been night, a candlelit night filled with soft music and silvery moonglow. Yet somehow it seemed right that he love her, this first time, in the morning, when the sun was growing stronger in a deep blue sky, and music came from the birds that flitted through her garden and the tinkling bells of the wind chimes she had at her windows.

"Where?" he asked her, and she gestured toward her bedroom door.

It smelled of her, a mix of female fragrances and perfumed powders—and something else, something he couldn't quite identify. Like smoke and flowers. The sun streamed gaily through billowing curtains and splashed the huge old bed with the towering carved headboard.

He skirted the trunk, charmed by the rainbow of colors refracted by colored crystals suspended from thin wire in front of each window. Rainbows instead of moonbeams, he thought as he laid her on the bed.

Foolish to be nervous now, she told herself, but her hands trembled lightly when she reached out to hold him against her. She wanted this. Wanted him. Still, the calm certainty she had felt only moments ago had vanished under a wave of nerves and needs.

He could see the need, the nervousness, in her eyes. Could she possibly understand that they were a mirror of his? She was so fragile and lovely. Fresh and untouched. His for the taking. And he knew it was vital for them both that he take with tenderness.

"Anastasia." Smothering his own fears, he lifted her

hand, pressed his lips to the palm. "I won't hurt you. I swear it."

"I know that." She linked her fingers with his, wishing she could be sure if it was fear of the moment a woman experiences only once in her life, or fear of the overwhelming depth of her love for him, that left her shaky and unsure. "Show me."

With rainbows dancing around them, he lowered his mouth to hers. A deep, drugging kiss that both soothed and enticed. Time spun out, drifted. Stopped. Still there was only his mouth against hers.

He touched her hair, his fingers combing through, tangling in the luxurious length of it. To please himself, he spread it over the pillow, where it lay like a pool of gold dust against soft Irish linen.

When his lips left hers, it was to take a slow, lazy journey of her face until he felt her nervous trembling fall away into pliancy. Even as she surrendered her fears to the light, sweet sensations he brought her, he kept the pace slow, so slow that it seemed they had forever just to kiss.

She heard him murmur to her, reassurances, lovely, lovely promises. The low hum of his voice had her mind floating, her lips curving in a quiet smile as they met his again.

She should have known it would be like this with him. Beautiful, achingly beautiful. He made her feel loved, cherished, safe. When he slipped the robe from her shoulders, she wasn't afraid, but welcomed the feel of his mouth on her flesh. Eager now, she tugged on his shirt, and he hesitated only a moment before helping her remove it.

A groan ripped out of him as his body shuddered. God,

the feel of her hands on his bare back. He fought back a wave of greed and kept his own hands easy as he parted her robe.

Her skin was like cream. Unbearably soft and fragrant with oils. It drew him like nectar, inviting him to taste. As he closed his mouth over her breast, the quiet, strangled sound she made deep in her throat echoed like thunder in his head.

Gently he used tongue and lips to take her to that next degree of pleasure, while his own passions licked at him, taunting him, demanding that he hurry, hurry, hurry.

Her eyes were so heavy, impossible to open. How could he know just where to touch, just where to taste, to make her heart shudder in her breast? Yet he did, and her breath sighed out between her lips as he showed her more.

Quiet whispers, a gentle caress. The scent of lavender and fairy roses thickening the air. Smooth sheets growing warm, skin dampening with passion. A rainbow of lights playing against her closed lids.

She floated there, lifted by the magic they made together, her breath quickening a little as he eased her higher, just higher.

Then there was heat, searing, torrid. It erupted inside her so quickly, so violently, that she cried out and struggled against him. "No. No, Boone, I—" Then a flash, a lightning spear of pleasure, that left her limp and dazed and trembling.

"Ana." He had to dig his fisted hands into the mattress to keep from plunging into her, driving them both where he knew the rewards were dark and desperately keen.

"Sweet." He kissed her, swallowing her gasping breaths. "So sweet. Don't be afraid."

"No." Rocked to the core, she held him close. His heart was thundering against hers, his body taut as wire. "No. Show me. Show me more."

So he slipped the robe away, driving himself mad with the sight of her naked in a pool of sunlight. Her eyes were open now, dark and steady on his. Beneath the passion just awakened, he saw a trust that humbled him.

He showed her more.

Fears melted away. There was no room for them when her body was vibrating from dozens of more vivid sensations. When he took her to the peak again, she rode out the storm, glorying in the flash of heat, desperate for the next.

He held back, gaining his pleasure from hers, stunned by the way she responded to each touch, to each kiss. Her innocence was his, he knew. With the breath laboring in his lungs, the blood pounding in his head, he entered her, braced for her to stiffen and cry out. Knowing he would have to stop, no matter how his body craved completion, if she asked it of him.

But she didn't stiffen, only gasped out his name as her arms came around him. The brief flash of pain was instantly smothered by a pleasure greater, fuller, than she had ever dreamed possible.

His, she thought. She was his. And she moved against him with an instinct as old as time.

Deeper, he slipped deeper, filling her, rocking her toward that final crest. When she did cry out, her body shuddering, shuddering from the glory of it, he buried his face in her hair and let himself follow.

* * *

He watched the dance of light against the wall, listening to her heart calm and slow. She lay beneath him still, her arms around him, her hands stroking his hair.

He hadn't known it could be like this. That was foolish, he thought. He'd had women before. More, he'd loved before, as deeply as anyone could. Yet this union had been more than he'd ever expected or experienced.

He had no way to explain it to her, when he was far from understanding it himself.

After pressing a kiss to her shoulder, he lifted his head to look at her. Her eyes were closed, and her face was flushed and utterly relaxed. He wondered if she had any idea how much had changed, for both of them, that morning.

"Are you all right?"

She shook her head, alarming him. Instantly concerned, he braced on his arms to remove his weight from her. Her lashes fluttered up so that he could see the smoky eyes beneath them.

"I'm not all right." Her voice was low and throaty. "I'm wonderful. You're wonderful." The smile curved beautifully on her lips. "This is wonderful."

"You had me worried." He brushed the hair away from her cheek. "I don't think I've ever been quite so nervous." Her lips were waiting for his when he bent his head to kiss her. "You're not sorry?"

Her brow arched. "Do I look sorry?"

"No." Taking his time, he studied her face, tracing it with a fingertip. "You look kind of smug." And the fact that she did brought him a rush of deep satisfaction.

"I'm feeling very smug. And lazy." She stretched a little, so he shifted to let her head rest on his shoulder.

"Happy birthday."

She chuckled against his throat. "It was the most… unique present I've ever been given."

"The thing about it is, you can use it over and over again."

"Even better." She tipped her head back, and now her eyes were solemn. "You were very good to me, Boone. Very good for me."

"It wasn't what I'd call an act of altruism. I've wanted this since the first time I saw you."

"I know. It frightened me—and excited me, too." She smoothed her palm over his chest, wishing for a moment they could stay like this forever, cocooned together in the sunlight.

"This changes things."

Her hand stilled, tensed. "Only if you want it to."

"Then I want it to." He sat up, bringing her with him so that they were face-to-face. "I want you to be a part of my life. I want to be with you, as often as possible— and not just like this."

She felt the old, niggling fear trying to surface. Rejection. Rejection now would be devastating. "I am part of your life. I always will be now."

He saw something in her eyes, sensed it in the tension suddenly blooming in the room with them. "But?"

"No buts," she said quickly, and threw her arms around him. "No ands. No anything now. Just this." She kissed him, pouring everything she could into it, knowing she was cheating them both by holding back. Not knowing how to offer it and keep him with her. "I'm here when you want me, as long as you want me. I promise you."

Rushing her again, he berated himself as she clung to him. How could he expect her to be in love just because they had made love? He wasn't even sure what he was feeling himself. It had all happened too fast, and he was riding on the emotion of the moment. He reminded himself, as he held Ana, that he didn't have only his own needs to consider.

There was Jessie.

What happened with Ana would affect his daughter. So there could be no mistaking, no acting on impulse, and no real commitment until he was sure.

"We'll take it slow," he said, but felt a twinge of resentment when Ana immediately relaxed against him. "But if anyone else comes to your door bearing gifts or needing a cup of sugar—"

"I'll boot him out." She squeezed him hard. "There's no one but you." Turning her head, she pressed her lips to his throat. "You make me happy."

"I can make you happier."

She laughed, tilting her head back. "Really?"

"Not like that." Amused, and flattered, he nipped her lower lip. "Not quite yet, anyway. I was thinking more along the lines of going down and fixing you lunch while you lazed around in bed and waited for me. And then making love with you again. And again."

"Well..." It was tempting, but she recalled too well what one of his meals did to a kitchen. And she had too many jars and bottles around that he might use incorrectly. "Why don't we do it this way—you wait for me while I fix lunch?"

"It's your birthday."

"Exactly." She kissed him before she slid out of bed. "Which is why I get to do everything my own way. I won't be long."

It was a pretty stupid man who wouldn't take a deal like that, Boone decided as he leaned back with his arms crossed under his head. He listened to her running water in the adjoining bath, then settled down to imagine what it would be like to spend the afternoon in bed.

Ana belted her robe as she walked downstairs. Love, she thought, did marvelous things for the spirit. Better, far better, than any potion she could brew or conjure. Perhaps in time, perhaps with enough of that love, she could give him the rest.

Boone wasn't Robert, and she was ashamed to have compared them, even for a moment. But the risk was so great, and the day so marvelous.

Humming to herself, she busied herself in the kitchen. Sandwiches would be best, she decided. Not terribly elegant, but practical for eating in bed. Sandwiches, and some of her father's special wine. She all but floated to the refrigerator, which was crowded now with Jessie's artwork.

"Not even dressed yet," Morgana said through the back screen. "I suspected as much."

With a boneless turkey breast in her hand, Ana turned. Not only was Morgana at her kitchen door, but crowded around her were Nash, Sebastian and Mel, too.

"Oh." She felt the flush blooming even as she set the lunch meat aside. "I didn't hear you drive up."

"Obviously too self-involved, with your birthday and all," Sebastian commented.

They piled in, bringing hugs and kisses and pushing ribboned boxes into her hands. Nash was already opening a bottle of champagne. "Find some glasses, Mel. Let's get this party started." He winked at his wife as she collapsed in a chair. "Apple juice for you, babe."

"I'm too fat to argue." She adjusted her weight—or tried to. "So, did you hear from Ireland?"

"Yes, a chest this morning. It's gorgeous. Glasses in the next cupboard," she told Mel. "Gifts inside. I talked to them…" Right before she'd gone upstairs to make love with Boone. Another flush heated her cheeks. "I, ah, I really need to…" Mel shoved a glass into her hand with champagne brimming up to the lip.

"Have the first glass," Sebastian finished for her. He cocked his head to the side. "Anastasia, my love, you look quite radiant. Turning twenty-seven certainly appears to agree with you."

"Keep out of my head," she muttered, and took a sip to give herself a moment to figure out how to explain. "I can't thank you all enough for coming by this way. If you'd just excuse me a minute."

"No need to get dressed for us." Nash poured the rest of the glasses. "Sebastian's right. You look fabulous."

"Yes, but I really need to—"

"Ana, I have a better idea." The sound of Boone's voice from just down the hall had everyone lapsing into silence.

"Why don't we—" Shirtless, barefoot and rumpled, he walked into the room, then stopped dead.

"Whoops," Mel said, and grinned into her glass.

"Succinctly put." Her husband studied Boone through narrowed eyes. "Dropping by for a neighborly visit, are we?"

"Shut up, Sebastian." This from Morgana, who rested both hands on her tummy and smiled. "We seem to have interrupted."

"I think we would have if we'd been any earlier," Nash murmured into Mel's ear, and made her choke back a chuckle.

Ana aimed one withering glance at him before she turned to Boone. "My family's brought along a little party, and they're all quite amused at the idea that I might have a private life—" she looked over her shoulder meaningfully "—that doesn't concern them."

"She always was cranky when you got her out of bed," Sebastian said, resigned to accepting Boone. For now. "Mel, it appears we'll need another glass of champagne."

"Already got it covered." Smiling, she stepped forward and offered it to Boone. "If you can't beat 'em," she said under her breath, and he nodded.

"Well." He took a long sip and sighed. It was obvious that his plans for the rest of the day would have to be adjusted. "Anybody bring cake?"

With a delighted laugh, Morgana gestured toward a large bakery box. "Get Ana a knife, Nash, so she can cut the first piece. I think we'll dispense with candles. She appears to have gotten her wish already."

Chapter 8

Ana was much too accustomed to her family to be annoyed with or embarrassed by them for long. And she was simply too happy with Boone to hold a grudge. As the days passed, they moved slowly, cautiously, toward cementing their relationship.

If she had come to trust him with her heart, with her body, she had not yet come to trust him with her secrets.

Though his feelings for her had ripened, deepened into a love he had never expected to experience again, he was as wary as she of taking that final step that would join their lives.

At the center was a child neither would have harmed by putting their own needs first.

If they stole a few hours on bright afternoons or rainy mornings, it was theirs to steal. At night Ana would lie alone and wonder how long this magic interlude would last.

As Halloween approached, she and Boone were caught

up in their own preparations. Now and again her nerves would jump out at the idea of her lover meeting the whole of her family on the holiday. Then she would laugh at herself for acting like a girl on the point of introducing a first date.

By noon on the thirty-first, she was already at Morgana's, helping her now greatly pregnant cousin with preparations for the Halloween feast.

"I could have made Nash do this." Morgana pressed a hand against the ache in the small of her back before she sat down to knead bread dough from a more comfortable position at the kitchen table.

"You could make Nash do anything simply by asking." Ana cubed lamb for the traditional Irish stew. "But he's having such fun setting up his special effects."

"Just like a layman to think he can outdo the professionals." She winced and moaned and had Ana's immediate attention.

"Honey?"

"No, no, it's not labor, though I damn well wish it was. I'm just so bloody uncomfortable all the time now." Hearing the petulance in her own voice, she winced again. "And I hate whiners."

"You whine all you like. It's just you and me. Here." Always prepared, Ana poured some liquid into a cup. "Drink it down."

"I already feel like I'm going to float away—like Cleopatra's barge. By the goddess, I'm big enough." But she drank, fingering the crystal around her neck.

"And you already have a crew of two."

That did the trick of making her laugh. "Talk to me

about something else," she begged, and went back to her kneading. "Anything to take my mind off the fact that I'm fat and grumpy."

"You're not fat, and you're only a little grumpy." But Ana cast her mind around for a distraction. "Did you know that Sebastian and Mel are working on another case together?"

"No, I didn't." And it served to pique her interest. "I'm surprised. Mel's very territorial about her private investigation business."

"Well, she's lowered the gate on this one. A runaway, only twelve years old. The parents are frantic. When I talked to her last night, she said they had a lead, and she was sorry she couldn't take this afternoon off to give you a hand."

"When Mel's in the kitchen, it's more like giving me a foot." There was affection for her new in-law in every syllable. "She's wonderful with Sebastian, isn't she?"

"Yes." Smiling to herself, Ana layered the lamb with potatoes and onions in Morgana's big Dutch oven. "Tough-minded, hardheaded, softhearted. She's exactly what he needs."

"And have you found what you need?"

Saying nothing at first, Ana added herbs. She'd known Morgana would work her way around to it before the day was over. "I'm very happy."

"I like him. I had a good feeling about him from the first."

"I'm glad."

"So does Sebastian—though he has some reservations."

Her brows knit, but she kept her voice light. "Particularly after he cornered Boone and picked through his brain."

Ana's lips thinned as she adjusted the heat on the stove. "I haven't forgiven him for that yet."

"Well." Morgana shrugged and set the dough in a bowl to rise. "Boone didn't know, and it soothed Sebastian's feathers. He wasn't exactly pleased to have walked in on your birthday and found you fresh out of bed."

"It's certainly none of his business."

"He loves you." She gave Ana's arm a quick squeeze as she passed the stove. "He'll always worry about you more because you're the youngest—and simply because your gift makes you so vulnerable."

"I'm not without my defenses, Morgana, or common sense."

"I know. Darling, I..." She felt her eyes fill and brushed hastily at the tears. "It was your first time. I didn't want to probe before, but... Lord, I never used to be so sentimental."

"You were just able to hide it better." Abandoning her cooking for the moment, Ana crossed over to take Morgana into her arms. "It was beautiful, and he's so gentle. I knew there was a reason I had to wait, and he was it." She drew back, smiling. "Boone's given me more than I ever imagined I could have."

With a sigh, Morgana lifted her hands to Ana's face. "You're in love with him."

"Yes. Very much in love with him."

"And he with you?"

Her gaze faltered. "I don't know."

"Oh, Ana."

"I won't link with him that way." Her eyes leveled again, her voice firmed. "It would be dishonest when I haven't told him what I am, and haven't the courage to tell him how I feel myself. I know he cares for me. I need no gift to know he cares for me. And that's enough. When there's more, if there's more, he'll tell me."

"It never fails to surprise me how damn stubborn you are."

"I'm a Donovan," Ana countered. "And this is important."

"I agree. You should tell him." She gripped Ana's arms before her cousin could turn away. "Oh, I know. I despise it when someone gives me advice I don't want to hear. But you have to let go of the past and face the future."

"I am facing the future. I'd like Boone to be in it. I need more time." Her voice broke, and she pressed her lips together until she felt she could steady it. "Morgana, I know him. He's a good man. He has compassion and imagination and a capacity for generosity he isn't even aware of. He also has a child."

When Ana turned away this time, Morgana was forced to brace herself on the table. "Is that what you're afraid of? Taking on someone else's child?"

"Oh, no. I love her. Who wouldn't? Even before I loved Boone, I loved Jessie. And she's the center of his world, as it should be. There's nothing, absolutely nothing, I wouldn't do for either of them."

"Then explain."

Stalling, Ana rinsed the hard-cooked eggs she was going to devil. "Do you have any fresh dill? You know how Uncle Douglas loves his deviled eggs with dill."

On a hiss of breath, Morgana slapped a jar on the counter. "Anastasia, explain."

Emotions humming, Ana jerked off the tap. "Oh, you don't know how fortunate you are with Nash. To have someone love you that way no matter what."

"Of course I know," Morgana said softly. "What does Nash have to do with this?"

"How many other men would accept one of us so completely? How many would want marriage, or take a witch as a mother for his child?"

"In the name of Finn, Anastasia." The impatience in her voice was spoiled a bit by the fact that she was forced to sit again. "You talk as if we're broomstick-riding crones, cackling while we curdle the milk in a mother's breast."

She didn't smile. "Don't most think of us just that way? Robert—"

"A pox on Robert."

"All right, forget him," Ana agreed with a wave of her hand. "How many times through the centuries have we been hunted and persecuted, feared and ostracized, simply for being what we were born to be? I'm not ashamed of my blood. I don't regret my gift or my heritage. But I couldn't bear it if I told him, and he looked at me as if—" she gave a half laugh "—as if I had a smoking cauldron in the basement filled with toads and wolfsbane."

"If he loves you—"

"If," Ana repeated. "We'll see. Now I think you should lie down for an hour."

"You're just changing the subject," Morgana began, then looked up as Nash burst in. There were cobwebs in his hair—simulated, fortunately—and an unholy gleam in his eyes.

"You guys have got to see this. It's incredible. I'm so good, I scare myself." He snatched a celery stalk from the counter and chomped. "Come on, don't just stand there."

"Amateurs," Morgana sighed, and hauled herself to her feet.

The two women were admiring Nash's hologram ghosts in the foyer when Ana heard a car drive up.

"They're here." Filled with delight at the prospect of seeing her family, she took one bounding leap toward the door. Then stopped dead. She was already whirling around when Morgana sagged against Nash.

Instantly he went as pale as his ghosts. "Babe? Are you—? Oh, boy."

"It's all right." She let out a long breath as Ana took her other arm. "Just a twinge, really." Leaning back against Nash, she smiled at Ana. "I guess having twins on Halloween is pretty appropriate."

"Absolutely nothing to worry about." Douglas Donovan was reassuring Nash. Like his son, he was a tall man, and his mane of raven hair was only lightly silvered. He'd chosen black tie and tails for the occasion, and had set them off with orange neon sneakers that pleased him enormously by glowing in the dark. "Childbirth. Most natural thing in the world. Perfect night for it, too."

"Right." Nash swallowed the lump in his throat. His house was full of people—witches, if you wanted to get technical—and his wife was sitting on the sofa, looking as if she weren't the least bit concerned that she'd been in labor for over three hours. "Maybe it was a false alarm."

Camilla wafted by in a sequined ball gown and tapped Nash on the shoulder with her feather fan. "Leave it to Ana, dear child. She'll take care of everything. Why, when I had Sebastian, I was in labor for thirteen hours. We joked about that, didn't we, Douglas?"

"After you'd stopped shouting curses at me, dear heart."

"Well, naturally." She wandered toward the kitchen, thinking she'd check on the stew. Ana never used quite enough sage.

"Would have turned me into a hedgehog if she hadn't been otherwise occupied," Douglas confided.

"That makes me feel better," Nash muttered. "Heaps."

Delighted to have helped, Douglas slapped him heartily on the back. "That's what we're here for, Dash."

"Nash."

Douglas smiled benignly. "Yes, indeed."

"Mama." Morgana gave her mother's hand a squeeze. "Go rescue poor Nash from Uncle Douglas. He's looking a little queasy."

Bryna obligingly set aside her sketchpad. "Shall I have your father take him out for a walk?"

"Wonderful." She gave a sigh of gratitude as Ana continued to rub her shoulders. "There isn't anything for him to do quite yet."

Ana's father, Padrick, plopped down the moment Bryna vacated the seat. "How's the girl?"

"I'm really fine. It's all very mild as yet, but I'm sure it'll get rolling before too much longer." She leaned over to kiss his plump cheek. "I'm glad you're all here."

"Wouldn't be anywhere else." He put a pudgy hand on her belly to soothe and gave his daughter one of his elvish grins. "And my own little darling. You're pretty as a picture. Take right after your da, don't you?"

"Naturally." Ana felt the next contraction start and kept her hands steady on Morgana's shoulders. "Long, relaxed breaths, love."

"Will you want to give her some blue cohosh?" he asked his daughter.

Ana considered, then shook her head. "Not yet. She's doing well enough. But you could get me my pouch. I'll want some crystals."

"Done." He rose, then flipped his hand over. In the palm was a sprig of bell heather in full flower. "Now where did this come from?" he said, in the way he had since the laboring woman had been a babe herself. "Take care of this for me. I've business to tend to."

Morgana brushed the heather against her cheek. "He's the dearest man in the world."

"He'll spoil these two if you let him. Da's a pushover for children." With the empathic link, she knew Morgana was in more discomfort than she was letting on. "I'll have to take you upstairs soon, Morgana."

"Not yet, though." She reached over her shoulder for Ana's hand. "It's so nice being here with everyone. Where's Aunt Maureen?"

"Mama's in the kitchen, probably arguing with Aunt Camilla over the stew by now."

On a little groan, Morgana shut her eyes. "Lord, I could eat a gallon of it."

"After," Ana promised, and looked up as the rattle of

chains and the moans of the suffering filled the room. "Somebody at the door."

"Poor Nash. He can't relax long enough to appreciate his own handiwork. Is it Sebastian?"

Ana craned her neck. "Uh-huh. He and Mel are critiquing the holograms. Whoops, there goes the smoke machine and the bats."

Sebastian strode in. "Amateurs."

"And Lydia was so scared she screamed and screamed," Jessie said, relating the chills and thrills of the elementary school's haunted house. "Then Frankie ate so much candy he threw up."

"Sounds like a red-letter day." To forestall exactly the same eventuality, he'd already hidden away half of the treats Jessie'd collected in her goodie bag.

"I like my costume best of all." As they got out of the car in front of Morgana's, Jessie twirled so that the starry pink material floated around her. Rather pleased with himself, Boone crouched to adjust her wings of aluminum foil. It had taken him the better part of two days to figure out how to tack and baste and tie the fairy costume together. But it was worth it.

She tapped her father's shoulder with her cardboard wand. "Now you're the handsome prince."

"What was I before?"

"The ugly toad." She squealed with laughter as he tweaked her nose. "Do you think Ana's going to be surprised? Will she recognize me?"

"Not a chance. I'm not sure I recognize you myself." They'd opted to dispense with a mask, and Boone had painted her cheeks with rouge, reddened her lips, and smudged her eyelids up to her eyebrows with glittery gold shadow.

"We're going to meet her whole family," she reminded her father—as if he needed reminding. He'd been worrying about the event all week. "And I get to see Morgana's cat and dog again."

"Right." He tried not to be overly concerned about the dog. Pan might look like a wolf—disconcertingly so—but he'd been gentle and friendly with Jessie the last time they'd visited.

"This is going to be the best Halloween party in the whole world." Rising to her tiptoes, she pushed the doorbell. Her mouth fell open in a soundless gasp when the moans and clanking chains filled the air.

A husky man with thinning hair and jolly eyes opened the door. He took one look at Jessie and spoke in his best ghoul's voice. "Welcome to the haunted castle. Enter at your own risk."

Her eyes were big blue saucers. "Is it really haunted?"

"Come in...if you dare." He squatted down until he was at eye level with her, then pulled a fluffy stuffed bunny from up his sleeve.

"Ooh..." Charmed, Jessie pressed it against her cheek. "Are you a magician?"

"Certainly. Isn't everyone?"

"Uh-uh. I'm a fairy princess."

"That's good enough. And is this your escort for the evening?" he asked, glancing up at Boone.

"No." Jessie laughed gaily. "He's my daddy. I'm really Jessie."

"I'm really Padrick."

He straightened, and though his eyes remained merry, Boone was sure he was being measured. "And you'd be?"

"Sawyer." He offered a hand. "Boone Sawyer. We're Anastasia's neighbors."

"Neighbors, you say? Well, I doubt that's all. But come in, come in." He exchanged Boone's hand for Jessie's. "See what we have in store for you."

"Ghosts!" She nearly bounced out of her Mary Janes. "Daddy, ghosts!"

"Not a bad attempt for a layman," Padrick said kindly enough. "Oh, by the way, Ana's just taken Nash and Morgana upstairs. We've having twins tonight. Maureen, my passion flower, come meet Ana's neighbors." He turned to Boone as a striking amazon in a scarlet turban came striding down the hall.

"I imagine you'd like a drink, boyo," Padrick said to Boone.

"Yes, sir." Boone blew out a long breath. "I believe I would."

Hesitant and uneasy, Mel knocked on the door of Morgana's bedroom, then poked her head in. She wasn't sure whether she'd expected the clinical—and, to her mind, frightening—aura of a delivery room or the mystical glow of a magic circle. Either one she could have done without.

Instead, there was Morgana propped up in a big, cozy-looking bed, flowers and candles all around. Harp and flute music was drifting through the room. Morgana looked a bit flushed, Nash more than a bit pale, but the basic normality of it all reassured Mel enough to have her crossing the threshold when Ana gestured to her.

"Come on in, Mel. You should be an expert at this now. After all, you helped Sebastian and me deliver the foal just a few months ago."

"I feel like a horse," Morgana muttered, "but that doesn't mean I appreciate the comparison."

"I don't want to interrupt, or get in the way or— Oh, boy," she whispered when Morgana threw her head back and began to puff like a steam engine.

"Okay, okay." Nash gripped her hand and fumbled with a stopwatch. "Here comes another one. We're doing fine, just fine."

"We, hell," Morgana said between her teeth. "I'd like to see you—"

"Breathe." Ana's voice was gentle as she placed crystals over Morgana's belly. They hovered in the air, gleaming with an unearthly light that Mel tried to take in stride.

After all, she reminded herself, she'd been married to a witch for two months.

"It's all right, babe." Nash pressed his lips to her hand, wishing desperately for the pain to pass. "It's almost over."

"Don't go." She gripped his hand hard as the contraction began to ease. "Don't go."

"I'm right here. You're wonderful." As Ana had instructed him, he cooled Morgana's face with a damp cloth. "I love you, gorgeous."

"You'd better." She managed a smile and let out a long, cleansing breath. Knowing she had a ways to go, she closed her eyes. "How am I doing, Ana?"

"Great. A couple more hours."

"A couple—" Nash bit off the words and fixed on a smile that was sick around the edges. "Terrific."

Mel cleared her throat, and Ana glanced over. "I'm sorry. We got a little distracted."

"No problem. I just thought you'd want to know Boone's here—with Jessie."

"Oh." Ana mopped her own brow with her shirtsleeve. "I'd forgotten. I'll be right down. Would you send Aunt Bryna up?"

"Sure. Hey, Morgana, we're all with you."

Morgana's smile was just a tad wicked. "Great. Want to change places?"

"I'll pass this time, thanks." She was edging toward the door. "I'll just get out of your way."

"You're not going to be gone long." Struggling against panic, Nash rubbed the small of Morgana's back and looked pleadingly at Ana.

"Only a minute or two. And Aunt Bryna's very skilled. Besides, we need some brandy."

"Brandy? She's not supposed to drink."

"For you," Ana said gently as she slipped out of the room.

The first thing Ana noted when she reached the parlor was that Jessie was being very well entertained. Ana's mother was laughing her lusty, full-bodied laugh as Jessie recounted her class's escapades at the school Halloween party. Since Jessie was already cuddling two stuffed animals, Ana deduced that her father had already been up to his tricks.

She certainly hoped he'd been discreet.

"Things are well upstairs?" Bryna said quietly as they passed in the doorway.

"Perfect. You'll be a grandmother before midnight."

"Bless you, Anastasia." Bryna kissed her cheek. "And I do like your young man."

"He's not—" But her aunt was already hurrying upstairs.

And there was Boone standing by the fireplace, where the flames crackled cheerily, drinking what was surely one of her father's concoctions and listening, with an expression of fascinated bemusement, to one of her uncle Douglas's stories.

"So, naturally, we took the poor soul in for the night. Storm being what it was. And what did he do but go screeching out in the morning, shouting about banshees and ghosts and the like. Touched," Douglas said sadly, tapping a finger to his head, where an orange silk hat now resided. "A sad and sorry tale."

"Perhaps it had something to do with you clanging about in that suit of armor," Matthew Donovan commented, warming a brandy in his long-fingered hands.

"No, no, a suit of armor doesn't resemble a banshee in the least. I imagine it was Maureen's cat screeching that did it."

"My cats do not screech," she said, insulted. "They're quite well behaved."

"I have a dog," Jessie piped up. "But I like cats, too."

"Is that so?" Always willing to oblige, Padrick plucked a yellow-striped stuffed kitten from between her fairy wings. "How about this one?"

"Oh!" Jessie buried her face in its fur, then delighted

Padrick by climbing onto his lap and kissing his rosy cheek.

"Da." Ana leaned over the sofa to press her lips to his balding head. "You never change."

"Ana!" Jessie bounced on Padrick's lap and tried to hold up her entire menagerie at once. "Your daddy's the funniest person in the world!"

"I like him myself." She tilted her head curiously. "But who are you?"

"I'm Jessie." Giggling, she climbed down to turn in a circle.

"No, really?"

"Honest. Daddy made me a fairy princess for Halloween."

"You certainly sound like Jessie." Ana crouched down. "Give me a kiss and let's see."

Jessie pressed her painted lips to Ana's, flushing with pleasure at her costume's success. "Didn't you know me? Really?"

"You fooled me completely. I was certain you were a real fairy princess."

"Your daddy said you were his fairy princess 'cause your mama was a queen."

Maureen let out another peal of laughter, and winked at her husband. "My little frog."

"I'm sorry I can't stay and talk," Ana told Jessie.

"I know. You're helping get Morgana's babies out. Do they come out together or one at a time?"

"One at a time, I hope." She laughed, tousling Jessie's hair, and looked over at Boone. "You know you're welcome to stay as long as you like. There's plenty of food."

"Don't worry about us. How's Morgana?"

"Very well. Actually, I came down to get some brandy for Nash. His nerves are about shot."

With an understanding nod, Matthew picked up a decanter and a snifter. "He has my sympathy." When he passed them to her, she felt a jolt of his power and knew that, however calm his exterior, his mind and his heart were upstairs with his daughter.

"Don't worry. I'll take care of her, Uncle Matthew."

"No one better. You are the best I've known, Anastasia." His eyes held hers as he flicked a finger over the bloodstone she wore around her neck. "And I've known many." Then a smile touched his lips. "Boone, perhaps you'd walk Anastasia back up."

"Be glad to." Boone took the decanter from Ana before they started out.

"Your family," Boone began, shaking his head at the foot of the stairs, unaware that she'd stiffened.

"Yes?"

"Incredible. Absolutely incredible. It isn't every day I find myself plopped into the center of a group of strangers, with a woman about to give birth to twins upstairs, a wolf—because I swear that dog is no dog—gnawing what looks like a mastodon bone under the kitchen table, and mechanical bats flying overhead. Oh, I forgot the ghosts in the foyer."

"Well, it is Halloween."

"I don't think that has much to do with it." He stopped at the top of the stairs. "I can't remember ever being more entertained. They're fabulous, Ana. Your father does these magic tricks—terrific magic tricks. For the life of me I couldn't figure out how he pulled it off."

"No, you wouldn't. He's, ah...very accomplished."

"He could make a living at it. I've got to tell you, I wouldn't have missed this party for the world." He cupped his free hand around her neck. "The only thing missing is you."

"I was worried you'd feel awkward."

"No. Though it does kind of scotch my plans to lure you into some shadowy corner and make you shiver with some bloodcurdling story so you'd climb all over me for protection."

"I don't spook easily." Smiling, she twined her arms around him. "I grew up on bloodcurdling."

"And uncles clanging around in suits of armor," he murmured as he brushed his lips over hers.

"Oh, that's the least of it." She leaned against him, changing the angle of the kiss. "We used to play in the dungeons. And I spent an entire night in the haunted tower on one of Sebastian's dares."

"Courageous."

"No, stubborn. And stupid. I've never been more uncomfortable in my life." She was drifting into the kiss, losing herself. "At least until Morgana conjured up a blanket and pillow."

"Conjured?" he repeated, amused by the term.

"Sent up," she corrected, and poured herself into the embrace so that he would think of nothing but her.

When the door opened beside them, they looked around like guilty children. Bryna lifted her brows, summed up the situation and smiled.

"I'm sorry to interrupt, but I think Boone is just what we need right now."

He took a firmer grip on the brandy bottle. "In there?"

She laughed. "No. If you'd just stay there, and let me send Nash out for a moment or two. He could use a little man talk."

"Only for a minute," Ana cautioned. "Morgana needs him inside."

Before Boone could agree or refuse, she slipped away. Resigned, he poured a snifter, took a good swallow himself, then refilled it when Nash stepped out.

He pressed the snifter on Nash. "Have a shot."

"I didn't think it would take so long." After a long breath, he sipped the brandy. "Or that it would hurt her so much. If we get through this, I swear, I'm never going to touch her again."

"Yeah, right."

"I mean it." Despite the fact he knew it was an expectant-father cliché, he began to pace.

"Nash, I don't mean to interfere, but wouldn't you feel better—safer—if Morgana was in a hospital, with a doctor and all that handy medical business?"

"A hospital? No." Nash rubbed a hand over his face. "Morgana was born in that same bed. She wouldn't have it any other way with the twins. I guess I wouldn't, either."

"Well, a doctor, then."

"Ana's the best." Remembering that relaxed him slightly. "Believe me, Morgana couldn't be in better hands than hers."

"I know midwives are supposed to be excellent, and more natural, I imagine." He moved his shoulders. If Nash was content with the situation, it wasn't up to him to worry about it. "I guess she's done it before."

"No, this is Morgana's first time."

"I meant Ana," Boone said on a chuckle. "Delivering babies."

"Oh, yeah. Sure. She knows what she's doing. It's not that. In fact, I think I'd go crazy if she wasn't here. But—" He took another swallow, paced a little more. "I mean, this has been going on for hours. I don't know how she can stand it. I don't know why any woman stands it. Just seems to me she could do something about it. Damn it, she's a witch."

Manfully masking another chuckle, Boone gave Nash an encouraging pat on the back. "Nash, it's not a good time to call her names. Women get a little nasty when they're in labor. They're entitled."

"No, I mean—" He broke off, realizing he was going over the edge. "I've got to pull myself together."

"Yep."

"I know it's going to be all right. Ana wouldn't let anything happen. But it's so hard to watch her hurting."

"When you love someone, it's the hardest thing in the world. But you get through it. And, in this case, you're getting something fantastic out of it."

"I never thought I could feel this way, about anybody. She's everything."

"I know what you mean."

Feeling better, Nash passed the snifter back to Boone. "Is that how it is with Ana?"

"I think it might be. I know she's special."

"Yeah, she is." Nash hesitated, and when he spoke

again he chose his words with care. Loyalty, split two ways, was the heaviest of burdens. "You'd be able to understand her, Boone, with your imagination, your way of looking beyond what's considered reality. She is a very special lady, with qualities that make her different from anyone you've ever known. If you love her, and you want her to be a part of your life and Jessie's, don't let those qualities block you."

Boone's brows drew together. "I don't think I'm following you."

"Just remember I said it. Thanks for the drink." He took a steadying breath, then went back in to his wife.

Chapter 9

"Breathe. Come on, baby, breathe!"

"I am breathing." Morgana grunted out the words between pants and couldn't quite manage to glare at Nash. "What the hell do you call this if it's not breathing?"

Nash figured he was past his own crisis point. She'd already called him every name in the book, and had invented several more. Ana said they were nearly there, and he was clinging to that as desperately as Morgana was clinging to his hand. So he merely smiled at his sweaty wife and mopped her brow with a cool cloth.

"Growling, spitting, snarling." He touched his lips to hers, relieved when she didn't bite him. "You're not going to turn me into a slug or a two-headed newt, are you?"

She laughed, groaned, and let out the last puff of air. "I can come up with something much more inventive. I need to sit up more. Ana?"

"Nash, get in the bed behind her. Support her back. It's going to go quickly now." Arching her own back, which echoed the aches in Morgana's, she checked one last time to see if all was ready. There were blankets warmed by the fire, heated water, the clamps and scissors already sterilized, the glow of crystals pulsing with power.

Bryna stood by her daughter's side, her eyes bright with understanding and concern. Images of her own hours in that same bed fighting to bring life into the world raced through her head. That same bed, she thought blinking at the mists in her eyes, where her child now labored through the last moments, the last pangs.

"No pushing until I tell you. Pant. Pant," Ana repeated as she felt the contraction build within herself—a sweet and terrible pang that brought fresh sweat to her skin. Morgana stiffened, fought off the need to tense, and struggled to do as she was told. "Good, good. Nearly there, darling, I promise. Have you picked out names?"

"I like Curly and Moe," Nash said, panting right along with Morgana until she managed to jab him weakly with an elbow. "Okay, okay, Ozzie and Harriet, but only if we have one of each."

"Don't make me laugh now, you idiot." But she did laugh, and the pain eased back. "I want to push. I have to push."

"If it's two girls," he continued, with an edge of desperation, "we're going with Lucy and Ethel." He pressed his cheek against hers.

"Two boys and it's Boris and Bela." Morgana's laughter took on a slightly hysterical note as she reached back to link her arms around Nash's neck. "God, Ana, I have to—"

"Bear down," Ana snapped out. "Go ahead, push."

Caught between laughter and tears, Morgana threw her head back and fought to bring life into the room. "Oh, God!" Outside, lightning shot across a cloudless sky and thunder cracked its celestial whip.

"Nice going, champ," Nash began, but then his mind seemed to go blank as glass. "Look! Oh, Lord, would you look at that!"

At the foot of the bed, Ana gently, competently turned the tiny, dark head. "Hold back now, honey. I know it's hard, but hold back just for a minute. Pant. That's it, that's the way. Next time's the charm."

"It's got hair," Nash said weakly. His face was as wet with sweat and tears as Morgana's. "Just look at that. What is it?"

"I haven't got that end out yet." Ana sent a glittering smile to her cousin. "Okay, this is for the grand prize. Bear down, honey, and let's see if we've got Ozzie or Harriet."

With laughter, Morgana delivered her child into Ana's waiting hands. As the first wild, indignant cry of life echoed in the room, Nash buried his face in his wife's tangled hair.

"Morgana. Sweet Lord, Morgana. Ours."

"Ours." The pain was already forgotten. Eyes glowing, Morgana held out her arms so that Ana could place the tiny, wriggling bundle into them. In the language of her blood, she murmured to the babe, as her hands moved gently to welcome.

"What is it?" With a trembling hand, Nash reached down to touch the tiny head. "I forgot to look."

"You have a son," Ana told him.

* * *

At the first lusty wail, conversation in the parlor downstairs cut off like a switch. All eyes shifted to the stairs. There was silence, stillness. Touched, Boone looked at his own child, who slept peacefully on the sofa, her head nestled in Padrick's comfortable lap.

He felt a tremor beneath his feet, saw the wine slosh back and forth in his glass. Before he could speak, Douglas was removing his top hat and slapping Matthew on the back.

"A new Donovan," he said, and snatched up a glass to lift in toast. "A new legacy."

A little teary-eyed, Camilla walked over to kiss her brother-in-law's cheek. "Blessed be."

Boone was about to add his congratulations when Sebastian crossed the room. He lit a white candle, then a gold one. Taking up a bottle of unopened wine, he broke the seal, then poured pale gold liquid into an ornate silver chalice.

"A star dawns in the night. Life from life, blood through blood to shine its light. Through love he was given the gift of birth, and from breath to death will walk the earth. The other gift comes through blood and bone, and is for him to take and own. Charm of the moon, power of the sun. Never forgetting an it harm none."

Sebastian passed the cup to Matthew, who sipped first. Fascinated, Boone watched the Donovans pass the chalice of wine from one to the other. An Irish tradition? he wondered. It was certainly more moving, more charming, than passing out cigars.

When he was handed the cup, he was both honored and

baffled. Even as he began to sip, another wail sounded, announcing another life.

"Two stars," Matthew said in a voice thickened with pride. "Two gifts."

Then the solemn mood was broken as Padrick conjured up a party streamer and a rain of confetti. As he blew a celebratory toot, his wife laughed bawdily.

"Happy New Year," she said, gesturing toward the clock that had just begun to strike twelve. "It's the best All Hallows' Eve since Padrick made the pigs fly." She grinned at Boone. "He's such a prankster."

"Pigs," Boone began, but the group turned as one as Bryna entered the room. She moved directly to her husband, who folded her tightly within his arms.

"They're all well." She brushed at happy tears. "All well and beautiful. We have a grandson and a granddaughter, my love. And our daughter invites us all upstairs to welcome them."

Not wanting to intrude, Boone hung back as the group piled out of the room. Sebastian stopped in the doorway, arched a brow. "Aren't you coming?"

"I think the family..."

"You were accepted," Sebastian said shortly, not certain he agreed with the rest of the Donovans. He hadn't forgotten how deeply Ana had once been hurt.

"An odd way to phrase it." Boone kept his voice mild to counteract a sudden flare of temper. "Particularly since you feel differently."

"Regardless." Sebastian inclined his head in what Boone interpreted as both challenge and warning. But when Sebastian glanced toward the sofa, he softened. "I imagine Jessie would be disappointed if you didn't wake her and bring her up for a look."

"But you'd rather I didn't."

"Ana would rather you did," Sebastian countered. "And that's more to the point." He moved to the doorway again, then stopped. "You'll hurt her. Anastasia sheds no tears, but she'll shed them for you. Because I love her, I'll have to forgive you for that."

"I don't see—"

"No." Sebastian nodded curtly. "But I do. Bring the child, Sawyer, and join us. It's a night for kindness, and small miracles."

Uncertain why Sebastian's words angered him so much, Boone stared at the empty doorway. He damn well didn't have to prove himself to some overprotective, interfering cousin. When Jessie shifted and blinked owlishly, he pushed Sebastian out of his mind.

"Daddy?"

"Right here, frog face." He bent and lifted his child into his arms. "Guess what?"

She rubbed her eyes. "I'm sleepy."

"We'll go home soon, but I think there's something you'd like to see first." While she yawned and dropped her heavy head on his shoulder, he carried her upstairs.

They were all gathered around, making a great deal more noise than Boone imagined was the norm even for a home delivery room. Nash was sitting on the edge of the bed beside Morgana, holding a tiny bundle and grinning like a fool.

"He looks like me, don't you think?" he was asking of no one in particular. "The nose. He's got my nose."

"That's Allysia," Morgana informed him, rubbing a cheek over her son's downy head. "I've got Donovan."

"Right. Well, *she's* got my nose." He peeked over at his son. "He's got my chin."

"The Donovan chin," Douglas corrected. "Plain as a pikestaff."

"Hah." Maureen was jockeying for position. "They're both Corrigans through and through. Our side of the family has always had strong genes."

While they argued over that, Jessie shook off sleep and stretched forward. "Is it the babies? Did they get born? Can I see?"

"Let the child in." Padrick elbowed his brother out of the way. "Let her have a look."

Jessie kept one arm hooked around her father's neck as she leaned forward. "Oh!" Her tired eyes went bright as Ana took a babe in each arm to hold them up for Jessie to see. "They look just like little fairies." Very delicately, she touched a fingertip to one cheek, then the other.

"That's just what they are." Padrick kissed Jessie's nose. "A brand new fairy prince and princess."

"But they don't have wings," Jessie said, giggling.

"Some fairies don't need wings." Padrick winked at his daughter. "Because they have wings on their hearts."

"These fairies need some rest and some quiet." Ana turned to tuck the babies into Morgana's waiting arms. "And so does their mama."

"I feel wonderful."

"Nevertheless…" Ana shot a warning look over her shoulder that had the Donovans reluctantly filing out.

"Boone," Morgana called out. "Would you wait for Ana, drive her home? She's exhausted."

"I'm perfectly fine. He should—"

"Of course I will." He settled the yawning Jessie on his shoulder. "We'll be downstairs whenever you're ready."

It took another fifteen minutes before Ana was assured that Nash had all her instructions. Morgana was already drifting off to sleep when Ana closed the door and left the new family alone.

She was exhausted, and the powers of the crystals in her pouch were nearly depleted. For almost twelve hours, she had gone through the labor of childbirth with her cousin, as closely linked as it was possible to be. Her body was heavy with fatigue, her mind drugged with it. It was a common result of a strong empathic link.

She staggered once at the top of the stairs, righted herself, then gripped her bloodstone amulet to draw on the last of its strength.

By the time she reached the parlor, she was feeling a little steadier. There was Boone, half dozing in a chair by the fire, with Jessie cuddled against his chest. His eyes opened. His lips curved.

"Hey, champ. I have to admit I thought this whole setup was a little loony, but you did a hell of a job up there."

"It's always stunning to bring life into the world. You didn't have to stay all this time."

"I wanted to." He kissed Jessie's head. "So did she. She'll be the hit of school on Monday with this story."

"It's been a long night for her, and one she won't forget." Ana rubbed her eyes, almost as Jessie had before falling asleep again. "Where is everyone?"

"In the kitchen, raiding the refrigerator and getting drunk. I decided to pass, since I already had more than my share of wine." He offered a sheepish grin. "A little while ago I could have sworn the house was shaking, so I switched to coffee." He gestured toward the cup on the table beside him.

"And now you'll be up half the night. I'll just run and tell them I'm going, if you'd like to go put Jessie in the car."

Outside, Boone took a deep gulp of the cool night air. Ana was right, he was wide awake. He'd have to work a couple of hours until the coffee wore off, and he'd more than likely pay for it tomorrow. But it had been worth it. He glanced over his shoulder to where the light glowed in Morgana's bedroom. It had been well worth it.

He slipped Jessie's wings over her shoulders, then laid her on the back seat.

"Beautiful night," Ana murmured from behind him. "I think every star must be out."

"Two new stars." Bemused, Boone opened the door for her. "That's what Matthew said. It was really lovely. Sebastian made a toast about life and gifts and stars, and they all passed around a cup of wine. Is that an Irish thing?"

"In a way." She leaned her head back against the seat as he started the car. Within seconds, she was asleep.

When Boone pulled up in his driveway, he wondered how he was going to manage to carry both of them to bed. He shifted, easing his door open, but Ana was already blinking awake.

"Just let me carry her inside, and I'll give you a hand."

"No, I'm fine." Bleary-eyed, Ana stepped out of the car. "I'll help you with her." She laughed as she gathered up the store of stuffed animals. "Da always goes overboard. I hope you don't mind."

"Are you kidding? He was great with her. Come on, baby." He lifted her and, in the way of children, she remained utterly lax. "She was taken with your mother, too, and the rest, but your father was definitely the hero. I expect she'll be bugging me to go to Ireland now, so she can visit him in his castle."

"He'd love it." She took the silver wings and followed him into the house.

"Just set those anywhere. Do you want a brandy?"

"No, really." She dropped the animals on the couch, put the wings beside them, then rolled her aching shoulders. "I wouldn't mind some tea. I can brew some while you settle her in."

"Fine. I won't be long."

A low growling emerged from under Jessie's bed when Boone carried her in. "Great watchdog. It's just us, you blockhead."

Desperately relieved, Daisy bounded out, tail wagging. She waited until Boone had removed Jessie's shoes and costume, then leapt onto the bed to settle at Jessie's feet.

"You wake me up at six and I'll staple those doggie lips closed."

Daisy thumped her tail and shut her eyes.

"I don't know why we couldn't have gotten a smart dog while we were at it," Boone was saying as he walked into the kitchen. "It wouldn't have been…" and then his words trailed off.

The kettle was on and beginning to steam. Cups were set out, and the pot was waiting. Ana had her head pillowed on her arms at the kitchen table, and was deep in sleep.

Under the bright light, her lashes cast shadows on her cheeks. Boone hoped it was the harshness of the light that made her look so delicately pale. Her hair spilled over her shoulder. Her lips were soft, just parted.

Looking at her, he thought of the young princess who had been put under a spell by a jealous fairy and made to sleep a hundred years, until wakened by true love's gentle kiss.

"Anastasia. You're so beautiful." He touched her hair, indulging himself. He'd never watched her sleep, and he had a sudden, tearing urge to have her in his bed, to be able to open his eyes in the morning and see her there beside him. "What am I going to do?"

Sighing, he let his hand fall away from her hair and moved to the stove to shut off the kettle. As gently as he had with Jessie, he lifted her into his arms, and, like Jessie, she remained lax. Gritting his teeth against the knots in his stomach, he carried her upstairs and laid her on his bed.

"You don't know how much I've wanted you here," he said under his breath as he slipped off her shoes. "In my bed, in the night. All night." He spread the covers over her, and she sighed, shifting in sleep and curling into his pillow.

The knots in his stomach loosened as he bent to touch his lips to hers. "Good night, princess."

In her panties and T-shirt, Jessie padded into the bedroom before dawn. She'd had a dream, a bad one about the haunted house at school, and wanted the comfort and warmth of her father.

He always made monsters go away.

She scurried to the bed, and climbed in to burrow against him. It was then that she noted it wasn't her father at all, but Ana.

Fascinated, Jessie curled up. Curious fingers played with Ana's hair. In sleep Ana murmured and tucked Jessie under her arm to snuggle her close. Odd sensations tugged through Jessie's stomach. Different smells, different textures, and yet she felt as loved and safe as she did when her father cuddled her. She rested her head trustingly against Ana's breast and slept.

When Ana woke, she felt arms around her, small, limp arms. Disoriented, she stared down at Jessie, then looked around the room.

Not her room, she realized. And not Jessie's. Boone's.

She kept the child warm against her as she tried to piece together what had happened.

The last thing she remembered was sitting down after she'd put on water for tea. Tired, she'd been so tired. She'd rested her head for a moment and...and obviously had fallen fast asleep.

So where was Boone?

Cautiously she turned her head, unsure whether she was relieved or disappointed to find the bed beside her empty. Impractical, of course, given the circumstances, but it would have been so lovely to be able to cuddle back against him even as the child cuddled to her.

When she looked back, Jessie's eyes were open and on hers.

"I had a bad dream," the girl told her in hushed morning whispers. "About the Headless Horseman. He was laughing and laughing and chasing me."

Ana snuggled down to kiss Jessie's brow. "I bet he didn't catch you."

"Uh-uh. I woke up and came to get Daddy. He always makes the monsters go away. The ones in the closet and under the bed and at the window and everywhere."

"Daddies are good at that." She smiled, remembering how her own had pretended to chase them away with a magic broom every night during her sixth year.

"But you were here, and I wasn't scared with you, either. Are you going to sleep in Daddy's bed at night now?"

"No." She brushed a hand through Jessie's hair. "I think you and I both fell asleep, and your father had to put both of us to bed."

"But it's a big bed," Jessie pointed out. "There'd be room. I have Daisy to sleep with me now, but Daddy has to sleep all alone. Does Quigley sleep with you?"

"Sometimes," Ana said, relieved at the rapid change of topic. "He's probably wondering where I am."

"I think he knows," Boone announced from the doorway. He was wearing only jeans, unsnapped at the waist, and he looked bleary-eyed and harassed, with the gray cat winding between his legs. "He howled and scratched at the back door until I let him in."

"Oh." Ana shoved her tumbled hair back as she sat up. "Sorry. I guess he woke you."

"Right the first time." He tucked his thumbs in his

pockets while the cat leapt onto the bed and began to mutter and complain to his mistress. The knots in his stomach were back, doubled. How could he explain what he felt on seeing Ana cuddled with his little girl in the big, soft bed? "Jessie, what are you doing?"

"I had a bad dream." She leaned her head against Ana's arm and stroked the cat's fur. "So I came in to get you, but Ana was here. She made the monsters go away just like you do." Quigley meowed plaintively and made Jessie giggle. "He's hungry. Poor kitty. I can feed him. Can I take him down and feed him?"

"Sure, if you'd like."

Before Ana had finished the sentence, Jessie was bounding off the bed, calling to the cat to follow.

"Sorry she woke you." Boone hesitated, then moved over to sit on the edge of the bed.

"She didn't. Apparently she just climbed right on in and went back to sleep. And I should apologize for putting you to so much trouble. You could have given me a shake and sent me home."

"You were exhausted." He reached out, much as Jessie had, to touch her hair. "Incredibly beautiful, and totally exhausted."

"Having babies is tiring work." She smiled. "Where did you sleep?"

"In the guest room." He winced at the crick in his back. "Which makes getting a decent bed in there a top priority."

Automatically she pressed her hands on his lower back to massage and ease. "You could have dumped me in there. I don't think I would have known the difference between a bed and a sheet of plywood."

"I wanted you in my bed." His gaze met hers and locked. "I very much wanted you in my bed." He tugged on her hair to bring her closer. Much closer. "I still do."

His mouth was on hers, not so patient now, not so gentle. Ana felt a quick thrill of excitement and alarm as he pressed her back against the pillows. "Boone—"

"Just for a minute." His voice took on an edge of desperation. "I need a minute with you."

He took her breast, searing her flesh through the thin silk of her rumpled blouse. While his hands skimmed over her, his mouth took and took, swallowing her muffled moans. His body ached to cover hers, to press hard against soft, to take quickly, even savagely, what he knew she could bring to him.

"Ana." His teeth scraped down her throat before he gathered her close, just to hold her. He knew he was being unfair, to both of them, and he struggled to back off. "How long does it take to feed that cat?"

"Not long enough." With a shaky laugh, she dropped her head on his shoulder. "Not nearly long enough."

"I was afraid of that." He drew back, running his hands down her arms to take hers. "Jessie's been after me to let her spend the night at Lydia's. If I can work it out, will you stay with me? Here?"

"Yes." She brought his hand to her lips, then pressed it to her cheek. "Whenever you like."

"Tonight." He forced himself to release her, to move away. "Tonight," he repeated. "I'll go call Lydia's mother. Beg if I have to." He steadied himself and slowed down.

"I promised Jess we'd go get some ice cream, maybe have lunch on the wharf. Will you come with us? If it all works out, we could drop her off at Lydia's, then go out to dinner."

She pushed off the bed herself, brushing uselessly at the wrinkles in her blouse and slacks. "That sounds nice."

"Great. Sorry about the clothes. I wasn't quite brave enough to undress you."

She felt a quick thrill at the image of him unbuttoning her blouse. Slowly, very slowly, his fingers patient, his eyes hot. She cleared her throat. "They'll press out. I need to change, go check on Morgana and the twins."

"I could drive you."

"That's all right. My father's going to pick me up so I can get my car. What time did you want to leave?"

"About noon, in a couple hours."

"Perfect. I'll meet you back here."

He caught her to him before she reached the doorway, then stopped her heart with another greedy kiss. "Maybe we could pick up some takeout, bring it back and eat here."

"That sounds nice, too," she murmured as she shifted the angle of the kiss. "Or maybe we could just send out for pizza when we get hungry."

"Better. Much better."

By four o'clock, Jessie was standing in Lydia's doorway waving a cheery goodbye. Her pink backpack was bulging with the amazing assortment of necessities a six-year-old girl required for a sleepover. What made the entire matter perfect in her eyes was that Daisy had been invited along for the party.

"Tell me not to feel guilty," Boone asked as he cast one last glance in the rearview mirror.

"About?"

"About wanting my own daughter out of the house tonight."

"Boone." Adoring him, Ana leaned over to kiss his cheek. "You know perfectly well Jessie could hardly wait for us to drive away so she could begin her little adventure at Lydia's."

"Yeah, but... It's not packing her off so much, it's packing her off with ulterior motives."

Knowing what those motives were brought a little knot of heat to Ana's stomach. "She isn't going to have less of a good time because of them—particularly when you promised her she could have a slumber party in a couple of weeks. If you're still feeling guilty think about how you're going to feel riding herd on five or six little girls all night."

He slanted her a look. "I kind of figured you'd help—since you have ulterior motives, too."

"Did you?" The fact that he'd asked pleased her enormously. "Maybe I will." She laid a hand over his. "For a paranoid father riddled with guilt, you're doing a wonderful job."

"Keep it up. I'm feeling better."

"Too much flattery isn't good for you."

"Just for that I won't tell you how many guys gave themselves whiplash craning their necks to get a second look at you when we were walking on the wharf today."

"Oh?" She skimmed back her blowing hair. "Were there many?"

"Depends on how you define many. Besides, too much flattery isn't good for you. I guess I could say I don't know how you could look so good today after the night you put in."

"It could be because I slept like a rock." She stretched luxuriously. A bracelet of agates winked at her wrist. "Morgana's the amazing one. When I got there this morning, she was nursing both of the twins and looking as if she'd just spent a reviving week at an expensive spa."

"The babies okay?"

"The babies are terrific. Healthy and bright-eyed. Nash is already a pro at changing diapers. He claims both of them have smiled at him."

He knew that feeling, too, and had just realized he missed it. "He's a good guy."

"Nash is very special."

"I have to admit, I was stunned when I heard he was married. Nash was always the go-it-on-your-own type."

"Love changes things," Ana murmured, and carefully screened all wistfulness from her voice. "Aunt Bryna calls it the purest form of magic."

"A good description. Once it touches you, you begin to think nothing's impossible anymore. Were you ever in love?"

"Once." She looked away, studying the shimmering ice plants along the banks. "A long time ago. But it turned out the magic wasn't strong enough. Then I learned that my life wasn't over after all, and I could be perfectly happy alone. So I bought my house near the water," she said with a smile. "Planted my garden, and started fresh."

"I suppose it was similar for me." He grew thoughtful as they made the final turn toward home. "Does being happy alone mean you don't think you could be happy with someone?"

Unease and hope ran parallel inside her. "I guess it means I can be happy as things stand, until I find someone who not only brings me the magic, but understands it."

He turned into the drive, shut off the engine. "We have something together, Ana."

"I know."

"I never thought to feel anything this powerful again. It's different from what I had before, and I'm not sure what that means. I don't know if I want to know."

"It doesn't matter." She took his hand again. "Sometimes you just have to accept that today is enough."

"No, it's not." He turned to her then, his eyes dark, intense. "Not with you."

She took a careful breath. "I'm not what you think I am, or what you want me to be. Boone—"

"You're exactly what I want." His hands were rough as he dragged her against him. Her startled gasp was muffled against his hard, seeking mouth.

Chapter 10

A whip of panicked excitement cracked through her as he tore her free of the seat belt and yanked her across his lap. His hands bruised, his mouth branded. This was not the Boone who had loved her so gently, taking her to that sweet, sweet fulfillment with patient hands and murmured promises. Her lover of quiet mornings and lazy afternoons had become something darker, something dangerous, something she was helpless to resist.

She could feel the blood sizzling under her skin as he took those rough, impatient hands over her. This was the wildness she had tasted that first time, in a moonlit garden with the scent of flowers ripe and heady. This bursting of urgent needs was what he had only hinted at under all that patience and steady control.

In mindless acquiescence she strained against him, willing, eager and ready to race along any path he chose.

Her body shuddered once, violently, as he dragged her over a ragged edge. He heard her muffled cry against his greedy mouth, tasted the ripeness of it as her fingers dug desperately into his shoulders. The thought ran crazily through his mind that he could have her here, right here in the car, before reason caught up with either of them.

He tore at her blouse, craving the taste of flesh. The sound of ripping seams was smothered by her quick gasp as he feasted on her throat. Beneath his hungry mouth, her pulse hammered erratically, erotically. The flavor of her was already hot, already honeyed with passion.

On a vicious oath, he shoved the door open, yanking her out. Leaving it swinging, he half carried, half dragged her across the lawn.

"Boone." Staggered, she tried to gain her feet and lost her shoes. "Boone, the car. You left your keys—"

He caught her hair, pulling her head back. His eyes. Oh, Lord, his eyes, she thought, trembling with something much deeper than fear. The heat in them seared through to her soul.

"The hell with the car." His mouth swooped down, plundered hers until she was dazed and dizzy and fighting to breathe. "Do you know what you do to me?" he said between strangled gasps for air. "Every time I see you." He pulled her up the steps, touching her, always touching her. "Soft, serene, with something smoldering just behind your eyes."

He pushed her back against the door, crushing, conquering, those full, luscious lips with his. There was something more in her eyes now. He could see that she was afraid. And that she was aroused. It was as if they both were fully aware that the animal he'd kept ruthlessly on a choke chain for weeks had broken free.

With the breath coming harsh through his lips, he caught her face in his hands. "Tell me. Ana, tell me you want me. Now. My way."

She was afraid she wouldn't be able to speak, her throat was so dry and this new need so huge. "I want you." The husky sound of her voice had the flames in his gut leaping higher. "Now. Any way."

He hooked his hands in her blouse, watched her eyes go to smoke just before he rent it in two. When he kicked the door open, she staggered back, then was caught up in a torrid embrace. Like her blouse, his control was in shreds. His hands tight at her waist, he lifted her off her feet to take her silk-covered breast in his mouth. As crazed now as he, she arched back, her hands fisted in his hair.

"Boone. Please." The plea sobbed out, though she had no idea what she was asking for. Unless it was more.

He lowered her, only so that he could capture her mouth again. His teeth scraped erotically over her swollen lips, his tongue dived deep. Then his heart seemed to explode in his chest as she began to tug frantically at his clothes.

He stumbled toward the stairs, shedding his shirt as he went. Buttons popped and scattered. But his greedy hands reached for her again, yanking the thin chemise down to her waist as they reached the landing. "Here." He dragged her down with him. "Right here."

At last, he feasted, racing his mouth over her quivering flesh, ruthlessly exploiting her secrets, relentlessly driving her with him where he so desperately needed her to go. No patience here, no rigid control for the sake of her fragility. Indeed, the woman writhing beneath him on the stairs was anything but fragile. There was strength in the hands that gripped him, searing passion in the mouth that tasted him so eagerly, whiplike agility in the body that strained under his.

She felt invincible, immortal, impossibly free. Her body was alive, never more alive, with heat pumping crazily through her blood. The world was spinning around her, a blur of color and blinding lights, whirling faster, faster, until she was forced to grip the pickets of the banister to keep from falling off the edge of the earth.

Her knuckles whitened against the wood as he tore her slacks away, then the thin swatch of lace beneath. His mouth, oh, his mouth, greedy, frantic, fevered. Ana bit back a scream as he sent her flying into hot, airless space.

Her mindless murmurs were in no language he could understand, but he knew he had taken her beyond the boundaries of the sane, of the rational. He wanted her there, right there with him as they catapulted into the madness of vivid, lawless passion.

He'd waited. He'd waited. Now her slim white body bucked. A thoroughbred ready to ride. Quivering like a stallion, he mounted her, driving himself into that wet, waiting heat. She arched to meet him and, hips moving like lightning, raced with him into the roaring dark.

Her hands slid weakly off his damp back. She was too numb to feel the slap of wood against them as they fell against the stairs. She wanted to hold him, but her strength was gone. It wasn't possible to focus her mind on what had happened. All that came were flashes of sensations, bursts of emotions.

If this was the darker side of love, nothing could have

prepared her for it. If this terrible need was what had lived inside him, she couldn't comprehend how he could have strapped it back for so long.

For her sake. She turned her damp face into his throat. All for her sake.

Beneath his still-shuddering body, she was as limp as water. Boone struggled to get a grip on reality. He needed to move. After everything else he'd done to her, he was probably crushing her. But when he started to shift, she made a little sound of distress that scraped at his conscience.

"Here, baby, let me help you."

He eased away, picking up a tattered sleeve of her blouse with some idea to cover her. Biting off an oath, he tossed it down again. She'd turned slightly on her side, obviously seeking some kind of comfort. For God's sake, he thought in disgust, he'd taken her like some kind of fiend, and on the stairs. *On the stairs.*

"Ana." He found what was left of his own shirt and tried to wrap it around her shoulders. "Anastasia, I don't know how to explain."

"Explain?" The word was barely audible. Her throat was wild with thirst.

"There's no possible... Let me help you up." Her body slid like wax through his arms. "I'll get you some clothes, or... Oh, hell."

"I don't think I can get up." She moistened her lips, and tasted him. "Not for a day or two. This is fine, though. I'll just stay right here."

Frowning at her, he tried to interpret what he heard in her voice. It wasn't anger. It didn't sound like distress.

It sounded like—very much like—satisfaction. "You're not upset?"

"Hmmm? Am I supposed to be?"

"Well, for... I practically attacked you. Hell, I *did* attack you, almost taking you in the front seat of the car, tearing off your clothes, dragging you in here and devouring what was left of you on the stairs."

With her eyes still closed, she drew in a deep breath, then let it out again on a sigh through curved lips. "You certainly did. And it's the first time I've been devoured. I don't think I'll ever go up and down a staircase the same way again."

Gently he tipped a finger under her chin until her eyes opened. "I had intended to at least make it to the bedroom."

"I guess we'll get there eventually." Recognizing concern, she put a hand on his wrist. "Boone, do you think I could be upset because you wanted me that much?"

"I thought you might be upset because this wasn't what you're used to."

Making the effort, she sat up, wincing a little at the aches that would surely be bruises before much longer. "I'm not made of glass. There's no way we could love each other that wouldn't be right. But..." She linked her arms around his neck and her smile was wicked around the edges. "Under the circumstances, I'm glad we made it into the house."

He skimmed his hands down to her hips for the pleasure of bringing her body against his. "My neighbor's very open-minded."

"I've heard that." Experimentally she caught his lower

lip between her teeth. Remembering how much pleasure it gave her to feel his lips cruise over her face and throat, she began a lazy journey over his. "Fortunately, my neighbor's very understanding of passions. I doubt anything would shock him. Even if I told him I often fantasize about him at night, when I'm alone, in bed."

It was impossible, but he felt himself stir against her. The deep, dark wanting began to smolder again. "Really? What kind of fantasies?"

"Of having him come to me." Her breath began to quicken as his mouth roamed over her shoulder. "Come to my bed like an incubus in the night, when a storm cracks the air. I can see his eyes, cobalt blue in a flash of lightning, and I know that he wants me the way no one else ever has, or ever will."

Knowing very well that if he didn't take some kind of action now they'd remain sprawled on the stairs, he gathered her up. "I can't give you the lightning."

She smiled as he carried her up. "You already have."

Later, hours later, they knelt on the tumbled bed, feasting on pizza by candlelight. Ana had lost track of time and had no need to know if it was midnight or approaching dawn. They had loved and talked and laughed and loved again. No night in her life had been more perfect. What did time matter here?

"Guinevere was no heroine." Ana licked sauce from her fingers. They had discussed epic poetry, modern animation, ancient legends and folklore and classic horror. She wasn't sure how they had wound their way back to Arthur

and Camelot, but on the subject of Arthur's queen, Ana
stood firm. "And she certainly wasn't a tragic figure."

"I'd think a woman, especially one with your compassion, would have more sympathy with her situation."
Boone debated having a last piece from the cardboard
box they'd plopped in the center of the bed.

"Why?" Ana picked it up herself and began to feed it
to him. "She betrayed her husband, helped bring down
a kingdom, all because she was weak-willed and self-
indulgent."

"She was in love."

"Love doesn't excuse all actions." Amused, she tilted
her head and studied him in the flickering light. He looked
gloriously masculine in nothing but a pair of gym shorts,
his hair tousled, his face shadowed with stubble. "Isn't
that just like a man? Finding excuses for a woman's infi-
delity just because it's written about in romantic terms."

He didn't think it was precisely an insult, but it made
him squirm a little. "I just don't think she had control of
the situation."

"Of course she did. She had a choice, and she chose
poorly, just as Lancelot did. All that flowery business
about gallantry and chivalry and heroism and loyalty,
and the two of them justified betraying a man who loved
them both because they couldn't control themselves?"
She tossed her hair back. "That's bull."

He laughed before he sipped his wine. "You amaze me.
Here I've been thinking you were a romantic. A woman
who picks flowers by moonlight, who collects statues of
fairies and wizards, and she condemns poor Guinevere
because she loved unwisely."

She fired up. "Poor Guinevere—"

"Hold on." He was chuckling, enjoying himself immensely. It didn't occur to either of them that they were debating about people most considered fictional. "Let's not forget some of the other players. Merlin was supposed to be watching over the whole business. Why didn't he do anything about it?"

Fastidiously she brushed crumbs from her bare legs. "It's not a sorcerer's place to interfere with destiny."

"Come on, we're talking about the champ here. One little spell and he could've fixed it up."

"And altered countless lives," she pointed out, gesturing with her glass. "Skewed history. No, he couldn't do it, not even for Arthur. People—witches, kings, mortals— are responsible for their own fates."

"He didn't have any problem abetting adultery by disguising Uther as the duke of Cornwall and taking Tintagel so that Igraine conceived Arthur in the first place."

"Because that was destiny," she said patiently, as she might have to Jessie. "That was the purpose. For all Merlin's power, all his greatness, his single most vital act was bringing Arthur into being."

"Sounds like splitting hairs to me." He swallowed the last bite of pizza. "One spell's okay, but another isn't."

"When you're given a gift, it's your responsibility to know how and when to use it, how and when not to. Can you imagine how he suffered, watching someone he loved destroyed? Knowing, even as Arthur was being conceived, how it would end? Magic doesn't divorce you from emotion or pain. It rarely protects the one who owns it."

"I guess not." He'd certainly had witches and wizards

suffering in the stories he wrote. It gave them a human element he found appealing. "When I was a kid, I used to daydream about living back then."

"Rescuing fair maidens from fiery dragons?"

"Sure. Going on quests, challenging the Black Knight and beating the hell out of him."

"Naturally."

"Then I grew up and discovered I could have the best of both worlds, living there up here—" he tapped his head with a fingertip "—when I was writing. And having the creature comforts of the twentieth century."

"Like pizza."

"Like pizza," he agreed. "A computer instead of a quill, cotton underwear. Hot running water. Speaking of which…" he said, fingering the hem of the T-shirt he'd given her to wear. He moved on impulse, and had her shrieking out a laugh as he tossed her over his shoulder and climbed out of bed.

"What are you doing?"

"Hot running water," he repeated. "I think it's time I showed you what I can do in the shower."

"You're going to sing?"

"Maybe later." In the bathroom, he opened the glass shower doors and turned on the taps. "Hope you like it hot."

"Well, I—" She was still over his shoulder when he stepped inside. With the crisscrossing sprays raining, she was immediately drenched, front and back. "Boone." She sputtered. "You're drowning me."

"Sorry." He shifted, reaching for the soap. "You know, this shower really sold me on the house. It's roomy." He slicked the wet bar of soap up her calf. "Pretty great having the twin shower heads."

Despite the heat of the water, Ana shivered when he soaped lazy circles at the back of her knee. "It's a little difficult for me to appreciate it from this position." Then she shoved her dripping hair out of her face and noticed that the floor was mirrored tiles. "Oh, my."

He grinned, and moved slowly up to her thigh. "Check out the ceiling."

She did, tilting her head and staring at their reflections. "Ah, doesn't it just steam up?"

"Treated glass. Does get a little foggy if you're in here long enough." And he intended to be in there just long enough. He began sliding her down his body, inch by dangerous inch. "But that only adds to the atmosphere." Gently he pressed her against the back wall, cupping her breasts through the clinging shirt. "Want to hear one of my fantasies?"

"It— Oh." He was rubbing a thumb over an aching nipple. "Seems only fair."

"Better idea." He brushed his lips over hers, teasing, retreating, until her breath began to hitch. "Why don't I show you? First we get rid of this." He dragged the wet shirt over her head, tossing it aside. It landed with a plop that had another tremor jerking through her system. "And I start here." Toying with her mouth, he rubbed the slick soap over her shoulders. "And I don't stop until I get to your toes."

She had a feeling showers were going to join staircases in the more erotic depths of her imagination. Gripping his hips for balance, she arched back as he circled wet, soapy hands over her breasts.

Steam. It was all around her, it was inside her. The thick, moist air made it all but impossible to breathe. A tropical storm, water pounding, heat rising. The creamy soap had flesh sliding gloriously against flesh when their bodies moved together. Her hands foamed with it as she ran them over his back, over his chest. Even as his mouth raced to possess, his muscles quivered at her touch, and her laugh was low and softly triumphant.

If she burned, so did he. That was power clashing against power. There was no longer any doubt that she could give back the wild, wanton, wicked pleasure he brought to her. A pleasure so much sweeter, so much richer, because it grew from love, as well as passion.

She wanted to show him. She would show him.

Her hands slid down him, over strong shoulders, the hard chest. She murmured in approval as she traced fingertips over his rib cage and down to the flat plane of his stomach.

He shook his head to try to clear it. He had expected to seduce her here, yet he was being seduced. The delicate hands flowing over his slick skin were shooting arrows of painful need through his system.

"Wait." His hands groped for hers, held them firm. He knew that if she touched him now he would never be able to hold back. "Let me…"

"No." With the new knowledge brimming inside, her mouth seared over his and conquered. "Let me."

Her fingers closed around him, sliding, stroking, squeezing lightly, while his breath sounded harshly in her ear. A fresh flash of triumph exploded inside her as she felt his quick, helpless shudder. Then greed, to have him, all of him, deep inside her.

"Ana." He felt the last wisps of reality fading. "Ana, I can't—"

"You want me." Delirious with power, she threw her head back. Her eyes were hot with challenge. "Then take me. Now."

She looked like a goddess newly risen from the sea. Wet cables of hair slicked like dark gold over her shoulder. Her skin glowed, shimmered with water. In her eyes were secrets, dark mysteries no man would ever unlock.

She was glorious. She was magnificent. And she was his.

"Hold on to me." Bracing her against the wall, he lifted her hips with his hands. "Hold on to me."

She locked her arms around him, keeping her eyes open. He took her where they stood, plunging into her as the water showered over them. Gasping out his name, she let her head fall back. Through the rising mists, she saw their reflections—a wonderful tangle of limbs that made it impossible to see where he left off and she began.

On a moan of inexpressible pleasure, she dropped her head to his shoulder. She was lost. Lost. Thank God for it. "I love you." She had no idea if the words were in her head or had come through her lips. But she said them again and again until her body convulsed.

He emptied himself into her, then could only stand weakly against the wall as the strength ran out of him. His heart was still roaring in his ears as he closed his hands over her shoulders.

"Tell me now."

Her lips were curved, but she swayed a little and stared up at him through clouded eyes. "Tell you what?"

His fingers tightened, making her eyes clear. "That you love me. Tell me now."

"I... Don't you think we should dry off? We've been in the water quite a while."

With an impatient jerk, he switched off the taps. "I want to look at you when you say it, and have at least some of my wits about me. We're going to stay right here until I hear you say it again."

She hesitated. He could have no idea that he was forcing her to take the next step toward having him—or losing him. Destiny, she thought, and choices. It was time she made hers. "I love you. I wouldn't be here with you, couldn't be here, if I didn't."

His eyes were very dark, very intense. Slowly his grip lightened, his face relaxed. "I feel as though I've waited years to hear you say that."

She brushed the wet hair away from his brow. "You only had to ask."

He caught her hands in his. "You don't." Because she was beginning to shiver, he drew her out of the stall to wrap her in a towel. He caught it close around her, then wrapped his arms tight for more warmth. "Anastasia." Tenderness swelled inside him as he touched his lips to her hair, her cheek, her mouth. "You don't have to ask. I love you. You brought something I thought I'd never have again, never want again, back into my life."

On a broken sigh, she pressed her face to his chest. This was real, she thought. This was hers. She would find a way to keep it. "You're everything I've ever wanted. Don't stop loving me, Boone. Don't stop."

"I couldn't." He drew her away. "Don't cry."

"I don't." The tears shimmered, but didn't spill over. "I don't cry."

Anastasia sheds no tears, but she'll shed them for you.

Sebastian's words rang uncomfortably in Boone's head. Resolutely he blocked them out. It was ridiculous. He'd do nothing to hurt her. He opened his mouth, then closed it again. A steamy bathroom was no place for the proposal he wanted to make. And there were things he needed to tell her first.

"Let's get you another shirt. We need to talk."

She was much too happy to pay any heed to the curl of uneasiness. She laughed when he took her back to the bedroom and tugged another of his shirts over her head. Dreamily she poured two more glasses of wine while he pulled on a pair of jeans.

"Will you come with me?" He held out a hand, and she took it willingly.

"Where are we going?"

"I want to show you something." He took her down the shadowy hall, into his office. Delighted, Ana turned a circle.

"This is where you work."

There were wide, uncurtained windows framed with curving cherrywood. A couple of worn, faded scatter rugs had been tossed on the hardwood floor. Starshine sprinkled through the twin skylights. An industrious-looking computer, reams of paper and shelves of books announced that this was a workplace. But he'd added charm with framed illustrations, a collection of dragons and knights that intrigued her. The winged fairy he'd bought from Morgana had a prominent place on a high, carved stool.

"You need some plants," she decided instantly, thinking of the narcissus and daffodils she was forcing in her greenhouse. "I imagine you spend hours in this room every day." She glanced down at the empty ashtray beside his machine.

Following her gaze, he frowned. Odd, he thought, he hadn't had a cigarette in days—had forgotten about them completely. He'd have to congratulate himself later.

"Sometimes I watch out the window when you're in your garden. It makes it difficult to concentrate."

She laughed and sat on the corner of his desk. "We'll get you some shades."

"Not a chance." He smiled, but his hands went nervously to his pockets. "Ana, I need to tell you about Alice."

"Boone." Compassion had her rising again to reach out. "I understand. I know it's painful. There's no need to explain anything to me."

"There is for me." With her hand in his, he turned to gesture at a sketch on the wall. A lovely young girl was kneeling by a stream, dipping a golden pail into the silver water. "She drew that, before Jessie was born. Gave it to me for our first anniversary."

"It's beautiful. She was very talented."

"Yeah. Very talented, very special." He sipped his wine in an unconscious toast to a lost love. "I knew her most of my life. Pretty Alice Reeder."

He needed to talk, Ana thought. She would listen. "You were high school sweethearts?"

"No." He laughed at that. "Not even close. Alice was a cheerleader, student body president, all-around nice girl who always made the honor roll. We ran in different crowds, and she was a couple of years behind me. I was going through my obligatory rebellious period and kind of hulked around school, looking tough."

She smiled, touched his cheek where the stubble was rough. "I'd like to have seen that."

"I snuck cigarettes in the bathroom, and Alice painted scenery for school plays. We knew each other, but that was about it. I went off to college, ended up in New York. It seemed necessary, since I was going to write, that I get myself a loft and starve a little."

She slipped an arm around him, instinctively offering comfort, waiting while he gathered his thoughts.

"One morning I was in the bakery around the corner from where I was living, and I looked up from the crullers and there she was, buying coffee and a croissant. We started talking. You know...what are you doing here, the old neighborhood, what had happened to whom. That kind of thing. It was comforting, and exciting. Here we were, two small-town kids taking on big bad New York."

And fate had tossed them together, Ana thought, in a city of millions.

"She was in art school," Boone continued, "sharing an apartment only a couple of blocks away with some other girls. I walked her to the subway. We just sort of drifted together, sitting in the park, comparing sketches, talking for hours. Alice was so full of life, energy, ideas. We didn't fall in love so much as we slid into it." His eyes softened as he studied the sketch. "Very slowly, very sweetly. We got married just before I sold my first book. She was still in college."

He had to stop again as the memories swam back in force. Instinctively his hand closed over Ana's. She opened herself, giving what strength and support she could.

"Anyway, everything seemed so perfect. We were young, happy, in love. She'd already been commissioned to do a painting. We found out she was pregnant. So we decided to move back home, raise the child in a nice suburban atmosphere close to family. Then Jessie came, and it seemed as though nothing could ever go wrong. Except that Alice never seemed to really get her energy back after the birth. Everyone said it was natural, she was bound to be tired with a new baby and her work. She lost weight. I used to joke that she was going to fade away." He closed his eyes for a minute. "That's just what she did. She faded away. When it had gone on long enough for us to worry, she had tests, but there was a mess-up in the lab and they didn't detect it soon enough. By the time we found out she had cancer, it was too late to stop it."

"Oh, Boone. I'm sorry. I'm so sorry."

"She suffered. That was the worst. She suffered and there was nothing I could do. I watched her die, degree by degree. And I thought I would die, too. But there was Jessie. Alice was only twenty-five when I buried her. Jessie had just turned two." He took a long breath before he turned to Ana. "I loved Alice. I always will."

"I know. When someone touches your life that way, you never lose it."

"When I lost her, I stopped believing in happy-ever-after, except in books. I didn't want to fall in love again, risk that kind of pain—for myself or for Jessie. But I have fallen in love again. What I feel for you is so strong, it makes me believe again. It's not the same as I felt before. It's not less. It's just…us."

She touched his cheek. She thought she understood. "Boone, did you think I would ask you to forget her? That I could resent or be jealous of what you had with her? It only makes me love you more. She made you happy. She gave you Jessie. I only wish I had known her."

Impossibly moved, he lowered his brow to hers. "Marry me, Ana."

Chapter 11

She froze. The hands that had reached up to bring him close stopped in midair. Her breath seemed to stall in her lungs. Even as her heart leapt with hope, her mind warned her to wait.

Very slowly, she eased out of his arms. "Boone, I think—"

"Don't tell me I'm rushing things." He was amazingly calm now that he'd taken the step—the step he realized he'd already taken in his head weeks before. "I don't care if I'm moving too fast. I need you in my life, Ana."

"I'm already in your life." She smiled, trying to keep it light. "I told you that."

"It was hard enough when I only wanted you, harder still when I started to care. But it's impossible now that I'm in love with you. I don't want to live next door to you." He took a firm grip on her shoulders to keep her still. "I don't want to have to send my child away so I can spend the night with you. You said you loved me."

"I do." She gave in to desperate need and pressed herself against him. "You know I do, more than I thought I could. More than I wanted to. But marriage is—"

"Right." He stroked a hand down her damp hair. "Right for us. Ana, I told you once I don't take intimacy lightly, and I wasn't just talking about sex." He drew her back, wanting to see her face, wanting her to see his. "I'm talking about what's inside me every time I look at you. Before I met you, I was content to keep my life the way it was. But that's no good anymore. I'm not going to keep running through the hedges to be with you. I want you with me, with us."

"Boone, if it could be so simple." She turned away, struggling to find the right answer.

"It can be." He fought against a quick flutter of panic. "When I walked in this morning and saw you in bed, with your arms around Jessie—I can't tell you what went through me at that moment. I realized that was what I wanted. For you to be there. Just to be there. To know I could share her with you, because you'd love her. That there could be other children. A future."

She shut her eyes, because the image was so sweet, so perfect. And she was denying them both a chance to make the image reality, because she was afraid. "If I said yes now, before you understand me, before you know me, it wouldn't be fair."

"I do know you." He swept her around again. "I know you have passion, and compassion, that you're loyal and generous and openhearted. That you have strong feelings for family, that you like romantic music and apple wine. I know the way your laugh sounds, the way you smell. And I know that I could make you happy, if you'd let me."

"You do make me happy. It's because I don't want to do any less for you that I don't know what to do." She broke away to walk off the tension. "I didn't know this was going to happen so quickly, before I was sure. I swear, if I'd known you were thinking of marriage..."

To be his wife, she thought. Bound to him by handfast. She could think of nothing more precious than that kind of belonging.

She had to tell him, so that he would have the choice of accepting or backing away. "You've been much more honest with me than I with you."

"About?"

"About what you are." Her eyes closed on a sigh. "I'm a coward. So easily devastated by bad feelings, afraid, pathetically afraid, of pain—physical and emotional. So hatefully vulnerable to what others can be indifferent to."

"I don't know what you're talking about, Ana."

"No, you don't." She pressed her lips together. "Can you understand that there are some who are more sensitive than others to strong feelings? Some who have to develop a defense against absorbing too much of the swirl of emotion that goes on around them? Who have to, Boone, because they couldn't survive otherwise?"

He pushed back his impatience and tried to smile. "Are you getting mystical on me?"

She laughed, pressing a hand to her eyes. "You don't know the half of it. I need to explain, and don't know how. If I could—" She started to turn back, determined to tell him everything, and the sketchpad on his desk slid off at the movement. Automatically she bent to pick it up.

Perhaps it was fate that it had fallen faceup, showing a

recently completed sketch. An excellent one, Ana thought on a long breath as she studied it. The fierce and wicked lines of the black-caped witch glared up at her. Evil, she thought. He had captured evil perfectly.

"Don't worry about that." He started to take it from her, but she shook her head.

"Is this for your story?"

"*The Silver Castle,* yes. Let's not change the subject."

"Not as much as you think," she murmured. "Indulge me a minute," she said with a careful smile. "Tell me about the sketch."

"Damn it, Ana."

"Please."

Frustrated, he dragged a hand through his hair. "It's just what it looks like. The evil witch who put the spell on the princess and the castle. I had to figure there was a spell that kept anyone from getting in or out."

"So you chose a witch."

"I know it's obvious. But the story seemed to call for it. The vindictive, jealous witch, furious with the princess's goodness and beauty, casts the spell, so the princess stays trapped inside, cut off from love and life and happiness. Then, when true love conquers, the spell's broken and the witch is vanquished. And they live happily ever after."

"I suppose witches are, to you, evil and calculating." Calculating, she remembered. It was one of the words Robert had tossed at her. That, and much, much worse.

"Goes with the territory. Power corrupts, right?"

She set the sketch aside. "There are those who think it." It was only a drawing, she told herself. Only part of a story he'd created. Yet it served to remind her how large a span they needed to cross. "Boone, I'll ask you for something tonight."

"I guess you could ask me for anything tonight."

"Time," she said. "And faith. I love you, Boone, and there's no one else I'd want to spend my life with. But I need time, and so do you. A week," she said before he could protest. "Only a week. Until the full moon. Then there are things I'll tell you. After I do, I hope you'll ask me again to be your wife. If you do, if you can, then I'll say yes."

"Say yes now." He caught her close, capturing her mouth, hoping he could persuade her by his will alone. "What difference will a week make?"

"All," she whispered, clinging tight. "Or none."

He didn't care to wait. It made him nervous and impatient that the days seemed to crawl by. One, then two, finally three. To comfort himself, he thought about the turn his life would take once the interminable week was over.

No more nights alone. Soon, when he returned restlessly in the dark, she would be there. The house would be full of her, her scent, the fragrances of her herbs and oils. On those long, quiet evenings, they could sit together on the deck and talk about the day, about tomorrows.

Or perhaps she would want them to move into her house. It wouldn't matter. They could walk through her gardens, under her arbors, and she could try to teach him the names of all of her flowers.

They could take a trip to Ireland, and she could show him all the important places of her childhood. There would be stories she could tell him, like the one about the witch and the frog, and he could write about them.

One day there would be more children, and he would see her holding their baby the way she had held Morgana and Nash's.

More children. That thought brought him up short and had him staring at the framed picture of Jessie smiling out at him from his desktop.

His baby. Only his, and his only, for so long now. He did want more children. He'd never realized until now how much he wanted more. How much he enjoyed being a father. It was simply something he was, something he did.

Now as his mind began to play with the idea, he could see himself soothing an infant in the night as he had once soothed Jessie. Holding out his arms as a toddler took those first shaky steps. Tossing a ball in the yard, holding on to the back of an unsteady bike.

A son. Wouldn't it be incredible to have a son? Or another daughter. Brothers and sisters for Jessie. She'd love that, he thought, and found himself grinning like an idiot. He'd love it.

Of course, he hadn't even asked Ana how she felt about adding to the family. That was certainly something they'd have to discuss. Maybe it would be rushing her again to bring it up now.

Then he remembered how she'd looked with her arm cuddling Jessie in his bed. The way her face had glowed when she held two tiny infants up so that his daughter could see and touch.

No, he decided. He knew her. She would be as anxious as he to turn their love into life.

By the end of the week, he thought, they would start making plans for their future together.

For Ana, the days passed much too quickly. She spent hours going over the right way to tell Boone everything. Then she would change her mind and struggle to think of another way.

There was the brash way.

She imagined herself sitting him down in her kitchen with a pot of tea between them. "Boone," she would say, "I'm a witch. If that doesn't bother you, we can start planning the wedding."

There was the subtle way.

They would sit out on her patio, near the arbor of morning glories. While they sipped wine and watched the sunset, they would talk about their childhoods.

"Growing up in Ireland is a little different than growing up in Indiana, I suppose," she would tell him. "But the Irish usually take having witches in the neighborhood pretty much for granted." Then she'd smile. "More wine, love?"

Or the intellectual way.

"I'm sure you'd agree most legends have some basis in fact." This conversation would take place on the beach, with the sound of the surf and the cry of gulls. "Your books show a great depth of understanding and respect for what most consider myth or folklore. Being a witch myself, I appreciate your positive slant on fairies and magic. Particularly the way you handled the enchantress in *A Third Wish for Miranda*."

Ana only wished she had enough humor left to laugh

at each pitiful scenario. She was certainly going to have to think of something, now that she had less than twenty-four hours to go.

Boone had already been more patient than she had a right to ask. There was no excuse for keeping him waiting any longer.

At least she would have some moral support this evening. Morgana and Sebastian and their spouses were on their way over for the monthly Friday-night cookout. If that didn't buck her up for her confrontation with Boone the following day, nothing would. As she stepped onto the patio, she fingered the diamond-clear zircon she wore around her neck.

Obviously Jessie had been keeping an eagle eye out, for she zipped through the hedge, with Daisy yipping behind her. To show his indifference to the pup, Quigley sat down and began to wash his hindquarters.

"We're coming to your house for a cookout," Jessie announced. "The babies are coming, too, and maybe I can hold one. If I'm really, really careful."

"I think that could be arranged." Automatically Ana scanned the neighboring yard for signs of Boone. "How was school today, sunshine?"

"It was pretty neat. I can write my name, and Daddy's and yours. Yours is easiest. I can write Daisy's, but I don't know how to spell Quigley's, so I just wrote *cat*. Then I had my whole family, just like the teacher told us." She stopped, scuffed her shoes, and for the first time since Ana had known her, looked shy. "Was it okay if I said you were my family?"

"It's more than okay." Crouching down, Ana gave Jessie a huge hug. Oh, yes, she thought, squeezing her eyes tight. This is what I want, what I need. I could be a wife to him, a mother to the child. Please, please, let me find the way to have it all. "I love you, Jessie."

"You won't go away, will you?"

Because they were close, because she couldn't prevent it, Ana touched the child's heart and understood that Jessie was thinking of her mother. "No, baby." She drew back, choosing her words with care. "I would never want to go away. But if I had to, if I couldn't help it, I'd still be close."

"How can you go away and still be close?"

"Because I'd keep you in my heart. Here." Ana took the thin braided gold chain with the square of zircon and slipped it over Jessie's neck.

"Ooh! It shines!"

"It's very special. When you feel lonely or sad, you hold on to this and think of me. I'll know, and I'll send you happiness."

Dazzled, Jessie turned the crystal, and it exploded with light and color. "Is it magic?"

"Yes."

Jessie accepted the answer with a child's faith. "I want to show Daddy." She started to dash off, then remembered her manners. "Thank you."

"You're welcome. Is— Ah, is Boone inside?"

"Uh-uh, he's on the roof."

"The roof?"

"'Cause next month is Christmas, and he's starting to put up the lights so we know how many we have to buy. The whole house is going to be lit up. Daddy says this is going to be the most special Christmas ever."

"I hope so." Ana shielded her eyes with the flat of her hand and looked up. There he was, sitting on top of the house, looking back at her. Her heart gave that quick, improbable leap it always did when she saw him. Despite nerves, she smiled, lifting one hand in a wave while the other rested on Jessie's shoulder.

It would be all right, she told herself. It had to be.

Boone ignored the tangle of Christmas lights beside him and pleased himself by watching them until Jessie raced back across the yard and Ana went inside.

It would be all right, he told himself. It had to be.

Sebastian plucked a fat black olive from a tray and popped it into his mouth. "When do we eat?"

"You already are," Mel pointed out.

"I mean real food." He winked down at Jessie. "Hot dogs."

"Herbed chicken," Ana corrected, turning a sizzling thigh on the grill.

They were spread over the patio, with Jessie sitting in a wrought-iron chair carefully cradling a cooing Allysia in her lap. Boone and Nash were deep in a discussion on infant care. Morgana had Donovan at her breast, comfortably nursing, while she listened to Mel relate the happy ending of the runaway she and Sebastian had tracked down.

"Kid was miserable," she was saying. "Sorry as hell he'd taken off, scared to go back. When we found him— cold, broke and hungry—and he realized his parents were scared instead of angry, he couldn't wait to get home. I think he's grounded till he's thirty, but he doesn't seem to care." She waited until Morgana had burped her son. Her hands had been itching to touch. "Want me to put him back down for you?"

"Thanks." Morgana watched Mel's face as she lifted the baby. "Thinking about having one of your own. Or two?"

"Actually." Mel caught the special scent of baby and felt her knees go weak. "I think I might…" She cast a quick look over her shoulder and saw her husband was busy teasing Jessie. "I'm not sure yet, but I think I may have already started."

"Oh, Mel, that's—"

"Shh." She leaned down, using the baby for cover. "I don't want him to know, or even suspect, or I'd never be able to stop him from looking for himself. I want to be able to tell him about this." She grinned. "It'll knock his socks off."

Gently Mel laid the child in his side of the double carriage.

"Allysia's sleeping too," Jessie pointed out, tracing a finger over the baby's cheek.

"Want to put her down with her brother?" Sebastian leaned over to help Jessie stand with the baby. "That's the way." He kept his hands under hers as she laid Allysia down. "You'll be an excellent mother one day."

"Maybe I can have twins, too." She turned when Daisy began to bark. "Hush," she whispered. "You'll wake the babies."

But Daisy was lost in the thrill of the chase. Heading for open ground, Quigley shot through the hedges into the next yard, yowling. Delighted with the game, Daisy dashed after him.

"I'll get him, Daddy." Making as much racket as the animals, Jessie raced after them.

"I don't think obedience school's the answer," Boone commented, tipping back a beer. "I'm thinking along the lines of a mental institution."

Panting a bit, Jessie followed the sounds of barks and hisses, across the yard, over the deck, around the side of the house. When she caught up with Daisy, she put her hands on her hips and scolded.

"You have to be friends. Ana won't like it if you keep teasing Quigley."

Daisy simply thumped her tail on the ground and barked again. Halfway up the ladder Boone had used to climb to the roof, Quigley hissed and spat.

"He doesn't like it, Daisy." On a sigh, she squatted down to pet the dog. "He doesn't know you're just playing and wouldn't really hurt him ever. You made him scared." She looked up the ladder. "Come on, kitty. It's okay. You can come down now."

On a feline growl, Quigley narrowed his eyes, then bounded up the ladder when Daisy responded with another flurry of barks.

"Oh, Daisy, look what you've done." Jessie hesitated at the foot of the ladder. Her father had been very specific about her not going near it. But he hadn't known that Quigley would get so scared. And maybe he'd fall off the roof and get killed. She stepped back, thinking she would go tell her father to come. Then she heard Quigley meow.

Daisy was her responsibility, she remembered. She was supposed to feed him and watch him so he didn't get in trouble. If Quigley got hurt, it would be all her fault.

"I'm coming, kitty. Don't be scared." With her lower lip caught between her teeth, she started up the rungs. She'd seen her father go right on up, and it hadn't looked hard at all. Just like climbing the jungle gyms at school, or up to the top of the big sliding board. "Kitty, kitty," she chanted, climbing higher and giggling when Quigley stuck his head over the roof. "You silly cat, Daisy was only playing. I'll take you down, don't worry."

She was nearly to the top when her sneakered foot missed the next rung.

"Smells wonderful," Boone murmured, but he was sniffing at Ana's neck, not the chicken she'd piled on a platter. "Good enough to eat."

Nash gave him a nudge as he reached for a plate. "If you're going to kiss her, move aside. The rest of us want dinner."

"Fine." Slipping his arms around a flustered Ana, he closed his mouth over hers in a long, lingering kiss. "Time's almost up," he said against her mouth. "You could put me out of my misery now, and—"

The words shut off when he heard Jessie's scream. With his heart in his throat, he raced across the yard, shouting for her. He tore through the hedges, pounded across the grass.

"Oh, God! Oh, my God!"

Every ounce of blood seemed to drain out of him when he saw her crumpled on the ground, her arm bent at an impossible angle, her face as white as linen.

"Baby!" Panicked, he fell beside her. She was too still—even his fevered mind registered that one terrifying fact. And when he reached down to pick her up, there was blood, her blood, on his hands.

"Don't move her!" Ana snapped out the order as she dropped beside them. She was breathing hard, fighting back terror, but her hands clasped firmly over his wrists. "You don't know how or where she's hurt. You can do more harm by moving her."

"She's bleeding." He cupped his hands on his daughter's face. "Jessie. Come on, Jessie." With a trembling finger, he searched for a pulse at her throat. "Don't do this. Dear God, don't do this. We need an ambulance."

"I'll call," Mel said from behind them.

Ana only shook her head. "Boone." The calm settled over her as she understood what she had to do. "Boone, listen to me." She took his shoulders, holding tight when he tried to shake her off. "You have to move back. Let me look at her. Let me help her."

"She's not breathing." He could only stare down at his little girl. "I don't think she's breathing. Her arm. She's broken her arm."

It was more than that. Even without a closer link, Ana knew it was much more than that. And there was no time for an ambulance. "I can help her, but you have to move back."

"She needs a doctor. For God's sake, someone call an ambulance."

"Sebastian," Ana said quietly. Her cousin stepped forward and took Boone's arms.

"Let go of me!" Boone started to swing and found himself pinned by both Sebastian and Nash. "What the hell's wrong with you? We have to get her to a hospital!"

"Let Ana do what she can," Nash said, fighting to hold his friend and his own panic back. "You have to trust her, for Jessie's sake."

"Ana." Pale and shaken, Morgana passed one of her babies into Mel's waiting arms. "It may be too late. You know what could happen to you if—"

"I have to try."

Very gently, oh, so gently, she placed her hands on either side of Jessie's head. She braced, waiting until her own breathing was slow and deep. It was hard, very hard, to block out Boone's violent and terrified emotions, but she focused on the child, only the child. And opened herself.

Pain. Hot, burning spears of it, radiating through her head. Too much pain for such a small child. Ana drew it out, drew it in, let her own system absorb it. When agony threatened to smother the serenity needed for such deep and delicate work, she waited for it to roll past. Then moved on.

So much damage, she thought as her hands trailed lightly down. Such a long way to fall. A perfect image clicked in her mind. The ground rushing up, the helpless fear, the sudden, numbing jolt of impact.

Her fingers passed over a deep gash in Jessie's shoulder. The mirror image sliced through her own, throbbed, seeped blood. Then both slowly faded.

"My God." Boone stopped struggling. His body was too numb. "What is she doing? How?"

"She needs quiet," Sebastian muttered. Stepping back from Boone, he took Morgana's hand. There was nothing they could do but wait.

The injuries inside were severe. Sweat began to bloom on Ana's skin as she examined, absorbed, mended. She was chanting as she worked, knowing she needed to deepen the trance to save the child, and herself.

Oh, but the pain! It ripped through her like fire, making her shudder. Her breath hitched as she fought the need to pull back. Blindly she clutched a hand over the zircon Jessie still wore and placed the other over the child's quiet heart.

When she threw her head back, her eyes were the color of storm clouds, and as blank as glass.

The light was bright, blindingly bright. She could barely see the child up ahead. She called, shouted, wanting to hurry, knowing that one misstep now would end it for both of them.

She stared into the light and felt Jessie slipping further away.

"This gift is mine to use or scorn." Both pain and power shimmered in her voice. "This choice was mine from the day I was born. What harms the child bring into me. As I will, so mote it be."

She cried out then, from the tearing price to be paid for cheating death. She felt her own life ebb, teetering, teetering toward the searing light as Jessie's heart began to beat tremulously under her hand.

She fought back, for both of them, calling on every ounce of her strength, every vestige of her power.

Boone saw his daughter stir, watched her lashes flutter as Ana swayed back.

"Jess—Jessie?" He leaped forward to scoop her into his arms. "Baby, are you all right?"

"Daddy?" Her blank, unfocused eyes began to clear. "Did I fall down?"

"Yeah." Weak with relief and gratitude, he buried his face against her throat and rocked her. "Yeah."

"Don't cry, Daddy." She patted his back. "I'm okay."

"Let's see." He took a shaky breath before he ran his hands over her. There was no blood, he discovered. No blood, no bruise, not even the smallest scratch. He held her close again, staring at Ana as Sebastian helped her to her feet. "Do you hurt anywhere, Jessie?"

"Uh-uh." She yawned and nestled her head on his shoulder. "I was going to Mommy. She looked so pretty in all the light. But she looked sad, like she was going to cry, when she saw me coming. Then Ana was there, and she took my hand. Mommy looked happy when she waved goodbye to us. I'm sleepy, Daddy."

His own heart was throbbing in his throat, thickening his voice. "Okay, baby."

"Why don't you let me take her up?" When Boone hesitated, Nash lowered his voice. "She's fine. Ana's not." He took the already dozing child. "Don't let common sense get in the way, pal," he added as he took Jessie inside.

"I want to know what happened here." Afraid he'd babble, Boone forced himself to speak slowly. "I want to know exactly what happened."

"All right." Ana glanced around at her family. "If you'd leave us alone for just a minute, I'd like to…" She trailed off as the world went gray. Swearing, Boone caught her as she fell, then hoisted her into his arms.

"What the hell is going on?" he demanded. "What did she do to Jessie?" He looked down, alarmed by the translucent pallor of Ana's cheeks. "What did she do to herself?"

"She saved your daughter's life," Sebastian said. "And risked her own."

"Be quiet, Sebastian," Morgana murmured. "He's been through enough."

"He?"

"Yes." She laid a restraining hand on her cousin's arm. "Boone, Ana needs rest, a great deal of rest and quiet. If you'd prefer, you can bring her home. One of us will stay and take care of her."

"She'll stay here." He turned and carried her inside.

She was drifting in and out, in and out of worlds without color. There was no pain now, no feeling at all. She was as insubstantial as a mist. Once or twice she heard Sebastian or Morgana slip inside her deeply sleeping mind to offer reassurance. Others joined them, her parents, her aunts and uncles, and more.

After a long, long journey, she felt herself coming back. Tints and hues seeped back into the colorless world. Sensations began to prickle along her skin. She sighed once—it was the first sound she had made in more than twenty-four hours—then opened her eyes.

Boone watched her come back. He rose automatically from the chair to bring her the medication Morgana had left with him.

"Here." He supported her, holding the cup to her lips. "You're supposed to drink this."

She obeyed, recognizing the scent and the taste. "Jessie?"

"She's fine. Nash and Morgana picked her up this afternoon. She's staying with them tonight."

With a nod, she drank again. "How long have I been asleep?"

"Asleep?" He gave a half laugh at her prosaic term for the comalike state she'd been in. "You've been out for twenty-six hours." He glanced at his watch. "And thirty minutes."

The longest journey she'd ever taken, Ana realized. "I need to call my family and tell them I'm well."

"I'll do it. Are you hungry?"

"No." She tried not to be hurt by his polite, distant tone of voice. "This is all I need for now."

"Then I'll be back in a minute."

When he left her alone, she covered her face with her hands. Her own fault, she berated herself. She hadn't prepared him, had dragged her feet, and fate had taken a hand. On a tired sigh, she got out of bed and began to dress.

"What the hell are you doing?" Boone demanded when he walked in again. "You're supposed to rest."

"I've rested enough." Ana stared down at her hands as she meticulously buttoned her blouse. "And I'd just as soon be on my feet when we talk about this."

His nerves jittered, but he only nodded. "Have it your way."

"Can we go outside? I could use some air."

"Fine." He took her arm and led her downstairs and out on the deck. Once she was seated, he took out a cigarette, struck a match. He'd hardly closed his eyes since he'd carried Ana upstairs, and he'd been subsisting on tobacco and coffee. "If you're feeling up to it, I'd appreciate an explanation."

"I'm going to try to give you one. I'm sorry I didn't tell you before." Ana linked her hands tight in her lap. "I wanted to, but I could never find the right way."

"Straight out," he said as he dragged deeply on smoke.

"I come from a very old bloodline—on both sides. A different culture, if you like. Do you know what wicca is?"

Something cold brushed his skin, but it was only the night air. "Witchcraft."

"Actually, its true meaning is wise. But witch will do." She looked up, and her clear gray eyes met his tired, shadowed ones. "I'm a hereditary witch, born with empathic powers that enable me to link emotionally, and physically, with others. My gift is one of healing."

Boone took another long drag on his cigarette. "You're going to sit there, look me in the face and tell me you're a witch."

"Yes."

Furious, he flung the cigarette away. "What kind of a game is this, Ana? Don't you think after what happened here last night I deserve a reasonable explanation?"

"I think you deserve the truth. You may not think it reasonable." She held up a hand before he could speak. "Tell me how you would explain what happened."

He opened his mouth, closed it again. He'd been working on that single problem for more than twenty-four hours without finding a comfortable solution. "I can't. But that doesn't mean I'm going to buy into this."

"All right." She rose, laid a hand on his chest. "You're

tired. You haven't had much sleep. Your head's pounding and your stomach's in knots."

He lifted a brow derisively. "I don't think you have to be a witch to figure that out."

"No." Before he could back away, she touched a hand to his brow, pressed the other to his stomach. "Better?" she asked after a moment.

He needed to sit down, but he was afraid he wouldn't get up again. She'd touched him, barely touched him. And even the shadow of pain was gone. "What is it? Hypnotism?"

"No. Boone, look at me."

He did, and saw a stranger with tangled blond hair billowing out in the wind. The amber enchantress, he thought numbly. Was it any wonder it had reminded him so much of her?

Ana saw both shock and the beginning of belief on his face. "When you asked me to marry you, I asked you to give me time so that I could find the right way to tell you. I was afraid." Her hands dropped away. "Afraid you'd look at me exactly the way you're looking at me now. As if you don't even know me."

"This is bull. Look, I write this stuff for a living, and I know fiction from fact."

"My skill for magic is very limited." Still, she reached into her pocket, where she always carried a few crystals. With her eyes on Boone's, she held them out in her palm. Slowly they began to glow, the purple of the amethyst deepening, the pink of the rose quartz brightening, the green of the malachite shimmering. Then they rose, an inch, two inches, up, circling, spinning in the air and flashing with light. "Morgana is more talented with such things."

He stared at the tumbling crystals, trying to find a logical reason. "Morgana is a witch, too?"

"She's my cousin," Ana said simply.

"Which makes Sebastian—"

"Sebastian's gift is sight."

He didn't want to believe, but it was impossible to discount what he saw with his own eyes. "Your family," he began. "Those magic tricks of your father's."

"Magic in its purest form." She plucked the crystals out of the air and slipped them back in her pocket. "As I told you, he's very accomplished. As are the rest of them, in their own ways. We're witches. All of us." She reached out to him, but he backed away. "I'm sorry."

"You're sorry?" Rocked to the core, he dragged both hands through his hair. It had to be a dream, a nightmare. But he was standing on his own deck, feeling the wind, hearing the sea. "That's good. That's great. You're sorry. For what, Ana? For being what you are, or for not finding it important enough to mention?"

"I'm not sorry for being what I am." Pride stiffened her spine. "I am sorry for making excuses to myself not to tell you. And I'm sorry, most sorry of all, that you can't look at me now the way you did only a day ago."

"What do you expect? Am I supposed to just shrug this off, pick up where we were before? To accept the fact that the woman I love is something out of one of my own stories, and think nothing of it?"

"I'm exactly what I was yesterday, and what I'll be tomorrow."

"A witch."

"Yes." She folded her hands at her waist. "A witch, born to the craft. I don't make poisoned apples or lure children into houses of gingerbread."

"That's supposed to relieve my mind?"

"Even I don't have the power to do that. As I told you, all of us are responsible for our own destinies." But she knew he held hers in his hands. "You have your choice to make."

He struggled to get a grip on it, and simply couldn't. "You needed time to tell me. Well, by God, I need time to figure out what to do about it." He started to pace, then stopped dead. "Jessie. Jessie's over at Morgana's."

Ana felt the crack in her heart widen. "Oh, yes, with my cousin the witch." A single tear spilled over and ran down her cheek. "What do you think Morgana's going to do? Cast a spell on her? Lock her in a tower?"

"I don't know what to think. For Lord's sake, I've found myself in the middle of a fairy tale! What am I supposed to think?"

"What you will," Ana said wearily. "I can't change what I am, and I wouldn't. Not even for you. And I won't stand here and have you look at me as if I were a freak."

"I'm not—"

"Shall I tell you what you're feeling?" she asked him as another tear fell. "Betrayed, angry, hurt. And suspicious of what I am, what I can do, or will do."

"My feelings are my own business," he shot back, shaken. "I don't want you to get inside me that way."

"I know. And if I were to step forward right now, reach out to you as a woman, you'd only back away. So I'll save us both. Good night, Boone."

When she walked off the deck, into the shadows, he couldn't bring himself to call her back.

Chapter 12

"I guess you're still a little dazed." Nash lounged against the rail of Boone's deck, enjoying a beer and the cool evening breeze.

"I was never a *little* dazed," Boone told him. "Look, maybe I'm just a narrow-minded sort of guy, Nash, but finding out the lady next door is a witch kind of threw me off stride."

"Especially when you're in love with the lady next door."

"Especially. I wouldn't have believed it. Who would? But I saw what she did with Jessie. Then I started piecing other things together." He laughed shortly. "Sometimes I still wake up in the middle of the night and think I dreamed the whole thing." He walked over to the rail, leaning out toward the sound of water. "It shouldn't be real. She shouldn't be real."

"Why not? Come on, Boone, it's our business to stretch the envelope a little."

"This blows the envelope wide open," Boone pointed out. "And what we do, we do for books, for movies. It's entertainment, Nash, it's not life."

"It's mine now."

Boone blew out a breath. "I guess it is. But didn't you... don't you even question it, or worry about it?"

"Sure, I did. I thought she was pulling my leg until she tossed me up in the air and left me hanging there." The memory made him grin, even as Boone shut his eyes. "Morgana's not the subtle type. Once I realized the whole thing was on the level, it was wild, you know?"

"Wild," Boone repeated.

"Yeah. I mean, I've spent most of my life making up stories about this kind of thing, and here I end up marrying an honest-to-goodness witch. Elfin blood and everything."

"Elfin blood." The term had Boone's head reeling. "It doesn't bother you?"

"Why should it bother me? It makes her who she is, and I love her. I have to admit I'm a little dubious about the kids. I mean, once they get going, I'll be outnumbered."

"The twins." Boone had to force his mouth to close. "Are you telling me those babies are...will be..."

"A pretty sure bet. Come on, Boone, they aren't going to grow warts and start to cackle. They just get a little something extra. Mel's expecting, too. She just found out for sure. She's the most down-to-earth lady I know. And she's handling Sebastian as if she's been around a psychic all her life."

"So you're saying, 'Loosen up, Boone. What's your problem?'"

Nash dropped down on the bench. "I know it's not that easy."

"Let me ask you this.... How far into the relationship were you when Morgana told you about her—what do I call it?—her heritage."

"Pretty much right off the bat. I was researching a script, and I'd heard about her. You know how people are always telling me about weird stuff."

"Yeah."

"Not that I believed it, but I thought she'd make a good interview. And—"

"What about Mel and Sebastian?"

"I can't say for sure, but she met him when a client of hers wanted to hire a psychic." Nash frowned into his beer. "I know what you're getting at, and you've got a point. Maybe she should have been straight with you earlier."

He gave a choked laugh. "Maybe?"

"Okay, she should have been. But you don't know the whole story. Morgana told me that Ana was in love with this guy a few years back. She was only about twenty, I think, and really nuts about him. He was an intern at some hospital, and she got the idea that they could work together, that she could help him. So she told him everything and he dumped her. Hard. Apparently he was pretty vicious about it, and with her empathic thing she's really vulnerable to, well...bad vibes, let's say. It left her pretty shaky. She made up her mind she'd go it alone." When Boone said nothing, Nash blundered on. "Look, I can't tell you what to do, or how to feel. I just want to say that she wouldn't have done anything to hurt you or Jessie on purpose. She's just not capable of it."

Boone looked toward the house next door. The windows were blank and dark, as they had been for more than a week. "Where is she?"

"She wanted to get away for a little while. Give everybody some room, I guess."

"I haven't seen her since the night she told me. For the first few days, I figured it was better if I stayed away from her." He felt a quick pang of guilt. "I kept Jessie away from her, too. Then, about a week ago, she took off."

"She went to Ireland. She promised to be back before Christmas."

Because his emotions were still raw, Boone only nodded. "I thought I might take Jessie back to Indiana before the holidays. Just for a day or two. Maybe I'll be able to work all this out in my head by the time we all get back."

"Christmas Eve." Padrick sampled the wassail, smacked his lips and sighed. "No better night in the year." Filling a cup, he handed it to his daughter. "Put color in your cheeks, my darling."

"And fire in my blood, the way you make it." But she smiled and sampled. "Isn't it incredible how the twins have grown?"

"Aye." He wasn't fooled by the bright note in her voice. "I can't stand to see my princess so sad."

"I'm not." She squeezed his hand. "I'm fine, Papa. Really."

"I can turn him into a purple jackass for you, darling. I'd be pleasured to."

"No." Because she knew he was only half joking, she kissed his nose. "And you promised we wouldn't have to talk about it once everyone got here."

"Aye, but—"

"A promise," she reminded him, and moved away to help her mother at the stove.

She was glad her house was filled with the people she loved, with the noise of family. There were the scents she had always associated with this holiday. Cinnamon, nutmeg, pine, bayberry. When she'd arrived home a few days before, she'd thrown herself into a flurry of preparations. Tree trimming, present wrapping, cookie baking. Anything and everything to take her mind off the fact that Boone was gone.

That he hadn't spoken to her in more than a month.

But she would survive it. She had already decided what to do, and she refused to let her own unhappiness ruin the family celebration.

"We'll be pleased to have you home with us back in Ireland, Ana." Maureen bent to kiss her daughter's head. "If it's truly what you want."

"I've missed Ireland," Ana said simply. "I think the goose is nearly ready." After opening the oven and taking a heady sniff, she nodded. "Ten minutes more," she predicted. "I'll just go see if everything's on the table."

"Won't even discuss it," Maureen said to her husband when Ana slipped out.

"Tell you what I'd like, my dove. I'd like to take that young man and send him off to some nice frozen island. Just for a day or two, mind."

"If Ana wasn't so sensitive about such matters, I could brew up a nice potion to bring him around."

Padrick patted his wife's bottom. "You have such a delicate touch, Reenie. The lad would be bound by handfast before he could blink—which would be the best thing to happen to him and that darling child of his." He sighed, nibbling his way up his wife's arm. "But Ana would never forgive us for it. We'll have to let her work this out her own way."

Frustrated by a day of canceled flights and delays, Boone slammed the car door. What he wanted was a long hot bath, and what he had to look forward to was an endless night of dealing with those terrifying words. *Some Assembly Required.*

If Santa was going to put in an appearance before morning, Boone Sawyer was going to have to put in some overtime.

"Come on, Jess." He rubbed his tired eyes. He'd been traveling for more than twelve hours, if you counted the six he'd spent twiddling his thumbs in the airport. "Let's get this stuff inside."

"Ana's home." Jessie tugged on his arm and pointed toward the lights. "Look, Daddy. There's Morgana's car, and Sebastian's, and the big black car, too. Everybody's at Ana's house."

"I see that." He felt his heart begin to trip a little faster. Then it all but stopped when he saw the For Sale sign in her front yard.

"Can we go over and say Merry Christmas? Please,

Daddy. I miss Ana." She closed her hand around the zircon she wore. "Can we go say Merry Christmas?"

"Yeah." Glaring at the sign, he gripped his daughter's hand. "Yeah, let's go do that. Right now."

Move away, would she? he thought as he strode across the lawn. In a pig's eye. Sell her house when he wasn't looking and just take off? They'd just see about that.

"Daddy, you're walking too fast." Jessie had to trot to keep up. "And you're squeezing my hand."

"Sorry." He drew in a long breath, then let it out again. He scooped her up and took the stairs two at a time. The knock on her door wasn't so much a request as a demand.

It was Padrick who answered, his round face wreathed in a fake white beard, and red stocking cap on his balding head. The minute he saw Boone, the twinkle in his eyes died.

"Well, well, look what the cat dragged in. Brave enough to take us all on at once, are you, boyo? We're not all as polite as my Ana."

"I'd like to see her."

"Oh, would you now? Hold it right there." He gave Jessie his charming smile and lifted her out of Boone's arms. "Looks like I got me a real elf this time. Tell you what, lass, you run right on in and look under that tree. See if there's not something with your name on it."

"Oh, can I?" She hugged Padrick fiercely, then turned back to her father. "Please, can I?"

"Sure." Like Padrick's, his smile faded as soon as Jessie raced inside. "I came to see Ana, Mr. Donovan."

"Well, you're seeing me. What do you think you'd do if someone took your Jessie's heart and squeezed it dry?"

Though he was more than a head shorter than Boone, he advanced, fists raised. "I won't use nothing but these on you. You've my word as a witch. Now put 'em up."

Boone didn't know whether to laugh or retreat. "Mr. Donovan…"

"Take the first punch." He stuck his whiskered chin out, looking very much like an indignant Santa. "I'll give you that much, and it's more than you'd be deserving. I've listened to her crying in the night over the likes of you, and it's boiled my blood. Told myself, Padrick, if you get face-to-face with that weasel of a man, you'll have to demolish him. It's a matter of pride." He took a swing that spun him completely around and missed Boone by a foot. "She wouldn't let me go after that other slimy bastard when he broke her poor heart, but I've got you."

"Mr. Donovan." Boone tried again, dodging the peppery blows. "I don't want to hurt you."

"Hurt me! Hurt me!" Padrick was dancing now, fueled by the insult. His Santa cap slipped over his eyes. "Why, I could turn your insides out. I could give you the head of a badger. I could—"

"Papa!" With one sharp word, Ana stopped her father's babbling threats.

"You go on inside, princess. This is man's work."

"I won't have you fighting on my doorstep on Christmas Eve. Now you stop it."

"Just let me send him to the North Pole. Just for an hour or two. It's only fitting."

"You'll do no such thing." She stepped out and put a warning hand on his shoulder. "Now go inside and behave, or I'll have Morgana deal with you."

"Bah! I can handle a witch half my age."

"She's sneaky." Ana pressed a kiss to his cheek. "Please, Papa. Do this for me."

"Could never refuse you anything," he muttered. Then he turned glittering eyes on Boone. "But you watch your step, mister." He jabbed out a plump finger. "You mess with one Donovan, you mess with them all." With a sniff, he went inside.

"I'm sorry," Ana began, fixing a bright smile on her face. "He's very protective."

"So I gathered." Since he wasn't going to have to defend himself after all, he could think of nothing to do with his hands but shove them in his pockets. "I wanted to—we wanted to say merry Christmas."

"Yes, Jessie just did." They were silent for another awkward moment. "You're welcome to come in, have some wassail."

"I don't want to intrude. Your family…" He offered what almost passed for a grin. "I don't want to risk my life, either."

Even the faint smile faded from her eyes. "He wouldn't really have harmed you. It's not our way."

"I didn't mean…" What the hell was he supposed to say to her? "I don't blame him for being upset, and I don't want to make you or your family uncomfortable. If you'd rather, I could just…" He turned slightly, and the sign on her lawn caught his eye. His temper rose accordingly. "What the hell is that?"

"Isn't it clear enough? I'm selling the house. I've decided to go back to Ireland."

"Ireland? You think you can just pack up and move six thousand miles away?"

"Yes, I do. Boone, I'm sorry, but dinner's nearly ready, and I really have to go in. Of course, you're welcome to join us."

"If you don't stop being so bloody polite, I'm going to—" He cut himself off again. "I don't want dinner," he said between his teeth. "I want to talk to you."

"This isn't the time."

"We'll make it the time."

He backed her through the doorway just as Sebastian came down the hall behind her. Placing a light hand on Ana's shoulder, he sent Boone a warning glance. "Is there a problem here, Anastasia?"

"No. I invited Boone and Jessie for dinner, but he isn't able to join us."

"Pity." Sebastian's smile glittered with malice. "Well, then, if you'll excuse us, Sawyer."

Boone slammed the door behind him, causing all the ruckus inside to switch off like a light. Several pairs of eyes turned their way. He was too furious to note that Sebastian's were now bright with amusement.

"Stay out of my way," Boone said quietly. "Each and every one of you. I don't care who you are, or what you are." More than ready to fight a fleet of dragons, he grabbed Ana's hand. "You come with me."

"My family—"

"Can damn well wait." He yanked her back outside.

From her perch under the Christmas tree, Jessie stared wide-eyed after them. "Is Daddy mad at Ana?"

"No." Happy enough about what she'd seen to burst

at the seams, Maureen gave the little girl a squeeze. "I think they've just gone off to take care of another Christmas present for you. One I think you'll like best of all."

Outside, Ana labored to keep up. "Stop dragging me, Boone."

"I'm not dragging you," he said as he dragged her through the side yard.

"I don't want to go with you." She felt the tears she'd thought she was finished with stinging her eyes. "I'm not going through this again."

"You think you can put up a stupid sign in your yard and solve everything?" Guided by moonlight, he tugged her down the rock steps that led to the beach. "Drop a bombshell on my head, then take off for Ireland?"

"I can do exactly as I please."

"Witch or no witch, you'd better think that one over again."

"You wouldn't even talk to me."

"I'm talking to you now."

"Well, now I don't want to talk." She broke away and started to climb back up.

"Then you'll listen." He caught her around the waist and tossed her over his shoulder. "And we're going to do this far enough from the house so that I know your family isn't breathing down my neck." When he reached the bottom, he flipped her over and dropped her to her feet. "One step," he warned. "You take one step away and I'll haul you back."

"I wouldn't give you the satisfaction." She struggled with the tears, preferring temper. "You want to have your say. Fine. Then I'll have mine, as well. I accept your position on our relationship. I deeply regret you feel it necessary to keep Jessie away from me."

"I never—"

"Don't deny it. For days before I left for Ireland you kept her at home." She picked up a handful of pebbles and threw them out to sea. "Wouldn't want your little girl too near the witch, after all." She whirled back to him. "For God's sake, Boone, what did you expect from me? Did you see me rubbing my hands together and croaking out, 'I'll get you, my pretty—and your little dog, too'?"

His lips quirked at that, and he reached out, but she spun away. "Give me some credit, Ana."

"I did. A little later than I should have, but I did. And you turned away. Just as I'd known you would."

"Known?" Though he was getting tired of the choreography, he pulled her around again. "How did you know how I'd react? Did you look in your crystal ball, or just have your psychic cousin take a stroll through my head?"

"Neither," she said, with what control she had left. "I wouldn't let Sebastian look, and I didn't look myself, because it seemed unfair. I knew you'd turn away because…"

"Because someone else had."

"It doesn't matter, the fact is you did turn away."

"I just needed to take it in."

"I saw the way you looked at me that night." She shut her eyes. "I've seen that look before. Oh, you weren't cruel like Robert. There were no names, no accusations, but the result was the same. Stay away from me and mine. I don't accept what you are." She wrapped her arms tight and cupped her elbows for warmth.

"I'm not going to apologize for having what I think was a very normal reaction. And damn it, Ana, I was tired, and half-crazy. Watching you lie there in bed all those hours, and you were so pale, so still. I was afraid you wouldn't come back. When you did, I didn't know how to treat you. Then you were telling me all of this."

She searched for calm, knowing it was the best way. "The timing was bad all around. I wasn't quite strong enough to deal with your feelings."

"If you had told me before—"

"You would have reacted differently?" She glanced toward him. "No, I don't think so. But you're right. I should have. It was unfair, and it was weak of me to let things go as far as they did."

"Don't put words in my mouth, Ana. Unless you're, what do you call it—linked? If you're not linked with me, you don't know what I'm feeling. It hurt that you didn't trust me."

She nodded, brushing a tear from her cheek. "I know. I'm sorry."

"You were afraid?"

"I told you I was a coward."

He frowned, watching the hair blow around her face as she stared out at the moon-kissed sea. "Yes, you did. The night you came across my sketch. The one of the witch. That upset you."

She shrugged. "I'm oversensitive sometimes. It was just the mood. I was…"

"About to tell me, and then I scared you off with my evil witch."

"It seemed a difficult time to tell you."

"Because you're a coward," he said mildly, watching her. "Let me ask you something, Ana. What did you do, exactly, to Jessie that day?"

"I linked. I told you I'm an empath."

"It hurt you. I saw." He took her arm, turning her to face him. "Once you cried out, as if it were unbearable. Afterward, you fainted, then slept like the dead for more than a day."

"That's part of it." She tried to push his hand away. It hurt too much to be touched when her defenses were shattered. "When the injuries are so serious, there's a price."

"Yes, I understand. I asked Morgana. She said you could have died. She said the risk was very great because Jessie..." He could hardly say it. "She was gone, or nearly. And you weren't just fixing some broken bones, but bringing her back from the edge. That the line is very fine, and it's very easy for the healer to become the victim."

"What would you have had me do? Let her die?"

"A coward would have. I think your definition and mine are different. Being afraid doesn't make you a coward. You could have saved yourself and let her go."

"I love her."

"So do I. And you gave her back to me. I didn't even thank you."

"Do you think I want your gratitude?" It was too much, she thought. Next he would offer her pity. "I don't. I don't want it. What I did I did freely, because I couldn't bear to lose her, either. And I couldn't bear for you—"

"For me?" he said gently.

"For you to lose someone else you loved. I don't want to be thanked for it. It's what I am."

"You've done it before? What you did with Jessie?"

"I'm a healer. I heal. She was…" It still hurt to think of it. "She was slipping away. I used what I have to bring her back."

"It's not that simple." His hands were gentle on her arms now, stroking. "Not even for you. You feel more than others. Morgana told me that, too. When you let your defenses down, you're more vulnerable to emotion, to pain, to everything. That's why you don't cry." With his fingertip, he lifted a teardrop from her cheek. "But you're crying now."

"You know everything there is to know. What's the point of this?"

"The point is to take a step back to the night you explained it all to me. The point is for you to take another chance and open yourself up. For me."

"You ask too much." She sobbed the words out, then covered her face. "Oh, leave me alone. Give me some peace. Can't you see how you hurt me?"

"Yes, I can see." He wrapped his arms around her, fighting to soothe while she struggled for release. "You've lost weight, you're pale. When I look into your eyes, I see every ounce of pain I caused you. I don't know how to take it back. I don't know how your father kept himself from cursing me with whatever was in his arsenal."

"We can't use power to harm. It's against everything we are. Please let me go."

"I can't. I almost thought I could. She lied to me, I told

myself. She betrayed my trust. She isn't real." He kept a firm grip on her arms as he pulled her away. "It doesn't matter. None of it matters. If it's magic, I don't want to lose it. I can't lose you. I love you, Ana. All that you are. Please." He touched his lips to hers, tasting tears. "Please come back to me."

The shaft of hope was almost painful. She clung to it, to him. "I want to believe."

"So do I." He cupped her face, kissing her again. "And I do. I believe in you. In us. If this is my fairy tale, I want to play it out."

She stared up at him. "You can accept all of this? All of us?"

"I figure I'm pretty well suited to do just that. Of course, it might take a while for me to convince your father not to do something drastic to my anatomy." He traced his fingers over her lips as they curved. "I didn't know if you'd ever smile for me again. Tell me you still love me. Give me that, too."

"Yes, I love you." Her lips trembled under his. "Always."

"I won't hurt you again." He brushed away tears with his thumbs. "I'll make up for everything."

"It's done." She caught his hands. "That's done. We have tomorrow."

"Don't cry anymore."

She smiled, rubbing her fists across her cheeks. "No, I won't. I never cry."

He took those damp fists and kissed them. "You said to ask you again. It's been longer than a week, but I'm hoping you haven't forgotten what you said your answer would be."

"I haven't forgotten."

"Put your hand here." He pressed her palm to his heart. "I want you to feel what I feel." He linked his free hand with hers. "The moon's almost full. The first time I kissed you was in the moonlight. I was charmed, enchanted, spellbound. I always will be. I need you, Ana."

She could feel the strength of that love pouring into her. "You have me."

"I want you to marry me. Share the child you gave back to me. She's yours as much as mine now. Let me make more children with you. I'll take you as you are, Anastasia. I swear I'll cherish you as long as I live."

She lifted her arms to him. Hair like sunlight. Eyes like smoke. Shafts of moonglow shimmered around her like torchlight.

"I've been waiting for you."

Epilogue

Alone on a wild crag facing a stormy sea stood Donovan Castle. This dark night, lightning flashed and shuddered in the black sky, and the wind set the leaded glass to shaking in the diamond panes.

Inside, fires leaped and glowed in the hearths. Those who were witches, and those who were not, gathered close, waiting for the indignant wail that would signal a new life.

"Are you cheating, Grandda?" Jessie asked Padrick as he perused his cards.

"Cheating!" He gave a merry laugh and wiggled his brows. "Certainly I am. Go fish."

She giggled and drew from the pile. "Granny Maureen says you always cheat." She tilted her head. "Were you really a frog?"

"That I was, darling. A fine green one."

She accepted this, just as she accepted the other wonders of her life with the Donovans. She petted the snoring Daisy, who rested her big golden head in Jessie's lap. "Will you be a frog again sometime, so I can see?"

"I might surprise you." He winked and changed her hand of cards into a rainbow of lollipops.

"Oh, Grandda," she said indulgently.

"Sebastian?" Mel hustled down the main stairs and shouted into the parlor, where her husband was sipping brandy and watching the card game. "Shawn and Keely are awake and fussing. I have my hands full helping with Ana."

"Be right there." The proud papa of three months set down his snifter and headed up to change diapers.

Nash bounced one-year-old Allysia on his knee while Donovan sat in Matthew's lap, playing with his pocket watch. "Be careful he doesn't eat it," Nash commented. "Or make it disappear. We're having a little trouble keeping him in line."

"The lad needs to spread his wings a bit."

"If you say so. But when I went to get him out of his crib the other day, it was full of rabbits. Real ones."

"Takes after his mother," Matthew said proudly. "She ran us ragged."

Allysia leaned back against her father and smiled. Instantly Daisy woke and trotted over. Within seconds, every dog and cat in the house was swarming through the room.

"Ally," Nash said with a sigh. "Remember how we said one at a time?"

"Doggies." Squealing, Ally tugged gently on the ears of Matthew's big silver wolf. "Kittycats."

"Next time just one, okay?" Nash plucked a cat off his

shoulder, nudged another off the arm of the chair. "A couple of weeks ago she had every hound within ten miles howling in the yard. Come on, monsters." He rose, tucking Allysia, then Donovan, under his arms like footballs. They kicked and giggled. "I think it's time for bed."

"Story," Donovan demanded. "Uncle Boone."

"He's busy. You'll have to settle for one from your old man."

He was indeed busy, watching a miracle. The room was scented with candles and herbs, warmed by the fire glowing in the hearth. He held tight to Ana as she brought their son into the world.

Then their daughter.

Then their second son.

"Three." He kept saying it over and over, even as Bryna settled an infant in his arms. "Three." They'd told him there would be triplets, but he hadn't really believed it.

"Runs in the family." Exhausted, elated, Ana took another bundle from Morgana. She pressed her lips gently to the silky cheek. "Now we have two of each."

He grinned down at his wife as Mel settled the third baby in the crook of Ana's arm. "I think we need a bigger house."

"We'll add on."

"Would you like the others to come up?" Bryna asked gently. "Or would you rather rest awhile?"

"No, please." Ana tilted her head so that it rested against Boone's arm. "Ask them to come up."

They crowded in, making too much noise. Ana made

room in the big bed for Jessie to sit beside her, then placed a baby in her arms.

"This is your brother, Trevor. Your sister, Maeve. And your other brother, Kyle."

"I'm going to take good care of them. Always. Look, Grandda, we have a big family now."

"You do indeed, my little lamb." He blew heartily into his checked kerchief. He wiped his runny eyes and looked mistily at Boone. "Just as well I didn't flatten you when I had the chance."

"Here." Boone held out a squealing infant. "Hold your grandson."

"Ah, Maureen, my cheesecake, look at this. He has my eyes."

"No, my frog prince, he has mine."

They argued, with the rest of the Donovans throwing their weight to one side or the other. Boone slipped his arm around his wife, held his family close as his son suckled greedily at his first taste of mother's milk. Lightning flashed against the windows, the wind howled, and the fire leapt high in the grate.

Somewhere deep in the forest, high in the hills, the fairies danced.

And they lived happily ever after.

* * * * *

Get ready to meet the MacKade family...

'The most successful
author on planet Earth'
—*Washington Post*

www.millsandboon.co.uk

Introducing
the Stanislaskis...

**Fall under the spell of *New York Times*
bestselling author**

Nora Roberts

www.millsandboon.co.uk

STANISLASKIS